Head Over
Heels

Books by Jennifer Dawson

Head Over *Heels*

JENNIFER DAWSON

ZEBRA BOOKS
KENSINGTON PUBLISHING CORP.
http://www.kensingtonbooks.com

ZEBRA BOOKS are published by

Kensington Publishing Corp.
119 West 40th Street
New York, NY 10018

All Kensington titles, imprints, and distributed lines are available at special quantity discounts for bulk purchases for sales promotion, premiums, fund-raising, educational, or institutional use.

Special book excerpts or customized printings can also be created to fit specific needs. For details, write or phone the office of the Kensington Sales Manager: Attn.: Sales Department. Kensington Publishing Corp., 119 West 40th Street, New York, NY 10018. Phone: 1-800-221-2647.

Zebra and the Z logo Reg. U.S. Pat. & TM Off.

First Printing: October 2017
ISBN-13: 978-1-4201-4015-6
ISBN-10: 1-4201-4015-9

eISBN-13: 978-1-4201-4016-3
eISBN-10: 1-4201-4016-7

10 9 8 7 6 5 4 3 2 1

Printed in the United States of America

Chapter One

No amount of spin in the world could save this situation.

Not even a public relations genius like herself could turn this disaster into gold.

Life as she knew it was over.

Sophie Kincaid watched with an odd sense of detachment as the FBI agents swarmed the downtown Chicago office of the formally prestigious multimedia ad company where she worked, digging through files and shouting orders at each other.

Calm as could be, almost as though she watched a movie, she sat on her office chair, drinking her venti Red Eye, observing the proceedings like someone else's life was being blown up. As though her life, and livelihood, weren't collapsing around her Stuart Weitzman stilettos.

In retrospect, she supposed she should have suspected something was amiss. Her boss, Walter Poole, had been erratic and paranoid lately. But she'd thought he was stressed because they were pitching a national ad campaign to American Express, and if they won the bid, it would put them in the big leagues.

How was she to know he'd turned into a raging, embezzling cokehead? He had a house in Kenilworth, a sweet beautiful wife, and four postcard-perfect kids. He even had a dog, a cute little cocker spaniel, with adorable floppy ears, that wore red and green bows in their Christmas card.

Honestly, Sophie had no idea people even did coke anymore. It seemed like a throwback drug during a time where popping prescription Oxycontin was the addicts' vice of choice.

Mind lost in a cotton cloud in spite of chaos reigning around her, she pondered his drug of choice. It was such an inconsequential detail, but she couldn't stop thinking about it. Had the drug experienced a revival with the rest of the eighties? If people could love neon again, it wasn't out of the realm of possibility.

Personally, she stuck to cocktails, wine, champagne, and maybe the occasional IPA beer. She was completely out of touch with the drug scene.

"Ms. Kincaid." A male voice shocked her out of her haze.

She blinked at the man standing in front of her. He was around her age, with close-cropped hair and a blue windbreaker with the letters "FBI" spread across it in yellow. If Sophie wanted to cast an FBI agent, he'd be exactly who she'd look for with his hard eyes, strong jaw, and broad shoulders. Maybe not as the lead, because he lacked a certain amount of charisma, but as the sidekick for sure.

"Ms. Kincaid," the agent said again.

She took a sip of her coffee. "Yes?"

"We're going to need to take you down to the station for questioning." His voice was authoritative but soft.

The words caught her attention. Surely she couldn't help; she had no information to impart. She straightened and put her hand on her chest. "Why? I had nothing to do with this."

He nodded, his features impassive and unreadable. She wondered if they taught them that at Quantico. Did they practice in the mirror? Were they tested? Graded?

He crossed his arms over his chest. "We're questioning all the vice presidents."

She tittered, and it was high pitched and nervous sounding. She shook her head. "But I'm just the PR girl."

She didn't know why she described herself that way, as though she was an intern, but she just couldn't seem to attach herself to these events.

His blank expression didn't even flicker and he nodded again. "It's not a request."

Suddenly, the gravity of her situation took hold of her. The world blared into crystal-clear focus, knocking her out of her detached apathy with a two-by-four spiked with nails. All the shouting, the people and flurry of paper and boxes screeched around her, rattling her out of her calm. Her heart started to pound a rapid beat, slamming against her ribs as her palms turned sweaty. The magnitude of her situation finally sank in.

She had nothing to do with this, but she was an executive at this company. What if they didn't believe her? What if she couldn't prove her innocence? What if she got thrown in jail? She'd just watched the new season of *Orange Is the New Black*, and she didn't think she was cut out to be a prison girlfriend.

Okay. She took a deep breath. She needed to think. She wasn't helpless. Maybe she didn't have a family she could depend on like most people, but she had people that could help her. She had something better than family, she had powerful friends.

Despite having nothing to do with this, she was smart

enough to know she shouldn't talk to anyone without representation.

She lifted her cell phone. "Can I make a quick call?"

He narrowed his eyes for a second and then shrugged. "Sure, but make it fast."

She didn't know which of her best friends to call first, Maddie, whose husband used to be a big-time defense attorney and now worked for the State Department but lived hours away in the small town of Revival, or Penelope, who was connected to practically anyone who was anyone in the city and married to a former Chicago football star turned coach.

In the end she opted for Penelope, who moved with the efficiency scientists in the future would study to replicate. And, Penelope was in Chicago, unlike Maddie, who wouldn't be able to do anything for hours.

She pushed the number, and when Penelope didn't answer, Sophie ended the call and dialed again. Penelope was COO of her husband's brother's commercial real estate company and always busy. But if she called enough, Penelope would know something was wrong and answer.

Sophie called her three more times before Penelope picked up. "What's wrong?"

Sophie was often called spirited, but she certainly wasn't prone to dramatics. "Sorry to bother you, but I need help."

"Is everything okay?" Penelope's voice was all business.

"No." Sophie's throat tightened and she shook her head before clearing it. "I'm being taken to the Chicago FBI office over on Roosevelt. I need a lawyer to meet me there."

There was ten seconds of complete silence before Penelope sprang into action. "What happened?"

"I don't know." The agent made a wrap-it-up signal with

his hand. "Best-case scenario, I'm out of a job. Worst case, I'm going to be arrested."

"We'll be right there." Then Penelope was gone.

Sophie took another sip of her coffee, set it on her former desk, and stood, smoothing out her black skirt. Sure, her entire life was ruined, but that was no excuse for wrinkles.

Head held high, she squared her shoulders. "I'm ready."

Chapter Two

One month later

Flanked by her best friends, Sophie stared at the tiny, thousand-square-foot house on Sycamore Street, located a few blocks away from the small downtown area of Revival, Illinois.

She wasn't sure how something four blocks long, with absolutely no significant shopping, could be considered downtown, but there it was.

Downtown Revival. This was her life.

No more busy Chicago traffic, no more noise, no more Nordstrom, Starbucks, or late-night clubbing.

Teeth grinding, she listened and heard nothing familiar. She could barely make out the rumble of a car. In fact, there was hardly any noise. How would she sleep without background noise?

Panic whooshed through her veins. What was she supposed to do with quiet? Think about her life? But she didn't want to think; she wanted to be out there in the busy world, acting. She took a deep breath. Okay, she needed to relax. This was temporary.

All she needed was a positive spin. There were worse

fates than spending time in Revival. The small town was certainly better than prison. It was better than crashing in Penelope's guest room because she couldn't pay her rent and was a bit . . . unemployable at the moment. And she'd always had fun when she'd visited. The weekends flew by, so how hard could it be? She'd do six months and be back where she belonged.

Eventually people had to forget. Right? After all, she'd done nothing wrong. All she needed was time. The world lived in a twenty-four-hour news cycle; the reporters had to move on sooner rather than later. It would just take a little time before her former company's name at the top of her résumé didn't send her email straight into the trash.

Maddie's arm was around her waist, and Penelope's was around her shoulders. They both squeezed. They were driving Sophie crazy. Of course they meant well, but all their relentless optimism made her want to scream or break out into uncontrollable sobbing. She did neither. She merely endured in suffocating silence.

Sophie refused to cry. Especially when she was lucky compared to some of her other coworkers.

Yes, her reputation was presently tainted. She'd lost her job and put her *Chicago After Dark* blog on hiatus. Since her name had continuously been in the papers as part of the company's executive team, she was a bit like a case of chlamydia. Not permanent, but distasteful enough that people wanted some distance. Given enough time, she'd recover. People had short memories, and when she got back home, she'd be back on top.

She needed to look on the bright side. This whole fiasco had taught her some valuable lessons. Namely, that life could change on a dime, and that sometimes it did pay to be prepared. It turned out designer shoes weren't actually an investment and money in the bank was important. Go figure. Maybe she wasn't practical and retirement savvy, but she was smart and wouldn't make that mistake again.

It wasn't all bad. While her savings were meager at best, she'd been able to get a job.

Yes, the position was in Revival, working for—she swallowed—the city government, but still. It was something. She wouldn't be homeless, have to live off her friends or, God forbid, be forced to go join her parents in their meditation commune in India. She didn't think she'd be good at commune life. She was too selfish. Too materialistic. Too American. She was everything her parents hadn't wanted her to be.

So she needed to focus on how lucky she'd been to land this job helping the city of Revival, population twenty five hundred, with their town revitalization project. As a bonus, she'd get to spend tons of time with Maddie, and that would be great.

So, see, she was blessed. It wasn't ideal, but it was work in her chosen profession, and for that she was grateful. She'd have time to regroup and reassemble.

It would be an adjustment, over before she knew it. If she kept busy, she'd blink and be home where she belonged, this whole mess like a faded bad dream.

"What do you think?" Maddie asked, waving her free hand at the frame porch, her long red hair blowing gently in the breeze, making her look like she was ready to film a shampoo commercial in a spring meadow.

Sophie studied what would be her home for the next six months. While the place was small, the white frame house looked like a cottage, with window boxes and a cute small front porch. It was a little run down and needed some landscaping, but it would do.

She smiled at her friend. They were both tiny, and eye level. At five-three, Maddie had Sophie beat by one inch.

Her friend had gone through so much trouble to find a place for her; Sophie refused to burst her bubble by whining about how she wanted to go home. "It's perfect, thanks."

It wasn't quite a lie, but it was an exaggeration.

It was charming enough, but Sophie was a city girl. She'd never lived anywhere with grass before. She took a deep breath. "Maybe I could learn to garden. Or at least mow the lawn. That's a thing, right?"

Maddie pointed to the garage in the back of the house. "The owner said there's a mower in the garage."

The grass needed to be cut. Once she'd read in *Real Simple* people found yard work therapeutic, so maybe it would help her feel better. More like she was at home instead of dropped into an alternative universe.

Penelope laughed. "Please call me when you do, because I'd really love to see that."

"Hey! Like you've ever mowed in your life." Sophie scowled good-naturedly at Penelope, a tall, willowy brunette and the good girl in their close group. Everyone knew she was the perfect one. The planner. The organized one. The woman that kept Maddie and Sophie out of jail when they were girls and from going off the deep end now as adults.

Penelope smiled. "But I could if I needed to."

"Well, so can I." Sophie squirmed, and her friends finally dropped their death hold on her. "How hard can it be?"

"I've done it." Maddie raised her hand like they were back in middle school. "It's kind of therapeutic. Like active meditation."

Just like *Real Simple* claimed. They wouldn't steer her wrong. Maddie's confirmation gave her hope.

If Maddie had reformed her wild ways and been domesticated, so could Sophie. How hard could it be? And Maddie loved Revival, had chosen to live here with her hot husband, Mitch, in their big farmhouse by the river. They even had a baby, a nine-month-old girl, Lily.

As the first child in their group of friends and family, she was spoiled rotten and universally deemed the prettiest baby any of them had ever seen. Lily had her mama's red hair and Cupid's bow mouth, combined with her daddy's amber eyes and golden skin. It was an unusual combination, and even now it was clear she was going to be a stunner. Already Mitch fretted over her being a teenager.

See, Maddie had completely adjusted to country life. In fact, she'd never move back to Chicago. If she could do it, Sophie could do it for six months.

Sophie wrinkled her nose. "I guess I'll find out."

Maddie gestured at the front yard. "We could put some hydrangea bushes in front of the house and plant the window boxes. It would be really pretty."

Oh. My. God. She was discussing gardening. How was this happening? She put on a happy face.

"Sure," she said absently, walking up the driveway. Time to stop avoiding and claim this as home.

"What time are the movers coming?" Penelope asked.

"They should be here within the next hour."

"We should get started cleaning, then." Penelope's voice took on that efficient edge, tinged with excitement. The woman lived for cleaning and organizing. Obviously Penelope was sick and twisted, but Sophie loved her anyway.

"Great." Her tone was dry. "I love cleaning."

Back home she'd paid a college girl to clean her apartment. She'd worked so much she wasn't about to waste her weekends on housework. But she couldn't afford that now. Her six-month contracted salary covered her rent, essentials, takeout, and one of those mutual funds thingies she was supposed to have by now. Something had to go, and it wasn't like she was going to start cooking.

She frowned. Did Revival have delivery?

Panic sliced through her and she took a deep breath. She'd worry about it later. Her friends were watching her every move, waiting to catch her the second she fell apart. She appreciated their love and relentless support but wanted no part of their sympathy. She'd freak out when she was alone and not a second before.

She dusted her hands on her jean shorts, smoothed down her red tank top, and squared her shoulders. Time to get down to the business of becoming a country girl.

Just then a loud roar rumbled through the quiet streets, interrupting the tranquility of the neighborhood. A big, black motorcycle turned the corner, the motor so loud it vibrated through her ears, and strummed through her blood, jolting the first signs of life from her.

Yes, of course motorcycles were dangerous, but Sophie had a tiny thing for danger she'd been trying to manage since college, and the Harley looked and sounded as dangerous as they came.

Sophie, Maddie, and Penelope all froze in the driveway, staring at the bike tearing a path through the street. She could tell the driver was a man by the breadth of his shoulders, but she couldn't make him out.

She waited for him to pass, but he pulled into the driveway next to hers and turned off the bike.

Sophie could only blink in shock. Her throat went dry. The driver wasn't just a man; he was *all* man.

Who in the hell was that?

The man didn't get off the motorcycle. Instead he sat there, watching her. At least she thought he watched her, but it was hard to tell behind his mirrored aviator sunglasses. He wore jeans, and the denim stretched over the powerful thighs straddling the beast of a machine. He took his hands off the handlebars, and the muscles in his forearms corded and flexed before biceps filled out his black T-shirt. His shoulders went on for miles, stretching the confines of the cotton.

That was just his body. But his face, holy shit his face. He had a strong jaw, hard features, and short dark brown hair. Sophie couldn't see his eyes, but he was ridiculously masculine and uncomfortably good-looking.

Sophie had nothing against hot men. In fact, she rather liked them. But she took one look at this one and immediately disliked him, for no rational reason or logical explanation other than he looked exactly like her type. And Sophie knew her type. Her type was nothing but trouble, heartache, and potential jail time. She'd given up her type a long time ago, and while it was a little boring, it was much safer.

She glared at the offending stranger. Why in God's name wouldn't he stop looking at her? Why didn't he get off his dumb bike? Why was he just sitting there?

"Hey, Ryder," Maddie called out, before giving her a huge, sly smile. "This is Sophie."

Her friend clearly knew exactly who he was but had failed to mention him.

Sophie frowned as he nodded in her direction before swinging his leg off the bike.

He straightened to his full height, and she gulped. He was a giant. Tall and broad with lean, tapered hips and a flat stomach. She'd bet every last dollar in her meager bank account he had a six-pack under his shirt.

And his name was Ryder. Gag. His mama didn't like him much, did she?

He walked across the grass.

Sophie scowled as her adrenaline kicked in and she had a sudden urge to flight.

Maddie waved a hand between them. "Sophie Kincaid, meet Ryder Moore."

He came to stand in front of her, tilting his strong jaw before raising his sunglasses to peer down at her.

Her scowl deepened.

His eyes were like nothing she'd ever seen before. They were gray, light and almost eerie.

He smiled and her heart skipped a beat. "Sophie, I've heard a lot about you."

She crossed her arms over her chest. She didn't want anything to do with this man. She didn't know what he was doing here, but she wanted him gone. "Why's that?"

He jerked a thumb over his shoulder. "I'm your neighbor."

Oh no. Why, God, why? Could this get any worse? What was Maddie thinking? She didn't want to live next to him.

He grinned down at her. "And your landlord."

Oh. My. God.

All those years of Catholic school, and *this* was how the heavens repaid her.

The tiny blonde stared at him as though he was a bug under her shoe. Arms crossed, she stood there, glaring at him like his very existence irritated her. Which, considering the deal he'd given her on rent, he didn't understand at all.

She should be grateful.

She should at least smile at him.

But she did none of those things.

Instead she glowered.

Maybe Maddie Riley had told her something bad, but that didn't seem right. He'd been a practical saint since moving to Revival. Maddie, her friends, and her family had been nothing but welcoming since he'd moved from a couple of towns over. Besides, he doubted they even knew about his trouble that had been the catalyst in his decision to start over fresh.

But the cute blonde he towered over clearly wasn't a fan.

Too bad, because she was a pretty little thing. With her hair pulled back in a ponytail, those big brown eyes of hers, and that sweet mouth, she should look soft and compliant. She didn't. She looked fierce, with a defiant tilt to her jaw and the set of her shoulders.

At six-four he stood more than a foot taller than her, but his height didn't appear to intimidate her, despite the disparity between them. Standing there, she was so small he had a sudden urge to pat her on top of her head. Certain that move wouldn't win him any favors, he resisted and said, "Rent's due on the first of the month."

Her frown deepened. "Fine."

He was intrigued. Rubbing women the wrong way wasn't really his thing. In fact, he had the opposite problem; women always liked him too much. With the right smile, he could get away with almost anything.

Not with this one, though.

He tried again, putting on his most charming grin. "Utilities are included."

She raised her brows. "Yeah, I know. I read the contract."

She had a bee in her bonnet, now didn't she? He jutted his chin in the direction of his house. "If you need anything, I'm right next door to help you out."

"I won't need anything." She huffed, waving a hand. "You won't even know I'm here."

He crossed his arms and mimicked her posture. "Somehow I doubt that, honey."

If anything, her stance grew more formidable. She locked her legs and slammed her hands on her hips, giving him the first clear view of a very nice rack. She had quite the chest on her for such a little thing. Not huge, not porn-star material, but soft, rounded, and full.

The snap of her voice refocused his attention back on her face. "My name is Sophie."

She really was cute all riled up. He raised a brow. "Are you sure you don't want me to call you Ms. Kincaid?"

She narrowed her eyes. "Since you won't know I'm here, you won't have to call me anything."

He laughed.

Maddie cleared her throat and came to stand next to her. She gave Ryder a huge, aw-shucks grin that raised the fine hairs on the back of his neck. *Never trust a redhead with a too-innocent smile; they're almost always up to something.* "Thanks so much for giving Sophie a short-term lease."

"Not a problem," he said, slowly. "You know I'm always happy to help."

She turned a pleading expression on Sophie. "Ryder gave you a great deal and did me a huge favor."

Sophie narrowed her eyes on him before tilting her chin even higher. "Thank you. I appreciate it."

Somehow he doubted that too. He glanced around. "Are your movers on the way?"

Before Sophie could speak, Maddie interjected, "They'll be here soon."

"You girls have help?" He scrubbed a hand over his stubble-covered jaw. It had been a hell of a night, and all he wanted was a shower and bed.

Sophie rolled her eyes. "We don't need help."

She was a sassy one. He shrugged one shoulder. "I wasn't offering, baby doll."

She gave him a disgusted huff. "Oh God, you're one of *those*."

Now this he had to hear. "One of what?"

"One of those guys that calls women insipid endearments

like honey, and baby, and sweetie, instead of humanizing her with an actual name."

Maddie opened her mouth to speak. "We—"

Sophie cut her off and kept right on going. "But I suppose with a name like Ryder Moore, I can't blame you."

He raised a brow. "What's wrong with Ryder?"

She rolled her eyes. "Did your mom watch too many soaps?"

"It's my granddaddy's name." He smirked. "I'll tell him you don't approve."

"Whatever." She waved a hand. "We've got work to do. Come on, girls." Without waiting to see if they followed, she turned around and sashayed her little ass away from him.

When she hit the top step of the porch, he called out helpfully, "Don't forget rent's due on the first, darlin'."

Without even looking back she gave him the finger, then stalked into the house, the door slamming behind her.

He looked at her two friends. Maddie he knew well, but the composed brunette, Penelope, he'd only met a few times. She was the wife of Evan Donovan, former wide receiver turned coach.

He cocked his head at them. "Well now, isn't she a hostile one."

Maddie shook her head. "Oh my God, I'm so sorry. I have no idea what got into her."

Penelope gave him a level stare. "She's had a hard go of it recently."

He nodded. "I see."

"I'm not sure she's a fan of the pet names." Penelope flashed him a smile that dazzled him for a second. He'd always thought her quietly pretty, but then she smiled or did something that made her heart-stopping. He'd heard bits of the story of her courtship with one of Chicago's most notorious football players, and when she hit Ryder with one of those looks he could see why Evan had fallen in love with her as a teenager and never fallen out.

He chuckled. "Really? What was your first clue?"

Penelope laughed. "I'm good at reading subtle body language."

Maddie shook her head. "Again, I'm really sorry. We'll talk to her."

He shrugged one shoulder. "No worries, she doesn't need to like me."

"She's really great, I promise," Maddie said, her voice a bit too cheerful.

"This is a big adjustment for her," Penelope added.

City girls were always the highest maintenance. He tilted his head in the direction of his house. "I'm gonna get some shut-eye. It's been a long night."

Maddie and Penelope exchanged one of those secret female looks that set his instincts on high alert.

Penelope cleared her throat. "We promise she'll be good."

Ah, now he saw what was going on.

Sophie Kincaid was a troublemaker.

A hellion living right next door. Well, wouldn't that make the neighborhood interesting?

At least he wouldn't be bored.

Chapter Three

The kitchen was nice enough. Nothing modern or fancy, but at least it was all white, so she could add her own touches. The wooden cabinets were plain, the appliances antiquated, and the counters some sort of boring ceramic tile. A blank slate she could make her own.

She went to her big laundry basket full of cleaning supplies—Penelope's idea of a house-warming present—and pulled on a pair of rubber gloves before grabbing the cleaner.

Might as well start with the sink. She tested the water, and it came out in a blast, surprising her. Back home she'd rented a brand-new condo where everything was low flow. She hadn't seen water pressure like this since the nineties. Clearly Revival didn't care about water conservation.

She sprayed down the sink and started to scrub, contemplating what she could do with the space. That would give her something to fill the time. She'd never considered herself a workaholic like Penelope, but until she'd lost her job she'd never realized how much actual time she'd spent working.

She needed projects to work on. Yes, she had the projects

with the city, but the hours didn't come close to what she was used to, so this house would have to do.

She hoped her landlord would appreciate her efforts.

She huffed. God, he rubbed her the wrong way. Realistically she didn't have a good reason other than gut instinct warning her off him. He just reminded her too much of the kind of man she'd given up a long time ago. She was older now. Wiser. She didn't care how good-looking he was. She didn't want to live next door to him, but she had no choice.

She was stuck. This was what she got for letting Maddie take care of all the details because she wanted to avoid the reality of her situation. What she should have done was come check out the place herself, but how could she have predicted Ryder Moore?

She scoured around the drain. She'd do what she always did and make the best of it. Of course she'd avoid him at all costs. It was only six months. And while she wouldn't be working seventy hours a week, she'd keep busy.

There was plenty to do. She had to come up with ideas on how to effectively utilize the new town square, to ensure new and existing businesses saw the positive effects and increased traffic and revenue, and she had two major events to plan and make a smashing success. The town square grand kickoff coincided with the Fourth of July, and that left her two months to make it so spectacular people would come from all over just to see it.

The mayor of Revival, Griffin Strong, had already given her the current plans, and she'd prepared a list of suggestions to make it a thousand times better. Then she'd have the Pumpkin Festival to keep her busy, and she'd be back home by Thanksgiving.

This might be a disaster, but she needed to remember to be grateful, because she was lucky to have a place to go, with friends to support her and work to do while she waited out the shit storm tainting her reputation back in Chicago.

She'd be grateful. Do her job. Keep away from her neighbor and go back home without causing a ripple.

Ryder Moore was a minor blip of annoyance she wouldn't pay any attention to.

Maddie and Penelope came barreling into the house, tumbling into the small kitchen. Sophie realized she'd been scrubbing the sink furiously for the past five minutes and stilled her frantic movements.

Maddie screeched. "What was that?"

Sophie flicked on the faucet and again marveled at how the water blasted out. She splashed the water around to get rid of the cleaning solution and said calmly, "What was what?"

"Now, Sophie," Penelope said in her calm, "let's discuss this reasonably" voice.

Sophie turned off the faucet and faced her friends. "What?"

Maddie, the more high-strung of the two, blew out an exasperated breath. "Why were you so unpleasant to Ryder? You need to be nice to him."

"I wasn't unpleasant." She picked up the cleaning product again. Sure she'd given him the finger, but her friends hadn't seen. Penelope gave her that look and Sophie grinned at her. "You know you're going to make a great mom someday."

Penelope shook her head. "Don't change the subject."

"What's the subject?" She didn't see what there was to talk about. She didn't want to spend one second of energy on stupid Ryder. Okay, yes, she was being a touch . . . unreasonable about him, but so what? She didn't have to like everyone, and she certainly didn't need to apologize.

Maddie ran a hand through her long red hair. "He's your

landlord, and your neighbor, it's best if you keep him on friendly terms. I don't even understand what your problem is. Ryder is a great guy. Everyone thinks so."

Of course they did. She couldn't imagine a single woman in Revival that wouldn't have heart palpitations when he walked by, but she wasn't so easily charmed. Her hormones were too smart to be fooled by all that testosterone. She was a South Side city girl; she could spot bullshit a mile away. She raised her hand and held up three fingers. "He called me pet names three times, Maddie. Three times! That's so obnoxious."

"He was clearly antagonizing you," Penelope said, as though that explained everything in a perfectly logical fashion.

Sophie threw up her hands. "Duh. That's my point."

Maddie sighed. "Only because you were being so snippy with him."

Sophie shrugged. "It doesn't matter. It's not like I'll see him."

Maddie chewed on her bottom lip. "He's a friend of ours. He's new in town. We invite him to things."

"It's no big deal. It will be fine." She'd avoid those things if he were around. Easy solution to a non-problem. The benefit of moving to the boonies was she didn't have to deal with anyone she wasn't interested in.

"Just remember, he gave you a great deal." Maddie put her hand on her chest. "As a favor to me."

Sophie wanted to stop talking about him. He made her itchy, and she had a million things to do today. She gave Maddie her best smile. "I promise I'll be good, Mom."

She was saved any more discussion when Mitch, Maddie's husband, called out from the foyer, "Anyone home?"

Maddie called back, "We're in the kitchen."

A second later Mitch Riley, Penelope's husband, Evan, and Shane, Maddie's oldest brother, stood in the foyer.

Maddie spun around and looked at her husband's empty arms. "Where's Lily?"

Mitch cocked his head and grinned. "What? Is she too young to be left alone?"

Maddie put her hands on her hips. "Where's my baby?"

Shane scoffed, "Relax, Mads. Ce-ce's got her."

Cecilia was Shane's wife, who also happened to be Mitch's sister, and was five months pregnant herself. Sometimes their complicated family gave Sophie a headache, and she felt one growing at the base of her skull right now. They were all so intertwined in a way that eluded her.

Like Penelope, Sophie was an only child. Unlike Penelope, Sophie had always liked it that way. Connection and attachments were complicated, and she liked to keep things simple. She'd grown up with decent parents who loved her and gave her a stable home and a roof over her head, despite a permanent case of wanderlust. Yes, they were a bit eccentric and flighty, and oh so new agey, always looking for the next step in an enlightenment they never seemed to find. As soon as they'd done their duty and she'd become a legal adult, they'd taken off to explore to their hearts' content. Her parents were hippie throwbacks, and they made their way around the globe by being international house sitters, living in communes, and taking on charity expeditions. Sometimes they stayed in a place for a month, sometimes years. Right now they were three months into their year in India. They left her alone to live her life, which was fine. Sophie wouldn't be able to handle the way Maddie's family always hovered over her.

Sophie talked to her parents once every couple of weeks on Skype, and occasionally they came home. As far as she was concerned, seeing them once a year was the perfect amount of parent time.

Sophie liked her freedom and had no desire to be tied down. She had no idea how Maddie put up with constant family involvement. It would drive her crazy.

The only people in this world she felt bonded to were Maddie and Penelope. Yes, she loved the rest of the group too, loved the Donovans and their big, crazy family, even though they were pains in the asses. But Maddie and Penelope were her rocks. The ones she'd do anything for.

They were more than enough for her. She didn't need more entanglements in her life. Sure, sometimes at Christmas when everyone was busy with celebrating with family she experienced a sense of wistfulness, but she solved that with nonstop activity. And they always included her, so it worked out.

Maddie's tension didn't seem to abate with her husband's reassurance. "Do you think she's okay? Maybe I should call Cecilia and make sure she knows the schedule."

Mitch walked over to his wife and put his hands on her shoulders, kissing her on the top of her head. "Maddie, relax. I took care of it."

Maddie worried her bottom lip. "I'm sorry I'm so paranoid. I just don't want anything to happen to her. She's so small and precious."

Evan snorted. "Please, that baby is a monster."

"Evan!" Penelope glared at her husband.

Maddie gasped, swinging in the direction of her brother. "You take that back."

Evan shrugged. "You are all smitten, but that kid is plotting world domination. You can see it in her eyes."

Sophie laughed. Evan was right. Lily Riley was a force to be reckoned with. She took spirited to a whole new level.

Maddie scowled. "Don't say that about my sweet baby."

Evan pulled Penelope in front of him, like she could shield him from his sister. "Penelope and I took her to the park, and I swear she was holding court in the sandbox. One of the babies threatened to crawl away and Lily cried until the poor kid came back. And then she smiled at me, all cunning."

"He might be exaggerating a touch," Penelope said, given she was required to be the most logical person in the room.

Mitch, however, chuckled. "That's my girl."

Maddie put a hand on her chest. "Our daughter is not cunning."

Everyone gave the proud mama a smile but remained silent.

There was a knock on the front door and Sophie sighed. Who could that be? Nobody she knew would knock. Everyone she knew would just walk right in. Bright pink gloves still on her hands, she took them off and excused herself, slowing as she saw who was at her door.

Ugh! It was *him*.

Their eyes met. And without all the distractions of other people, a spark of heat flared between them.

Yeah, screw that. Not in this lifetime.

When she reached the screen she gave him a narrow-eyed glare, but determined to do right by her friends, she said sweetly, "Can I help you, Mr. Moore?"

He opened the door and stepped inside like he owned the place. She went to call him on the invasion only to realize he actually did. Thinking of Maddie, and peace, she politely said nothing.

"Mr. Moore, huh?" He gave her another one of those wicked smiles he seemed to favor. A smile Sophie was sure got him anything his little black heart could desire.

"You're my landlord." She crossed her arms and huffed. "I'm supposed to be respectful."

"Ah, darlin', I wouldn't want you to go changing on my account." God, his voice was ridiculous. Like dripping honey.

Sophie bet he made more than one thing drip all over town. She put her hands on her hips. "I'm not rising to the bait."

Then he had the nerve to let his eyes take a long, leisurely stroll down her body. "What fun is that?"

The challenge, the spur of competition and thrill of banter raced through her blood, swift and sudden. She'd always been a sucker for sharp, witty repartee. It was like crack, and it made him a hundred times more attractive. Which was unfortunate considering he was far too attractive already.

She raised her chin and said in her most haughty tone, "I'm not here for fun. I'm here to work, keep my head down, and serve my time before I go back home."

He chuckled. "I'd bet good money you haven't had a quiet day in your entire life."

"Since you don't know me, you have no basis for your claim."

"I've got good instincts." He stepped closer and he was so big, so broad, and so freakin' gorgeous.

It was like every cell in her body came to startling, angry life. Why couldn't he be slow? A bit dim-witted like men who looked like him were supposed to be? She rarely met a tongue as sharp as her own, and she was enjoying this a little too much. Her vagina had terrible taste in men and notoriously steered her wrong, which was why she'd stopped listening to it years ago.

So instead of a retort that would send them further down the rabbit hole, she said, "Can I help you?"

His attention shifted to her mouth, settled for a bit

before moving back up to her eyes. He held out a ring with three keys on it. "These are the rest of the keys."

Well now, he actually had a purpose that didn't include sparring with her. Great. She held out her hand. "Thanks."

He didn't drop them into her palm; instead he raised the first one. "This is to the basement." He flicked the other one. "The back door." And the third. "This is to the garage."

"Got it."

He dropped the ring into her palm and she put the keys in her pocket.

Their gazes caught and held a little too long.

In his honeyed voice he said, "The garage can stick and be a little stubborn, so let me know if it gives you problems and I'll show you my tricks for easing your way in."

Was that dirty? It sounded dirty. She should be good. Say thank you and send him on his way. But instead, she smirked. "I'm a big girl, I assure you I know how to ease my way in just fine."

"I'm sure you do, honey."

What were they talking about here? Because it sure as hell wasn't keys.

She needed to put an end to this. She cleared her throat. "So are we done here? 'Cause I've got a lot to do."

He nodded. "You know where to find me in case you need help with how something works."

She flashed him her most winning smile. "I've been living on my own a long time. I promise you, your door is the last place I'll show up."

"Didn't your mama ever tell you not to make promises you can't keep?"

She put a hand on a cocked hip and wiggled her fingers. "Good-bye, honey."

He laughed, not remotely insulted. "Try not to make too much noise, I've got to get some sleep."

She huffed. "It's the middle of the day, you deadbeat."

He opened the door and said over his shoulder, "Late night."

"Those hookers wear you out?" Okay, she had to stay away because she couldn't seem to control her mouth.

He spun around and held out his arms. "Like I have to pay for sex. I mean, come on."

Then he turned and jogged down the stairs and across the front yard before she could get in the last word.

"I'm fairly certain he doesn't have to pay for sex," Penelope said, somehow standing next to Sophie.

When had she shown up? And why hadn't Sophie realized she was there? She put her arms over her chest. "You just shut up."

Penelope rose to her tiptoes trying to get a gander at his disappearing form. "Good God, that man is hot."

"He's obnoxious."

"And hot."

Sophie turned and glared at Penelope. "You're married, and everyone knows Evan is the most gorgeous man ever, so stop that."

"I'm married." Penelope grinned. "But I'm not dead."

"Well, I don't want to talk about him." She shook her head. "What was Maddie thinking?"

"I don't understand why you don't like him."

"Because I don't." She took off back toward the kitchen, determined to put Ryder out of her mind and not think about him again for the rest of her natural born life.

Chapter Four

Ryder had intended on staying away from Sophie Kincaid for at least the next couple days because despite their antagonistic sparring, he hadn't missed the chemistry between them. She liked arguing with him, and he sure as hell liked arguing with her. When it had been just the two of them standing in the living room, the sexual tension had buzzed like a live electrical wire.

The old him would have backed her against a wall and put all that heat to good use, but he'd turned over a new leaf, and acting rashly wasn't part of the package. Besides, with that fiery temper of hers, she'd probably kill him. Although he suspected it would be worth it.

But the way he figured it, putting his new tenant on her back less than twenty-four hours after he'd said hello probably wasn't a smart move. He had to live next door to her, and this was a small town. Used to a big city like Chicago, she might think she could avoid him, but he knew that was impossible.

There'd be no escaping the little blond firecracker, and being attracted to her wasn't a good enough reason to have sex with her and make things awkward. After the fiasco back home, he'd stopped making mistakes like Sophie.

So after he'd left her house, as he'd lain in bed, waiting for the adrenaline from the night to wash away and for sleep to claim him, he'd decided to stop whatever game they were playing. It was best to treat her like a proper neighbor and stay away from her as much as possible.

That plan went straight to hell about thirty seconds after he woke up to her cursing in the backyard.

He blinked his eyes open, glanced at the clock. It was nine a.m. He'd slept straight through the day and into the next morning, which didn't surprise him considering the last couple of days he'd had.

He heard a loud bang, followed by an exasperated female mutter. His bedroom was in the back corner of his house, closest to Sophie's yard. He reached over and lifted up the corner of his blackout shades to see her. Blond hair pulled back in a ponytail again, she wore tiny gray cotton shorts and a white tank top that made her look like a sexy, wholesome girl fantasy come to life.

She was trying to get the garage door open.

He smiled as she shoved against the side entrance. She was doing it all wrong. The harder she tried to force it, the more stuck it would become. He flipped the shade back down and put his hands behind his head.

The last thing he should do was go out there. And if he did go out there, it should be to help her, not taunt her.

"Goddamn it to hell!" she yelled, making him laugh.

Yeah, screw that.

He got out of bed. After putting on some coffee, he went to the bathroom, brushed his teeth, ran a hand through his hair, and threw on some gym shorts. He grabbed his cup and went out to the back.

At the sound of the screen door slamming shut, her

head shot up and she whirled to face him. She planted her hands on her small hips, her chest a rapid rise and fall from exertion.

Christ, she was a hot little thing.

He raised his mug to her. "Morning, Sophie."

"I am not asking you for help." Her voice was loud and indignant.

He shrugged. "Suit yourself." Then he settled himself on top of his picnic table to enjoy the show, taking a sip of coffee and letting the caffeine work its way through his system.

She stared at him.

He stared right back.

Next spring he planned on tearing down the house where Sophie stayed and building one big house that covered both lots so there was no fence between the two yards. When the lease ran out on his last tenants he'd told them he wasn't going to let them renew, and since nobody wanted a seven-month lease he'd planned on letting the house sit empty. Sophie had fallen right into his lap, and as they faced off Ryder couldn't figure out if that was a blessing or a curse.

She narrowed her eyes on him. "I knew you'd be ridiculous."

"I'm afraid you lost me."

She waved a hand over him. "Look at you with your abs and tats. You shouldn't be allowed out of the house."

He chuckled. "You don't like it, darlin', don't look."

She shook her head. "You're the absolute worst."

He put the cup down on the table and sat back, resting on his palms. The early May air was warm, the sun bright. Her eyes traveled the length of his bare chest, and she scowled at the tattoo on his shoulder and the one on his rib cage before shooting daggers at his stomach.

The corners of his mouth tilted as he repressed his grin. He kept in shape; he wasn't going to apologize.

Suddenly, her expression clouded and she ripped her gaze away, crossing her arms over her chest. She jutted her chin toward the garage door. "Do you happen to have one of those clicky things?"

He let the smile spread over his lips. "You mean a garage door opener?"

"Yes."

"Nope." He picked up his coffee and took a sip before saying, "It's manual."

She pointed to the two-seater Porsche convertible. "You mean I'm supposed to get out of my car and open the door . . . by hand?"

"Or you could keep your car in the driveway." He offered helpfully.

Her hand waved at her car. "You expect me to keep my baby in the driveway?"

He studied the Porsche and had to admit it was a cool car. It wasn't white and wasn't beige, but kind of a muted white tan color that probably had some name that eluded him. The creamy color highlighted the red leather seats and matching steering wheel. The combination was a surprise, unexpected, much like the woman in front of him trying very hard to work on her temper.

He shrugged. "It's an option."

"It's not an option."

"Then I guess you'll have to get out of the car and open the garage door."

She shook her head. "I'm in hell. You're the devil. And this is my punishment for all my misdeeds. That's the only logical explanation."

He let his gaze take a slow, lazy lap over her body

before saying, "Confess your sins, darlin', and maybe you can still be saved."

She sucked in a breath and heat flared between them before she frowned, all fierce and defiant. "Your dumb nicknames are getting redundant."

But they were effective. Despite her protests. He laughed. "Do you want me to show you how to open the door?"

She stared at him, her expression one of disbelief, as though she couldn't figure out how he could be such an idiot. Suddenly her features cleared and she got a sweet, bright smile on her lips. "No, no, that won't be necessary."

All the fine hairs on the back of his neck rose as she flashed him another brilliant smile before marching into the house.

He kept an eye on the back door, wondering what on earth she planned, having more fun this morning than he'd had in the last year.

After about five minutes she walked outside, carrying a sledgehammer over her shoulder.

"Now, Sophie," he said, getting up from the table. "Let's be reasonable."

She ignored him.

And before he could even get out another argument, calm as could be she went to the side door, swung, and smashed the door handle with a resounding crack.

The knob fell to the ground and she sighed happily before putting the hammer down and resting it against the garage. She pushed open the door and called out, "I'm in."

He shook his head. Thankfully, she faced away from him and couldn't see his huge grin. "Are you going to pay for that?"

"Yep." She walked into the garage. "Have a nice day, sweetie."

He laughed.

Yep, no doubt about it. Sophie Kincaid was nothing but trouble.

Somehow she'd managed to avoid Ryder for the rest of the day. Okay, she managed to avoid *talking* to him. Looking at him was a different matter entirely.

Oh sure, she'd made sure not to occupy the same air space as him, playing a game she was positive he was onto. When he was inside, she did work outside, and when he was outside, she went in.

But every time she heard the slam of his door she'd run to the window to look. Oh dear Lord, did she look.

Yesterday, she'd thought him ridiculously, eye-rollingly hot, but without a shirt, Ryder Moore should be outlawed. The man was completely ripped, in the very best way. And those tats. God, when she'd seen them this morning, highlighted by the sun, she'd about fainted with lust.

They were her weakness.

See, she had a secret. Yes, she'd reformed herself from a troubled rebellious teenager who'd had far too much freedom. Yes, she wore designer clothes, went to the best clubs, and drank trendy twenty-dollar cocktails. And yes, she went on dates with successful, nice, professional men. She did everything a responsible woman of thirty-one was supposed to do.

But deep down, it was men like Ryder that really flipped her switch. Men she could go toe-to-toe with. Men that would give her a run for her money. Men she didn't have to be nice to or sweet with. Men that picked you up, tossed you over their shoulder, and had their politically incorrect way with you.

Bad men so cocky you couldn't help screwing in the

bathroom an hour after you met them. Men that fucked so good they became an addiction.

The kind of men healthy women grew out of because they were nothing but trouble.

Ryder was that kind of man. She'd sensed it the second she'd met him and known for certain the moment their eyes had locked as he handed over his keys.

Yes, she sold her inability to keep a boyfriend as being picky . . . and she was picky, because the respectable men she was supposed to like bored her to tears. She just couldn't get excited about a guy that wanted to wake up early to get to Home Depot on Saturday.

She supposed someday she'd grow up and like the men she was supposed to, but Ryder had proved that today wasn't that day.

She took a sip of iced tea and sat on the porch swing, gently rocking it with her foot as she took in the quiet tree-lined street.

Why did he have to have tattoos? God, she loved ink. One scrolled across his right shoulder, bold and black, in an intricate pattern, and the other was along his rib cage and spelled "freedom." She wanted to lick them. Trace every single letter and curve with her tongue.

It was the worst.

If it was just his looks, she could handle it, but there was something far worse, far more dangerous than him being hotter than hell. She liked fighting with him. Like, really liked it. She was pretty certain grown women weren't supposed to get turned on by arguing, but Sophie couldn't help but love a good battle. There must be something wrong with her that when a man brought her flowers on a first date she had to repress the eye roll, and a man that fought with her made her want to jump him. She was messed up, she understood that and had paid the price.

A long time ago, she'd learned to ignore her urges, which actually wasn't that difficult. The kind of men that were her weakness didn't exactly grow on trees. Somewhere along the way she'd grown complacent in the fact that most men couldn't pull it out the way she needed. She'd made the mistake of thinking she was over it.

She gritted her teeth and shook her head.

It was like she was cursed. Ryder was her neighbor, her landlord, and she didn't like him. Well, she didn't like him the way she was supposed to. She didn't get it. In Chicago, a city with millions of people, she couldn't even find a man she wanted to date, let alone have sex with. But two minutes in Revival and her neighbor was a fucking god who was annoying as hell, and happened to push every single one of her bad girl, perverted buttons? How unfair was that?

It was so unfortunate. Obviously, she couldn't act on it.

How hard could it be? She'd managed to avoid him all morning, and thankfully he'd taken off on his motorcycle an hour ago. There was no sign of him.

Had he gone to a girlfriend's house for dinner? Not that it was any of her business.

What if he had a girlfriend? He'd clearly been out all night yesterday. Wasn't a girlfriend the logical reason? But things had definitely sparked between them, so if he was in a relationship, how serious could it be?

She shook her head. It. Did. Not. Matter.

Enough of this. She stood and the swing bounced. She had things to do. It was Friday. She had two days to get this house together and settle in before she started her job with the city of Revival on Monday.

She needed to get out of the house for a bit. She walked

in and grabbed her purse off the kitchen counter. First stop on the list, buy a proper, functioning door for the garage to replace the one she'd broken.

She smiled. Smashing that door had been so immensely satisfying, made even more so by the sound of Ryder's surprised laughter.

Which was why she was staying far away from him.

Two hours later she flew down the highway, top down on the best car in the entire world, listening to "Mama's Broken Heart" by Miranda Lambert and singing at the top of her lungs. She'd gone to the store, picked out a new door, bought a tape measure, and gone back home, because apparently all doors aren't the same, measured said door, then returned to the store.

It would be delivered tomorrow morning, and the guy would even install it for her. See, she didn't need one bit of Ryder's help.

Just as she hit the curve on the road and Miranda started singing about hiding your crazy, she flew past a car going the opposite direction, realizing too late it had the word "sheriff" scrolled in white along the side.

Her gaze flew to her speedometer, which read ninety-five. She eased off the gas and started praying, watching the cop car get farther away in her rearview mirror.

Please don't pull me over. Please don't pull me over. Please, please, please.

Just as she thought she was safe, the car did a U-turn and the lights started flashing.

Shit!

Heart pounding, she slowed down and eased to the side of the road. Was it too early to throw Charlie's name around?

Charlie Radcliff was the county sheriff, this cop's boss,

and they were friends. Didn't that mean she automatically got out of tickets? Would that even work? Okay, she'd feel out the cop and make a decision on the fly on whether to drop Charlie's name. Besides, she was good at talking her way out of trouble; maybe it wouldn't even be necessary.

She came to a stop and the car pulled in back of her.

Even if she didn't drop Charlie's name, she had a ready plan for handling the police. She was always prepared with her license and registration. She was extremely nice, cheery, and full of bright smiles. She never made excuses, was apologetic, and took full responsibility for her actions.

It got her out of tickets nine times out of ten.

While the cop got out of the car, Sophie busied herself getting out her license, registration, and current insurance card. She managed to get it all together and fix most of her brilliant smile on her lips as the shadow fell across her car.

"I'm so sorry, Officer," she said in her most sunny voice as she turned to the man in uniform. She looked up—and up and up.

The smile fell away as she stared into a pair of mirrored sunglasses and the face of her nightmares.

"You!"

Ryder cocked a grin. "Me."

No way. She glared at him. "There's no way you're a cop."

"But I am. Chief deputy sheriff, to be exact."

She could only stare at him in complete horror. "This has got to be a joke. I don't believe you. Let me see your badge."

He shook his head and took out a black leather case, flipping it open and handing it to her. "What, do you think I rented a uniform, complete with cop car, on the off chance I'd spot you on the road and could pull you over?"

Okay, that did sound ridiculous. But still, how in the

hell could Ryder be a cop? What kind of justice was there in this world? She studied the title under his name and handed it back, ignoring his barb. "What exactly is a chief deputy sheriff?"

He flashed her that wicked grin. "It means I'm the sheriff's second in command."

Why? Why is this happening to me? Stupidly, she sputtered, "But that's impossible."

Between Charlie and Ryder, the women in this town had to be begging to get arrested. Her mind instantly filled with a fantasy of late-night traffic stops on deserted roads, being handcuffed and pushed facedown on the hood, legs spread.

She shook it away. This was not the time.

"Afraid not." He put his arm on the edge of her window. "Do you know how fast you were going, darlin'?"

Oh God, this was some brand-new fresh version of hell.

Chapter Five

Sophie glared, her pretty face filled with fury and something else Ryder thought he recognized . . . excitement.

The license and registration she'd so graciously held out were snatched back as she gaped at him. Thank God he'd never told her his profession, because her expression right now was well worth it.

It had taken everything in him to not burst out laughing at her surprised horror.

She narrowed those big doe eyes at him. "You're not going to give me a ticket."

He cocked a brow. "You so sure about that?"

He wasn't, actually. He didn't pull people over anymore, and he hadn't had the radar on her, but as soon as he'd seen her speeding he hadn't been able to resist pulling her over.

Of course, he should have resisted, but so far the decision was hard to regret.

She tilted her chin. "I wasn't even speeding."

He let his gaze fall to her full mouth and thought of all the reasons he couldn't kiss her. He pushed away the idea of engaging in a very inappropriate abuse of power.

He held out his hands. "License and registration, ma'am."

She huffed and slapped it into his hands. "I'm going to tell Charlie about this."

"Go ahead. He'll side with me." He looked down at her license. So she was only five-two, and by the looks of her wasn't lying about her weight. But it was her picture that stopped him. It was, by far, the worst picture he'd ever seen. The DMV employee clearly had a grudge against her, because they'd caught her half-lidded, mid grimace. "I see they captured you on a good day."

"You just shut up."

"Is that any way to talk to a man that holds your insurance rates in his hands?"

She gripped the steering wheel tighter. "Is threatening a harmless citizen any way to correct the public perception of rampant police corruption?"

In his vast history with women, he'd never met any he liked arguing with this much. Every interaction with her was like a mini adventure. "Honey, you are the least harmless woman I've ever met."

She still wore the white tank top and gray shorts from that morning. She still looked hot as hell. Her eyes went wide and innocent as she put a hand on her fantastic chest. "Me? I'm like a quiet little mouse."

He raised a brow. "Tell that to my garage door."

"That door was asking for it." She waved a hand behind her. "Besides, I already ordered a brand-new proper one with a lock that doesn't need to be taken to dinner first before it allows me to enter."

He laughed. "Did anyone ever tell you that you have a sharp tongue?"

She reached out and plucked her license out of his hands. "Nope. Everyone else thinks I'm lovely."

"So they don't really know you."

She rolled her eyes at him. "You've known me for less than twenty-four hours, so you, sir, are no authority."

He wasn't quite sure about that. Something told him he was getting the real Sophie Kincaid, but before he could decide for certain he needed to see her react with other people. He snatched her license back and she made a grab for it, but he held it out of her reach. "If I run your license, what am I going to find?"

She smiled sweetly. "That I'm an excellent driver."

"So no tickets?"

"Hardly any."

He narrowed his eyes. Her expression was far too innocent. Far too pleasant. As though she hid something. "So you haven't been pulled over recently."

Her brows furrowed for a fraction of a second before she shrugged. "That's not what you asked. You asked if I have tickets."

"So you've been pulled over."

She shrugged again. "Maybe a few times."

"But you have no tickets."

"That's correct."

Ah, now he was getting the picture. "So you charm your way out of them?"

She smiled. "I'm a very charming person."

"You're walking, talking chaos." She was already causing him havoc wherever she went.

She peered up at him, that cocky smirk on her lips, and he wanted to kiss it right off her. Their gazes clashed, and heat and tension thickened the air around them, pushing out all the fun and replacing it with desire.

She sucked in a little breath.

He fought the urge to lean down and do dirty, filthy things to that mouth.

Her pink tongue darted out and wet her lips.

He had an image of pushing her over the hood of her car, peeling down those shorts, and using his mouth, hands, and cock to make her beg for him. In fact, he couldn't think of anything he'd like more than to listen to Sophie plead for him to take her.

Don't do it.

Her big doe eyes were dark now, her pupils dilated as though she followed his thoughts. There was no mistaking the chemistry that filled the air.

Don't do it.

Her chest rose and fell, shallow and wanting.

Don't do this.

He leaned down.

Her chin tilted and her lips parted.

Ah, fuck it.

His fingers slid up her arm, touching her for the first time. He practically groaned at the contact of her skin under him.

She shivered.

He wrapped his hand around the nape of her neck.

She craned to meet him.

"Chief, is everything okay?"

He jerked back, shaking his head to clear it from the cloud of lust she'd wrapped around him, to see his newest and youngest deputy standing there. Ryder had been so caught up in Sophie, he hadn't even seen the damn kid pull up. He sighed. "Everything's fine, Harold."

"We tried to get you on the radio." The kid, who looked like a cherub angel playing dress-up in his daddy's uniform, glanced at Sophie, back at him, then at Sophie again. He cleared his throat. "There's been an accident out on Route Twelve."

Great. Not another one. He hated the beginning of summer, when the weather got warm and kids were almost out of school and their brains were already on vacation. It made everyone stupid and reckless, and clearly he wasn't an exception.

He looked down at the woman already messing up his life. Did he not have a list of reasons to stay away from her? Was she not trouble? Did she not trigger all of his worst and baser instincts?

So what had he done with all his common sense? He'd gone to kiss her. It wouldn't have been a nice, gentlemanly kiss either. It would have been hot. Hungry. And messy.

If Harold hadn't shown up, his mouth would be on hers right now. He'd know just what she tasted like. He wouldn't entertain fantasies about firing Harold for his poor timing. It wasn't the kid's fault. Really, he should be thanking him for saving him from a grave mistake.

He handed her back the license and registration.

She took it from him, darted a glance behind her to Harold, then back at him before saying in a low voice, "Whatever that was, it didn't mean anything."

He appreciated a woman that didn't shy away from awkward situations. He nodded. "Agreed."

"I mean it. It was a moment of madness."

"I'm not arguing with you." It was a moment of something, all right. And it was probably best he didn't know what she felt like moving under him. Just sliding his fingers over her skin and through her hair had been bad enough.

"We're neighbors, and that's all we'll ever be." Her fingers tightened on her license.

Of course she was right. "I agree."

"I mean it, I'm never going to sleep with you." Her expression turned aggravated, and he knew right then she was looking for a fight. That she wanted him to argue with her. That a part of her liked the struggle.

He thought about it and decided to let her stew. "Sophie?"

She scraped her bottom lip with her teeth, and he almost groaned. "Yes?"

"Slow down." Then he turned and walked away before he could give in to the temptation of her.

Chapter Six

The first thing she did when she got home was call Penelope. She needed to process what the hell had just happened with Ryder, and the only way she knew how to do that was by talking. Penelope was the reasonable choice.

She was logical. Calm. Not prone to drama. But best of all, she didn't live here.

There was a knock on the screen door before Penelope called out, "Sophie?"

"In the kitchen." She rubbed her temples.

This was not good. Her heart still pounded, her skin still stretched too tight, and heat had settled low in her belly. And he'd barely touched her.

What if he kissed her? No, she couldn't let that happen.

Penelope walked in, wearing jeans, flats Sophie identified as Frye, and a gauzy, sleeveless white top. Even casual, Penelope looked pulled together and neat. The only time she wasn't neat was after Evan got his hands on her, so she'd been messed up considerably since they went public with their relationship. "Hey, what's up?"

Sophie handed her a glass of iced tea. "I have a problem."

Penelope sat down at the kitchen table and nodded. "Okay, let's see what I can do to help."

Just being in her presence calmed Sophie down. Made it possible to think. That's how, back in the day, a couple of wild girls like her and Maddie had Penelope as a best friend. Someone needed to be the calm one, and that someone was Penelope.

Sophie took a seat across from her. "You can't tell Maddie."

"My lips are sealed." She made a zipping motion and threw the imaginary key over her shoulder.

This wasn't a betrayal of her friendship with Maddie. This was how things worked. When they wanted to say fuck it, throw caution to the wind, and get someone to go along with the crazy, Maddie and Sophie went to each other. When they wanted common sense and practical, sensible discussion, they went to Penelope.

Besides, Maddie lived here, and ever since she'd become domesticated she'd been all gung ho on trying to set people up. The last thing Sophie wanted was for her to start getting ideas.

She folded her arms and rested her head on them. "I think I have the hots for Ryder."

Penelope laughed. "Oh, that was obvious the second he pulled up on his motorcycle."

Her head shot up. "Why would you even say that?"

Penelope took a sip of her iced tea. "You stared at each other for a minute flat. It didn't take a genius to figure out it was going to go down."

Boo. She'd hoped it was a figment of her imagination. "I don't like him."

Penelope gave a delicate shrug of her shoulder. "I don't think liking someone and attraction always go together."

"He's irritating. He argues with me. And he calls me

stupid names." Sophie threw up her hands, really getting into the spirit of the confession. "And he's a cop!"

Penelope picked up her glass and grinned. "I know. I met him before."

Sophie's mouth fell open. "You *met* him before? And this is the first you're telling me?"

"It didn't seem relevant."

"How could it not be relevant?" Being married to a Donovan boy, Penelope spent more time in Revival than Sophie had, but how could she have not mentioned Ryder?

Penelope rolled her eyes. "How was I supposed to know you'd develop a case of insta-lust for him?"

Sophie sucked in a breath. "You take that back. I don't have insta-lust, I'm just . . . just . . . having an unfortunate chemical reaction to him."

Penelope gave her a feigned look of sympathy and clucked her tongue. "Poor thing."

"You're such a bitch. Back to the topic." Sophie blew out a breath. "He pulled me over and almost kissed me."

"How did he look in his uniform?" Penelope asked.

Sophie blinked at her. "You're missing the point."

"I need a visual."

"How do you think he looked in his uniform?" She groaned, shaking her head. "Like a god. When he stood over me with that gun holster wrapped around his hips, I had about five hundred fantasies."

"That's rough." Penelope's tone was filled with amusement.

"Did you know he has tattoos?"

"No, I did not."

"On his shoulder and along his ribs." Sophie sighed. "It's like he was custom designed to bring out the slut in me."

Her thoughts had veered so inappropriately, so jarringly

pornographic, she'd had a hard time not breaking into a sweat as he stood there, staring down at her, looking broad in his uniform, those mirrored sunglasses highlighting his strong jaw. Sophie groaned. "He looked good in tan, Penelope. Tan! You know how much I hate men in tan. It should be outlawed."

Her friend's lips quivered. "I've heard the lecture."

"Well, he made it look good. Like 'strip me naked and do whatever you want to me' good."

"I see." Penelope calmly clasped her hands on the table. "And he almost kissed you?"

"Yes. We'd been arguing. He called me walking, talking chaos and I took offense. One second we were in the heat of battle, and the next it was all smoldering lust and too-long looks. Then I started breathing fast and he touched my arm, and it was like an electric shock actually traveled across my skin. Up my arm, Penelope! He leaned down to kiss me but his deputy, a baby that looked like he'd stepped off *The Andy Griffith Show*, came up and ruined the moment."

"How interesting." Penelope nodded as though everything made perfect sense. But it didn't make sense.

God, what was wrong with her? Why did fighting with him turn her on so much? How deranged was it that she got off arguing? Hadn't she learned her lesson back in college? Why couldn't she be a normal woman and like flowers and sonnets? She stared pleadingly at her friend, as though she could provide Sophie with the answers. "What should I do?"

"What do you want to do?" Penelope would have made a great therapist. She never gave advice but instead asked annoying, thought-provoking questions that made you want to hurl things at her before you hugged her.

Sophie knew what she'd *wanted*. She'd wanted Ryder to kiss her. She'd wanted him to put her in handcuffs and teach her a lesson. Ryder brought out that girl from her youth, and she was supposed to be above all that now. She was not supposed to want to star in her own porno of Breaking Bad Girls.

"You know guys like him and I don't mix."

"That was a long time ago. And how bad could he be? He's a cop, an upstanding member of society. It's hardly the same thing." That was Penelope for you, always pointing out the obvious.

His standing wasn't the problem. The way he made her feel, all wild and crazy, was the problem. She tried a more pragmatic approach. "He's going to be my neighbor. I don't need things to get awkward."

"So there's your answer," Penelope said reasonably.

Sophie frowned. "You aren't going to tell me to go for it?"

"What's the point in that?" Penelope tilted her head as though in thought. "You're right, he's your neighbor, and this town is small. You'll probably see him all over the place. It's only a couple of orgasms. Nothing you can't take care of yourself, right?"

Everything Penelope said irritated Sophie. Which meant she was 100 percent correct. Well, good. This was exactly why she'd called Penelope. To be sensible. She straightened in her chair. "You're right. Guys who look like that are never good in bed. Girls fall all over themselves to sleep with them, so they never cultivate any skills. I'm sure my vibrator is much better than him."

"I'm sure." Penelope nodded as though she agreed with everything Sophie was saying, but the light of mischief shone in her eyes.

Sophie frowned, thinking of Penelope's own gorgeous man, who clearly knew how to give orgasms. Despite Penelope not being much of a sharer, there was no way

Evan was bad in bed. Sophie cocked a grin. "I'm sure Evan is the *only* exception."

"I'm sure." Penelope smiled before waving her hand in the air. "So ignore your attraction and focus on your many arguments for why sex with Ryder isn't a good idea. If you keep reminding yourself, that should keep you in line."

Suspicious, Sophie narrowed her eyes. "I sense a trap."

"I don't see why." One dark brow rose. "Unless you're looking to be talked into it."

"Of course I'm not." But she was. That's what this conversation had shown her. That was the problem with her—guys like Ryder made her want to throw caution to the wind, and once she did, she slipped down the rabbit hole and lost herself. Guys like Ryder always went the same way: insane, spontaneous sex in every place that wouldn't lead to arrest, obsession, angst, anger, hurt, and eventually, abandonment. All leading to one giant clusterfuck she wanted no part of.

Penelope nodded. "Okay."

Well, now she knew the truth, and it only cemented her original instincts. Time to move off him as a subject. "It's settled, then. I'll avoid him while I'm here and focus on doing my job."

"Sounds like a solid plan," Penelope said, her lips curving into a soft smile.

"Exactly." Sophie put her head in her palms and sighed. "I can't believe I'm stuck here for six months."

"It's not that bad. Look on the bright side, you get to see Maddie all the time. You can slow down and enjoy yourself."

Sophie raised her head and sniffed. "I was enjoying myself just fine back home."

Penelope's brow furrowed. "I don't know. Between work

and traveling all over the city for your blog, you had to be getting burned out."

Sophie shook her head. "This from the ultimate workaholic?"

Penelope shrugged. "I'm just saying after your parents' last visit you seemed to go into hyperdrive and never shut off."

Granted, her parents' last visit had driven her crazy. All three of them trapped in her one-bedroom apartment. Their incessant going on about how her materialistic capitalism was a disappointment to them. Like her being successful and stable was a failure. But that had nothing to do with it.

"My blog really took off after they left. It was a coincidence and had nothing to do with them." Sophie put her hand on her chest. "And I was having fun doing something I loved."

"You weren't getting tired of going to all those clubs?" Penelope asked.

"No! Why would I?" Yes, maybe it had been a bit manic sometimes, but she'd still loved her life. She'd been busy, too busy to think about anything but how much fun she'd been having.

Just the way she liked it.

Ryder managed to avoid Sophie for the next twenty-four hours, but as the afternoon grew to a close he couldn't avoid the inevitable any longer. Somehow he didn't think she'd be too happy if he surprised her, so he sighed, vowed to keep his hands off her, and knocked on the screen door.

She emerged from the back of the house, where the bedroom was located, looking as fuckable as ever in a pair of frayed, cut off jean shorts and a yellow tank top with the word "princess" sprawled across her chest in glittery pink letters. Her hair was coiled into a messy bun on the top of her head, with tendrils spilling out onto her neck and framing her face.

God help him.

He told himself not to engage her and to refer to her by name. *Get in, get straight to the point, and get out*. He gave her his most charming smile. "Hello, darlin'."

Okay, so he had no self-control.

Arms crossed, she glared at him through the screen. "What do you want, dumplin'?"

He laughed. "Darlin' is way better than dumplin'."

She rolled her eyes. "You're so clueless."

Oh, but he wasn't, and that was the problem. She liked that one in particular. Her eyes flashed every time he said it. Not that he intended to mention that piece of information and risk starting down a path that would probably lead to sexual innuendo, and him pushing her against the wall and ravishing her mouth.

The walk to her bedroom was a little too short.

And she was a little too tempting.

He put his hand on the door handle. "Can I come in?"

"Why?" The question was laced with suspicion.

"Because I wanted to talk to you about tonight."

"Tonight?"

"Sophie." He lowered his voice. "Let me in."

She sighed. "Fine, but keep your distance."

A smile quivered at his lips, but he nodded, all serious like, and stepped into the living room.

Her gaze flickered down his body, and she bit her lip before shaking her head. "You're in. What can I do for you?"

She could do any number of things, but all of them were off the table, so he kept it to business. "I assume you're headed to Mitch and Maddie's tonight."

"Of course. The Chicago group leave tomorrow and it's

tradition." Her eyes roamed over him again, as though she couldn't help herself.

He was right there with her because his brain was half on the conversation and half on the filthy things he'd like to do to her. He cleared his throat. *Stay on topic.* "I'm going, so I wanted to warn you."

She scowled. "Why are you going?"

He shrugged. "I was invited."

"Why?"

"Because I'm friends with Mitch and Maddie, I don't work tonight, and it's a party." He took a step toward her and she stepped back. The flare of anticipation in her gaze made him predatory, and hard. Which wouldn't do at all.

"But . . ." She trailed off, her expression filled with something he could only describe as panicked excitement. "I don't want you there."

He needed to stay sharp here, to not give in to this insatiable desire to bait her, but then his attention shifted to her mouth. "Don't you?"

She shook her head. "No. Of course not."

There was something addictive about the way they sparked. It went beyond chemistry or attraction. Beyond sex.

He raised a brow. "It won't make your night more *exciting*?"

She sucked in a little breath. "Don't be an egomaniac."

"It's got nothing to do with ego."

"How do you figure?"

Because she was consumed with the same lust he was, and being around her would sure as hell make his night a lot more interesting. But he ignored the question. He flashed her a smile. "Do you want a ride?"

Her eyes went wide and she sputtered, "Excuse me?"

He laughed. "To Mitch and Maddie's. In case you didn't notice, we live next door to each other. Seems kind of silly to go separately." Of course, driving together was down-right stupid, but he didn't plan on bringing that up. They both knew the danger. Unfortunately, they both seemed to like danger a little too much.

A pretty pink flush stained her cheeks. "Yes, well, um . . ."

Awww. He'd flustered her. With another woman he'd let her compose herself and ignore her misinterpretation of his statement, but this was Sophie, so he grinned. "I'm happy to give you the other kind of ride too. Just say the word, darlin'."

She gasped, her stance turning rigid. There was that temper.

"Not in this lifetime!" She stepped toward him and jabbed him in the chest with her finger. "I told you yesterday, I'm never having sex with you. Ever. So don't even think about getting ideas in your head."

She poked him again and he grabbed her hand. "The ideas are already there. It's what to do about them."

She snatched her hand away. "You will do nothing about them."

He glanced down. Her nipples were hard, her skin flushed, her eyes bright. Since his brain had taken leave the second she'd opened the door, he responded with what would drive her most crazy. He shrugged. "All right."

"All right?" Her lips were parted, ready.

He nodded. "All right, I'll do nothing about them."

She growled. Actually growled. It was adorable. "Good."

He repressed his smile. "So are you going to ride with me or what?"

"No. I'll go by myself."

"Because you're stubborn?"

"Because I want my freedom."

He raised his brow. "Are you sure it's not because you're afraid to be alone with me?"

"Ha! You wish." She huffed and put her hands on her hips. "You're the most harmless man I've ever met."

"Right back at ya, honey."

"Stop calling me those names."

He met her eyes. "Come with me."

Her pupils dilated and he realized too late how that sounded.

He lowered his voice. "We're going to the same place. Let me drive you. Look at the bright side, you can drink as much as you want and not have to worry about how you're going to get home."

Her brow furrowed. "Do you have a car? Or do you expect me to ride on the back of that motorcycle?"

"I have a car too." His fingers twitched with the desire to put his hands on her. Christ, she made him hard. "We'll take whatever you prefer."

Her chest was a rapid rise and fall as she seemed to think through her options.

He wondered if she thought through the same options as him—namely, the things he could do to her in a car versus the things he could do to her on his bike. Things he wasn't supposed to be thinking about.

"I'd think a car was safer," she said, ripping him away from his list of depraved acts.

That depended on what kind of safety she meant, but he nodded. "The car it is."

"Fine, I'll go with you." She held up a hand. "But only because I want to drink."

"Of course. No other reason."

"So we understand each other?"

"Perfectly." His gaze dipped to her mouth before rising to meet her eyes. "We'll meet out front at six."

"All right."

Neither moved.

God help him. Somewhere in the next couple of hours he needed to shore up his self-control. He was going to have to do something to take the edge off because he sure as hell couldn't be around her like this and keep his hands to himself. "I'll see you soon, Sophie."

"Yes." The muscles in her throat worked as she swallowed hard. "Soon."

He turned and got the hell out of there.

Sophie spent the rest of the afternoon frantically unpacking to work off her excess energy and trying to figure out what to wear. Before Ryder showed up at her door, her outfit hadn't been a thought in her head, but now she obsessed on it. Her brain told her to dress very conservatively—like maybe a nice pair of jeans and a blousy top—but her slut told her to make Ryder sweat.

As she stood, fresh from her shower, in a pair of panties and no bra, staring at her closet, she knew which part of her was winning. He made her want to be risky, be daring. And he was right—his being at Mitch and Maddie's had upped the excitement quotient by a thousand.

Why did he have to be so hot and infuriating?

She blew out an exasperated breath, tried to grab a pair of jeans, and at the last second veered to the left, picking out a flirty, sexy Bohemian-style white sundress.

She'd bought it a couple of weeks ago, but hadn't worn it. Nor had she tried it on. But it was perfect for tonight. Casual, and revealing, but it didn't look like she was trying too hard.

Praying it fit, she slipped it over her head, and the second she turned to the mirror she was in love. It was in a wrinkled cotton fabric that fell high on her thighs, with a jagged eyelet hem. The spaghetti straps flattered the curve of her shoulders before the dress dipped down, scooping low across her cleavage. It looked awesome with her newly tanned skin. She paired it with a thick tan woven belt and UGG flip-flops to maintain the casual vibe.

More than satisfied with the dress, she spent the next thirty minutes working her hair into an "I've just been to the beach" mess and applying light makeup that highlighted her eyes, cheekbones, and mouth while looking like she barely had anything on.

At the end, she surveyed her results. Sometimes the gods smiled upon you, and this was one of those times.

Okay, so she wasn't wearing a bra . . . but how could she with her dress?

It didn't mean anything.

She was just being fashionable. She was a very fashionable woman.

Really.

She glanced at her clock. It was six, and she was right on time. Her stomach did a little dance, which she ignored. She was cool, not excited. Not brimming with anticipation.

She walked to the front of the house and out the door, turning to lock it before swiveling around to find him already waiting for her, watching.

She took two steps and froze, her throat going dry.

Holy mother of God.

She wasn't religious, but she'd gone to Catholic school all her life, and she resisted the urge to make the sign of the cross and pray for strength.

She was going to need it.

He stood, wearing worn jeans, a black T-shirt, and his aviators and leaning against a kick-ass black classic Ford Shelby Mustang.

Sophie almost had an orgasm on the spot.

She could only stare at him, looking like a total badass, hotter than any man she'd ever laid eyes on.

And he stared right back.

While she couldn't see behind his sunglasses, she could practically feel his long once-over. Heat and chemistry shimmered along the air, and somehow she finally managed to make her way down the stairs.

Out of all the cars, why did he have to have this one? Muscle cars were her weakness. Well, that and tattoos.

Hell, everything about this man was her weakness.

She stepped next to him and rubbed the chrome. He had a classic Mustang and a big, powerful Harley. This man was sent from hell. Voice awed, she said, "It's so pretty. I can't believe you own one."

He smiled down at her. "1967."

She shivered. "That's the best year."

He shook his head and sighed.

She licked her lips. "What?"

"Do you have to be perfect?" The question came out thick, shivering down her spine.

So. Much. Trouble.

She'd had men tell her a lot of things. She'd been told she was gorgeous. Hot. Fun. Smart. When someone dated as long as she had, she'd heard practically every compliment under the sun. But this, right here, was the best one ever. Thirty seconds in his company and they were already veering. She shrugged. "I could say the same for you."

"Could you?" His voice had turned low, intimate.

Tilting her head, she smirked. "You're a pretty lethal combination, as I'm sure you're well aware."

He shifted, turning slightly more toward her. "Maybe, but this isn't typical."

She wanted to ignore the trap he was laying for her, but she seemed unable to stop herself. "What does that mean?"

He moved closer, and she didn't step away, even though she should. "It means this isn't about thinking the other person is hot." He crooked a finger and ran it down her bare arm. Gooseflesh broke out over her skin, and her nipples tightened. "Although you're so fucking hot I can't think straight."

A low throb took up residence in her belly. She hissed, "Stop that."

They were facing each other head-on now, and Sophie didn't know how it happened, but they were much, much too close. He slid his hand over the roof of the car. "We seem to have a visceral attraction."

They did. The most dangerous of all attractions. Something she'd experienced a few times, but Ryder blew every single one of them out of the water.

In an effort to maintain some semblance of sanity, she crossed her arms. "Which is why we are going to stay neighbors."

"Darlin', my head couldn't agree more."

While what burned between them might be impossible to ignore, she needed to be clear that nothing would come from it. "This isn't a date. This is a carpool. Nothing more. Nothing less."

"I can do that." He nodded.

She shifted away from him. "So we're on the same page, right? Because crazy chemistry only leads to disaster."

His jaw jumped. "Agreed."

A frustrated disappointment settled in her sternum. She wanted him to fight her on it. Fight her, overpower her, and then take her. She wanted him to be a caveman. And the more she thought about it, the hotter she got.

She never learned, did she?

Hoping to clear the lust, she shook her head. "We should get going."

"Sophie?"

She sucked in a breath at her name on his lips. "Yes?"

He glanced down at her chest, making her hyperaware of her peaked nipples. "Is there any way in hell I can get you to put on a bra?"

That would be rational. She looked up at him and shook her head. "No."

"That's what I thought." He dragged his hand through his hair. "Christ."

"What?"

"Nothing."

He wasn't going to say it, so she held out her hand. "Can I drive?"

"Not in a million years."

She puffed out her bottom lip. "Pretty please?"

He growled. "Not going to work."

"Next time." She grinned.

"Never."

"I'm driving this car." She needed to check it off her bucket list. It had nothing to do with him.

His voice dropped. "What are you willing to do for the privilege?"

For one second she let herself say what she really wanted. She batted her lashes. "The things I would do to drive this car are illegal and depraved."

He shook his head. "You are all kinds of trouble."

What was it about him that clouded her brain? She licked her lips, unable to resist the flirtation. "You have no idea."

He pointed to the car. "Get in before I throw you over the hood."

"Like you'd ruin the paint." She flipped her hand and

turned her back on him, walking around the car to the passenger's side.

He looked at her over the roof. In the late sun his cheekbones looked cut from granite. "It might be worth it."

The impulse to say something wicked sat in her throat, but she'd indulged enough. So she smiled. "Ryder?"

"Yes, Sophie?" A muscle clenched in his jaw.

"I'm driving this car."

Chapter Seven

There was a flurry of greetings, hugs, and cheek kisses, which suited Ryder fine. After the ride over, he needed a fucking minute to compose himself. He'd barely been able to stay on the road as her legs crossed and uncrossed in the passenger's seat, working the hem of her dress high on her thighs.

It had been pure hell.

As he made the rounds in Mitch and Maddie's packed kitchen, he kept an eye on Sophie, who seemed intent on torturing him. And that dress. All he wanted to do was rip it off her. She wasn't even wearing a bra. How could he get any blood to his brain with her nipples visible under that thin, crinkly cotton? One good hard tug on those straps and he could have her exposed, her breasts bare.

He shook his head to clear the thoughts.

Shane Donovan, Maddie's brother and corporate million-aire, slapped him on the back. "How's life with the new neighbor? I heard you guys got off to a rocky start, but it looks like she came around."

"I think that's generous," he said.

Mitch handed him a beer, and he took a long swallow before glancing at the woman in question. When he'd moved to Revival, he'd given up casual relationships after the last one went wrong. He'd determined he was old enough and had sowed enough oats, so it was time to start searching for the kind of relationship his parents had. Loving, generous, and calm. Sophie sure as hell didn't fit the bill. Sure, he had no idea about the loving and generous part, but she wasn't calm. And she was temporary. She'd kick the dust off this town the second she got a chance.

"That good, huh?" Mitch said, interrupting his thoughts.

"It's . . ." He fought to find the right word before he settled on, "Interesting."

Shane kicked back against the distressed white cabinets with trendy golden brown granite countertops and grinned. "Soph always was a wild child."

Evan walked over and shook hands with Ryder before settling into the spot next to his oldest brother.

Shane hit Evan in the stomach with the back of his hand. "Remember the time when Sophie and Maddie dragged poor Penelope to a party in the woods and they got her arrested?"

Somehow this didn't surprise Ryder one bit.

Evan laughed. "You had to bail them out. Penelope was not pleased."

"I wasn't pleased about what?" the brunette asked, sidling up to her husband.

He hooked his finger into the loop of her jeans and tugged. "We're just talking about your juvenile record, baby."

She huffed and tossed her hair over her shoulder. "Please. I was an angel."

He smiled. "You were the least angelic good girl I knew."

Penelope shook her head and grinned at Ryder. "Don't believe them. I'm always the good one, ask anyone."

Ryder laughed. "I believe you." After all, he knew who the troublemaker was.

The kitchen was crowded and loud. All of the Donovans and their significant others were there. Sam Roberts, who lived next door, and Charlie Radcliffe, Ryder's boss and one of his best friends, were talking in the corner with the high school football coach, Bill Williams. Sophie and Maddie stood by the big kitchen table talking to Harmony Jones, Gracie's right hand woman at her bakery, and Cheryl Miller, the nurse that had moved to town not too long ago.

The only couple that seemed to be missing was the mayor, Griffin Strong, and his wife, Darcy, but that wasn't a surprise. Griff had told him they had to go to a charity event tonight.

Sophie caught his gaze before skirting back to the girls.

Maddie set a big bottle of tequila on the table next to a shaker of salt and a big bowl of limes. She looked at it lovingly and smiled. "I am officially done breastfeeding, so you know what that means, don't you?"

"Oh, this is going to be bad," Mitch mumbled under his breath.

Maddie picked up the small glasses on the table and lined them in front of her makeshift tequila stand. "Shots." She wagged her finger around the room, her red hair loose down her back, her green eyes flashing, practically daring anyone to defy her. "I haven't had a drink in twenty months, my child is with her grandmothers where she will be spoiled, worshiped, and most important, staying until morning. We are getting drunk, so don't even think about saying no to me."

"But—" Penelope started and Maddie held up her hand, cutting her off.

"There will be no buts." She picked up the bottle of alcohol and poured the liquid into the shot glasses in one seamless stream before turning to her sister-in-law Cecilia.

"I'm sorry you can't have one, but I promise we'll do the same for you when you can drink again."

Cecilia laughed. "You have fun for me."

Cecilia was tall and lithe, built like a supermodel and just as pretty. At five months pregnant she hardly showed.

Shane, who'd gone over to her in the commotion, pulled his wife close and kissed her temple before rubbing her barely-there belly. "I'm sure the kid will appreciate it."

She covered his hand with hers, lacing their fingers together. She craned her neck to look at him. "I'm sure."

Maddie clapped her hands. "Any non-pregnant women, get over here."

Gracie Donovan swung around, planted her hands on curvy hips, and shook her head at her husband, Maddie's brother James. "Your sister is making me drink."

James, a serious-minded professor, nodded and said in a dry tone, "I'm sure it will be a real hardship for you."

"It will be." Gracie tilted her chin, her blonde curls bouncing. "I might be forced to strip for you later."

Gracie was the very definition of bombshell, and most men would have a heart attack at the prospect, but James's expression didn't even flicker. "The sacrifices I make for you."

Gracie laughed and gave him a big long kiss before pulling away and sashaying over to the rest of the girls huddled around the table. "Okay, let's do some damage."

"That's the spirit," Maddie said.

Penelope sighed but took her glass.

When Sophie raised her shot, Ryder forgot everyone else in the room. As though sensing his stare, she looked over at him. They locked in on each other and the hyper-awareness they seemed to share made the room go quiet as the blood rushed in his ears.

Without breaking eye contact, she licked her skin on the top of her hand.

His fingers tightened on his bottle.

She liked muscle cars, tequila shots, and arguing.

He was in fucking trouble.

Eyes still on him, she shook salt and licked her skin again, slow and evil.

The erection he'd finally tamed roared back to life.

She downed the tequila before sucking on the lime.

He'd lusted after plenty of women in his time, but never quite like this. Never so hard he doubted his control over the situation. He took a sip of his beer and aggressively roamed the length of her body over the bottle.

"Again," Maddie said, shaking him from his haze.

Mitch shook his head. "Madeline."

She looked at him, her long red hair like flame around her face. "Yes?"

"Since we're baby free tonight, I have things in mind that don't include you throwing up."

Her lips tilted and she held up a glass. "You know what tequila does to me."

"I do." He laughed when she took another shot. Then he turned back to the guys. "This night is going to either be very good or very bad, and there's no telling which way it's going to go."

Ryder couldn't have said it any better himself.

Ryder had a mellow buzz as they were all outside, sitting in comfortable chairs in a big circle around a huge chat pit littered with citronella candles and a low-burning fire to take some of the late-spring chill out of the air.

The alcohol flowed freely, and by silent, mutual agreement Ryder and Sophie kept their distance. Well, *kind of* kept their distance.

Maybe they didn't talk directly, but they practically burned up the place with long, lingering looks. They sat across from each other, and Gracie leaned over to whisper something in Sophie's ear that had her throwing her head back.

In the low golden light of the fire he couldn't take his goddamn eyes off her. He didn't know what it was about her, but he fucking wanted her with a ferocity he didn't quite know what to do with.

From across the table the laughter died down and her gaze slid to his. Locked and held.

She picked up her drink and sipped it while they pretty much screwed on the table. He kept telling himself what a bad idea she was, but his body wasn't getting the message.

"Oh, I know," Maddie said in a too-loud voice.

He jerked his attention from Sophie and onto the red-head, who now sat in her husband's lap.

She straightened, jabbing her elbow into Mitch's stomach. He winced. "Ouch!"

She giggled. "Sorry."

He narrowed his eyes on her. "Why don't I believe you?"

She lowered her lashes. "Because you're super smart."

"Flattery will get you everywhere, Princess." Mitch grinned at his wife with exasperated affection.

She winked at him and then turned back to the group. She looked at Sophie, Ryder, Bill, and Cheryl, swinging a beer bottle in their direction. "I have an idea."

Ryder straightened, his instincts kicking in. Wherever this was going wasn't going to be good.

"Since you four are all new in town, you guys should all go out together. Like a double date." She grinned and looked at Sophie. "I'm sure Bill would love to show you around town."

Sophie's gaze slid to Ryder's, then yanked away.

Bill really was a nice guy. All wrong for Sophie, but still nice. Contemplating murder was probably unreasonable.

Bill held up his hands and laughed. "No pressure. I mean, I'll be happy to take you out for a night. But don't feel obligated with Maddie putting you on the spot."

Ryder would not kill him. He wouldn't. He was duty bound to protect and serve, not maim.

Sophie tucked her hair behind her ear and straightened.

Maddie clapped her hands. "Oh, come on, you guys will have so much fun."

Cheryl, the cute brunette nurse, bit her lip and gave Ryder a shy smile. "This is really awkward."

Maddie did her best to look contrite. "I know I'm terrible. But I think you'd have a fun time, and it will be a great way to meet people."

Cheryl was also very nice and sweet. Since they'd met, she'd been giving him very subtle clues that she was interested in him. He'd thought about asking her out. She seemed like the kind of woman he was supposed to date now that he'd decided to settle down and be good. He'd see her out or at a night like tonight, and they'd chat. After they parted ways, he'd tell himself he'd call her.

Only he kept forgetting.

Apparently Maddie thought a double date with his new neighbor was just the thing to put them on the path to cordial friendship.

He looked at Sophie.

She looked back at him.

Everyone waited. Bill and Cheryl had made it clear they were game, and how would it look if they said no? What good reason did they have to say no?

None.

Sophie shrugged, putting on a bright smile. "That would be great. Thanks."

"Sounds fun." It didn't sound fun at all. Ryder took a drink of his beer. What kind of special hell was this?

"Great, it's settled, then," Maddie said. "How about next Friday?"

Mitch pinched her. "You're moving into pushy territory."

She laughed. "I'm drunk and I can do what I want."

"Great," Bill said, winking at Sophie. "I'll get your number before I leave."

"Fantastic." Her voice was filled with cheer.

Ryder gritted his teeth. Yeah, really fucking fantastic.

Okay, so Sophie had a bit of a buzz. She couldn't figure out what was worse, that she couldn't stop thinking about screwing Ryder, or that she'd somehow been roped into going on a double date with the very nice, very agreeable, very good-looking football coach. She'd been right to be suspicious of the way Maddie kept talking up Bill whenever she had the chance. Why she failed to talk up Ryder was anyone's guess.

If that wasn't bad enough, she had to watch Ryder go on a date with that *nurse*, who, let's be honest, was far too nice for him. Ryder needed a woman who'd challenge him, not give him sweet, shy smiles, blush when he glanced sideways at her, and giggle.

But oh, joy, they were going on a double date. She'd throttle Maddie, but that would reveal her lust for Ryder, which she wasn't supposed to be acting on even though they'd been eye-fucking each other all night.

She kept meaning to stop, really she did, but she'd had so many shots, and her defenses were at an all-time low. Somehow she kept catching his gaze and getting lost in the heat of those silver eyes that promised so many dirty things.

To cool off, she sucked down a big glass of water in the kitchen.

Just as she put her glass in the sink, the back door opened and her heart picked up as her belly heated. Anticipation surged hot and thick in her blood. She spun around only to deflate in disappointment.

It was just Penelope.

Sophie knew right then hydration had nothing to do with her trip to the kitchen. Subconsciously, she'd been hoping Ryder would follow her.

Which was wrong.

Carpool, Sophie. This is a carpool. Oh, and he was her new double-date buddy.

God, she was in hell.

Penelope leaned back against the counter. "You look so sad to see me."

Sophie glowered, mimicking Penelope's casual stance. "Don't be crazy."

Her friend smirked. "So, how's it going?"

"Good."

The smirk turned into a grin. "Your date sounds fun."

Sophie pointed at her. "You just shut up."

"Your faces." Penelope broke out in a laugh, sounding like a hyena. "Priceless."

Sophie dragged a hand through her hair. "I guess my only consolation is it isn't obvious I have a serious case of lust for the wrong guy."

Penelope chuckled and wiped tears of mirth from under her lashes. "Oh, it's obvious. At least to me, but I'm looking for it. I can ask Evan."

"Don't you dare!"

"By the way, nice dress," Penelope said, her gaze a little glassy eyed, but other than that there was no sign the drinking affected her.

Sophie's chin tilted. "It's super comfortable."

Penelope nodded. "And it has nothing to do with seducing Ryder?"

She should say something jokey and casual, but screw that. She was too buzzed for subtle. She straightened. "Why? Do you think he's seduced?"

Penelope raised a brow. "I thought you didn't want to sleep with him."

"I said I *shouldn't* sleep with him. Not that I didn't want to." Sophie ran a hand through her hair. "I mean, have you looked at him?"

Penelope laughed. "I have."

"Pen, you have to help me." Sophie bit her lip. "I want him. I want him so bad I'm having a hard time not going over to him and begging him to take me."

"Awww . . . You poor thing, how rough it must be for you."

Her brain was fuzzy, and what little filter she had was gone. "Do you think he fucks rough?"

"I'd say that's a distinct possibility," Penelope said, her voice prim.

Sophie scowled. "You're not helping."

"You asked me."

"You're supposed to lie."

"Well, I didn't know that." Penelope crossed her arms. "You know I'm not a good liar."

"Penelope," Sophie wailed. "I'm going on a double date with him, what am I going to do?"

"If you don't want to sleep with him, this would be a good way to go about it."

That was true. Maybe she could go on a date with Bill but kidnap Cheryl and hide her in the storage shed so she couldn't touch Ryder.

No. Wait. The double date was supposed to be a good thing.

Evan chose that moment to come into the kitchen, saving Sophie from an answer. Penelope and Sophie immediately straightened.

He looked back and forth between them. "What are you up to?"

"Nothing," Penelope said, giving him a bright smile. "What could we be up to?"

Evan's gaze narrowed. "Something."

Penelope rose to her tiptoes and brushed her mouth against Evan's. "Nothing."

Evan's hand moved around her neck and he pulled her back to him, kissing her more deeply.

Even though they were married now, it was still weird to see them together. They'd always kept such a distance from each other, careful never to even look in each other's direction, so to see them all gropey and affectionate sometimes jarred Sophie. Especially when they were talking about Penelope, who Sophie had always deemed a bit of a prude because she was so conservative and proper.

Penelope kind of was a prude . . . unless Evan was involved.

They were still kissing and it was getting obnoxious, so she said, "For God's sake, would you stop."

Evan lifted his head and, still looking into Penelope's eyes, said, "Sorry, Soph."

Then he leaned down and whispered something in Penelope's ear that made her suck in her breath.

The door opened and Ryder came into the kitchen, making Sophie suck in her own breath. Without thinking Sophie said, "Thank God you're here. I think they're going to have sex right in front of me."

Penelope scowled. "Stop being dramatic."

"Yeah, I was suggesting the bathroom, not right in front of you," Evan said.

Ryder's lips twitched and his gaze flickered down Sophie's body, leaving a trail of lust in his wake. "Not much of a voyeur, are we, darlin'?"

His "darlin'" was starting to make her shiver with desire instead of irritate her. Jesus, just the sight of him made her hot and her stomach heat. Just looking at him made her wet. And she couldn't remember when that had ever happened.

If her brain wasn't clouded by tequila she'd cross her arms over her chest or do something decent, but instead she put her hands on the counter and leaned back, the motion raising her breasts and making them strain against the fabric.

He definitely took notice because he zeroed in on her nipples and his jaw hardened.

She shrugged. "There are some things I'd watch, but not that."

His attention fell to her mouth and he said in that honeyed voice, "Such as?"

Oh, she had a list and every item included him, but she wasn't about to volunteer that information. She was buzzed, not stupid. Sophie waved a hand at Evan and Penelope. "Stop trying to get me to talk dirty in front of my friends, you pervert."

Evan laughed.

Penelope covered her mouth with her hand to hide her smile.

Ryder cocked a brow. "I see tequila makes you sassy."

He made her sassy. "Have you met me?"

He skimmed a path down her body. "You're making your presence quite known."

Evan looked first at Sophie, then at Ryder. "Didn't you two agree to date other people?"

"Yep," Ryder said, still devouring Sophie with his eyes.

"It's gonna be a super-fun time," Sophie said, leaning back farther, shivering at his dark, hot expression.

His gaze traveled from her lips, down to her breasts, and over her hips and legs before gliding back up again. "The best."

"I see." Evan turned to Penelope. "Poor Bill and Cheryl."

"Indeed," Penelope said.

Sophie's breath kicked up.

Someone cleared their throat, Sophie didn't know who, but it wasn't Ryder, because they hadn't stopped staring at each other.

"Yes, well, I'm sure you have . . . things to discuss," Penelope said.

"Yeah, things, like where you're going to take Bill and Cheryl," Evan said, amusement in his tone. "We'll be back."

Without taking his eyes off Sophie, Ryder said, "Have fun."

"Be good," Penelope said.

Sophie was pretty sure she was past being good. Why had she forgotten how tequila makes her stupid?

The door swung closed and they were alone.

The temperature in the room increased by fifteen degrees. He crossed his arms over his chest. "Are you drunk?"

"I'm a little buzzed." *Come to me.*

He stayed where he was.

She picked up the tequila. "Do you want a shot?"

His gray eyes darkened to a storm cloud. "That depends."

"On what?" She gulped, excitement beating fast in the pulse of her neck.

"Do I get to lick the salt from your skin?"

She practically melted into a puddle. "That seems fair."

He uncrossed his arms and walked to her, slow, steady, and predatory. So much hotter than if he'd hurried.

Her heart pounded in her ears.

When he stood in front of her, he slid his hands onto her hips before lifting her onto the counter. Sophie might burst into flames.

Eyes a dark gray filled with intent, he picked up the salt shaker. He met her eyes. "Where should I put it, Sophie?"

Her voice was husky when she spoke. "Drinker's choice."

He curled his free hand around her neck, letting his fingers tangle in her hair. All thoughts of stopping this madness between them evaporated into thin air. Besides, who was she kidding? It had been game on since they laid eyes on each other. With his thumb, he trailed a path down her jaw before brushing it over her mouth. Her lips parted and he hissed out a breath as he swept over their wetness, making her tingle all over.

His expression turned feral and he fisted her hair and pulled her head back.

She moaned and braced herself on the counter.

With slow, deliberate movements, he leaned down and slowly licked right where her collarbone and neck met.

Oh dear God.

Her legs parted, and when he stepped between them, her thighs tightened on his hips.

This, right here, was the hottest thing that had ever been done to her. One touch and he'd blown sex out of the water.

His teeth scraped over her skin, and he licked again and she clutched the counter.

Not letting go of her hair, he pulled back and shook the salt onto her wet skin before his tongue fluttered over her pulse.

She was about to come on the spot.

He pulled back, releasing his grip on her hair so the base of her neck tingled.

He straightened and, eyes never leaving hers, drank from the bottle. How gray eyes could look so hot was a mystery, but he burned her up.

He didn't bother with the lime. Instead he put down the bottle and put a hand on either side of her on the counter. He shook his head. "This is not good."

She was going to hyperventilate. "Not good at all."

"What are we going to do about this, Sophie?"

She bit her lip. "I don't know, Ryder."

He rested his big hands on her hips. "No ideas?"

"Stop?" Voice so breathless it belied the word.

"You want me to stop?" He gripped her tighter.

"Yes." Her fingers came up and clutched the cotton on his shirt.

"You know what I think?" His tone was a low rasp that sent desire rushing through her veins.

"What?"

He leaned forward, raising one hand to tangle in her hair. "I think you like to say no because you want me to overpower you."

She groaned. That was exactly what she wanted. What she craved. "Why would you think that?"

Their breathing had increased considerably.

His hand tightened at the nape of her neck. "The way your breath hitches when we fight. The way your nipples get hard." He tugged and she gasped, feeling it low in her belly. "The way you're rocking your pussy right now."

Only then did she realize she was unconsciously lifting to meet him. "Oh God."

In answer, he thrust back. "That's right, you're so hot, you're ready to beg, aren't you, darlin'?"

"Yes." She had no pride.

His hard cock rubbed against her clit, sending tiny shock waves across her skin.

He leaned down and bit her lower lip. "You're such a cocktease."

His mouth was so close she let her tongue flick along the seam of his lips. "Sorry, not sorry."

He growled. "You're not going to let Bill touch you, are you?"

"No."

They were all gasping moans and harsh breathing.

"Good," he whispered in her ear. "He's too nice to ever be able to handle you."

Her fingers tightened on his shirt. "Are you nice, Ryder?"

"When it comes to you"—he scraped his teeth against her jaw—"I'm as bad as they come."

Then his mouth crashed on hers.

And it was like an explosion.

There were no calm getting-to-know-you caresses. No soft, gentle teasing.

No, they went at it. With hard mouths, bruising lips, and thrusting tongues. They kissed exactly how she felt.

Like she couldn't get enough.

Like she was starving.

Desperate for the taste of him to be imprinted on her skin.

It was like he brought out everything primal and consuming inside her. Like he awakened the sleeping beast she'd kept locked tight inside her.

She put her hands on the counter and used it as leverage to rub against his cock shamelessly while their tongues dueled.

He bit her.

She bit back.

He growled and fisted her hair, hard enough that pain

pricked along her neck, and it was the best thing she'd felt in forever.

Lust and wicked addictive chemistry stormed through her.

They kissed harder. Hotter. Their lips were fierce, almost punishing.

She clutched at his shirt with one hand while she tangled her hand in his hair and pulled him closer.

His head slanted.

The kiss deepened. Became wetter. Messier.

One big hand fell to her breast and swiped across her nipple. Once, twice, three times, before he plucked it with his thumb and forefinger.

Low in her belly, everything clenched and tightened.

Her lungs strained as their lips parted for a fraction of a second before coming together again in a harsh collision of explosive passion.

He teased her nipple, his fingers moving in time with their tongues and thrusting bodies. Her breasts had always been sensitive, and every stroke made her clamp down, making her feel empty. Demanding to be filled.

There was nothing tentative about him.

Breath coming fast, she ripped away to draw air into her lungs.

Their lips brushed in almost angry swipes as they panted hard, their movements too frantic to maintain consistent contact.

"We have to stop." Her whispered words were harsh and ragged.

"Yes."

Their mouths came together hard and demanding.

God, she wanted him. She wouldn't have to pretend with him. Wouldn't have to restrain herself. She could give as good as she got.

She wanted his cock. Pounding inside her. Thrusting. Impal—

"Sophie!" There was a loud clapping noise. "Sophie!"

They jerked apart, gasping for air, and stared into Penelope and Evan's amused faces.

Penelope shook her head. "I've been calling your name."

She wiped her mouth with her hand. "Oh."

Ryder dragged his fingers through his hair. "Can we help you?"

"Nope." Evan kicked back against the counter before shrugging. "Just trying to prevent a scandal."

"Helpful," Ryder said dryly.

"We were just . . ." Sophie tried to think of what she could say, but her mind was blank. She was still so hot, so on fire. And she wanted him so bad.

"Being neighborly," Ryder supplied.

Sophie guessed that was one way to look at it.

Chapter Eight

The hour had grown late, Sophie was officially intoxicated, and after the kitchen she'd stayed as far away from Ryder as possible.

That kiss had shaken her. And it had shaken her badly.

The force of her lust, her longing, her willingness to forgo all her rational common sense when it came to him worried her. Scared her. Her reaction to him—it was too strong, too volatile, their chemistry too out of control to be comfortable.

He reminded her too much of the bad decisions she'd sworn off when she was in college and was addicted to a guy that was no good for her. Tony had been her first real boyfriend. She'd always been reckless, up for anything and flying by the seat of her pants. Back then, she'd loved anything wild, and when she'd met him as a sophomore in college he'd called to everything inside her. She still cringed when she remembered her devotion, ignoring all the red flags and everyone's warnings that he was no good. When he'd finally grown bored with his psychological warfare, his abandonment had left her with a hole she'd thought would never fill. It had, but she'd sworn never again, and she'd kept her promise.

Less reckless and wild. Less willing. She'd stuck to her vows and cleaned up her act, and she'd never regretted it.

Yes, sometimes it made life a little too safe, a little too predictable, but it was a hell of a lot better than suffering that kind of loss. Better than ending up with some guy that didn't treat her the way she deserved because she was too obsessed with him to walk away.

Ryder reminded her too much of how she'd been, all that rushing, crazy chemistry and wild abandon. Which was why she needed to stay away from him. The right path was a guy like Bill. Guys that inspired white picket fences and school districts. Not guys that made her want to go down on them in the kitchen at a party.

Ryder had tried to corner her later on, but she'd slipped away from him. Penelope had tried to corner her too, but she'd avoided her, not wanting to talk about or explain her actions.

Now she stood in the powder room of Maddie's house and tried to figure out how to drive home with him and not attack him. The problem was she had no self-control around him. Nowadays if she slept with a man it was because she wanted to, because she liked him and he was skilled and fun. Not because it was compulsion. Aching need.

She knew what she had to do. She ran her hands through her hair and gazed in the mirror.

Her eyes were glassy, her cheeks flushed, and even all these hours later she could feel the hard press of his mouth on her. She shuddered.

God, had she ever been kissed like that?

She couldn't remember.

She didn't think so.

The best thing to do was go on the offensive.

As soon as she got in the car she'd tell him that kiss was

a mistake. Because it didn't matter how much she wanted him. Ryder Moore made her crazy. And craziness like that, never ended well, so she couldn't even start. If she broke the seal she'd be lost.

So she couldn't break the seal.

Secure in her plan, she took a deep breath and left the bathroom, taking the small hallway to the kitchen and out the back door to the yard.

As soon as she stepped out of the house, his gaze flickered down her body.

Instinctively, she shivered, feeling him everywhere. The sensation of him between her thighs imprinted on her skin. "You ready, Sophie?"

No she wasn't ready, but it was time to go home. She nodded. "Sure. I'm going to sleep for a week."

She hugged Penelope, who whispered in her ear, "I'll be calling you tomorrow."

"Yes, Mom." Sophie smacked a kiss on her cheek.

She hugged the rest of the group, and when she reached Maddie, she smiled. "I'm drunk. Mission accomplished."

Maddie laughed. "Good. Me too. Isn't it awesome?"

"It is." Except for all the stupid decisions she wanted to make.

Maddie pulled back and beamed. "Do you know how excited I am that we can have lunch next week?"

"Me too." The one good thing that came from the disaster of her life was she got to see Maddie all the time. Whenever she wanted. Just like the old days when they were teenage hellions and they'd go out after school and make mischief. She leaned back and slanted a sly glance at Maddie's husband, Mitch. "You are so screwed, because we are going to cause so much trouble."

"God help us all." Mitch shook his head, but his expression was amused.

"Indeed," Ryder said from behind her.

She looked over her shoulder. Why did he have to look like that . . . *Stop thinking about it.*

She pulled away from Maddie, shifting her attention to Ryder, and putting her hands on her hips. "What have you got to complain about, I've been an angel."

He raised a brow. "You murdered my door."

"I replaced it."

"That door is boring."

"That door is fantastic and it works. You should thank me." She was doing it again. Engaging him. Provoking. No control.

His gaze flickered down her. "We should go."

Evan laughed and put his arm around Penelope.

Sophie ignored him and flipped her hair. "Fine."

"Oh wait," Bill said, stepping forward.

Sophie blinked at him. Shit. She'd forgotten he was there. "Oh, hi."

He smiled. "I need your number."

"Right." She bit her lip and refused to look at Ryder. Bill handed her his phone and she input her number before handing it back to him.

"Great, I'll call you this week. Maybe we could have coffee."

She studied him without the cloud of Ryder getting in her way. He was tall, broad, and very nice to look at. His eyes were a pretty bright blue, and he had a killer smile. Coffee with him was exactly what she should do. She beamed her best smile. "Sure, but I'll have to play it by ear, I start at City Hall Monday and I have no idea what to expect. I'll need to see how the week plays out."

Bill gave her an affable shrug. "No worries." He shifted his attention to Ryder. "I'll give you a call to figure out where we're going to take these lovely ladies Friday."

Ryder gave her a sideways look. "I have some ideas."

None of them were proper. Of that she was certain.

She glanced at Cheryl, who looked at Ryder like a six-year-old girl looks at a Barbie Dream House, and then back at Ryder. She waved a hand at the pretty nurse with her soft smile and smitten expression. "Aren't you going to get Cheryl's number?"

Ryder snaked his hands into his jeans and pulled out his keys. "Already have it."

"Oh." Sophie wasn't an expert or anything, but wanting to roundhouse kick the nurse in the stomach might not be an appropriate response. Not that she was jealous, she just . . . wasn't a fan of people who helped other people. So what?

Ryder smirked at her. "You coming, Sophie?"

She sucked in a breath. That rotten bastard. She narrowed her eyes, glaring at him before shaking her head. "You're the worst."

"Just trying to get you home safely." His voice was far too sweet, filled with fake innocence.

God, she wanted to fight with him. She wanted to fight with him so damn bad. And then she wanted to spend hours aggressively and inappropriately sweating out their differences until she was finally exhausted and boneless.

She clucked her tongue. "Aren't you, like, the best neighbor ever?"

"Absolutely." His gaze was hot on her.

She shivered and tried to shake off his spell, and refusing to look in Penelope and Evan's direction, waved. "Have a good night."

As they walked to the car Sophie gave herself a pep talk. In her head she ran down her list of reasons he was a terrible idea. Reasons she wanted to chuck into the wind. Which was why he was dangerous.

When she got to the car she put her hand on the door handle and looked at him. One look at his gorgeous face, chiseled features, and broad shoulders had heat flooding her, pooling in her belly and tightening her nipples.

Oh, for the love of God. She was so screwed.

She needed to say something now. Right now before she stepped foot in his awesome car that just screamed *have sex in me.* "Ryder."

He looked at her.

She shook her head. "What happened in the kitchen was a mistake."

His gaze narrowed. "We'll talk about it in the car."

"I mean it, I'm not going to sleep with you." Her voice even sounded certain. Good for her.

He put his hands on the hood and cocked his head. "You want me to argue with you about this, Sophie. And that's all you need to realize."

She bit her bottom lip. "What does that mean?"

His attention drifted to her lips. "It means you're making these statements because you want me to prove you wrong."

"I'm making these statements because they're true. Because you and I are a bad combination. And there are a million reasons to stay away from each other."

A muscle in his jaw tightened. "There's no part of you that doesn't want me to stalk over there, take you by the arms, push you up against the car and say, 'You and I are going to fuck, it's just a matter of when before I kiss you, slide my leg between yours, and show you exactly what I can make you do for me'?"

Well, of course she did. Her thighs clenched at his words and she might hyperventilate. The reasons were all true, but deep down, under all her justifications, that was exactly what she wanted. What she hoped for. But she couldn't admit that—it was a horrible thing to admit.

She shouldn't want that. She was thirty-one, too old to be playing this game.

This time when she spoke, the word didn't come out certain at all. "No."

"You sure about that, Sophie?" His gaze bored into her and his tone was deep, slow, and seductive. "Because I think that's exactly what you want."

She cleared her throat. "You're wrong."

She held her breath, waiting to see if he'd prove her wrong.

They stared at each other, the knowledge of how easy it would be for him to do just that sitting between them, filling the air.

He shrugged. "Fair enough."

He got in the car, and Sophie tried to contain her disappointment.

She was so twisted.

Ryder turned over the engine and fought his baser impulses.

Sophie sat next to him with her bare legs and peaked nipples, in that little white dress with straps he could snap with the slightest tug.

In silence, he pulled out of the spot, down the drive, and onto the main road.

The tension was pulled tight, too tight, like a rubber band waiting to snap. If he pulled over, hauled her on top of him, she wouldn't refuse. He'd have her dress above her hips, and she'd be riding him.

All he wanted was to get inside her.

But he didn't pull over. He just kept driving toward home, his fingers tight on the steering wheel.

Because she was right. It was lust clouding his brain.

That kiss. It fucked with his head. He was supposed to be playing it safe now. He was thirty-three; it was time to start thinking about settling down, giving his mom and dad those grandkids they wanted. Sophie was here for six months, and then she'd go back to Chicago where she belonged.

Even if he put his life on hold to get inside her, what were the chances they'd even last six months? There was nothing calm about their chemistry. Nothing calm about the woman sitting next to him. Why make things messy? Better he stick to his first instinct and stay the hell away from her.

He'd tasted her mouth. Had his hands on her. Felt her rocking along his cock.

That was enough.

His grip tightened on the steering wheel even further as he gritted his teeth.

He didn't appreciate the way she made him feel.

Which was why it was best to stay away.

They drove for three blocks before the quiet got to be too much for her. Sophie cleared her throat. "I just think it's better to be neighbors."

"Agreed." The word a hard bite.

She shifted in the seat, and her skirt inched up. He wanted to reach over and slide his hands up her thighs. His hands would look good against her lightly tanned, smooth skin.

"You sound angry."

"I'm not."

"We should clear the air."

He shot a sharp glance at her. "Clear the air about what, Sophie? That if your friends hadn't come into the kitchen we wouldn't have stopped?"

Her hands clasped tight in her lap. "I don't know what happened. I'm not even sure I like you."

He pulled up to a stop sign in the middle of Main Street. "That's bullshit."

She shook her head. "It's not. I swear. Do you even like me?"

He narrowed his gaze. "You've been nothing but a pain in the ass since the second I laid eyes on you."

Her attention shifted to his mouth. "So this is good. Being neighbors?"

He returned his focus to the road and stepped on the gas, shifting the car into first and then second before he said, "Yep, fucking great."

She fell silent, but there was nothing peaceful about a silent Sophie. Her silence was loud. Restless and agitated.

He pulled into his driveway and pressed the garage door opener.

She pointed. "Why do you get a garage door and I don't?"

"You do have a garage door."

"Not one that goes up and down the way it's supposed to."

He pulled into the garage. "It does go up and down."

"Not by a click of the button."

A smile twitched at his lips. "Think of it as character building."

She huffed. "It's still unfair."

"You could move."

Her brows furrowed. She put her hand on the handle but made no move to open it. She licked her lips. "Do you want me to move?"

"And sic you onto some poor, unsuspecting citizen of Revival? I took an oath to protect and serve."

She jerked her head up to glare at him. "I'm not that bad."

Their eyes met. Heat flared to life, filling the small space that separated them.

He growled. "Get out of the car, Sophie."

"Okay." She made no move to exit.

He smirked and tilted his head. "I know how bad you want it."

"That's arrogant." Her breath kicked up a notch.

He skimmed a path down her body. "It's not arrogant if it's true."

"I need to go." She glanced over his shoulder in the direction of her house, and then back at him. "I'm buzzed and not my best right now."

"Nobody's stopping you from getting out of the car." He leaned back against his door. "No matter how badly you want it to be true."

She stared at him, unblinking for a good fifteen seconds before she blew out a breath. "I didn't mean for this to happen."

Isn't that the truth? If he'd had any idea what awaited him he would have sent Maddie Riley on her way when she'd suggested he rent the house to Sophie. He could live without upgraded appliances. He nodded. "It's unfortunate."

Her brows furrowed. "My life, it's such a mess right now."

Her confession surprised him, made him stop thinking about sex and start thinking about her. "Do you want to tell me about it?"

She shook her head. "Not really."

He waited. The car was silent. Neither of them made an effort to leave the small space.

She blew out a breath. "I had this great, glamorous career in Chicago where I was invited to all the best places and got to do all sorts of fun things. Then the president of the company decided to get greedy and extort money. Overnight it was all gone."

"I'm sorry." That had to be rough. He hadn't known her long, but with all her energy he could understand how hard it must be to go from the rush of city life to plunked down in a small town of twenty-five hundred people.

"I just want everything to go back the way it was." She scraped her bottom lip with her teeth.

There was an air of desperation in her voice that didn't sit well with him. Like she was trying too hard to convince herself, of what, he didn't know, but it was something. He nodded. "I'm sorry."

She shrugged. "Me too."

"Is there more?" Because it seemed like there was more.

She sighed. "I don't want the distraction of you. All I want is to do my time and get back home."

"Fair enough." It was the smart move. They had lives moving in different directions.

He needed to focus on what he needed to do, cementing his life in Revival. She wanted to get back to Chicago. They had chemistry and heat, but something about the way they mixed made her uneasy.

And the truth was, it made him uneasy too. He just didn't know why. He didn't know her well enough to understand the meaning behind the gut reaction.

She wrinkled her nose. "I've always had an impulsive streak."

"That doesn't surprise me one bit."

She sighed. "And giving into it has never led me anywhere good."

He narrowed his eyes and looked past her into the darkened garage. "I can relate."

"You can?" She shifted in her seat, glancing at him.

"I can. I've been burned by my impulsiveness before."

She nodded. "Me too."

Seeing no way to have his cake and eat it too, he conceded the point. "It's okay, Sophie. You're right. I won't kiss you again."

"It's for the best."

"It is."

"So do you think we can be friends?"

No way in hell, but there didn't seem to be a lot of other options. He shrugged. "Yeah, of course. We're going to be neighbors, it's best to get along."

Their gazes met. Held too long for friendship.

She looked away first. "I guess it's time to say good night."

"Guess so."

"So I'll see you later?"

"You will."

She sat there for a few more moments, her fingers restless in her lap. Then she straightened her shoulders and put her hand on the door. "Have a good one, Ryder."

"You too, Sophie."

Then she climbed out of the car, taking her little white dress with her.

Chapter Nine

Sophie's phone rang on her bedside table at nine o'clock, startling her from a dream. The second her eyes flew open her head started a low throb. She whispered a groggy "Hello?"

"Did I wake you?" Maddie's far-too-cheerful voice rang over the line. The girl never did get hangovers.

"Why are you calling at the crack of dawn? And why are you so happy?" Her temples had miniature jackhammers beating away, and there was a dull ache behind her eyes. It wasn't just the alcohol; it was the lack of sleep. She'd stayed up far too late thinking about her neighbor, vacillating between mourning a sexual experience she'd never get to have and cheering her smart decision-making skills.

Maddie laughed. "Um, this is the latest I've slept in forever. I feel like I caught up on a year's worth of sleep. I feel like a brand-new woman."

Oh no. Maddie was perky and optimistic about the world. Sophie could not handle perky. And she absolutely couldn't deal with optimism. She rubbed the sleep from her eyes. "Why are you calling me again?"

"Breakfast. Ce-ce and Gracie already headed back to Chicago, so this is the perfect chance for Penelope, you, and me to talk before she hits the road in a few hours. Evan says he'll pick her up from the restaurant and they'll leave from there."

As much as Sophie would love to, there was no way she could say no. While Sophie loved their now-large group, Penelope and Maddie were her oldest and bestest friends. Getting time with just the three of them was at a minimum. She sighed. "How much time until you get me?"

"Can you be ready in thirty?"

Ugh. "I'll be ready."

At least she'd get coffee and grease. That would take care of her hangover.

The rest of her life, though, was still up for grabs. God only knew what tomorrow would bring.

Might as well enjoy her last day of being unemployed.

She climbed out of bed, determined to make the best of her situation, and her new life in Revival.

The three of them tumbled into Earl's Diner. Sophie's eyes still hurt, so she kept her oversized Chanel sunglasses in place. The second she walked through the door she spotted Ryder sitting with Charlie Radcliffe, the local sheriff.

She gritted her teeth.

Wasn't that just great.

Why in the hell would anyone want to live in a small town? This was why she loved Chicago; it was hard to run into people in a city with two and a half million people. Unlike Revival. She'd lived here three days and she couldn't escape Ryder.

The bell jingled and he looked toward the door.

Their gazes immediately locked.

Shoving her sunglasses to the top of her head, she rolled

her eyes at him before smoothing down her coral tank top and white shorts.

He grinned and gave her a wink.

Her heart did a fast little double tap.

He was so obnoxious. And so, so gorgeous.

She stuck her tongue out at him before flouncing into the booth, realizing too late she'd picked the wrong side. Now she could stare at him from across the room. Those broad shoulders, his wide chest. That chiseled jaw. She shuddered. She needed to get her mind out of the gutter. Gutter thoughts would not help her resolve.

Maddie waved at Ryder and Charlie before turning to Penelope and her. "I'll say hi and be right back."

The waitress called out, "You girls want coffee?"

Sophie would sell her soul for coffee.

Maddie yelled back, "Yes, please. Thanks, Mabel."

Sophie rubbed her temples. "Everyone knows each other. And, you know, talks to each other."

"I know, isn't it fun?" Penelope picked up her laminated menu.

"No! It's not fun. I like walking down the street and being ignored." Sophie sounded as sulky as she felt. She already missed home.

"You'll get used to it," Penelope said, her voice unconcerned.

Sophie sniffed. "Easy for you to say, your career has always been perfect." To her horror, her eyes welled with tears just as Maddie sat back down.

"Oh no." Maddie's forehead furrowed. "What happened?"

"Nothing." She picked up a napkin and wiped under her lashes.

"Talk to us," Penelope said.

"Yes." Maddie put her hand over Sophie's. "We're here for you."

"I'm fine." Sophie blinked the wetness away. "It sounds weird, but I think it's finally hitting me. You'd think being dragged off by the Feds would have made the disaster real. You think carrying all my stuff from the building, or my silent phone and empty email, would have made it all sink in. But it didn't. It's all seemed like one big dream I'd wake up from. But today, I'm staying instead of going with Penelope, I have a hangover, and everyone's so cheerful, and it's finally hitting me."

Penelope clucked like the mother hen she was while Maddie patted Sophie's hand.

Maddie squeezed her fingers. "I promise we'll have fun. I'll make it fun. You won't even miss Chicago. And when you go back home, this mess will be over and everyone will have forgotten and you can start again. It's going to be okay, because you're Sophie, and you're always okay."

Sophie nodded and tried to take in the pep talk. "Okay. You're right."

"And you're going to be great for Revival," Penelope said. "You'll blow them away, and it will restore your confidence and remind you how awesome you are at your job. Who knows, maybe it will even be good for you."

"Chicago is good for me," she said. Penelope and Maddie exchanged a look and she frowned. "What?"

Maddie's brow furrowed. "Nothing."

"What? Tell me." Sophie experienced a strange thump in her heart.

Another glance passed between her friends. Penelope shrugged one delicate shoulder. Despite the night of drinking, she appeared completely together in a gauzy white blouse, her chestnut hair perfect. "It's just that you keep making it sound like everything in Chicago was perfect."

"It was perfect." Sure, since her best friends had gotten married and Maddie had moved away, she got a little lonely. But she'd taken care of that by filling her life in other ways.

"But—" Maddie began, but thankfully, the waitress came with coffee, saving Sophie from a conversation she was sure she didn't want to have.

She wiped under her lashes once more and looked up, straight into Ryder's gaze. From across the room, he watched her, a frown on his lips.

She put on a bright, sassy smile. The last thing she wanted was for him to see her upset.

His eyes narrowed, his frown deepening.

She turned her attention to the menu. He was so arrogant he probably thought she cried over him.

It felt good to latch onto righteous indignation instead of sadness. She didn't like sadness and avoided it at all costs.

Penelope peeked over her shoulder at Ryder and then back at her. "Anything interesting happen last night?"

Sophie scowled. "No."

"You sure?" Penelope gave her a wide-eyed innocent look.

Maddie looked back and forth between them. "What's going on?"

Sophie shook her head. "Nothing. Not one thing."

Penelope smiled. "Evan and I caught Sophie and Ryder making out in the kitchen."

"You bitch!" Sophie hissed. "You're not supposed to say anything."

"You never said that."

"I did too!"

Maddie gasped, darting a surprised glance over her shoulder, and Sophie smacked her. "Stop looking at him."

Maddie jerked her attention back to the table. "Really now?"

"They were going at it too," Penelope said helpfully.

"We were not. It was just a kiss." Sophie tucked her hair behind one ear. "To . . . um . . . cut the tension."

Penelope laughed. "Is that what the kids are calling it these days?"

"Shhhh!" Sophie gave her friends the evil death glare. "Be quiet. He'll know we're talking about him."

Sophie glanced over. Now he watched her, but now there was amusement etched into the lines of his cheeks instead of concern.

Sophie growled. "Let's change the subject. There's nothing to discuss. We fought. We kissed. We talked, cleared the air, and agreed to be good neighbors. End of story."

Maddie giggled. "Why did you let me set you up?"

"You gave me no choice," Sophie exclaimed. She waved a hand. "Besides, it's fine because there's nothing between Ryder and me. I'm excited to go out with Bill. He seems like such a great guy." Well, right now he seemed a boring guy, but that was because she compared him to Ryder.

But boring was good. Boring was very good.

Just what she needed to get back on the right track.

"So, Sophie, huh?" Charlie asked in his sly voice, the hint of a Southern drawl still present even after all these years.

Ryder jerked his attention off the woman driving him to distraction. "What?"

"You have the hots for Sophie." It was a statement.

Charlie might be his boss, but they'd become good friends since he recruited Ryder from the next county over.

Griffin and Charlie were his closest friends in town. But that didn't mean he wanted to confess his fixation on Sophie.

He shrugged. "She's my new neighbor."

Charlie gave him a sly grin. "She's a hot little thing."

Ryder shook his head. "Not falling for that one."

Charlie laughed. "You don't think she's hot?"

"I think she's very hot, but if you were going to do anything about it, you would have done it a long time ago." He scrubbed a hand over his jaw and glanced at her. God, she was bitable in that little tank top and shorts. This morning she appeared exactly what she was: sexy, wild, and fun.

"True," Charlie said, his voice amused. "I never moved on her because she had too many ties and lived in Chicago. My dick's not that big."

Ryder rolled his eyes, still not falling for the bait Charlie laid before him.

Charlie continued, "But she's here now, and with her leaving to go back home at some point, she might work quite nicely."

Ryder knew when he was being played, but it didn't stop the rush of adrenaline. Still, he played it cool. He raised a brow. "What would Felicia say about that?"

As far as Ryder could tell, Charlie did not get emotionally involved with women and only did friends with benefits. Felicia Hayes being the current friend of choice. It was before his time, but from what he understood, Charlie had been with Gracie Donovan for years, and when she'd broken it off, he'd moved on to Felicia and stayed.

Charlie shrugged. "She's getting restless."

That caught Ryder's attention. "Oh?"

Another shrug from across the table. "She's starting to hint she wants more."

The only person this surprised was Charlie. Everyone in town knew Felicia was in love with him, and Ryder couldn't help feeling a little bad for her. He wasn't sure what made Charlie so leery of emotional entanglements, but he knew enough to know that wanting a commitment from the guy was the kiss of death for their non-relationship.

Ryder glanced back at the table of women, his eyes on Sophie. Earlier, she'd been upset. And that made him stop thinking about her naked and start wondering why. Had something happened? He shouldn't care. She'd made herself clear last night that she was off-limits. That they were going to be strictly neighbors.

Still, he wanted to know why she'd had tears in her eyes, because Sophie didn't strike him as a crier. He liked her sassy, not weeping.

"You're staring again." Charlie's voice was wry.

Ryder yanked his focus back to the table and took a sip of coffee. Time to stop thinking about her. Time to get back to work. He and Charlie often met at Earl's Diner before the start of the week to discuss priorities before the craziness of the office distracted them.

"How do you think Harold is doing?" Ryder named their newest deputy, who'd interrupted him that day with Sophie and was just barely out of the academy.

Charlie grimaced. "Green, overeager, and a pleaser."

Ryder laughed. "In other words, he bugs the shit out of you."

"Pretty much."

Once upon a time Charlie had been a field agent for the FBI before he left city life for small-town law enforcement. He didn't have a lot of tolerance or patience for wide-eyed innocence.

That's where Ryder came in. He was the oldest child, with two younger sisters. Growing up, he'd helped them with their schoolwork, taught them how to throw a baseball and ride their bikes. He had patience to spare and an easy nature that complemented Charlie's more hard-assed demeanor.

Charlie was who the deputies cowered before.

Ryder was who they talked to about their problems and if they wanted their birthday off.

They made a good team, and Ryder didn't regret making the move to Revival one bit. Not only had he needed a change in his life, he'd been stuck in his old department. The establishment guard hadn't been inclined to move on or make changes to modernize the department.

The opportunity for Chief Deputy Sheriff had come along, Charlie and he had met over beers and hit it off, and the rest was history.

In his mind he had the best of both worlds: His family was close enough to see for dinner whenever he wanted, but now he didn't have to worry about arresting any of them. Not that his sisters were troublemakers.

They were good girls. Or so he liked to believe.

There was a chorus of female laughter, and Ryder looked over at the table where Sophie sat. She appeared happier. And that made him happy.

He grinned at her.

She wrinkled her nose.

It was bad enough he was attracted to her, but why did she have to go and be so much fun?

"Did you tell her yet?" Charlie asked, once again pulling Ryder's gaze from Sophie.

Ryder didn't have to ask what Charlie referred to, because he already knew. "Nope. I thought it would be more fun to surprise her."

"That's a stupid idea."

"Probably, but it hasn't exactly come up in conversation." He'd been too busy thinking other, more . . . interesting things.

"I've never seen it, but it's rumored Sophie has quite the temper."

He laughed. "That's what makes her fun."

Charlie shook his head. "You're twisted."

"Yeah, pretty much." And that's when it hit him, part of her appeal, beyond the obvious. Since he'd decided to clean up his ways, he'd gone out of his way to date women that aligned with his relationship goals. Someone nice and stable, to balance out the crazy he'd experienced when the woman he'd been just having some fun with decided to fixate on him and refuse to let go. When he went out with a woman now, he made no move to seduce her. He did what he was supposed to do—get to know her, learn about her—but he hadn't realized until that moment how exhausting he found all that good, polite behavior. Careful and safe was work for him. An effort.

He didn't have to do that with Sophie. He didn't have to tone it down.

It was like that kiss. He'd never had a first kiss like that. They'd held nothing back. There'd been no caution. No getting to know you. It had just been instant, filthy making out, full of tongue and teeth and unfiltered lust.

He couldn't remember the last time he'd experienced that with a woman. Probably never.

Despite all his internal warnings, the second he was with her he flew on instinct, bantering and goading her. He hadn't even known that was missing for him. It didn't change his goals or where he wanted his life to go, but it did refine his perception of what he needed in a woman.

It didn't change anything between Sophie and him because that same instinct told him she was a bad idea. Both of them wanted to stay away from each other. Neither thought an affair would work. But since he had a better handle on the balance he desired, he could try the whole neighborly friend thing.

He glanced over at her. She was laughing, her eyes bright. She was fun. He liked her temper. Liked her sharp tongue. She'd been in town only a few days, and she already livened up the place.

Friends was worth a shot.

Chapter Ten

Laying out in a white string bikini had nothing to do with Ryder Moore.

It didn't. All it had to do with was her hangover.

When she'd gotten home from breakfast with her friends, she'd tried for a total of five minutes to be productive before giving up. It was Sunday, and she started her job tomorrow. Everything could wait.

Today she'd relax.

For May, it was nice and hot, the sun bright, and she was tired. So she slathered on sunscreen, dragged out a lawn chair she'd found in the garage, grabbed a book, and there she was.

So see, her bikini was all about her and nothing about Ryder.

She wasn't preoccupied with her neighbor.

She heard the roar of a motorcycle and her heart leapt into her throat. She clutched at her book and pretended to be thoroughly engrossed in the storyline.

As he pulled into the driveway she forced herself not to look up. She was reading. The book was so good she didn't even notice him.

The engine died and the backyard fell silent.

She turned the page. See? Totally, completely engrossing.

She sucked in a breath.

She focused on the heroine's name and realized her nipples were hard now at the thought of him watching her. Oh, good grief, this was ridiculous.

She turned another page.

A shadow fell over her, and excitement rushed Mach 10 through her veins. Without looking up she said, "Do you mind? You're in my sun."

"UV rays are bad for you." Ryder's voice was filled with amusement.

She turned another page. "I have sunscreen on."

"Did you get your back?"

No, she hadn't. She bit her lip, imagined his big hands roaming all over her skin. She knew what they felt like. Strong and slightly rough, but not too rough. Just rough enough to know you were touched by a man.

She turned another page. "I'm good."

"I wouldn't want you to burn. Or look like a pancake." That voice, his low, honeyed voice.

Sophie couldn't resist and finally peered up. His large frame blocked out the sun, casting him in a golden glow. "Pancake?"

He smiled. "Yeah, that's what my sisters call it. When you're burnt on one side and pale on the other. Like a pancake."

She blinked up at him. "You have sisters?"

"I do." He held up two fingers. "Younger sisters. I also have a mom and dad."

How normal of him. She bit her lip. "Do they live in Revival?"

"They live a couple towns over." He leaned back against the deck railing. "How about you?"

Should she be engaging in this kind of behavior? But

wasn't this what good neighbors did? She knew all about her neighbor in Chicago—a cute pixie princess who looked like a cross between Twiggy and Esmeralda. She was a graphic artist. She was the middle child of three girls, and her parents lived in Arlington Heights. See, this was what neighbors did. She cleared her throat. "I'm an only child."

"And your parents?" he asked.

She couldn't read his expression behind his sunglasses, but she saw her reflection staring back at her. Damn, but she did rock this swimsuit. "My parents are in India living in a meditation commune for the year."

He laughed. "Oh really?"

She couldn't help the quiver of a smile at the corners of her lips. "Yeah, really. I think next year they plan on going to Nigeria to paint." She wrinkled her nose. "They're what people like to call 'free spirited.'"

"How'd you turn out like you did?"

"What's that supposed to mean?"

"You wear Chanel sunglasses."

"How do you know they're Chanel?"

"I have two sisters that are label whores."

She laughed before shrugging. Maybe friends was possible. "I don't know. My parents are weird as hell, but when my mom got pregnant with me, even they couldn't figure out how to drag a newborn all over the world. My dad's from the South Side of Chicago, and when my grandma died, she left him her house that had been sitting empty. So they put aside their traveling and settled until I was eighteen and could fend for myself. So in some ways I had a very traditional childhood, except my parents cleansed the house with sage, chanted a lot, took in visitors from strange lands, and didn't believe in rules."

He raised his sunglasses to perch on top of his head. "What do you mean by until you were eighteen?"

They'd taken off the second she'd left for college, but she didn't want to make a big deal about it. After all, she'd grown up listening to them talk about all the things they wanted to do once they were free, so it hadn't exactly been a surprise. Wanting to change the subject, she shrugged. "They had things to do and places to see. What about you? What were your parents like?"

Silent for a moment, he studied her like he had questions before his expression cleared. "I grew up with a traditional family filled with a disgusting amount of love and support."

She wondered what that was like. Her parents loved her, of course. They were great, as long as you didn't expect anything parental from them. Over the years she'd begun to think of them as friends she was happy she didn't have to see a lot of. She put on a bright smile. "That must have been nice."

"It was." His voice lowered. "What was a teenage Sophie like without rules?"

"Exactly how you'd expect me to be," she said.

Silence hung in the air before he said, "So about your back."

She gulped. "What about it?"

"Turn over and let me get it for you. I wouldn't want all that pretty skin of yours to burn."

She went tingly all over thinking about him rubbing his hands over her skin. "That's not necessary."

He smiled. "Don't tell me you're afraid for me to touch you."

Her brows slammed together. "Oh my God, you're not honestly trying to dare me, are you?"

"Of course I am."

"Well, it's not going to work."

"That's a shame." He gazed down at her with those searing gray eyes. How their coolness burned so bright was beyond her, but he left a trail of fire in his wake. Oh right, she needed to concentrate on making him a friend. Maybe friends that flirted a little. If she could just shift her perception to something like the way she viewed Charlie, it could work. Charlie was gorgeous, and sure they flirted sometimes, all good-natured and sexy, but it didn't mean anything. She'd always looked at him as a wrong time, wrong place kind of guy.

Not too different from Ryder.

"Maybe I should come lay out with you. I have some reading to catch up on."

She needed to say no, but instead she shrugged. "It's a free country."

How could they establish an easy friendship if she avoided him? She thought of using her list of things to do as an excuse but abandoned the idea. It was Sunday. Sunday was designed around no rules, no obligations, and all play. Wasn't that why they called it Sunday Funday?

"In that case, I'll be back." He turned and jogged down the steps.

She tried not to notice his perfect ass in faded jeans.

What would he look like in a bathing suit?

She counted to ten. Slowly she inhaled and exhaled, trying to talk herself out of the giddy prospect of him shirtless. Up close. Where she could study his tattoos.

When that didn't work she started to list all the bathing suit options that would cool her desire.

Speedos were absolutely on the top of the list. If he came out in a Speedo, all her problems would be solved because no self-respecting man wore a bathing suit like that.

Next on the list was plaid. Plaid swimsuits were for

grandfathers and three-year-olds named Bradley. If you weren't in either of those camps, you didn't belong in plaid.

Jean shorts. Sure, they were cool back in the day, cruising the Chicago forest preserves on the back of a truck. Now, at their age, they indicated a man had never grown up and still had the fashion sense of a sixteen-year-old burnout.

Next—the door opened.

She jerked to look at him.

Her mouth went dry. Oh dear God. Deliver her from the evil temptation of this man.

His aviators were back in place, and he carried a file of papers and an iPad. Shirtless, his skin golden and muscled, his abs ridiculous, the black ink on his skin only highlighting his perfection. He wore red board shorts that hung low on his hips, emphasizing the cut between muscle and bone.

She had the irrational desire to punch him.

He ran up the steps, put his stuff on the small table where she had her glass of iced tea and her now-discarded book, and flashed her a smile. "Be right back."

He jogged back down the stairs to his garage and disappeared inside before returning with a lawn chair and setting it up on the other side of the table.

When he stood, she glared at him.

"What?" His voice was a touch too innocent.

She waved a hand over him. "You're so obnoxious."

He chuckled, not even pretending to be indignant. "You're pretty obnoxious yourself, darlin'."

She rolled her eyes. "Is that the stupid dismissive pet name you settled on?"

He stretched out on his back, and all his glorious muscles glimmered in the sun. He picked up her sunscreen. "Yep."

"Why's that?" She really needed to look away, but she stared transfixed as he slathered sunscreen over his chest.

He winked at her. "That's the one you like best."

"It is not!" Her tone was full of outrage. But she couldn't lie; his body distracted her. She wanted to bite his hip bone, then lick it, before she licked other things. Namely, she wanted to trace the word "freedom" written across his ribs with her tongue.

Wrong train of thought, and not at all helpful.

"Well, even if it's not, I don't really care." His hand slid down his stomach, over the chiseled muscles. "I like the way your eyes flash."

Sophie tried not to think about her body's response. She looked up at the sun. "I can't believe how warm it is today."

His hand kept gliding over his skin. "It's hotter here than up north where you live."

She closed her eyes and let the warmth kiss her skin. "Did you ever think about living in Chicago?"

Moving from small-town Illinois to the big city was a common occurrence because of job opportunity and growth.

"Nope. I've always liked living in a small town. I've been there, but it's not for me."

"Why not?" She didn't understand how anyone chose anything else.

When he spoke, his voice was thoughtful. "I guess I like knowing people. I like them knowing me. And I wouldn't want to be that far away from my family."

Lashes fluttering open, she turned her head to look at him. "It's not that far. Look at James and Gracie, they spend time in both places."

He grinned at her, his expression a little chagrined. "Does it make me weird that I like seeing my family for Sunday dinner?"

Sophie couldn't imagine, so she smiled and said, "Yeah, totally."

Ryder laughed. She was such a little brat, and holy shit did she look fantastic in a swimsuit. A fact he chose to ignore. He shrugged. "I'm not going to apologize."

"Nor should you." She sighed, sounding a bit wistful.

He couldn't help wondering about her childhood and her familial relationship and how that might have affected her. He'd wanted to question her, but the second she mentioned her parents, her shoulders had gone completely rigid and her face pursed with defensiveness. It was an interesting reaction, given her words had been delivered with a light breeziness. In his profession he'd learned how to read body language, learned to watch for tells in a person's actions. Sophie's tells had reminded him of a cornered animal with its hackles raised.

So despite his curiosity, he'd decided not to press and ask a question he already knew the answer to. "What about you? Ever think of leaving the big, bad city for the quiet life?"

She shook her head. "God no. I'd hate it."

"How do you know that?"

"I like the constant activity, the fast pace. Being able to go to any store I want and go out to dinner at all the best restaurants."

He got that, but those were all things. Not connections. There was no mention of friends, or even her job. Another observation he intended to investigate deeper, but for now he kept the conversation light. "Maddie mentioned you ran a Chicago entertainment blog. What made you decide to do that?"

She lifted her head to the sun before stretching a little and letting her shoulders drop.

He ignored the lithe movements of her body.

She sighed again, appearing to grow lazy in the sun. "I worked in PR for a media company, and it just made sense. I had a lot of connections, and I love to go out and try new things, love making all those discoveries off the beaten path and sharing them with other people." She laughed a little. "I started it on a whim, actually. I did it for fun and didn't expect anything to come from it. But I'm really good at my job, and in a year, places all over Chicago were begging me to feature them. So I got to go to all these great, exciting fun places and get paid for doing it." Her brow furrowed.

"What?" he prompted, wanting her to continue and hopeful she would if he didn't interrupt her.

"Oh nothing." She waved a hand in the air. "It's nothing."

"Tell me." When she didn't answer, he tried again. "I really want to know."

She shook her head a little. "I was on track to quit my job at the end of the year and focus on that full-time." She cast him a furtive glance. "Promise you won't tell anyone?"

He wanted her secrets. "I promise."

She bit her lip a little. "I'd even made a business plan— and I'm not a planner."

He got it. She'd had hope. Carefully, he asked, "Did your company's scandal hurt the blog that much?"

"Yeah, it did. Maybe it would have been okay if I hadn't been a VP, but every time it was mentioned anywhere, they named the executives and how they'd all been investigated. Chicago likes its corruption, and even though I'd been cleared of any suspicion, my name kept getting tangled." She wrinkled her nose. "Not great for PR, you know?"

"I can imagine." It wasn't just her job she'd lost but her plans for the future.

She shrugged, like she was trying to roll away the bad memories. "I can probably rebuild once a little time has passed and people have forgotten. We'll see. I don't know if I have it in me to start again."

"Sophie?"

"Yes?" She glanced at him.

"Thanks for telling me."

"It was nothing." She turned her attention toward the yard. "Shit happens. We deal and go on."

It was something, but she was done talking and, from her dismissive tone, seemed to want to lighten the mood. So he'd help her along. He grinned at her and asked her a question only a muscle head would get excited about. "Wanna wash our kick-ass cars?"

"Absolutely." Her expression brightened and she practically jumped out of the lawn chair.

He laughed. She didn't disappoint. He hadn't underestimated her love of fine automobiles.

Right then and there, he vowed to do his best to give her a good last day before she started what she clearly saw as her sentence in Revival.

Chapter Eleven

After Sophie threw on a pair of shorts, she and Ryder got to work. They washed her car first, and Sophie had to admit she was having a great time. She'd always loved cars, attracted to the rev of the engine and the jerk of speed when she switched from one gear to another. Sometimes on Sundays, she'd head out of the city north toward Wisconsin, just to drive fast on the deserted back highways while the wind whipped through her hair. It was her private escape for when she needed to think and be quiet.

She also loved to baby her Porsche, a present to herself when she got promoted. And why not? She could be frivolous, she had no kids or mortgage to support. No one to depend on her.

She rarely got to wash her car because she lived in the city, so she took extreme pleasure in it now.

She glanced over at Ryder, spreading wax over her hood, his muscles glossy and glittering in the sun. She didn't know why she'd told him about her plans to quit, plans she hadn't even told her best friends. She'd been happy when he let it go and didn't press for further information, even though the desire to probe had sat heavy in the way he'd studied her.

He circled over the creamy hood and she called out, "You're doing it wrong again." He wasn't, but they'd fallen into a rhythm of antagonistic teasing as they worked to establish a relationship that didn't include ripping each other's clothes off.

He glanced up at her, that quirk on his lips. "I am not. Who's the expert here? Me or you?"

"Me." The word was sassy as she planted her hands on her hips.

Sophie had managed to learn a lot about Ryder over the course of the afternoon. She learned his mom and dad had a great marriage. That he loved his baby sisters. How he'd been recruited to work in Revival, that she suspected was half a story by the way he hurried through it. That Charlie was more than his boss, he was also a friend.

She also learned the only reason this house was for rent was because he planned on tearing it down next year and building one big house, which made her think he had plans for a family, although he hadn't said as much.

She tried to picture some woman coming out onto the deck and calling him in for iced tea, or maybe washing the cars with him like she was doing. She envisioned Ryder's future wife as her exact opposite, tall, lithe, and brunette. Maybe she'd bake cookies and wear an apron. Maybe she'd have gray-eyed little children tugging at her skirt.

Sophie immediately hated her.

Cloth still in hand, he straightened. "I wax my car weekly. How many times have you waxed yours?"

"Never." She flipped her hair. "I've watched plenty of YouTube videos. I know what's up."

He laughed. "YouTube."

"What's wrong with that? They are very instructional and informational."

"All right, then." He tossed another cloth on the hood. "Get started, darlin'."

"You don't think I can do it, do you?"

"I have faith in you that you can rub circles." He winked at her. "I just think it's a lot more laborious than you believe."

She walked over to stand next to him, picking up the soft cloth. He glanced down at her, and his expression darkened as their eyes met.

It had been like this too. That spark of chemistry was not easily contained, but they both seemed content to ignore it and work on the plan they'd laid out last night.

She jerked her attention away and got to work, slowly working the wax into the paint before wiping it away. Fifteen minutes later her arms ached in a way that told her she'd been slacking during her workouts.

She also found it boring.

She straightened. "You finish up, I'll get started on hosing down your car."

"Is that an order?" He smirked at her.

"Yes." She tossed the cloth to him. It hit his stomach and fluttered to the ground. She swung on her heels and walked over to pick up the hose before turning back to him. "Get to it, boy."

One dark brow slowly rose up his forehead. "And this has nothing to do with your biceps burning?"

She tilted her chin. "Of course not. I'm being efficient."

His gaze dipped. "You don't fool me one bit."

That was part of the problem. She didn't think she did, and she wasn't sure she wanted to be seen. She flashed him a smile and snapped her fingers. "Chop chop."

He shook his head. "God, you're a brat."

"Uh-huh." Without giving it another thought, she sprayed him with the hose.

He jerked as the icy water hit his skin. "Hey! What was that for?"

Sophie gave him her best wide-eyed, innocent "you can't blame me because I'm too cute" face. "It was an accident."

He narrowed his gaze. "You are a troublemaker, Sophie Kincaid. Pure and simple."

She smiled, lifted the hose, and blasted him. "Oops. I slipped."

He dropped the cloth he'd been using into the soapy water and came for her. Heart racing, she screamed, flung the hose, and ran across the yard.

She was fast, but he was faster and taller, and he caught her with ease, wrapping his arm around her waist and tackling her. They tumbled to the ground, and he shifted so he took the brunt of the impact with her on top of him before he flipped them both over so she was on the grass, trapped beneath him.

He growled. "You are going to pay for that."

"I'm sorry!" she screeched, laughing. "I promise I'll be good."

His whole body covered hers, and it was fucking awesome.

He imprisoned her wrists in one hand and held them captive over her head. "I don't believe you."

"It's true!"

"Liar."

Then he started to tickle her, and she thrashed and squirmed and laughed hysterically, gasping out, "Ryder! Oh my God, stop."

"No." He dug his fingers into her ribs, and she bowed up and screamed.

"Stop, I'm sorry." She giggled. Desperately trying to get away from him, she arched and his legs slid between hers, and all of a sudden she became acutely aware they were practically naked, and he was on top of her.

She felt his erection against her hip and stilled. All the laughter died away.

His hands stopped torturing her, curving around her rib cage. Both of them breathing heavy, their eyes met.

Everything turned on a dime.

He shifted, and his cock slid just where she wanted him.

"Oh," she said on a small gasp.

He looked down at her mouth and whispered, "Are you going to be a good girl?"

"Yes."

"I think you're incapable of being good."

Her breath caught. "You're wrong."

His hand slid down her body, cupping her hip.

She was trapped under him, and it clouded her brain and made her lose all reason. All their progress from the day evaporated in an instant.

His hips flexed, nudging her, and she bit back a moan. Unbidden, she pressed against him.

He sucked in a strangled sound. "Christ."

She inhaled sharply.

A voice came from the opposite side of the yard. "Oh!! Shit. Sorry!"

Sophie jerked her attention away from Ryder to see Maddie standing there holding Lily, a huge smile across her face.

She looked from Ryder to Sophie and put a hand over her daughter's eyes. "Don't look, Lily, this is grown-up stuff."

Ryder rolled off Sophie, who scrambled to her feet and smoothed down her hair, which had grass and dirt in it. "That . . . um . . . wasn't what it looked like."

Maddie laughed, shifting her redheaded little daughter to her opposite hip. "Say hi to Auntie Sophie, Lily."

The baby chewed on her fist and looked at Sophie skeptically.

Sophie gestured toward the cars in the driveway. "We were just washing the car, I swear."

Ryder came up next to Sophie. "We're totally just friends."

Maddie smiled and nodded. "No need to explain."

"But—" Sophie began.

"Great," Ryder said.

Maddie tilted her head. "I was in the neighborhood and thought I'd stop by and ask you to dinner."

Sophie appreciated the offer, but she was worn out on people. All she wanted was to sit on the couch, eat takeout, and veg. Wait . . . did Revival have takeout that delivered? She had no idea. She'd worry about that later.

She smiled. "Thanks, Mads, but I want to take it easy tonight. Big day and all that, plus it's been a crazy weekend."

"I get it. I figured, but since I was in the neighborhood I'd thought I'd drop by and ask."

"Well, I love you, but all I want is to sit on my couch and watch Netflix."

"Understood." Maddie glanced a Ryder, a sly expression on her face. "Would you like to come?"

"I've got work to finish," Ryder said, smooth and calm. As though they hadn't been caught wrestling inappropriately on the ground.

"No worries," Maddie said, her words breezy. She tucked a lock of flame-red hair behind her ear and grinned. "Make sure you call me after work to tell me how it went."

"Will do." Sophie figured that wasn't all Maddie would want to hear about.

"Talk to you soon." Maddie waved her daughter's hand. "Say bye-bye, Lily."

Lily shook her head.

Maddie laughed. "She's a stubborn little thing."

"Gee, I wonder where she gets that from," Sophie said, dryly.

Maddie winked. "Her daddy, of course." She waved and turned to walk away, calling out over her shoulder, "You two have fun."

"Wait. No." But the justifications were lost as Maddie disappeared into the front yard. Sophie whipped around to Ryder. "Now do you see what you did?"

Ryder folded his arms over his broad chest. "Darlin', *you* rubbed your pussy against *me*."

She slammed her hands on her hips. "I did not. You held me down and trapped me. I was trying to get away."

"And getting turned on in the process."

"As if," she retorted, responding to the thrill of arguing with him. "Like you're all pure and innocent. I swear, how do you walk around with that thing?"

He laughed. "You do know how to make a man feel good."

"It wasn't a compliment." So he had a huge cock. Whatever.

"That's why you were all hot and needy, 'cause it was so awful. I get it."

"You are so full of yourself."

He inched forward. He leaned down, and she could almost feel his lips on hers. He shrugged. "Fair enough."

She was going to punch him in the face. But instead she said calmly, "Good. We've got that cleared up. By the way, does Revival have delivery?"

He chuckled. "No."

She looked at him in horror. "What am I supposed to eat?"

"There's a grocery store, you could try that."

She huffed. "You want me to go to the grocery store? On a Sunday night . . . and cook?"

He nodded. "It's an option."

"God, this town is the worst." She huffed and stomped away to the sound of his laughter following her all the way in.

Two hours later, after she'd showered and put on her most comfortable gray cotton shorts and a red tank top, she stared at her empty refrigerator and cursed Revival. She hadn't even thought about food. Why would she? In Chicago if she wanted to eat and she didn't have anything at home she just ordered takeout, regardless of the time.

She supposed she could do the unthinkable and run to the grocery store as Ryder suggested, but that would require at least putting on a bra, and how horrible did that sound? She sighed and closed her fridge. If she wanted to eat, that's what she needed to do.

She glanced at the counter. A jar of peanut butter and a loaf of bread sat there. Well, her options were clear—peanut butter and the couch, or a bra and the grocery store.

It wasn't really a contest.

She opened her silverware drawer and pulled out a knife, grabbed a paper plate, and returned to her meager dinner. She untied the loaf of bread when the doorbell rang.

There were only two people it could be—Maddie or Ryder—and since her best friend assumed she was already with Ryder and not to be disturbed, it could only be him.

She put down the knife, affixed a feigned indignant expression on her face, and went to the door.

He stood there, wearing gray cargo shorts and a white T-shirt and holding a bag.

She leaned against the door frame and eyed the brown sack. "What's that?"

He held it out, giving her that wicked grin. "Takeout."

Her pretend indignation fell away and she squealed in excitement and clapped. "You're a god among men."

He laughed and pushed toward her. "I hear that all the time."

How could she resist a man that brought food? She was only a mere mortal.

"Stop bragging." She snatched the bag and stood aside as he entered the house.

He peered at her newly decorated living room and shook his head. "You're such a girl."

She'd decided on distressed white cottage-type furniture accented with light blues and deep grays. She laughed. "Isn't it awesome?"

"I'm afraid to sit on the couch."

It was the color of dove's wings, slouchy and super comfortable. She clucked. "Don't be such a pussy."

He jerked his head to glare at her. "Good God, you're sassy."

She grinned. "Yeah? So?"

"So nothing." He skimmed down her body and sighed. "Again with no bra?"

"In fairness, you arrived uninvited, and what I do in the privacy of my own home is my business."

"True. But still. Have pity on me."

"What fun would that be?" She swung around and called out, "I'll get the plates and silverware. Start setting up on the coffee table."

"Yes, ma'am." His tone was full of sarcasm.

As she walked away he muttered something under his breath that sounded suspiciously like "bossy little thing."

She smiled. She'd think about how much she liked him later.

She got to her kitchen and called out, "Oh no, I don't have anything to drink."

A second later he called back, "I got you wine, darlin'."

She was starting to believe Ryder Moore was too good to be true. She returned to the living room holding napkins, paper plates, and silverware. "What'd you bring?"

"Italian. I didn't know what you'd like so I ordered a bunch of different things." He pointed to the now-open containers. There was bruschetta, a salad, calamari, and three different kinds of pasta. "I'm not picky, I'll eat whatever you don't or we can share."

Suddenly his thoughtfulness overwhelmed her. It filled her chest, expanded, and made pleasure bloom across her skin. It was unexpected and rare. No one had ever taken care of her. Even as a kid she'd fended for herself. She blinked and met his eyes. "Thank you."

He gave her that killer smile. "You're welcome."

She sat down next to him, putting the stuff she carried on the now-crowded table. Their knees brushed together, skin to skin, and it was like an electric shock.

He picked up the bottle of wine and poured it into two glasses before handing her one. "I assume you don't have much of a hangover."

"Not anymore." She took a sip and glanced at the TV. "What should we watch?"

She didn't ask if he was staying. It was already clear he was, and that was exactly what she wanted.

She couldn't remember the last time she'd had so much fun with anyone, and despite their unfortunate chemical reaction to each other, she liked being around him. She just needed to not wrestle with him again. She picked up the remote and turned it on.

"Anything but *Say Yes to the Dress* or *Real Housewives*," he said.

She grinned at him. "Sisters?"

He rolled his eyes. "Sisters."

"Have you seen *Making a Murderer*?"

He shook his head. "What's that?"

She furrowed her brow. "Huge hit on Netflix?"

His gaze dipped to her lips. "I don't have Netflix."

She gaped at him in horror. "Why? Are you living under a rock?"

"I don't watch much TV."

"Don't be insane."

"The only thing I have is HBO so I can watch *Game of Thrones*."

"At least I know you're not completely a lost cause." Sophie started pressing buttons. "It's a true crime documentary, you'll like it."

"If you say so." He picked up a plate. "What do you want?"

"Everything. I love food and I'm starving."

He shook his head.

"What?"

He scooped a little bit of everything onto her plate. "I love a girl who likes to eat."

"Then, Ryder Moore, you have met your match."

The words were flippant, but as soon as they left her mouth there was a stilling. An awkwardness that filled the air and spoke what neither of them dared to say.

That maybe he had, and that maybe she had too.

She saw now that she'd been wrong about him. He wasn't bad, not really; he was fun and made her think risky things, but *he* was a good man.

Not only had he'd brought her dinner, but he'd taken care of everything. In her vast dating experience, she'd learned most men half-assed things, wanting her to do most of the work and planning. They called for a date and immediately left the plans up to her by asking so many questions she ended up with all the decisions in her lap.

But Ryder had taken care of everything. He'd done all the work for her.

She'd been right to think him dangerous.

Only now she realized it was for all the wrong reasons.

Well now, wasn't this surreal?

If anyone had told Ryder he'd be in this situation four days ago, he'd have told them they were crazy. But here he was, stomach full, wine consumed, and sitting on Sophie's couch.

Dinner was long over, they'd drunk two bottles of wine, cleared the table, laughed, talked, and now they were sitting on her couch, three episodes into *Making a Murderer*.

He was mildly buzzed as he suspected Sophie was too, considering how she lazily took up most of the couch. He was more than a foot taller than her and scrunched into the corner.

Neither had acknowledged how they'd ended up here, ignoring the scene in the yard as though it had been an aberration.

"Oh my God!" Sophie yelled at the TV before she turned to him, gesturing wildly. "Can you believe this? You're in law enforcement. Explain how this is possible?"

Ryder figured if he had Sophie around to watch TV with all the time, he'd spend a lot more time watching. She was fun as hell. She yelled obscenities at the screen. Had arguments with the characters, bossed them around, and let out huffs of exasperation.

He could watch her all day.

She scowled, her expression fierce. "Well?"

He raised a brow. "Are you really asking? Or do you have an opinion formed and are not interested in changing your mind?"

She kicked him in the thigh. "Of course I'm not going to change my mind."

He laughed and shook his head. It was a good thing, because he had no fucking clue what was going on in the documentary. He'd been too busy watching her, studying her to pay attention.

He gestured toward her. "Sophie, how can one small person take up the entire couch?"

She flashed him a grin. "Aren't you comfortable?"

"I could be more comfortable."

She clucked her tongue. "Poor baby."

He rolled his eyes. "If you were any kind of hostess you'd make room for me. I did buy you dinner after all."

"Because I'm awesome."

He laughed. "Yeah, kind of."

"No kind of about it."

He flashed a smile, and the words were out of his mouth before he could stop them. "You could let me stretch out too."

She stared at him for a good ten seconds before she said slowly, "I could."

Their eyes met and he shook his head. "But you shouldn't."

She bit her lip and her foot brushed his thigh. "No, I shouldn't."

Transfixed by her, he encircled her ankle, stroking over the bone. "A horrible idea."

"Worst idea on the planet." Her tone was breathless now.

He took in her tumbled, messy hair, skimpy clothes, and tanned skin and questioned his sanity.

Time to back away. He released his hold on her. "Agreed."

A frown fluttered over her lips for a flash of an instant before she pushed back up in a seated position. She glanced back at the TV. "Ryder?"

"Yes, Sophie?"

"Thank you for today. This is a big transition for me, and you made it fun." She cleared her throat. "I appreciate it."

A pretty blush spread across her cheeks, and his chest gave a hard thump. He'd never seen her blush before. He'd seen her flushed with passion but not from embarrassment. "You're welcome. It was a good day."

She nodded. "It was."

He put his arm on the back of the sofa to keep from reaching for her. "Ignored everything I was supposed to do today."

"Me too." Her teeth slid over her bottom lip.

"Sophie?"

She glanced at him. "Yes?"

"It was worth it."

Their eyes met.

Lust thickened the air, filling up all the space and demanding attention. It was so fucking hot between them, simmering right under the surface, ready to come to a boil.

Neither looked away.

Her breath quickened.

His did the same.

She jerked her attention away, swinging her legs off the couch and standing up. "I have to go to the bathroom."

"Okay."

She hurried to the back of the house, and a second later a door slammed shut.

He turned back to the TV, sitting forward and resting his

elbows on his knees before dragging a hand through his hair. He muttered under his breath, "Christ."

Okay, when she came back in he'd get his ass up and go home. It had been a great day, but it was time for it to end. They'd made a lot of progress today. They were on the right track. They just needed to stick with it.

The bathroom door opened and she made her way back to the living room. He forced himself off the couch. "I should probably go."

She nodded. "Probably, early day tomorrow."

She brushed past him and he followed, keeping his gaze off her little shorts. When they got to the front door, an awkwardness settled between them.

"Thanks again," she said, not looking at him.

"It was my pleasure." He put his hand on the handle.

She smiled, her attention darting toward the door. "Good night."

"Good night."

Neither moved.

Her tongue swept over her lips. She fussed with her hair, her movements agitated before her hands settled back to her sides.

He needed to twist the handle and walk away. Instead he said, "Sleep well."

"You too."

He wasn't quite sure what happened next. One second he was turning the knob, and the next he had her pinned to the wall, almost surprised to find himself there.

She let out an oomph, and then a moan.

He didn't think, he just acted, covering her mouth with his.

She threw her arms around his neck, her lips as desperate and wanting as he felt. He groaned and she answered in response. The heat that had been driving him crazy kicked up another notch.

The kiss grew wetter, more insistent. Demanding and consuming.

Body tight with desire, he devoured her as she squirmed against him.

He shoved her harder against the wall, trapping her.

Her legs parted and he slid between them, lifting her legs to wrap around him.

She arched.

He surged.

Breathing hard. They rocked, hips urgent and questing. He needed to stop, but she was just so damn hot. So damn perfect.

She gripped his hips, digging her nails into his shoulders.

He grunted.

She moaned, the sound vibrating on their lips.

Their kiss turned ruthless.

His tongue invaded and captured her.

Desire pounded in his blood.

It was too much, spiraling out of control faster than he could think. Perched on the very edge of arousal, he couldn't clear his head.

He shifted and his cock thrust in the most torturous way. She whimpered against his mouth and clutched him with her thighs to hold him there.

Her nails dug into his back as he ground against her.

The air turned humid, hot and sticky with sex and lust.

She gripped him tighter, their breathing coming so fast it was hard to maintain the press of their mouths. Panting against each other, full of tongue and teeth.

He was out of control, consumed by the rush of mad, fucking crazy lust. He needed to stop. Right now.

He pressed one more hungry kiss against her lips,

growling low in his throat before forcing himself to pull away. Expending more willpower than he had in his entire life, he gentled his hold, putting his hands on her thighs before he whispered, "I should go."

She blinked open glassy eyes, and slowly her legs slid from his waist. "Yes."

He stepped away, gaze snagging on her swollen lips. "Sleep well."

She crossed her arms over her chest. "You too."

This time he didn't hesitate.

Chapter Twelve

The following morning, Sophie twisted and turned in the mirror she'd hung in her bedroom to check out how she looked in her work attire. She wore a black dress in a slim cut, with a square neck and three-quarter sleeves and her favorite stilettos.

She looked good, probably too urban for Revival, but she didn't care. She dressed how she dressed, and after being out of work all this time it was nice to look like her former self.

She stared at her reflection, her mind returning to that kiss in her hallway. She touched her lips. It had been hot, desperate, and dirty.

She had no idea what to make of it.

There was a knock on the door, saving her from having to dwell on it.

The knocking became louder and more insistent. She called out, "I'm coming!"

It was probably Maddie, stopping by this morning to check in on her before she left.

She opened the door, but her friend wasn't standing there. Instead it was Ryder, looking illegally hot in his sheriff's uniform. He smiled at her and held out a venti Starbucks. "Good morning."

As she stared at the coffee, her heart skipped a beat. "The nearest Starbucks is ten miles from here." She knew because the first thing she'd done when she settled in was look at the app to see where the closest one was. She'd wanted to run back to Chicago when she saw it was way too far to go to on her way to work.

"Yeah, I know." His gaze raked down her body. "Is that what you're wearing?"

Still floored by the gesture, she nodded absently. "You drove ten miles to get me coffee?"

He shrugged. "You kept complaining about how far it was, and how you needed your triple-shot Red Eye every morning. I wanted you to have a good first day."

At a loss for what to say, she took the cup. Diamonds wouldn't have made her this happy. There was nothing better he could have done for her. There he went, being thoughtful again. "Thank you."

"You're welcome." He stepped inside the house. "You didn't answer my question."

God, he smelled good, like he'd come from the shower and rolled in a bucket of summer. "What question?"

"Is this what you're wearing?"

She tilted her chin up to gaze at him. "Yes. What's wrong with it?"

His fingers tightened on her hips. "You look like a city girl."

"I am a city girl."

A muscle jumped in his jaw. "You're going to fucking stop traffic."

Pleasure warmed her chest, making her smile. "I think that's probably an exaggeration."

"Nope."

Their eyes met. Holding far too long.

To break the tension, she raised her cup. "What did I do to deserve this?"

His head tilted. "It's a peace offering."

"For what?" She tightened her fingers, not wanting to talk about what happened last night.

"There's something you need to know before you go to work today." His gaze flickered.

She took a sip of coffee. "That sounds ominous."

He smiled, all smooth and slick. "You're not going to like it."

Oh no. She raised a brow. "Like what?" She couldn't fathom what he possibly needed to tell her before work.

He eyed the coffee. "Would you consider putting the cup down?"

"Why?" There was no sense of alarm, only intrigue.

"I don't want to risk getting hot coffee tossed in my face."

She cocked her hip. "Ryder, there's not one thing in this world you could tell me that would make me waste perfectly good coffee."

He sighed. "All right, so here's the thing . . . I'm kind of going to be your boss."

Surprise flashed through her and she sputtered, "Excuse me?"

"I'm going to be your boss," he repeated as though it explained everything and she was too dense to understand.

She shook her head. "Griffin's my boss."

"Well, yeah, but I'm the head of the town square grand opening project."

Oh. My. God. This could not be happening. So, not only was Ryder her neighbor and current fixation, he was going to manage her work too! Was there no justice in this world? Eyes wide, she asked, "But how? You're a cop."

He shook his head. "I'm the chief deputy, a leader in the

community. Small-town government isn't all separated and segmented out into defined departments the way it would be in Chicago."

She could not believe this. She put down her coffee and turned to face him.

His expression grew wary.

She clenched her fist. "So you're saying after all this time that you failed to mention I was going to be *working* with you?"

He scrubbed a hand over his jaw, before shrugging. "I . . . um . . . thought it would be a fun surprise."

"A *surprise*?" Her voice notched up an octave on the last word.

He gave her a smile she was sure charmed every woman he came in contact with. "Bad idea?"

"Bad idea, Ryder!" she yelled, then stalked up to him and jabbed him in the chest with her finger. "Mark my words, you are going to pay for this."

"It's not that big a deal."

She screeched and jabbed at him again. "Not a big deal? Not only do I have to live next door to the most infuriating man on the planet, now I have to work for him too!"

"Well, when you put it that way." His lips quivered.

She clenched her teeth. "I swear to God, if you laugh you're a dead man."

His expression turned serious but his eyes danced with amusement. He held up his hands. "I brought you coffee to make up for the omission."

She poked him again. "That doesn't absolve you."

"I know."

She let out a scream. She could not get away from this man. "I want to slap you across the face right now."

The smile threatened again. "Would that make you feel better?"

"Yes." She needed something physical to work out all her pent-up frustration.

He nodded. "Okay, go ahead."

Something wrong and thrilling passed between them, settling in her belly. She narrowed her eyes. "You don't think I'll do it, do you?"

"Sure I do. I know you have it in you." He offered his cheek, pointing at the stubbled jaw. "Go ahead, darlin', right here."

"I'll do it." Excitement sparked across her nerve endings.

"Give it your best shot."

A devil took hold of her, and she raised her hand and struck. Of course he caught it, deflecting it easily.

But before she could retaliate further, he swept in and claimed her mouth, his tongue tangling with hers as he sucked her in and under the current of the most relentless desire she'd ever known.

She could kiss him forever.

It was like her lips had never had such a perfect fit. When they met, it was no mere press of mouths. No, they fused together, melded and yielding, burning until they were impossible to separate.

He groaned. Shifted them and walked back until she hit the wall.

Everything turned hotter. Wetter. Messy and slick and insistent.

His head slanted.

Her chin tilted.

He fisted her hair.

She clutched at his shoulders.

Their breath came fast, hands roamed.

The world tilted, her body surged, and the kiss spiraled out of control.

He lifted his head to pant against her lips, "We have to stop."

"I know." She pulled him back down.

He cursed and kissed her again.

Harder and more frantic. His body flush against hers as she squirmed to get closer.

He ripped away. "You're going to be the death of me."

She took a deep breath and her lashes fluttered open. "You need to stop kissing me."

"Believe it or not, I'm trying."

She shook her head to clear it from the lust making her stupid.

He rubbed his thumb over her lower lip. "It's time to go to work."

She sagged against the wall. "It is."

He met her eyes. "Are we good?"

She sighed. "Do I have any other choice?"

"You can choose to be mad, but I'll still be the project manager."

She glared at him. "Don't think you're going to tell me what to do."

He laughed. "I'd never."

"Yeah, right."

"Sophie?"

"Yes."

"I—" He stopped and got a look in his eye that made all the air in her lungs stall. Jaw hardening, he raised his hand and worked the collar of her dress to the side before slowly lowering his head to her neck.

"What are you doing?" Her tone was far too uneven.

In answer he brushed his lips along the curve between her shoulder and throat, a soft, gentle caress. She closed her eyes, letting the sensation flutter over her.

Then he bit her. Not a nip, not a playful tug, but a bite.

She gasped as his teeth sank into her flesh, hard enough to leave a mark. Her knees literally went weak.

She might have an orgasm right here.

He wrapped his hand around her waist to steady her, then released her skin and licked over the spot that stung before pulling her dress back in place. Like it was the most normal thing in the world to sink his teeth into her before she left the house.

He stood back, a satisfied expression on his face. "There. I feel better now."

"Oh my God, did you just try and mark me?" Her tone filled with exasperation despite the bone-deep thrill he'd given her.

He grinned. "Yeah. Sorry, I couldn't help it."

It might be the hottest thing anyone had ever done to her, but she couldn't let it pass without making a remark. She raised a brow. "Do you want to pee on me later?"

He laughed. "Would you let me?"

She slapped him. "That's gross."

"Biting you is way more effective."

She rolled her eyes and shrugged as though it wasn't true, even though they both knew the truth.

"Have a good day, darlin'." He tucked a lock of her hair behind her ear. "I'll see you soon."

And with that, he was gone, and she could only stare after him in amazement.

The morning passed in a blur, filled with paperwork, building tours, and meeting far too many people to count. Sophie barely had time to think, let alone obsess over Ryder. Although every time she thought of him, the spot on her neck tingled and her belly heated.

Thus proving how effective his strategies really were.

But she'd think about that later.

Right now, she had to concentrate on the plans and ideas she wanted to present to the mayor of Revival, Griffin Strong. When Sophie pictured mayors, she pictured loose-jowled old white guys with bellies.

Griffin couldn't be any further from that picture.

Quite simply, the man was gorgeous. Tall and broad, with dark sandy hair and melting chocolate brown eyes. He was charming, charismatic, and likable, not to mention he seemed to be single-handedly dragging Revival into the modern century. From what she understood, the town had been floundering until he came along, and with him at the helm there was slow, steady improvement. People weren't leaving, unemployment had dropped, and local businesses had improved.

Sophie had no problem seeing how he'd won the last election in a landslide.

A week ago, upon meeting him, she would have bemoaned the handsome mayor's new marital status, claiming all the good ones were taken, but today she didn't even give it a passing thought.

How could she with Ryder making her so crazy?

She took a chair opposite his desk, ready to get down to business. She couldn't deny how good it felt to be productive again. It was funny, Sophie had never considered herself to be career obsessed—Penelope had always won that spot—but she hadn't realized until it was all gone how much she enjoyed her job. It was such a part of her identity, seeping into the very fabric of her life from friends, to parties, to what to wear. She'd taken it for granted, but not anymore. She was grateful to have projects that fired up her brain cells.

"So, how's your first day going?" Griffin asked with a smile.

"Great, everyone has been very friendly," she said.

He raised a brow. "Even Mrs. Weller?" Naming his very scary secretary, who looked at Sophie as though she might be a Russian spy.

She laughed, tilting her head. "She's a good gatekeeper."

"That's one way of putting it." He gestured to his computer screen. "I've read over your report outlining ideas for the Fourth Festival and was suitably impressed. There wasn't anything in your plans I have issue with, but the next step is to run them past the project team. What I am really interested in was your thoughts on the tourism proposal. You're from Chicago, if we're able to implement successfully, do you think overstressed workaholics would come out here to relax for the weekend?"

On their initial call Griffin had gone over his current objectives, but it had been clear the tourism trade was what he was most excited about, so Sophie had done some initial research. With the town right next to the river and not horribly far from Chicago, the revenue could help grow the town. It was a good plan.

She nodded. "Yes—"

There was a knock at the door, and Griffin called, "Yes?"

Mrs. Weller opened the door. "The chief is here."

Sophie's heart started a rapid, excited pounding. Oh no, she was in so much trouble.

Griffin pointed to the phone on his desk. "You know there's an intercom."

The secretary shushed him. "Nobody wants to talk face-to-face any more."

Griffin expelled a long sigh. "Send him in."

Sophie stifled her smile.

Griffin rubbed the bridge of his nose. "She was my teacher in grade school, and I was a hellion back in the day.

She hasn't quite forgiven me." Griffin raised his head and stood, a wide, friendly smile on his face. "There he is. Sophie Kincaid, I'd like you to meet our chief deputy sheriff, Ryder Moore."

She rose and turned to face him. The bite on her neck warmed and pulsed as a flush spread over her cheeks.

He held out a hand, a big, arrogant grin on his face as their palms slid together and electricity ran up her arm. "Sophie and I know each other, actually. We're neighbors."

Griffin laughed. "Of course, what was I thinking? I'd forgotten she rented the house next to you." He smiled at Sophie. "I know you've only been in town a few days, so I wasn't sure if you had a chance to meet."

"We have." Ryder's voice sounded sly, cunning.

Sophie extracted her hand and willed the heat to cool. She cleared her throat. "It's good to see you again, Ryder."

His gaze dropped to her neck. "You too."

Griffin glanced at the two of them and then offered a bright smile. "Since you're well acquainted, I suppose we can skip the whole getting-to-know-you chitchat and get down to business."

"Exactly," Sophie said, refusing to look at Ryder.

Griffin gestured to a round table. "Let's sit over there. I was about to ask Sophie her thoughts on expanding tourism as a potential avenue of revenue."

They all sat down, and under the table, Sophie's knee bumped Ryder's.

For good measure, she shot him a death glare.

He smiled innocently. "And what were your thoughts, Sophie?"

She met his gray eyes, which danced with amusement. He thought he could throw her, and he wasn't wrong, he could.

Only when it came to her job, she didn't intend to let him.

* * *

Ryder grinned as Sophie squared her shoulders, shot him a "you'd better behave or you're a dead man" glare, and opened her oversized iPad pro. It didn't surprise him that she had the latest and greatest technology. She was that kind of woman.

Yes, this was business, but she looked so good he wanted to rip her dress off her. She drove him crazy. So crazy he bit her. Unable to help himself, his gaze skimmed down to settle on her neck. He wanted to bite her again. Somewhere everyone could see it.

But he had to play it cool. Griffin was his friend and the city project was his baby. He'd been excited over the opportunity to hire Sophie, hoping she'd bring fresh ideas and a big-city perspective.

Ryder was going to take a wild guess and assume Griffin most likely wouldn't appreciate his behavior toward her these last couple of days. Especially when Ryder had known they'd be working closely together.

She flipped the screen toward Ryder and Griffin, showing them a map of Revival, focusing on the river section of town.

"I think it's a great idea," she began in a rock-solid professional voice. "It has a lot of potential, but your problem right now is opportunity. You don't have any resorts or places people wanting a break from the city would want to stay." She circled three houses on the map. "These are for sale." She drew arrows to two. "But these are smack in the middle of the residential section of the river. Families live here because this is a small town and they get to leave their doors unlocked and know all their neighbors. They're not going to want to have some strangers renting out the house next to them to party all weekend."

Damn. Ryder was impressed. She'd done her homework. As a group, they'd been focused on the town square and the events that would follow, figuring they'd pay attention to the how later.

On the other hand, Sophie had done significant research.

She glanced at them to ensure she had their attention. She pointed to the house at the other end of the map. "This house has potential, but the house next to it has been in the same family for over a hundred years, which limits possible expansion." She slid her finger over the screen and recentered the image. "But this land might work. It's big and undeveloped. It has room for a small resort that would allow people to get away from it all." She flashed them a smile. "It's a great mix of riverbed and forests."

She sat back in her chair, and Ryder glanced at Griffin, who looked like he might jump out of his skin with excitement.

She gave Ryder a smug look, twirling her pen. "The land would need to be rezoned, but it's doable. You'll have a better pulse on how the citizens of Revival will take it. But assuming they are on board, that leads us to the next problem on the list: investors. You're asking them to take a risk on an idea, on the potential of the town."

Griffin nodded. "And you don't think they'll go for it?"

She shrugged. "I don't know. It's a trend, that's for sure. People are tired and they want to get away. But why come here instead of Lake Geneva?"

Captivated by her, Ryder interjected. "Lake Geneva is a hell of a lot more crowded."

She pointed at him. "Exactly." She sat forward. "So here's what we need to do. We need to build a story. We need to come up with a campaign that will sell Revival as the anti-Wisconsin lake town. Then we need to invite people to Revival and test the story. Once we do that, we'll know what we're dealing with."

Ryder could only stare at her in wonder. In the past four days—Christ, had it only been four days?—he'd lusted after her body, her face, her quick wit, biting tongue, and sassy retorts. He'd been impressed by her banter, her comebacks, and her lack of fear. He'd known she was intelligent, but he'd had no idea how off-the-charts smart she was.

This woman knew her shit. It wasn't that Griffin had never talked about this stuff. He had. They knew they didn't have actual places for people to visit, but they'd been focused on building up the town, driving business and community. Those were in the final phases, and it was time to start looking at the next piece of the puzzle.

Sophie had made it concrete and actionable.

Ryder had no doubt in his mind if Griffin decided to sic Sophie on this, she'd move faster than anyone else in this town ever dared.

Griffin sat back in his chair. "Wow."

"Thank you," Sophie said, grinning ear to ear. "In addition to this, I have plans that could work to help grow the town. You sent me the town's current initiatives, so I developed the beginning outlines for each of the projects."

"I'm impressed," Griffin said.

"That's what you're paying me for." She shrugged, as though it wasn't a big deal, but Ryder wasn't fooled. She was well aware she'd just hit a home run.

"And worth every penny, I see," Griffin said, his voice amused.

The truth was they'd never had anyone this good before. At the last meeting, someone suggested a direct mail campaign. Even Ryder, who knew virtually nothing about public relations and marketing, knew that was a shitty, outdated idea.

"I'm glad you're happy," she said graciously, although Ryder would bet a hundred dollars she was thinking *you bet your ass I am.*

"Hey," Griffin said, breaking Ryder from his thoughts. "My wife, Darcy, is very active in the community, but she actually spent a lot of years living in New York. Not only would she love to meet you, but she'd love to hear the ideas as well. She's a good sounding board for stuff like this. I know this is your first week in town and it's probably crazy, but maybe you'd have dinner with us next week once you're settled in?"

Sophie beamed and folded her hands. "That would be lovely. I'd love to meet her."

"Great." Griffin turned to Ryder. "Can you make it too?"

Wild horses couldn't drag him away. He met Sophie's gaze. "We'll be there."

"She's fucking impressive," Griffin said to Ryder.

Sophie had left for another meeting, leaving Griffin and him alone.

Ryder nodded. "She is."

"I researched her background before we talked, and until the mess with her company, she was hot shit. She knows everyone." Griffin ran a hand through his hair. "Maddie told me she was the person people called when they wanted into the most exclusive party. That she knows how to get people eating out of the palm of her hand. Being her best friend, I thought she was exaggerating. Clearly I was wrong."

"She'll get stuff done." An understatement.

There was a moment of silence before Griffin cleared his throat. "Are you sleeping with her yet?"

Ryder jerked with shock. "What? No."

Griffin smiled good-naturedly, holding up his hands. "Technically this isn't my business, but I don't want things to get messy either. We need to keep her as long as we can."

Ryder shook his head. "Why would you even think that?"

Griffin laughed. "Do you want a list?"

"Yeah." He was a fucking cop, he wasn't supposed to have tells.

Griffin shrugged. "One, she flushed the second you walked in the room. Two, you looked at her like you were contemplating screwing her on the desk in front of me. Three, I practically choked on the sexual tension between you. Four, you kept looking at her neck and she kept touching her neck in the same spot. Five, you said 'we'll' be there. Six—"

Ryder held up his hand. "All right, I get the picture."

Griff chuckled. "I didn't even need the other stuff. I knew the second you shook hands there was something going on between you."

Technically, they'd agreed there was nothing between them. Only he couldn't seem to stop kissing her and she couldn't seem to stop kissing him back. He decided on the simplest and most factual statement. "I'm not sleeping with her."

Griffin smirked. "Well, in fairness, she's only been in town a few days."

And she was already causing havoc wherever she went. Ryder shrugged. "We're neighbors."

"And it's your business. You might be the project manager, but she works directly for me. You're not even on the same payroll as her, and there's no rule against . . . dating her. As the mayor I'd ask you to be careful because I'd like to keep her around for as long as possible." He propped his elbows on the table. "As your friend, let me say nice job. She's . . . something else."

She was. But despite marking her, he had no real claim on her and couldn't pretend otherwise. He reiterated, "Just neighbors."

Griffin chuckled before pointing at the door. "That kind of skill set, with her charisma, it's only a matter of time before her association with that disaster wears off and people start clamoring for her. We need to get as much out of her as we can before she goes back to Chicago."

"Understood." A pit grew in Ryder's stomach. Griffin was right. Now that he'd seen her in action, there was no way Chicago wasn't coming for her.

He'd be lucky if she even lasted through the Halloween festival.

Hell, he'd be lucky if she lasted the summer.

At some point Sophie was going back to Chicago where she belonged.

Ryder was pretty sure that, after forty-eight hours, the knowledge wasn't supposed to feel like a kick in the gut. Fuck. He liked her. Not wanted her, not was amused by her, but *liked* her.

He was so screwed.

Chapter Thirteen

Thankfully, in government, everyone locked up their offices and vacated the building at exactly five o'clock. So Sophie was able to stop by Maddie's by 5:15 for a first day recap.

She sat down at the table and smiled at Maddie's happy, devious baby. "Hey, Lily, what kind of trouble did you get into today?"

Lily picked up a toy on her high chair and screamed, "Ba!" then chucked it across the room.

Very seriously, Sophie nodded. "I see. That is crazy, girl."

Lily gave her a big gap-tooth, droolly smile. "Ba, ba, ba!"

"You don't have to tell me." Sophie patted the little baby's hand. "You're preaching to the choir."

Maddie laughed, putting a couple of Cheerios on Lily's tray before she sat down. "So, how was your first day?"

"Good." It surprised her. It hadn't been nearly as dreadful as she'd feared. She'd actually found herself having fun. She'd always loved meeting new people and taking on new challenges, and she'd assumed she'd be bored. But that wasn't the case. Instead she wanted to dig in, get her hands dirty, and start tackling obstacles.

The festivals she could do in her sleep, but it was the tourism project that really got her juices flowing. She'd known Griffin had it in his objectives, so she'd prepared properly, but she hadn't realized how high it was on his wish list for the small town until they'd started talking. To organize something of that magnitude, to build and sell the story, come up with creative solutions would be a huge accomplishment.

It would take a lot of work and far more time than she had in Revival, but the prospect of getting it going on the right foot excited her.

Maddie picked up a slice of apple and bit, chewing before she swallowed. "Was everyone nice to you?"

"Yes. They were great." Everyone had been warm and gracious and excited to have her. Which was a nice change of pace from the cold shoulder she had been getting back home. "It was more fun than I thought."

Maddie beamed. "See, I told you! I'm not going to lie and say moving here wasn't an adjustment at first, even though it was what I wanted, but I love it now."

Sophie took a sip of iced tea and grabbed her own apple slice from the bowl between them. "How could you not want to move back to Chicago?"

Maddie laughed, waving a hand. "What's so great about Chicago?"

Sophie frowned. "What do you do for shopping?"

"Well, there's plenty of stores, and there's an outlet mall not too far from here." Maddie's eyes went wide. "And I'm not sure if you've heard, but there's this new thing called the Internet where you can buy practically anything you want and have it delivered to your door."

Sophie laughed.

Maddie continued. "Besides, I get back to the city enough to keep my palate sophisticated and my shoes current."

It might not be Sophie's dream, but she couldn't be happier for her friend. "I'm glad you finally found your place."

"Me too." Lily gurgled and threw a toy on the floor. Maddie dutifully picked it up and handed it back to her daughter, her face practically glowing with love for the little girl. "And what did you think of Griffin? Think you can work for him?"

Sophie fanned herself. "Good God, you have one hot mayor."

Maddie chuckled. "Yeah, he's been awesome for the town too."

"I can see why. He's got a laundry list of ideas, and I think if he could, he'd implement them all at the same time."

"So you think you can be happy here for a while?"

"Yeah, I think I can. It's a good challenge and the time will fly by with so much to do."

Maddie nodded. "Good. I really think if you give it a chance, it might be good for you."

Sophie frowned. Both Maddie and Penelope had said that several times now, and she didn't understand it. "Why do you guys keep saying that?"

Maddie shrugged. "Because I know you."

"But I was super happy before it all came crashing down." She had been, she'd barely had a second's free time, but she'd been happy.

"That's what you kept saying, but I don't know . . ."

"I'm good, Mads." Sophie patted her hand. "I promise."

"Good, because we're your family, you know that, right?"

"Of course," she said automatically. She understood they all thought that, even though she'd always considered herself a bit removed. Never assimilated the way Penelope had been.

The light of mischief lit her friend's expression. "Soooo, do I have to bring up Ryder? Or will you?"

Sophie swallowed a bite of her apple. And here they were, at the man invading her life from every angle. "Did you know he's kind of my boss?"

Her friend laughed. "No way. How's that even possible?"

"Apparently he's the project lead on the festivals." Sophie's eyes narrowed. "Like you didn't know. This is a small town, I thought everyone knew everyone else's business."

"Well, yeah, sure." Maddie laughed, hearty and warm. "But I don't know who's on what project team."

Finished with her snack, Sophie dragged a hand through her hair. "Now I've got to live next door to him *and* work with him. It's hell."

"Hmmm . . . It didn't look like you were suffering too much yesterday when I found him on top of you."

"Ha!" Sophie waved a hand. "That just shows what you know."

"That bad, huh?" Maddie's voice was filled with feigned sympathy.

"It's terrible."

"So what's going on?"

"Nothing." The word was quick and unconvincing. She thought of the mark on her neck, left by his teeth sinking into her flesh. The way her knees quivered and she'd wanted to clutch at him. "He kissed me a few times, no big deal. Right now we're working on being friends."

Maddie nodded. "Sounds like a plan."

Something that felt a lot like disappointment welled in her chest. A part of her wanted Maddie to press, if only so she could make sense of her emotions. Sophie was an extrovert. Talking it out helped her process. Only without direct questions, she didn't know what to say.

Sophie scowled at her friend. "You should have warned me about him."

Lily kicked her legs against the base of her high chair and Maddie pushed a Cheerio at her. "It didn't occur to me."

Sophie stared at her wide-eyed. "I know you're all blissfully married, but have you seen him? Even Penelope made a comment."

"You're totally right, I don't know what I was thinking." Maddie's lips twitched. "Disclosing your hot landlord should have been the first thing on my list to discuss with you."

"Exactly!" Sophie pressed her hand to her hot cheeks. "Maddie?"

In answer, her friend tilted her head.

She blew out a deep breath and confessed what she'd refused to even admit to herself. "He brought me dinner. And drove ten miles out of his way to bring me coffee. I think I like him."

"Oh," Maddie said.

Sophie looked away, studying Maddie's beautiful kitchen with all its handmade cabinets and state-of-the-art appliances. They'd kept the decor true to the farmhouse's origins, and it was quite spectacular, although Sophie cared more about clothes than houses. She said softly, "Do you have any idea how long it's been since I liked someone?"

"Yeah, I do." Maddie's voice was soft.

Sophie wrinkled her nose. Her friends worried about her, fretted over her being the last one to fall in love. She'd tried not to mind, and really she hadn't. She didn't even think about kids and a family. She'd always liked being single. What she didn't like was the stuff that came with it. All those holidays people spent with their families, and her parents were in the far-off corners of the world. They always invited her, and she always went because she knew they'd be concerned if she didn't. But you don't bring a casual date to Christmas. She barely even talked about men these days because there hadn't been anyone worth mentioning in a long time.

She swallowed hard. "I don't like the way he makes me feel."

Maddie's head tilted. "How does he make you feel?"

"Wild and reckless." She licked her lips. "Like I want to go out and do something crazy."

"Is that wrong?"

Maddie had been her partner in teenage rebellion before her dad died in an accident that left her in a coma. When she'd woken up, she'd turned herself into a perfect daughter, sister, and girlfriend until she nearly suffocated with it. When it got too much for her, she'd climbed out the window on her wedding day and ended up in Revival and never looked back. For her, crazy and reckless had led her to the love of her life. Sophie had never been that lucky. Sophie blew out a breath. "You know my track record with wild and reckless, and it never ends well."

Maddie clucked her tongue. "Soph, Tony was a long time ago. You're not the same person you were then."

"I know, because I don't engage in that kind of behavior anymore."

Maddie frowned. "We all have that one guy that messes with your head. Eventually you have to move on."

"It's not that. I got over that asshole the second he overdrew my bank account and abandoned me." She shuddered, still able to recall the crushing loss of it. She shook the rush of emotion away. "It was more than messing with my head. I was so crazy about him, so desperately in love with him, I let him do whatever he wanted. But worse, I let him manipulate me. Let him isolate me from you and Penelope. Let him convince me that every red flag I saw was in my imagination. That every time he disappeared to screw some girl, *I* was the crazy one. And all because I was addicted to the way he made me feel."

There was silence for a bit before Maddie said, "I don't think Ryder is emotionally abusive, Soph."

"I know that." But it didn't matter; she had no desire to lose herself like that again. There was the truth of the matter. He had the potential to ruin her, and she couldn't let that happen. "It doesn't matter. I'm leaving. So I'm going to stay away."

"Okay," Maddie said, like it was so simple.

She sighed. "I only wish he didn't make me remember."

"Make you remember what?" Maddie asked.

"What abandon tastes like."

Ryder knocked on Sophie's door at six thirty, slightly embarrassed by his actions but unable to help himself.

She opened the door a minute later dressed in yoga pants and a tank top, her hair in a ponytail. She didn't say anything, she just looked at him, with shadows under her eyes.

He jerked a thumb over to his house and smiled. "I'm making dinner, I thought you might want to join me."

Her forehead furrowed and she peered over his left

shoulder, looking out on the quiet street before she shook her head. "I don't think that's a great idea."

Sadness creased her face and he frowned. He'd been in the last meeting with her and she'd been fine, all bright and full of sass. Had something happened between now and then? "Is everything okay?"

"Everything's great." But her voice lacked any of its customary verve. She shrugged. "I . . . I think we should keep our distance."

Okay, he'd kissed her and bitten her, but she'd seemed fine all day. He wanted to ask but didn't think she'd tell him. He shrugged. "It's just dinner, Sophie. I know you haven't been shopping, and Revival doesn't have delivery. I thought you might want to eat."

Her fingers tightened on the door frame. "That's what we always say."

She had him there.

She gazed out onto the street again. "Bill called, I'm having coffee with him Wednesday."

His jaw tightened, and an unfamiliar and unwelcome jealousy sat in his gut. "You don't want to go out with Bill."

She shrugged. "Why not? He's a nice guy."

"Because you'll eat him alive."

She raised a brow, putting a hand on her hip. "Like you'd give Cheryl a heart attack if you ever said boo to her."

"I never said I wanted to go out with Cheryl. Maddie put us on the spot and we went with it."

"Maddie must have believed there was some reason the two of you should go out." She met his eyes.

And here he thought asking her for dinner would be the simplest part of his evening. He sighed. "Yes, I thought about it, but I hadn't gotten around to it."

"Ryder?"

"Yes?" His cop instincts went on high alert.

"I don't think we are a good idea. And you don't think we are a good idea." A small smile flirted over her lips, but there was no joy in it. "We're only playing with danger because we like danger. That's all it is."

Was that it? Was that all it was? The adrenaline rush of her clouding his judgment? Because she was right, he kept saying he didn't want to tangle with her, but kept putting himself right in her path. Playing with fire.

He stared at her and she stared right back, her expression unwavering. He blew out a breath. "Be very careful what you wish for, Sophie, what you ask for, because I'll give it to you."

A frown curved over her lips, and her face darkened. "Is that a threat?"

Shoulders rigid, he said, "You don't think I know you say one thing and mean another? Do you think I haven't noticed?"

"Why are you fighting for this? To what purpose?"

The question stopped him cold. What was he fighting for? When he really thought about it, his reasons for staying away from her were flimsy as hell. Sure, he had this grand plan to stay away from reckless wild women, but Sophie wasn't a one-night stand.

She wasn't a future either.

His only excuse was he . . . liked her. He could be himself with her, and he didn't know the last time that happened. She made him feel clicked on and engaged, and fuck it, he wasn't ready to give that up. Even if that meant agreeing to friends only. For real this time.

But first he had to tell her the truth.

He shoved his hands in his pockets. "Last year, I had a one-nighter with a girl I met in a bar."

Her expression clouded with confusion but she nodded. "Okay?"

"I've always been a bit wild. It's not that I didn't ever want commitment, but more that I was young and had time and didn't want to tie myself down. I guess you could say I was your typical player. I was always up front. Always told the woman she couldn't expect anything from me." He sighed and pointed to the steps. "Can we at least sit down?"

She straightened. "Okay."

They sat on the top of the steps, her on one side, him on the other. He put his elbows on his knees and continued, "So this woman, we met at a bar, and I took her home after I'd laid out my normal ground rules."

"All right." She sounded interested now, and he supposed that was something.

"She wanted to exchange numbers, and I didn't see the harm, since we'd had fun and she seemed cool with what I wanted." He gave her a chagrined smile. "Even though I didn't intend to call her again."

She rolled her eyes. "Men."

"Yeah. Typical, huh?"

She laughed a little, and he was happy to see the sadness slip from her features.

He laced his fingers between his splayed knees. "She called me a few days later wanting a hookup, and I didn't see the harm."

"Of course. 'Cause sex."

He shook his head. "Pretty much. I was going through a pretty busy time at work, and she'd call, always very cool and relaxed, and I figured why not."

"Oh no." She shifted, propping against the rounded column. "You fell for it."

"Yep." He shook his head. "She was a head case. She must have watched too many soaps when she was in her formative years because she pulled out every trick in the book, including a fake pregnancy."

Sophie grimaced. "God, how horrible. How'd you find out it was fake?"

"I took her to the doctor and sat in the room with her."

Sophie smiled. "You were still giving her attention, though."

"I was." He sighed, looking at her. "It's the kind of nightmare guys always fear, and it was a nightmare for a good three months. Once I threatened her with a restraining order she seemed to snap out of it. But you know the lesson I learned?"

"What?"

"It was my fault. It happened because I was out for consequence-free sex and was entitled enough to think I was above paying the price. It wasn't her, it was me. I wasn't some victim, my actions were to blame." He held up two fingers. "It took two weeks for her crazy to show itself. Two tiny little weeks. If I'd done things the proper way, the way my parents had taught me, asked her on a date, gotten to know her, I would have seen what I needed to. But I wanted to have my cake and eat it too."

"I'm sorry, Ryder." Her voice was soft and low. "That really sucks."

"It did." It was a harsh lesson, but one he'd never forget. Actions had consequences. End of story. He sighed. "After it was over, I decided it was time for a change. I changed jobs, towns, and told myself I'd date a woman before I took her to bed."

"A solid plan."

He met her eyes. "Then you showed up and I took one

look at you and wanted to toss you over my bike and do filthy things to you."

She sucked in a little breath. "Yeah."

"It reminded me that my actions have consequences and that I should probably stay the hell away from someone who makes me want to forget all that."

That shadow passed over her face again and she nodded. "Yes."

"There's only one problem."

"What's that?"

"I like you, Sophie. I like you a lot. You're fun to be around, you make me laugh and think. I know you're going back to Chicago, but it's been a long time since a woman has engaged me the way you do. I find myself making excuses to spend time with you."

She sighed, long and deep. "I like you too, Ryder."

"But?" Because he knew there was a "but," he could hear it in her tone.

She shrugged. "I don't see how it ends well."

A muscle jumped in his jaw. "I think you're running scared and won't tell me why."

"I don't know, maybe."

Definitely. But she wasn't ready to talk. Well, it was time to put his money where his mouth was, so he took a deep breath and dived in. "There's no way for us to avoid each other. We'll see each other at work and at home. You'll see me at Maddie's house, and at Earl's Diner, and probably a couple of places in between."

"I'm figuring that out."

He tightened his fingers. "So, I'll leave it up to you. I told you where I stand. I will respect and abide by your wishes and parameters. Whatever they may be."

Truth was, the promise was hard to make. Not because

he wouldn't always respect what she wanted but because he knew how easy it would be to push her until she caved.

Appearing deep in thought, she looked out at the street. The sun was low now, settling into that purple-pink horizon before it set.

He waited, not enjoying the brilliant sky because he thought he already knew her choice.

Finally, she looked back at him. "I don't think we should spend time together."

"Are you sure?" One last time he needed to ask.

"I'm sure. It's for the best."

The confirmation went down like glass, but he nodded. Going against all his baser instincts, he rose. "Okay then, I'll leave you alone."

He paused, waiting to see if she spoke, but when she didn't, he walked down the steps and didn't look back.

He'd tried. That was all he could do.

Chapter Fourteen

Charlie walked into Ryder's office, shut the door, and sat down in the chair opposite his desk.

Not in the mood for conversation, Ryder didn't look away from his computer screen. "Yeah?"

"Everything okay?" Charlie's accent, which only hinted at his Southern roots normally, sounded more pronounced when he was concerned.

"Yep, everything's great." The words he'd intended to be flippant came out like a snarl. He cleared his throat. "What's up?"

"You bit Harold's head off at the morning huddle," Charlie pointed out, oh so helpfully.

Well, that was because he was in a shit mood.

Ryder shrugged. "You keep saying he needs to toughen up."

"Yeah, but I'm the bad cop, you're the good one. I thought he was going to cry."

Ryder turned away from his computer screen. "I wasn't that bad."

Charlie raised a brow. "He's moping around here like a kicked puppy. You know the kid hero-worships you, and this isn't how this operation works. I break their spirit, and it's your job to build it up again, stronger and better than before."

Ryder sighed. Charlie was right. He hadn't meant it, but he was short on sleep and patience, and he'd taken it out on the poor kid. "I'll fix it."

"Good."

Ryder waited for Charlie to leave, but instead he kicked back in the chair and stretched out his long legs.

"So what's wrong?"

"What makes you think anything's wrong?" Ryder didn't want to discuss what had happened with Sophie. He'd done the right thing, laid out his cards, and she'd made her decision. There were no more moves to be made.

Charlie laced his fingers over his stomach, making it clear he wasn't leaving until Ryder talked. That he was settling in and digging in his heels. "I've worked with you for almost a year now. You've been in a bad mood exactly one other time, and that was when you found out your mom's dog died. So being a crack detective, I put two and two together and figured something was wrong."

"I don't want to talk about it."

"I'm going to assume this is about Sophie."

"Fuck you." He delivered the words like bullets.

"Jackpot." Charlie smiled and laughed. "Just get it off your chest and you'll feel better."

Ryder scowled at him. "We're guys, we don't get things off our chest. That's not how being a man works."

Charlie just stared him down with the hawkeyed expression he used to elicit confessions. Since Ryder was a fan of the move himself, they squared off for a good three minutes before he broke down. With a sigh, he ran his hand through his hair. "She thinks it's best if we don't spend time together. Oh, but we're going out on a fucking double date Maddie so helpfully cornered us into. And I'm not going to lie, I'm really not interested in watching another guy hit on her all night."

"You like her, huh?"

Fucking guy was too observant for his own good. Ryder shrugged. "She doesn't want anything to do with me, so the point is moot."

"I'm sorry."

He let out a frustrated breath. "I should be thankful, because being with her is like being repeatedly blindsided by a truck."

Charlie chuckled. "I'm not sure I understand what that means."

"I'm not sure I understand either." Ryder scrubbed a hand over his jaw. "You know how with women you have to be on your best behavior all the time?"

Charlie nodded.

"Sophie is bored by my best behavior." Not that it mattered any longer.

"That's a pretty fantastic trait in a woman," Charlie said.

"Yeah, it is." Ryder's brows knitted as he thought through the last couple of days. He'd underestimated his emotions, and he didn't like it one bit. He'd hoped she'd agree to at least something, but she hadn't, and he'd promised. "It doesn't matter. I laid it out for her, and she asked me to stay away. What can I do?"

"Well, obviously something else is going on with her, because I know it's not lack of interest or chemistry."

Ryder narrowed his gaze. "How do you know that?"

Charlie laughed. "This is Revival. You guys are the talk of City Hall."

Ryder frowned. "We've kept it very professional."

Charlie nodded. "I don't doubt you believe that, but everyone else is waiting for you to go at it during the next project meeting. Griffin said you guys have so much tension, after every meeting he goes home to take the edge off with Darcy."

Ryder rolled his eyes. "So I'm helping Griffin get laid. Awesome."

"I'm not sure Griffin needs help getting laid by his wife, but the point is you guys reek of sex and it's making everyone horny."

Ryder pinched the bridge of his nose. "How is this helpful?"

"I'm just saying the evidence suggests she's in as bad a shape as you are. So there's other factors at work here."

Ryder shrugged. "Other than her saying it's not a good idea, she won't tell me."

Charlie's expression turned speculative.

Frowning, Ryder asked, "What?"

"This isn't consistent with the Sophie I know."

"What does that mean?"

"It means everything I've ever heard about Sophie is she never plays it safe. She's impulsive and spirited and confrontational. Maddie once told us a story about getting into trouble with some guys in high school and how Sophie tried to rescue her and take them all down herself. One of them tried to punch Sophie, and Maddie said she went ballistic on the guy, kicked him in the balls, and made him cry like a baby. Sophie rushes in and thinks later. So why is she thinking ahead now?"

Ryder scrubbed a hand over his jaw. "I have no idea. I can only take her at her word. If she wants to be neighbors, I'm not sure the reasons matter. I have to respect her decision."

Charlie sighed. "Guys with blue balls are such idiots."

"If you have something to say, just say it." He delivered the words through gritted teeth.

"She's running scared." Charlie smirked, cocking a brow. "And so are you."

Defensiveness immediately reared up, raising the hair on the back of Ryder's neck. "How do you figure? I'm the one that wanted to go for it."

"But you're playing it safe, which isn't your way and sure as hell isn't hers. Stop trying to manage your attraction to her."

"I'm not." Anger was like a hot poker in his side, letting him know Charlie was on to something. All his years in law enforcement had taught him volatile emotions always hid something. As soon as a suspect got riled, they were headed down the right path.

"You said she was bored by good behavior," Charlie pointed out.

"Yeah, so?"

"So why haven't you stopped the meeting and pulled her into the storage closet yet?"

His brow furrowed. Because . . . he was playing it safe.

And Charlie was right, he was scared. He'd never met anyone like Sophie, and she was leaving. He'd done the right thing, believing it was for her, but for the wrong reasons. He'd bullshitted himself. He blinked. "You're right."

"Of course I am, now what are you going to do about it?" Charlie's voice was full of smugness.

Ryder played with the mouse on his desk, thinking. He needed to make a decision, right here. Right now. He was either in or he was out.

He thought of her, looking up at him with those big brown eyes, the kitchen at Maddie's that night, the way she took a sledgehammer to the garage door and yelled at the television.

He thought of Cheryl, the kind of woman he'd been attempting to date since he moved to Revival. He hadn't even remembered to call her. How could he with Sophie on his mind? How could any woman compare to Sophie when she was right next door?

Yeah, she'd leave. As much as he'd love to delude himself, Sophie wouldn't stay in Revival. So, yes, he'd crash and burn and go down in a blaze, but so what? Women like Sophie came around once in a lifetime. Better to have her for six months than never have her at all.

He'd made a promise, one he had to stick to, but that didn't mean he had to make it particularly easy for her.

He sat forward and put his elbows on his desk. "First, I'm going to give her a chance to miss me, and then I'm going to take her on a double date with Bill and Cheryl."

A slow smile spread across Charlie's face. He nodded. "Interesting strategy."

He shrugged. "With Sophie, it's got to be."

After a miserable day, she drove up the driveway to find Ryder, shirtless, cutting his hedges. As he clipped away with big garden shears, she gritted her teeth. His muscles flexed and bunched in the late afternoon sun, making her mouth water and her heart ache. She'd done the right thing, she could tell because the words had been so hard to say. She lay against the steering wheel and watched him.

Skin golden, he gleamed with sweat.

Her mouth watered.

He swung to look at her.

Across the yard, their eyes met.

She held her breath.

They said nothing.

He nodded.

She nodded.

Finally, she got out of the car. She didn't have the energy

to fight with the garage door, so she grabbed her bag from the passenger's seat and started the trek to the house when he called, "Sophie."

Her heart leapt into her throat as her body surged in response to her name. She looked over her shoulder at him. "Yes?"

With the shears he pointed at her car. "It's supposed to rain tonight." Then he turned back toward his task without a backward glance.

Her shoulders sagged. She watched the way his shoulder blades moved under his skin, fighting the urge to drop her stuff and touch him. She dragged her attention away and trudged inside, sagging against the now-closed door. She'd deal with the car later, after he'd gone and no longer presented such a temptation.

Throat tight, she closed her eyes. All she wanted was to cross the yard and tackle him to the ground. Snarl and bait him until he consumed her.

She wanted something else too. Only, she had no name for what it was she craved. All she knew was he was the man to give it to her.

It was in the way he looked at her. Like he had plans. Understood things. Like he wasn't afraid to satisfy her.

She banged her head softly against the door. She was doing the right thing. If it hurt like this now, what would it feel like after months?

She took a couple of deep breaths and dropped her work bag on the kitchen table before digging her cell phone out of her purse. She needed to call Penelope. Her logical, practical friend who'd agree with all of Sophie's sound, adult reasoning.

She pressed her name and kicked off her shoes before padding into the bedroom. The phone rang and she unzipped her dress, shrugging out of it and lying down on the bed when Penelope answered.

The second she heard her friend's voice, tears slipped from the corners of her eyes. "Pen?"

"What's wrong?" Penelope sounded instantly alert.

Sophie swallowed, trying to contain her emotions. Trying to get them under control. This just confirmed she was right to back away. To disengage from him.

"Sophie, what happened?" Penelope's tone turned demanding.

She pressed her fingers into her eye sockets to quell the urge to sob and managed to spit out a shaky, "I'm okay."

"You're not okay. Talk to me so I can help you."

She bit down hard on her lower lip, enough to cause the sting of pain. It reminded her of when Ryder bit her. It had been aggressive, territorial, and arrogant as hell, but God, had she liked it. So much. She'd never felt claimed before. Not by anyone. Nobody had ever really seemed to want to, and she'd been on her own so long, she had no idea that was something she wanted.

"Soph." Penelope's soft voice brought her out of her haze. "Talk to me."

She sucked in a shuddered breath. "It's Ryder."

"Okay."

"I like him, Pen."

"From what I saw he likes you too."

"I know."

"That's bad?"

"I like him too much." She clenched her jaw. "So I pushed him away and told him to leave me alone."

Penelope clucked. "Oh, Sophie."

She shook her head. "I'm doing the right thing. I know I am. He's too . . . much."

There was a moment of silence before Penelope said,

"Once you told me Evan looked at me like I was a steak dinner and he was starving."

"I remember." It was the night Penelope had finally broken down, let out all her pent-up emotions and had a good long cry.

"You said you'd kill to have a guy look at you like that."

"I did." She didn't really mean it, though, because that wasn't something she anticipated happening.

"Ryder looks at you like that."

Sophie stared up at the ceiling. "But he's the wrong guy."

"Why's that?"

She couldn't stomach talking about her past mistakes, so she gave the easy answer. "Because he lives in Revival and I live in Chicago."

"Isn't it premature to be worried about that?"

"No." She swallowed hard and admitted the truth. "He's going to hurt me, Pen."

There was more silence before Penelope said, "All right."

"I can't set myself up for heartbreak. I just can't."

"I understand." Penelope sighed. "But just so you know, you can survive heartache. People do it every day."

Not her. She'd closed her heart off a long time ago. Or maybe, with the way she'd grown up with parents that loved each other more than they'd loved her, she'd never really opened it. Her whole life it had always been that way. She was used to living on the outskirts. That was her place. Where she belonged.

Ryder threatened that, but to what end? It wasn't like when she went back he'd choose her. His life was here, his family, friends, and job. He had roots. She was doing the right thing, for both their sakes.

She cleared her throat and said in a firm tone, "It doesn't

matter. It's done. I told him to leave and he left. I took care of it."

"So you're safe?" Penelope asked in a soft voice.

"Yeah, I'm safe." She'd made sure to ruin it.

"Now what?"

"I do the job I came here to do, have fun with Maddie, do my time, and come home."

"You have a plan."

"I do." She licked her lips. "I'm doing the right thing, right?"

Three beats passed before Penelope answered. "If you don't want to get hurt, you're doing the right thing."

"Exactly." She wiped her face. "I'm going to go watch Netflix." Not *Making a Murderer* because that would remind her of Ryder, but something else. Maybe *Penny Dreadful*. A dark, macabre story to fit her mood.

"Okay. If you need me, call."

"I will. Thanks."

She hung up but didn't feel any better. In fact, she felt worse.

She lay on her bed and stared unblinking at the ceiling. She wasn't sure how long she stayed like that, silent and pondering, but a knock at her back door startled her out of her trance. Her heart leapt and immediately started pounding a too-fast beat.

She looked down and remembered she was almost naked. With a sigh she got up, pulled on shorts and a T-shirt, and padded out of her bedroom and into the kitchen. Her throat went dry at the sight of him at the door through the glass.

He was still shirtless. Why was he doing this? She thought they'd agreed.

She opened the door but didn't speak.

Gaze narrowed, he swept down her body. A muscle in

his jaw clenched. He held out his hand. "Give me your keys and I'll put your car away."

Oh. The car. She'd already forgotten. She glanced over his shoulder. The sky had darkened, threatening rain at any minute. "I can do it."

"It will only take me a second. I already opened the door."

The tension between them was electric, making her nipples harden and her whole body tingle. She shrugged. "One second."

She walked over to the counter and retrieved her keys before walking back to hand them over. "Thanks."

He gripped them tight. "I'll be right back."

She leaned against the doorway, watching as he jogged over to her car. He got in and pulled it into the garage. A minute later the door shut and he was back in front of her. He handed her the keys.

Why did he have to be gorgeous and considerate?

She licked her lips. "Thank you."

He met her eyes. "I talked to Bill today."

A date was the last thing she wanted. She'd canceled coffee but was determined to go through with Friday. "All right."

"There's a slight problem. He suggested that since we live right next door, and he and Cheryl live on the opposite end of town, it made sense to meet them at the restaurant in the middle. Considering your desire to stay away from me, I wanted to run it by you."

Bill was the last thing on her mind. All her reasons were good, only when Ryder got in front of her, he made it hard to think. It was why she didn't want to be alone with him. She didn't trust herself. And she knew what happened when she didn't trust herself.

But he was here now. Standing in front of her. Real.

Unable to help it, she let her gaze roam over Ryder's chest, down his stomach to his lean hips. When she spoke, her voice came out husky. "I guess that makes sense."

"It's practical." Ryder's own gaze wandered, hooding when he reached her breasts.

He put his hand on the door frame, right above her head, and it brought him way too close. "So should we meet outside at seven?"

She sucked in a breath, inhaling the masculine, spicy scent of him. She had no idea what he was talking about. "What?"

When he spoke, his words came out low and intimate. "Our date, Sophie. On Friday."

"Oh." All she wanted was to step aside and let him in, but she stayed frozen in her spot. "Yes, that works."

He nodded. "I'll pick you up at seven."

Disappointment raged inside her, and she held her breath, waiting for him to slip, to say something very Ryder-like and suggestive.

But he didn't. He just turned on his heel and walked away.

With shaking hands she closed the door.

He'd taken her at her word. All right then, good.

Things would only get easier from here.

Chapter Fifteen

True to his promise, Ryder had stayed away. At home he only spoke to her when absolutely necessary. There'd been no more drop-bys, no more dinners, no nothing. At work he'd been polite and cordial. Not cool, exactly, but professional. He'd been receptive to all her ideas, praising her when he liked something, arguing with her when he didn't. But there was no sparking with her. No evil gleam in his eyes like when he sparred with her.

Sophie couldn't pretend. She missed him. Too much for comfort.

By Friday evening, Sophie had prepared herself for the night to come. Or as much as she could. She wore a flirty little sleeveless black cocktail dress with matching four-inch sandals that made her legs actually look long.

To her dismay, all day she'd been excited for all the wrong reasons. She wanted to see him, be forced to spend time with him. She ached for that hot, electric jolt he evoked in her. No matter how hard she'd tried, she'd been unable to talk herself out of it. With no idea what to expect, her instincts were on high alert, inappropriately thrilling her.

The doorbell rang and her heart leapt into her throat,

pounding in a rapid beat. As slowly as she could, she walked to the door and opened it.

Oh dear God.

Ryder stood in front of her wearing all black, his silvery eyes practically glowing in the porch light. She swallowed her lust, put on a bright smile, and said, "Hey, ready to go?"

He raked his gaze down her body, bold and aggressive, giving the first sign in forever that he still wanted her. "Ready."

The Mustang was in the driveway, looking as badass as its owner. She turned and grabbed her purse. "Great. Bill said we were going to Rock's Steakhouse?"

"That's the plan." He stepped aside.

Some of her tension eased as she slid past him. So far so good.

Behind her keys jingled. "You look nice."

Wasn't this all . . . civil. Good. Maybe this would be easier than she thought.

She climbed into the car, and as the doors shut she said, "So do you."

He smirked. "I'm sure Bill will be happy."

"Cheryl too."

Was this a game? It had to be a trick?

He turned over the engine, and it roared to life. "Did you have a good day?"

"Busy but good. Small-town government isn't as easy as I thought."

"There's a lot going on right now." He pulled out of the driveway. "The town square is important to people, and everyone I've talked to is happy with your contribution."

The niggling of disappointment poked in her sternum, frustrating her. It forced her to confront the truth: She'd been prepared for sabotage, and it had excited her.

Well, good. This was the best-case scenario.

She cleared her throat. "I'm glad. The Fourth of July Festival is in good shape and I've met with a lot of business owners in town, and I think given a little time I can increase sponsorships by thirty percent. The advance pre-order ticket sale promotion I came up with has been really well received, and with the strong sales, it can only help businesses see the benefits."

"I know." He shifted into third gear, and she tried not to get distracted by the muscles moving under his powerful thighs. "I get your daily reports."

"I wasn't sure if you read them."

"Every word."

The car fell silent.

She looked out the window. She could get through this night with him being nice and polite.

She thought of him, the way he kissed her and made her ache. She pressed her thighs together.

If he could be cool, so could she.

Ryder clenched the steering wheel and tried to think about baseball, puppies, and grandmothers. He had his plan and he needed to stick to it.

All week had been hell. Hell every time he treated her like a business associate. Hell every time he saw her in the backyard. All he wanted was to follow her inside and throw her across the kitchen table.

But he hadn't done that—because he wanted her to ache for him. He wanted her lying in bed, the covers twisted around her legs, restless.

Tonight he needed to show her she didn't want to be friends, didn't want to be just neighbors. And the only way he could think to do that was to show her exactly what being just neighbors looked like. To drive her right out of her mind with friendliness.

So it didn't matter if she looked spectacular.

It didn't matter how her legs looked in her dress.

Or how he wanted to wrap her thighs around his hips.

He gripped the gearshift tighter.

He would not slip his hands up her skirt and into her panties.

At least, not yet.

She moved restlessly in the seat.

"Is everything okay?" He kept his voice innocent.

"Everything is great." She shot him a scowl before her expression cleared. "I'm looking forward to my first night out in Revival."

"Rock's is an institution."

She laughed, a little too high pitched. "You're forgetting I live in Chicago, I have Gibsons and the Chop House."

But Chicago didn't have him. "You'll have to judge for yourself if it meets your standards."

She frowned. "Aren't you going to try and convince me it's better?"

"Nope." He wasn't going to engage her in any arguments at all.

Her brows furrowed deeper. "All right."

He pulled into the parking lot and found a spot before turning off the car. He took the keys from the ignition. "Ready for your big date?"

"Yep." Her chin tilted in defiance. "You?"

"Yep." Just as she was about to get out of the car, he grabbed her wrist.

She sucked in a breath. "What?"

He gave her his most winning smirk. "Try not to break Bill's heart."

He let her go and she jerked her arm away, huffing as she got out of the car and slammed the door.

Oh, this plan was working.

He smiled at her retreating form, shoulders all straight and thrown back in defiance.

Excellent.

God, he was the most frustrating man on the planet. Two could play this game.

Sophie plastered a pleasant expression on her face and walked through the restaurant, following as the hostess led them through tables to a corner booth where Bill and Cheryl were already seated.

Bill sat on one side of the booth, Cheryl on the other. They'd appeared deep in conversation, only stopping when Ryder and Sophie stood in front of them. The hostess put the menus on the table and stepped away.

Sophie waggled her fingers. "Hi."

Bill smiled at her. "Hey, you guys made it."

"We did," she said, nodding. She turned her attention to Cheryl, dressed in a cute floral sundress in pastels. A look Sophie could never pull off in a million years, but the other woman made it work. She was very pretty—sweet and innocent, but pretty. The right man would want to mess her up and defile her. Sophie smiled. "You look pretty." She craned over her shoulder to smirk at Ryder. "Doesn't she?"

His gaze flickered before he shifted to Cheryl. "Very much so. Like a breath of fresh air."

Cheryl appeared as though she might faint on the spot. Her lashes fluttered. "Thank you."

All wrong for Ryder, who needed someone who could go toe-to-toe with him.

Cheryl glanced at Sophie. "You look great too."

She hoped so, she'd worked damn hard at it. "Thanks."

"Have you been waiting long?" Ryder asked from behind her.

Cheryl cast a furtive glance at him, and a pretty flush broke out over her cheeks.

Sophie resisted an eye roll. God, could the woman stroke his ego a little harder? It was clear by the way she bit her lip and tried not to look at Ryder she had a crush on him. And why wouldn't she? The man was so seriously hot it was ridiculous. But she didn't have to be all blushy about it.

"Not at all," Bill said, his voice light and pleasant. Bill was no slouch in the looks department. He was built like a football player, tall and broad. He'd do quite well. She just had to shift her focus off Ryder.

Since Bill was her date, she slid into the booth next to him, and Ryder did the same next to Cheryl.

Their eyes caught and held.

Well, now, wasn't this cozy.

Sophie jerked her attention to the table. "This is fun. After trying to get acclimated, it's great to get out and let off some steam."

Bill shifted to the corner, sliding his arm along the back of the booth and behind Sophie's head. "I heard you've been getting rave reviews."

"She has," Ryder said, his gaze skimming over her. "Sophie's not only organized but she's charismatic. She's already met with half the town, it seems."

She held out her hands. "I'm just doing my job."

"It's great," Cheryl said, shifting toward Ryder and flashing him an angelic smile. "The whole town is excited about the Fourth of July Festival."

Sophie's belly tightened with what she refused to name as jealousy.

"It's fun to be involved, but it's not nearly as important as the work you do at the clinic," Sophie said, politely.

"Sophie's right." Ryder slanted a glance at Cheryl, whose cheeks pinkened with his gaze on her.

Poor girl, she might be crushing on Ryder hard, but she'd never be able to handle him. She'd die of shyness. Sophie's brows furrowed. What did they say about the quiet ones? That they were the most wild.

Sophie studied Cheryl with her demure sundress, neat hair, and restrained makeup. She couldn't imagine her wild. Couldn't imagine Ryder sliding between her legs and whispering dirty things in her ear. Couldn't imagine him kissing Cheryl the way he kissed her, like he'd eat her alive. Like he was trying to communicate how he planned to fuck her by his mouth alone.

Her core heated at the mere thought of it. *Stop*.

She needed to stop.

"Is it warm in here?" Bill asked, shaking Sophie from her haze. "I can see if they can jack up the air."

Sophie shifted in her seat, dismayed she appeared . . . heated. "Nope, I'm good. It's the perfect temperature."

Her gaze slid to Ryder, who smirked. As though he knew what she was thinking about.

Bill nodded. "So Ryder, how are you enjoying your new neighbor?"

Sophie tensed.

Ryder picked up his glass of water and took a sip. "She keeps things interesting."

The waiter showed up, saving Sophie from having to kick him under the table.

She beamed at him. "I'll have a double martini, straight up with olives."

Ryder cocked a brow.

"I'll have a white wine spritzer," Cheryl said, making Sophie look like a raving alcoholic.

But she didn't care. Girly wine spritzers wouldn't cut it. She needed alcohol. Lots and lots of alcohol.

This dinner . . . wasn't working out as Ryder had planned.

Sophie had quite the buzz going, and he wasn't exactly the most sober he'd ever been. Bill and Cheryl, on the other hand, kept it perfectly together. The sane ones in their little party of four.

The night was a recipe for disaster but had taught him one thing. Seeing Sophie and Cheryl side by side, he understood why he'd kept forgetting to ask Cheryl out. She was nice enough, and she was certainly pretty enough. And sweet. Very sweet.

But watching Sophie in her little black dress with her flashing eyes and death glares only brought home the fact that nice and sweet wasn't his kind of girl. When he'd decided to move to Revival and started to think about settling down, he'd thought he'd needed to change the kind of girl he dated, but now he understood the truth.

He needed someone like Sophie.

Someone who'd kick ass and take names. Someone who was as bored by convention as he was. Someone who'd make damn sure he didn't get away with anything. Before Sophie, he'd been limiting himself both ways.

Sophie had shown him. She was like him that way. A little too wild, too edgy to really quite fit into convention.

He'd feel bad about Cheryl, really he would, only he was doing her a favor. He wasn't any more suited for her than she was for him. He kept hoping she'd figure out she liked talking to Bill a hell of a lot more than she liked talking to him.

Cheryl laughed at something Bill said, but Ryder had no clue what they were talking about.

Bill grinned at Cheryl. "He told me he couldn't do burpees because it was against his religious freedom."

This made Bill and Cheryl roar with laughter.

Across the table Sophie looked at him, brow raised. He shrugged. She shifted in her seat, taking another sip of her drink and meeting his gaze over the rim. He knew that look. She wanted him as much as he wanted her. Under the table, he moved his foot, stretching out his leg so it slid next to her heel. She licked her lips and stayed.

In that moment, he confronted the truth. He would get emotionally attached to her—hell, he *was* emotionally attached to her. The smart thing to do was to save both of them from heartbreak. But he couldn't.

If he didn't just fucking take her and make her belong to him for as long as he had her, she'd be a regret.

And he didn't do regrets. He'd never played it safe in his entire life, and he wasn't about to start with Sophie. He'd never met another woman like her, and he didn't intend to let her go until he had to.

So he was going for it. Consequences be damned.

His eyes met hers. He moved his leg so his calf brushed against hers.

She sucked in a breath. Pressed against him.

She'd been drinking and her defenses were weak, he understood that. But he also understood all it meant was she allowed herself what she wanted.

Him.

"Everything okay?" Bill asked, seemingly oblivious to the tension between Sophie and him.

"Everything's great." Sophie's voice was a touch too breathless. Eyes on Ryder she asked, "Do you want to go dancing?"

"Yes," he said, because there was only one thing he wanted to do more, and he'd get that soon enough.

For now, he'd drive her wild.

Cheryl laughed, nervous and high, ripping Ryder's attention away from Sophie. She touched the hem of her dress. "I don't really know how to dance that well."

Oh no. Ryder started to frantically spin through the reasons he had to go dancing, but Sophie saved him.

She waved a hand. "It's all good. We'll show you. It will be fun."

Bill cleared his throat. "Well . . . I'm not much of a dancer either."

Figured.

Sophie clasped her hands in prayer. "Please? It will be fun, I promise."

Bill glanced down at her, a slight frown on his lips before he turned to Cheryl. "What do you say?"

Maybe the guy wasn't an idiot. There was no love match with Sophie, and his eyes seemed intent on Cheryl. She glanced at Ryder before her eyes flirted back to Bill. "If you're game."

Ryder looked at Sophie and without another thought to sanity slipped his hand under the table, leaning forward and touching her bare knee.

With a little jump, she shot him a furtive glance before parting her legs. His fingers played over the bare skin on the inside of her thigh. Her brown eyes darkened as he traced a finger over her skin.

She gave a radiant smile to Bill and Cheryl. "Are you guys in?"

Cheryl and Bill glanced at each other and then shrugged. Cheryl nodded. "Sure."

Sophie slid down a little in her seat and he gripped her leg. "Check?"

She picked up her drink, downed the last bit, and put it back on the table. "Check."

Chapter Sixteen

They walked across the street to the infamous Big Reds, and it being a Friday night, the place was packed. Throughout dinner, as the drinks had been consumed, as Ryder had treated Sophie with cordial respect befitting his neighbor, she'd come to a life-altering conclusion.

Fuck it.

She'd studied Ryder sitting next to Cheryl, looking all kinds of wrong sitting next to her, and decided she needed him. All the martinis she'd drunk had clarified everything in her mind.

The simple truth was, she needed the way he touched her. The way he looked at her. The way he baited her. The way he made her laugh. The way his tongue felt in her mouth, and a thousand other things.

So when his foot had rested against hers, she hadn't moved. And when his hand slid over her skin, she'd opened.

On a date with two other people was not the time or place to have this realization, but life wasn't interested in timing.

Besides, she had an idea of how to make amends.

She'd been watching Cheryl and Bill all night, and they belonged together. Their conversation with Ryder and

Sophie was awkward and tense, but they were easy and engaged with each other. All through dinner they'd paired off, only not with the person they were supposed to be on a date with. They thought they wanted people like Sophie and Ryder, but they didn't understand it would never work. They needed calm.

And Sophie and Ryder needed wild and chaos.

Sophie was going to get them together.

Ryder pushed them up to the bar and turned to her, his gaze flicking over her mouth before dipping his head and yelling in her ear, "What do you want, darlin'?"

She tilted her head back to say into his ear, "Let's do shots."

"Tequila?" The hand farther away from Bill and Cheryl strayed to her hip.

"Tequila."

They looked at Bill and Cheryl, who were shaking their heads.

Cheryl held up her hands. "I can't do shots. I'll take a white wine."

Bill waved them off. "Beer for me. I've got practice in the morning."

See? Utterly perfect for each other.

Ryder signaled the bartender and gave their order. A few minutes later, he'd handed Bill and Cheryl their drinks and turned back to Sophie.

He picked up the shot and handed it to her before taking one of his own. "Salt?"

His gray eyes heated. She shivered as she remembered the press of his tongue against her skin. She shook her head. "I'm good."

They clinked the tiny glasses together. "Bottoms up."

They downed the shots and put them back on the bar.

All Sophie wanted to do was jump him, but instead she said, "Let's dance."

He squeezed her hip. "Let's."

Cheryl smiled. "Do you mind if we sit this one out?"

Ryder tensed but then Bill said, "I'll sit with her, you guys go ahead."

Ryder didn't hesitate. He grabbed Sophie's hand and led her onto the dance floor, where a country song played. A second later he spun her into his arms and she was pressed flush against him.

It was a medium tempo, and he started gliding her through a two-step. She melded into him, not understanding how someone so much bigger than her could fit her so right.

He gripped her around the waist and looked down at her. "Have you learned your lesson, Sophie?"

She leaned back and raised her brows. "What lesson would that be, Ryder?"

He dipped his head a little lower. "That you don't want me as your friend."

"Is that what this is? Teaching me a lesson?"

"I was giving you what you claimed to want, and you don't like it one bit."

Her mouth dropped open and she could only gape at him. "You are so arrogant. And cocky. I can barely stand you."

The song shifted, slowed down, and he pulled her closer into his arms. She leaned in despite herself.

His erection brushed her belly and he whispered into her ear, "Admit it and I'll give you what you really want."

She bit her lip, her nipples puckering tight. "And what do you think I really want?"

"You want me to take away your options." He bent lower, nipped at her earlobe. "You want me to slam you up against the wall and take you. You don't care where we are.

How we won't even make it to bed. How we might not even make it out of this bar."

She sucked in a breath and clutched his shoulder.

He licked a spot on her neck before scraping his teeth over her skin. "I'll make it real dirty, darlin'. I'm going to do what you've been dying for since the day we met."

"What's that?" Her voice was all breathless and panting.

"I'm going to take you in hand, and I'm not going to fucking let go." His arm tightened around her waist. "Because that's what you want, Sophie. What nobody else has ever been able to give you. It's why you can't stay away from me no matter how much you try and talk yourself out of it."

Throat dry, she swallowed hard. "And why can't you stay away from me, Ryder?"

"That's easy." He lifted his head and looked into her eyes. "I know you can take it. I know you want it. But more, I know you won't settle for less. You're greedy and you're going to demand everything from me."

Just like that, it all made sense. How and why they fit. Because they needed the same thing.

He curled his hand around her neck. "Admit it."

She licked her lips. "I admit it."

He fisted her hair in his hand. "Here's how it's going to be. There will be no more dates with anyone else. No more backing away. No more trying to distance yourself. Because it's not going to work, Sophie. You and I are happening. You might leave, but you're sure as hell not going to forget me when you do, and we both just have to accept that."

Her heart slammed into her chest. "Aren't you high-handed?"

"Like I said, I'm giving you what you want. And don't even try and pretend it doesn't make you wet." His hold tightened, pricking pain along the back of her neck. "It makes you wet, doesn't it, Sophie?"

"Yes."

"Are your panties damp for me?"

"Yes."

"Should I take you to the bathroom and fuck you?"

"Yes." She didn't care what that made her.

"You don't care that the first time won't be in a bed?"

She rose to her tiptoes and whispered, "Ryder, anyone can fuck in a bed."

"Let's go." He released her, grabbed her hand, and started dragging her toward the back.

"Ryder."

"Yeah?"

"What about our dates?"

"Oh." His brow furrowed. "Them. We can deal with them after."

"But—"

"Sophie, they have to be blind, deaf, and dumb not to see there's something going on between us." He dragged his hand through his hair. "The whole town knows there's something going on between us."

"They do?"

"Yes."

"How?"

"I don't know, they just do." He started to tug her back, and as much as she wanted him, she held firm.

"Ryder, it's not right. We've already been total assholes, we can't make it worse."

He appeared ready to argue, but then he sighed. "What do you suggest?"

She was so on edge for him, she didn't want to say it, but she still wanted to do something right tonight. "Let's go back to the table, be nice for a few more minutes, and then take them aside separately and let them down easy."

"Are you fucking serious?"

It pained her, but she needed to do this as penance. "Let's do this one thing right. Then everything after can be wrong."

"Christ." He shook his head. "Fine."

When they returned to the table Sophie said, "Another round?"

Ryder had had more than enough. His main priority at this point was getting rid of their dates because he really didn't think he could take one more second of not touching her. Of pretending he had any interest in anyone but her.

Bill stood from his chair. "I'll go with you to the bar."

Ryder wanted to refuse him but thought better of it, as this gave him a chance to apologize to Cheryl and be done with this date from hell.

Sophie beamed at Bill and said, "Great."

Ryder experienced a possessive urge to kiss her before she went but resisted. The sooner they got this over with, the better. He nodded and sat down, turning to Cheryl as they walked off.

He opened his mouth to speak, but she surprised him by holding up her hands and smiling. "It's okay."

"Okay?" Ryder couldn't help glancing over her shoulder to where Sophie and Bill were swallowed up by the crowd.

She laughed and shrugged a shoulder. "You like Sophie."

"Like" was a mild word for what he felt, but he returned

his gaze to the pretty nurse and gave her the attention she deserved. He sighed. "I'm sorry."

"Hey, it's okay." She tucked a lock of hair behind her ear. "I had a feeling the night of the Rileys' party. But when you didn't cancel, I thought maybe I was wrong." She offered him another shy smile. "Tonight confirmed my initial impression."

Ryder ran his hand through his hair. "Again, I'm really sorry. I should have canceled."

She waved a hand. "No worries. You didn't ask me out, Maddie did. And you haven't led me on. You haven't taken your eyes off her all night."

"You're being far too nice about this." Because she was.

"Nice is underrated."

That was a matter of debate, but he agreed anyway. "True."

She smiled. "You belong with a woman like Sophie."

"I belong with Sophie." He didn't want to think about the day she'd leave. All he wanted to do was think about having her right now. Tonight.

Sophie and Bill returned to the table, and the four of them stared at each other awkwardly.

Bill cleared his throat then looked at Cheryl. "You ready to go?"

She shot up like she'd been catapulted from her seat. "Yes, I hate bars."

"God, me too," Bill said, before holding out a hand to Ryder. "It's been fun, despite the weirdness."

Ryder stood up and shook the guy's hand. "Yeah, sorry about that. I hope we can still be friends."

Bill shrugged one big shoulder. "It happens."

Ryder slid his hand over Sophie's hip. "If it makes any difference, she's a real pain in the ass."

Sophie turned on a dime and knocked his hand away. "You jerk. I'm a delight."

He grinned down at her. "You're a menace."

"I am not." She turned to Cheryl. "It's me who's saving you. He's pure evil."

Cheryl smiled. "He's always been a complete gentleman to me."

Sophie huffed. "Haven't you heard? The devil is always a gentleman."

Cheryl laughed. "Then I'll consider myself saved."

Sophie smirked up at Ryder. "And I'll consider myself damned."

His gaze flicked over her mouth. Oh, she was damned all right. He planned on multiple lines of torture. Just as soon as he had her first. Preferably within the next five minutes.

"Well, you two have fun, and good luck." Bill shook his head before saying to Cheryl. "You want to go for ice cream?"

"Sure, I'd like that," Cheryl said.

They waved and said good-bye.

Sophie turned to Ryder, and he raised a brow. "How'd he take it?"

"He already knew. He said it was obvious."

"Cheryl too."

She grinned. "I told him when he took Cheryl home he needed to make out with her in the car."

Ryder reached for her, sliding his hand around the nape of her neck, and she shivered. "What did he say to that?"

"That he'd already been planning to do just that."

He leaned down and nipped her bottom lip. He gripped her around the waist. "I hope those two find a way to have really fantastic vanilla sex."

She shuddered, her eyes going dark. "We're not going to have vanilla sex, are we?"

"Not in this lifetime, darlin'."

"Good, because I have a really short attention span."

He grabbed her wrist. "Time to go."

Chapter Seventeen

In silence, they walked through the parking lot, hands clasped, tension radiating in the space around them. Sophie had never been filled with such anticipation. Such mad excitement.

They reached his car and he walked around to the passenger's side. She reached for the door but he grabbed her wrist, spun her around, and pushed her against the car.

His mouth was on her in an instant, hard and demanding and furious.

She went to wrap her hands around his neck, but he gripped her wrists and held them both against the car.

Their tongues clashed.

His head slanted, deepening the contact.

She moaned against his lips.

Straining to get closer.

Arching.

Moving.

Squirming.

Desperate for him.

He tore his mouth away and traveled down her neck. "Sophie. Fuck. Sophie."

"Let me go."

He released her wrists, and her hands were on him. Touching him everywhere. Pulling him closer. His fingers snaked up under her dress, gripping her leg and lifting her up. He bent at the knees, and finally he was exactly where she wanted him to be.

He bit her neck, swearing viciously before yanking her hair back and whispering in her ear, "We have to get in the car."

She scraped her teeth along his jaw. "Okay, but only because we're civil servants."

He groaned, licked at the spot behind her ear. "Do you like the sound of that, my cock sliding into you in public?"

She jerked at the thought, pressing into his erection. "Yes. Maybe not the first time, but yes."

"I'm going to give you everything you could ever want." His breath was hot on her throat. "Get in the car before I lose what's left of my willpower."

She took a deep, steady breath and got in.

He jogged around the car, slid into the driver's seat, and turned the engine on. He looked at her, shook his head a little, and then his jaw flexed. "Take your panties off."

She didn't even hesitate. She was too hot to protest. Keeping her eyes on him, she slowly, seductively, dragged her dress up her thighs, stopping just before he saw anything. She parted her legs. The fabric rode high and she tilted her hips.

He growled.

She smirked.

She shimmied until the scrap of lace she wore dangled off one high-heeled foot, which she raised to the dashboard to slip the panties off before dropping them onto his lap.

He looked at the underwear and said in a harsh voice, "That's what you've been wearing all night?"

"Uh-huh."

He looked ready to attack, and it thrilled her. Made her feel alive with power.

"For Bill?"

She shook her head. Even in her denial she knew. "For you."

He reached over, dragged his fingers over her neckline, then tugged until her breasts spilled over the top. He ran his thumb over the front clasp of her bra before flicking it open and pulling her breasts free. She spilled over the top of her dress, and she looked hedonistic and wanton. Exactly how he made her feel.

He tugged at her nipple before rolling it.

As the sensation shot through her, she arched. She moved to drop her leg and he shook his head. "No. Stay like that."

She relaxed back into position, her breath coming fast.

He played with her nipples until the skin puckered and she moaned, rocking her hips. "Lift your skirt and show me."

She pulled the hem, exposing herself.

He leaned over and took one hard peak in his mouth, sucking it between his lips before laving it with his tongue.

She hissed, pressing her head back against the seat.

He released her and sat back. "Open your legs wider."

She did, so she was spread obscenely.

He leaned against the driver's seat door. "Touch yourself so I can see how wet you are."

She licked her lips. "I'd rather you touch me. I've been touching myself since I met you."

He emitted a feral noise. "If I touch you, I won't be able to stop until you come, and you're not coming until my cock's inside you."

"Ryder." His name was urgent on her lips. She dipped

her fingers between her legs, and she was so slippery she glided along swollen flesh. "I want you so bad."

"Show me."

She slid her fingers inside, rising to meet her hand before she pulled away. In the moonlight the evidence of her arousal shimmered.

He took her hand and brought it to his lips, sucking her fingers into his mouth with a tight suction before he released her. He reached over and rolled her nipple, pinching and pulling until she moaned and squirmed in her seat.

Never in her life had she been this crazy with lust. She burned for him.

While he played he said, "Later, after I've fucked you enough times to see straight, I'm going to tie you to the bed and see if I can make you come from playing with your nipples. I'll make sure you're spread-eagled because I don't want any friction to help you get off. How does that sound?"

Liked she'd died and gone to heaven. Or hell. She wasn't sure which, she just knew she was in ecstasy. She managed to pant out, "Ryder."

"What, darlin'?"

"Take me home."

His gaze flashed. "You stay sitting like that the whole way."

Oh God, she was ready. Ready to fall. Ready to surrender. This was going to be the best night ever.

Ryder had no idea how he managed to stay on the road with Sophie sitting like that. Wanton and on display. Wet and aching for him. He drove down the highway and glanced over at her. "Play with your pussy."

She groaned and slipped her fingers between her legs, lightly stroking the flesh.

He gritted his teeth. "That's right, keep it nice and light, baby."

She circled over her clit, her breasts rising and falling with her heavy breaths. She had the prettiest nipples, stained pink, and he couldn't resist reaching for her and rubbing the hard buds, matching her rhythm.

Eyes closed, her head lolled back as she moaned.

"Don't come, Soph. Whatever you do, don't come."

She cried out. "You have to stop that."

"No." He plucked at her, his cock pulsing as he kept one eye on the road and the other on her. "When you get too close, stop until you're calm enough to start back up."

He'd always liked control in the bedroom, a trait he'd held back and kept in check, but Sophie made him want to push it, push her.

She jerked back her fingers and, like lightning, she gripped his wrist as he still toyed with her. "You're going to push me over the edge."

He dropped his hand, once again taking her fingers in his mouth and licking her clean. She tasted like he'd imagined, sweet, wild, and addictive.

He released her and said, "Again."

She started to stroke again. "Ryder, you're killing me."

"Good. Because when we get home, there's going to be no preamble. I'm just going to fuck you on the first available surface."

She jerked her hand away.

He gave her thirty seconds to calm down, then ordered, "Again."

She made a whimpering noise that made his cock impossibly harder and did as she was told.

And he made her repeat it over and over again the entire

ride home, until she was panting and squirming in her seat, unable to touch for more than a few seconds without going over.

He roared into the driveway, turned off the motor, and was out of the car like an Olympic sprinter. He jogged around, and by the time he reached her, she was out of the door. He slammed her against the car, his mouth on hers before she could even shut it.

She was crazed, and he was right there with her. He fisted her hair and kissed her like he was dying for her, which wasn't far from the truth.

She made small, needy noises, tearing at his belt, and unfastened it with hurried fingers, pulling her mouth away long enough to say, "I want your cock."

Frantic fingers fought with his zipper, and when he sprang free, his erection slid against her wetness. He cursed out the filthiest, most wicked things.

She gripped his cock, positioned it at her entrance, and said, "Please. Fuck me."

He growled.

She was so perfect.

He gripped her hip, raised her leg, and thrust along her slick opening.

She cried out and he clenched his jaw, fumbling in his pocket to pull out a condom while still kissing her. Somehow, by the grace of God, he managed to sheath himself.

He bent. Lifting her up and holding her steady against the car, he impaled her wet, tight heat.

With no finesse, he pounded into her.

But it wasn't enough.

He needed deeper. With a feral sound, he pulled out and whipped her around, tumbling them to the grass in one jerky movement, before slamming back into her.

Her neck arched. "Ryder."

"Christ I've never felt anything as good as you." His words were a snarl.

Her nails raked down his back, digging into his skin.

He pounded into her. Harder and faster, with a determination that made his vision blur. His whole world narrowed down to how she felt clasped around him.

Her body quickened. Her legs clenched around his hips.

He took her harder, leaning down and saying in her ear, "I want to feel you come on my cock. I've been waiting for it since the second I saw you."

Her hips moved wildly. There was no choreographing here, no skill; no, this was just primal, animalistic sex. A claiming, so he called it what it was.

"Your pussy is mine." He bit her neck. "You're mine."

She jerked and seized and convulsed around him. He growled, losing himself in her body, in her taste, in the grip of her legs and pierce of her nails on his skin. He came in a blinding, heart-stopping rush that consumed his entire body, shuddering through him as he emptied inside her.

The aftershocks still racing through his blood, he collapsed on top of her in a heap.

Hearts pounding, breath panting, they stayed like that for God knew how long, until reality finally drifted back and he realized he must be crushing her. He rolled over onto his back, taking her with him so she sprawled on top of his chest. He blinked up at the sky.

A million stars twinkled in the inky blackness, and he ran his fingers up and down her spine. "We're on the ground."

She laughed. "I know."

"That was . . ." He trailed off, not knowing the words to adequately describe it.

She propped her arms on him and rested her chin on her hands to peer at him. "That was . . ."

"The best ever."

"Times a thousand."

He chuckled. "I think you're underselling it."

Lips swollen, she smiled at him and stole his very breath. He put an arm behind his head to prop it up and see her better. Her hair was a tumble around her shoulders, and he pushed it back with his fingers. "You are the most gorgeous woman I've ever laid eyes on."

Her smile grew. "Thank you."

"I am going to do filthy things to you."

"Promise?"

"Yes." He rubbed his thumb in the indentation at the back of her neck. "I think you should know my goal is to ruin you for anyone else."

She grinned. "Same."

Christ. By the time they were through, she was going to own him.

Maybe she already did.

Chapter Eighteen

Exhausted, Sophie plopped down in the booth at Earl's Diner across from her best friend, hair a mess, sunglasses still in place. She'd thrown on the first thing she'd stumbled upon and wore a pair of jean shorts and a pink T-shirt. She'd seen the mirror; she looked like she'd been on a bender.

And she had been. After two hours of sleep she'd jolted awake and jostled Ryder, whose arm had been draped over her stomach, trapping her, to yell, "I'm supposed to meet Maddie for breakfast in fifteen minutes."

He'd groaned and gripped her tighter. "You are not a peaceful woman to wake up to."

She'd squirmed under him. "You have to let me up. It's too late to cancel."

He yawned. "Seriously?"

"Seriously."

Without even opening his eyes, he'd kissed her, rolled over, and said in a sleep-rough voice, "Have fun, darlin'."

She'd scrambled out of bed, run across the yard in a towel she'd found in his bathroom, gotten dressed, and here she was.

Maddie raised a brow. "What happened to you?"

The real question was, what hadn't happened to her. Every single muscle in her body ached. She was sore everywhere, and she did mean *everywhere*.

A waitress came over, and she begged for coffee before turning back to Maddie. "I slept with Ryder last night."

Maddie put her hands on the table. "Oh. My. God."

Words she'd yelled about a thousand times last night. "Exactly."

"How was it?"

Sophie raised her glasses to the top of her head and rolled her eyes. "Have you seen that man? How do you think it was?"

"That good, huh?" Maddie grinned ear to ear.

She shook her head and sighed. "It was the most phenomenal sex on the planet. I literally have no idea how many orgasms I had. And he's so dirty, Maddie. He's the best."

She was addicted to him. Infatuated. Smitten, and all those other words, but it was more than that. They just fit—not just their bodies, but everything.

He terrified her. Excited her. Thrilled her. Made her nervous and happy. The complete gamut of emotions.

Maddie laughed. "So you had a good time?"

"Yes. So good."

"So now what?"

Sophie sighed. She missed their twenties, when nobody asked about intentions and you could sleep with someone without it having to mean anything or go anywhere. In your thirties, everyone seemed to be pointing to an imaginary clock and saying *tick tock*.

She shrugged. "I guess we're seeing each other until I go back home."

Maddie's brow wrinkled. "And you're okay with that?"

The waitress returned with coffee and Sophie said, "Oh, thank God." Then she tasted it and wanted to pray for death again. She remembered her first day of work, when Ryder had brought her Starbucks because he'd known it would make her happy.

She looked out the window onto the streets of Revival's downtown. Completely different from the view she was used to.

Saturday mornings in Revival were still busy, but without the congestion of Chicago. Families ambled down the streets pushing strollers, people walked their dogs or stopped and talked to each other. She recognized some of the faces now. Like Mary Beth Crowley, who was outside the auto garage she owned with her husband, and an endearing pain in Sophie's ass. She spotted Cindy, a librarian at the local branch who was part of the planning committee for the town project. And other people too.

"Soph?"

She turned back to Maddie and shrugged. "I'll have to be. I tried to stay away from him. It didn't work. I can't do it. He's impossible to resist."

He wasn't Tony. Ryder wouldn't take advantage of her vulnerable state, and she couldn't get consumed because there was a defined end. So she was giving herself the gift of him, and when she left to go back home, she'd close the door and not look back.

"I've never heard you say that about anyone before," Maddie said.

"That's because it never happened." She bit her lip. "I'm probably going to be in trouble."

"You really like him."

"I really do." Sophie picked up the menu. "And not just because he's fucking awesome in bed. Because he's awesome at everything. It feels like he knows me. Does that make sense?"

"Yeah, it does." She smiled. "That's how I feel with Mitch,

that I can be exactly who I am. Happy or sad, irrational, emotional, angry, excited, impulsive and crazy. Anything I want to be, he's good with."

Sophie's phone beeped and she looked down to see Ryder's name on her screen. She swiped her thumb over his name. There was a picture of her black dress lying in a haphazard heap on his floor, and his text read, *I hope you're not at Earl's naked.*

A huge grin spread over her face, so big her cheeks hurt. She could let herself enjoy him for six months, then let him go. She typed back, *And if I am?*

The phone beeped a few seconds later. *I'll come down there with my Sharpie and write Property of Ryder across your breasts.*

She sucked in a breath, heating in an instant. She suspected society would deem that unacceptable, but she liked the sound of that a little too much.

Another text popped up. *And Do Not Touch, across your stomach.*

Oh God.

The way her heart fluttered in her chest told her everything she needed to know about his effect on her. She turned her phone toward her, snapped a selfie. *I'm not naked.*

I might do it anyway, because I like the sound of it.

So did she, not that she was about to admit it. *Like I'd let you.*

I spent the night with you, I know exactly how much you like the idea.

Arrogant and correct. She ignored the comment. *Can I help you? I'm being rude.*

Yeah, I'm going to Mitch's to play basketball, so after breakfast you should head there instead of home.

What if I have stuff to do?

I'll help you.

She couldn't help it; she let out a dreamy sigh. *All right.*

Another text. *Oh, and Sophie, you look like you've been fucking all night.*

She laughed and put down her phone, looking up to see Maddie watching her, her eyes wide. "Wow."

"What?" She shifted in her seat.

"You're glowing."

"Shut up!" Sophie threw a napkin at her. "They're going to your house to play basketball."

Maddie rubbed her hands together. "This is going to be fun."

Sophie picked up her napkin. "So, I guess I'm doing this. I hope it's not a total disaster."

Maddie smiled. "Sometimes you just have to go for it, consequences be damned."

She lifted her coffee cup. "Cheers."

As Sophie and Maddie went out to the backyard, she sucked in a breath at the sight of Ryder, bare chested, body slicked with sweat, lunging for the ball.

Gracie waved them to the sidelines.

As they walked over, Sophie could only marvel at the scene before her. Screw professional sports, right here was a recipe for female fantasy. Mitch, Charlie, Sam, and Ryder were on the court, and holy hell, they were awesome. Hot men. Sweating. Swearing. Pushing and shoving. They did not play nice, which made Sophie all the more interested.

Until Ryder, she'd never given much thought to how much energy she put into curtailing her baser, wilder instincts and impulses. Until him, she hadn't realized she'd been struggling under the weight of it.

They pulled some chairs next to Gracie, who smiled at them, coffee in hand. "Isn't this fun?"

Maddie looked around. "Where's James?"

"Running. You know he's allergic to sports."

While James might not like sports, he had the body of a competitive athlete.

Gracie sighed. "It's marathon training season again."

Maddie wrinkled her nose. "But think of it this way. Last year you invented those power cookies, and now everyone wants them."

Gracie laughed. "True."

They kept talking, but Sophie's attention wandered to her current fixation. Her thighs ached pleasantly, reminding her how much time he'd spent between them. And as though he sensed her thoughts, he turned around and looked at her, his gaze sweeping down her body before he broke into a smile.

Oh God. She was in so much trouble.

He called time and jogged over to her.

She sucked in a breath, having no idea what he was going to do, but before she could say anything he leaned down, hauled her up to meet him, and kissed her. Not just a peck on the lips, but an open-mouth, full-tongue, dirty kiss. She tensed for a fraction of a second, thinking about everyone watching them, before she shrugged off propriety and gave into the heat of his mouth.

Her hand snaked around his neck, and even slicked with sweat she wanted to take him into the house and have her slutty way with him.

He finally pulled away, and as she attempted to catch her breath, she said, "Hi."

He chuckled, tugged her close, and whispered in her ear, "I'm going to fuck you in the shower later."

She whispered back, "But not before I go down on you."

"Tease." He kissed her again, this time quick and aggressive. "I'll be back."

Then he turned back to the game and said as casually as could be, "Ready?"

The men looked at him, then at Sophie, then back at Ryder before shrugging. A second later the game resumed.

Sophie didn't get off so easy. Gracie and Maddie stared at her open mouthed.

Sophie shifted in her chair. "What?"

Gracie pointed toward the court. "Did you just offer to go down on Ryder?"

Oops. She shrugged. "Do you blame me?"

Gracie laughed. "Hell no."

Maddie shook her head. "Girl, you are in trouble."

Yep, she totally was.

Late that night, Ryder ran a hand over Sophie's bare stomach, lightly tracing the dips and curves of her body with his fingers. One day with her and he was already addicted. After the Rileys' they'd come home, showered together, and spent the entire day doing shit around their houses and screwing like it was going out of style.

Ryder had picked up takeout and they'd watched three more episodes of *Making a Murderer* before going to bed, where she was game for literally anything he wanted to do to her. Now they lay there, and Ryder couldn't remember the last time he'd been so relaxed and happy.

He propped his head up on his hand. "Tell me about your childhood."

Her lashes fluttered open. "Now?"

"What's wrong with now?"

"Don't you want to bask in the afterglow?"

He laughed. "With the amount of sex we're having, if we only basked in the afterglow we'd never get out of bed, or off the floor, or out of the shower, the kitchen table . . ." He grinned. "Well, you get the idea."

She rolled her eyes. "You are such a bragger."

"Darlin', this is all you." He cupped her breast and stroked over her nipple, which rose to the occasion. "But back to the question."

He'd noticed she avoided talking about herself. That she didn't like it. It was like she tried to play everything about her past as inconsequential, which was usually a sign of avoidance.

She shrugged. "There's not much to tell. I was an only child. As you know, my parents are free spirits, but they held it together long enough to give me a stable, albeit eccentric childhood. When I turned eighteen, they took off to travel the world. End of story."

With the tensing of her body, he somehow doubted that but decided not to push for details. "How did you meet Maddie and Penelope?"

She smiled. "I met Maddie in junior high. We both got kicked out of English class and bonded in the hallway. Penelope came as part of the package with Maddie. They met in kindergarten."

He circled her nipple. "Penelope is the one that kept you guys out of trouble?"

She laughed. "Well, she tried, but we had minds of our own. She kept us out of jail a few times. Of course, we got her thrown in jail too, so you know, it all worked out in the end."

"Do you have a record?" Amused, he shook his head at her.

"Just some juvenile misdemeanor stuff. Nothing serious. Woods parties, underage drinking, stuff like that." She grinned at him. "Are you disappointed?"

"Kind of."

"You are such a pervert."

"If you are just figuring that out, you haven't been paying attention." He bent down and nipped at her bottom lip. "I'm imagining some very creative role-playing in our future."

Her face lit up with excitement. "Can I dress up?"

How could one woman be so perfect for him? She could show up in a burlap bag as far as he was concerned, but he was curious to see what she came up with. "What do you want to dress up as?"

"Of course there are standards, but I'm not sure yet." She pressed her shoulders into the bed. "What are your fantasies?"

They were countless. He traced a path over her ribs. "They all end with you naked."

"Will you tell me one?"

He narrowed his gaze. She wanted to divert the conversation away from her past, but maybe he could work with that. "How about we trade. You answer my questions, and I'll answer yours."

"That sounds fair." She slid her leg across his thighs. He expected a sex question, but she surprised him by asking, "Did you have a happy childhood?"

"I did. It was very idyllic. My parents loved each other, and us. We had fun, laughed around the dinner table. I have no complaints."

She tilted her head. "Not one complaint?"

He shrugged. "Nothing substantial. My only complaint was that I hated having no complaints. Which sounds like an entitled asshole thing to say, so I keep it to myself."

Her gaze darted away. "I can't imagine what that would be like. To be raised so normal. I mean, my parents weren't mean or anything, but I always felt . . ." She trailed off, her gaze darting away.

He smoothed a path over her stomach. "Always felt what?"

She shrugged. "They loved me, but they never really wanted me. They never said, but I'm pretty sure my mom got pregnant on accident. It was more like they were putting in time, that they couldn't wait for their responsibility to be done."

He frowned, thinking of his own encouraging childhood. He'd never once doubted his family's dedication. "That must have been hard."

She pushed a lock of hair from her face. "Not really. It was how it was. They are who they are, what's the point of wishing for someone different? I had Penelope and Maddie and all the freedom a teenager could possibly want. Sure, sometimes I'd walk into a group meditation session going on in the living room, but there's far worse things."

True, but he didn't like the idea that she'd felt like a responsibility instead of a blessing.

She touched his chest, her fingers a soft flutter over the scrolling black design on his skin. "Does this mean anything?"

He shook his head. "I got it on my eighteenth birthday, so it wasn't a well-thought-out plan. I picked the design out of a book because I thought it was cool."

She chuckled before tracing the word "freedom" on his ribs. "And this?"

He shrugged. "I got that one when I was twenty-one. As a reminder, I suppose."

"How do you mean?"

The thoughts of his twenty-one-year-old self seemed distant and unclear, but the word still resonated with him.

He tugged down the sheet, exposing her hip where he curved his hand around her soft flesh. "It's like I've always been a little too wild, a little too reckless for my own good. It's hard for me to feel content. I'm not sure if that makes any sense. It's to remind myself that most of the time when I feel restless, it's because I'm trying to put myself in a box." He laughed, slightly embarrassed. "Or, I don't know, something equally stupid."

Her eyes went wide. "I don't think that's stupid."

"No?"

She shook her head. "Some people just need to roam free."

A smile curved over his lips. "Exactly."

She furrowed her brow. "I'm surprised you decided on a career in law enforcement."

"Why's that?"

"It's a field governed by rules."

He nodded. "It is in some ways, but it's also not a traditional work environment. I'd go crazy working in a corporate job, and since my parents didn't raise me to be a good criminal, this seemed like a balance."

"Do you like it?"

"I do, very much. I can't imagine doing anything else."

Her gaze flickered to his face. "I know what you mean, about the wildness."

Somehow that didn't surprise him. He leaned down and brushed her lips. "Tell me more."

She bit her lips. "Like I said, I didn't have a lot of rules growing up, and Maddie was like my kindred spirit in causing trouble, with Penelope standing over us as the superego. And it worked. I needed Maddie and Penelope. Maddie to fulfill my bad girl, Penelope to fulfill my good. But then Maddie got in a terrible car accident that killed her father and left her in a coma, and when she woke up, she'd changed. It's a long story, but she felt a lot of guilt and decided the way to cope with it was to become perfect. I understood it. Even as a fifteen-year-old kid it made sense to me. But I lost my partner in crime. Now I had the superego standing over me, and the ego, and eventually my antics began to seem silly, like an annoyance. In college, I found new people to be wild with, and it came back to bite me. So I learned a lesson: to stop letting it control me. To be safe and responsible for it. Oh sure, I was still feisty and outgoing. Still the life of the party. And people think I'm the wild one. But I haven't felt wild in a long time."

Somewhere in that story was the truth of her. But he was smart enough to bide his time, so he asked softly, "Until me?"

She looked at him. "Yes. I like the way you make me feel. I like how I don't have to tuck myself into a contained ball around you."

"Thank you." He kissed her, soft and gentle. "I feel the same exact way about you."

"Really?"

"Really."

She averted her gaze. "I have a question."

"What's that?"

Her big brown eyes gazed up at him. "I promised Penelope I'd visit next month. Is it too soon to ask you to come with me?"

He slid his hand around her throat, feeling the fine muscles flex under his touch. "Not too soon. I would love that. We could make a long weekend out of it."

"Really?"

"Really."

She sat up in bed and beamed at him, and Ryder fell impossibly harder for her. "This is going to be fun. I have so many places to show you."

He laughed. "Sophie, you make everything fun."

She straddled him, sliding over his cock, which now paid attention. She leaned down and her hair cascaded over him as she bent to his ear. "You know I'll never say no to you."

"Never?"

She licked at his skin. "Never." She sat up, her breasts bare and beautiful in the soft glow of the moonlight streaming through the window. "Are you going to tell me a fantasy?"

His mind scrolled through a hundred different scenarios before he settled on one he thought would strike her fancy and sense of adventure. "I'm at a bar. We're strangers. Your dress is slutty and minuscule and your lips are red. We flirt, everyone knows we're circling each other, and I fuck you in the corner of the bar, quiet and discreetly, but in front of everyone."

She sucked in her breath, her nipples hardening at the suggestion.

He ran his thumbs over the hard peaks. "Do you like that idea?"

"Yes." Her hips twitched against him.

"Because you like danger. And getting caught."

"Yes." She rocked her hips against his now-hard shaft. "And so do you."

"I do." He tugged at her nipples. "Sophie."

"Yes?"

"I'll never say no to you either."

"Good." She reached over to the bedside table, its surface littered with condoms, and grabbed a packet. With her gaze heavy on his, she ripped it open with her teeth before sliding the condom down his shaft. Then she lifted her hips, grasped his cock, and impaled herself on him. They both groaned at the contact and she began a slow, steady grind. "Ryder."

"Yes?"

"I'm going to make you a very happy man."

She was already more than he could have ever asked for, more than he could have dared to hope for. He closed his eyes, gripping her hips to speed up her rhythm. Needing to get lost in her, so she felt like him.

Chapter Nineteen

Ryder watched Sophie stand and greet yet another Revival business owner, beaming at them with her killer smile and charming the socks off them. They were at dinner with Griffin and Darcy at the famous Rock's Steakhouse, and between the three of them they'd had almost nonstop visitors.

Even after sleeping with him for the last three weeks and spending all her free time with him, she managed to keep him surprised.

Of course, the entire town knew they were together, and Ryder couldn't help thinking about how seamlessly she fell into his life. They were dangerous thoughts he couldn't control. She was everything he could want in a woman. Fun and insatiable, and every day with her was an adventure.

He was addicted to her. And as one day bled into the next, he stopped thinking about her leaving and entertained the possibility that she'd stay. She seemed happy.

It might be a foolish thought, but as she kissed the cheek of Mary Beth Crowley, the town's matriarch and all-around hard-ass, and made her laugh, he couldn't help hoping.

Sophie had stopped complaining about the lack of Starbucks.

Stopped speaking of Nordstrom with longing.

Stopped talking about Chicago as home.

How could he not hope? Especially when they were so damn good together.

Sophie sat back down and Darcy, the first lady of Revival and fellow hellion, raised her dark brows. "You won over Mary Beth?"

With a smirk, Sophie picked up her menu. "She was easy once I figured out her only motivation was the success of the town."

"Well, you're a wonder," Darcy said, smiling. She took a sip of wine. "How are you liking Revival?"

Sophie tossed a sassy look in her direction. "It's hard to complain too much."

Darcy laughed, waving a hand. "When I first moved back from New York, I thought I was going to die."

Sophie shook her head. "I don't know how you did it."

"Well, it was different for me, I suppose. I grew up here." Darcy slid her hand over Griffin's, and their fingers entwined. "And there was this boy I never forgot."

Sophie bit her bottom lip. "Do you miss it?"

"Sometimes, but this is home now, and I truly feel this is where I'm meant to be."

An expression Ryder couldn't decipher slid over Sophie's face. "That must be a nice feeling."

I could be that for you, I could give you that, if you let me. The thought was hard and demanding, and truthfully a little frightening.

"It is." Darcy stroked her thumb over Griffin's palm. "After a while, I realized I missed the convenience of it. The noise and activity that allowed me not to think, if that makes sense."

"It does." Sophie's expression creased before clearing. "Griffin told me you run a blog."

Darcy's expression widened. "Did he now?"

"Yes, he said you're a freelance writer and write a blog," Sophie said.

"I do."

Sophie smiled. "I had a blog in Chicago. I miss it."

Darcy took a sip of wine. "Well, there's no reason you can't start one here."

Sophie shook her head. "I ran an entertainment blog, and since Revival doesn't have any entertainment, it would be kind of skimpy."

"True," Griffin said, rubbing a hand over his jaw. "All you need is a different angle."

Sophie jutted her chin toward Darcy. "What's your angle?"

"Sex." Darcy winked.

Sophie laughed. "Fun. Do tell."

Darcy shrugged. "I do advice, product reviews, how-to columns, stuff like that."

Sophie winked at Griffin. "Aren't you a lucky guy?"

"You have no idea," he said with a grin.

Darcy held her finger to her lips. "Shhh, don't tell anyone. It has to be our little secret."

Only a select few knew the origins of Darcy's blog, considering she was first lady of a small town. Ryder was surprised she'd told Sophie, but on the other hand, not surprised at all.

They were cut from the same cloth, after all.

Sophie made a locking gesture over her mouth and threw away the imaginary key. "I won't tell a soul."

"I trust you," Darcy said. "Look at all the good things you're doing for the town. That speaks volumes."

"I'm just doing my job," Sophie said.

"I disagree." Darcy beamed a smile. "Doing your job would be to keep everything that had been set up running smoothly and in an organized fashion. But you went out and made it better, increased revenue, publicity, community excitement."

Sophie shrugged. "To me that's my job."

Darcy tilted her head toward her husband. "I'm afraid Griffin might be in love with you."

Griffin rolled his eyes.

Ryder scrubbed his hand over his jaw. "I think Darcy is right." He winked at the pretty woman with her dark hair and dancing blue eyes. "What are we going to do to break up this love affair?"

Now it was Sophie's turn to roll her eyes.

The truth was, Griffin was a little in love with Sophie—not with her body but with her mind. He'd been desperate for someone with her considerable talents and planned on milking her for whatever he could.

Darcy's expression turned sly and she raised her glass, taking a sip of her martini before saying, "We could just have a four-way and let them get it out of their system."

Sophie laughed. Griffin had been taking a drink and started to choke. Darcy reached over and patted him on the back.

Ryder, however, looked at Sophie with utter seriousness and nodded. "If we must, we must."

Darcy put on a good appearance for the public, but she was a bad girl and never let Griffin forget it in safe company. Her lips twitched. "You guys could come back to our hot tub."

Sophie's expression danced with mirth. "Only if we're naked."

"Darlin', that's a given," Ryder said and put his hand

along the back of her neck, rubbing it softly. "I'm not about to pass up on a chance to see Darcy naked."

Sophie's gaze flicked over Darcy. "I can't say I blame you."

Darcy laughed and smirked at Ryder. "You'd better find a way to keep her, because she might be my new favorite person."

He was working on it. Because he wanted to keep her. Needed to keep her.

"Who knew small town America could be so fun," Sophie said, with a wicked grin.

Griffin and Darcy laughed.

Ryder reached over, pulled her close, and whispered in her ear, "You are trouble."

"Would you have it any other way?"

"Not in a million years."

The following afternoon, Sophie sent off a text to Ryder and smiled. *Can you meet me at that bar over in Shreveport tonight after work?*

She had to admit Revival was growing on her. Maybe it had to do with Ryder—okay, it probably had a lot to do with Ryder, but living in a small town was turning out to be more fun than she thought and certainly not the torture she'd envisioned when she took the job.

She got to see Maddie all the time.

The townspeople had been nothing but receptive and welcoming.

There was something fun about walking down the street and people calling her name.

And then there was Ryder. Gorgeous, hot Ryder who was not only the best sex partner she'd ever had but who brought her Starbucks during his lunch break and seemed to be up for anything she wanted.

Her phone pinged. *We can meet at home and go together.*

She licked her lips. That wasn't her plan. She had other plans. Surprises in store for him. She made an excuse. *I have a meeting. I'll meet you there at seven.*

Since she wouldn't be able to sneak into her house without his notice, she'd made arrangements to get ready at Maddie's.

Then we'll have two cars.

She shook her head. *But I'll already be there.*

A few seconds passed. *All right, if you insist.*

I'll meet you at the bar. She smiled. She'd make it worth his while. As hard as it was not to tease, she didn't want him on alert. She wanted him completely surprised. Shocked.

She could hardly wait.

This was what she loved about him.

She'd never had so much fun.

Never felt so free. Because not only did he indulge her, he encouraged her. Some of the things she'd done with him were probably illegal. And she couldn't get enough.

Griffin entered her doorway, his broad shoulder against the frame. He grinned at her. "Have you recovered?"

The hot tub had been very inappropriate, but they'd kept their clothes on, and while Darcy and Sophie teased them incessantly, they hadn't made out. The truth was, they all played a good game, but Sophie didn't want to kiss anyone but Ryder and she knew Darcy felt the same about Griffin.

But they'd made a good show and tormented without mercy. Flirted. All in good fun. By the time they'd left, Sophie was pretty sure Darcy had suffered the same fate as she had. She hadn't even gotten to the car before Ryder was on her, his hands in her wet underwear.

It had been awesome.

She laughed. "I'm one of those annoying people who recovers quickly."

"Good for you." He slid his hands into his pockets. "And how are you feeling?"

"Fuzzy." He flashed her a smile. "But it was too much fun to mind."

"Exactly." She gestured toward the seat across from her desk. "So I've been thinking of an idea I wanted to run past you."

He sat down and tilted his head. "What's that?"

"I know that you're not quite there yet, but I've been doing a lot of thinking about the tourist trade. I believe there's a real opportunity. We've already talked about the small-town getaway idea, but I decided to do some market research, and it turns out it's a growing trend. Disconnecting from city life is a huge selling point. You're close enough to Chicago to make it a great weekend getaway. You've got the river. And quiet. The town is undergoing changes, and I think you can attract more businesses if you try and capitalize on it."

He nodded, shifting forward in his chair a little. "I agree, but I want to be careful not to ruin those aspects of the town that make it home."

"I couldn't agree more. And after meeting a lot of the citizens of Revival I don't think they'd be happy with Revival, turning into a tourist town. They like what they have and don't want it to change. You want a happy medium, something that will make it attractive to small businesses but not so much that you ruin what's great about this place."

"And you think you have an idea?"

"I think I have the beginnings of an idea." She folded her hands on the desk. "What if, instead of some sort of smaller resort like we talked about earlier, we jump on the tiny house trend? I've looked at the land and talked to the city planner, and I think you could reasonably build fifteen tiny houses that will still feel really secluded. You could maintain the forest feel, preserve the trees and nature that would be ruined by a resort, and as an added bonus, we could build some awesome tree houses. I've looked, and people are really into this. It would be unique and different. I also think it would be attractive to people year-round because you're close to several skiing areas. It's also far enough away from the river citizens to make them not feel invaded."

She'd put a lot of thought into this and done a lot of research. This could work. She felt it in her bones. It would increase revenue to businesses but keep Revival intact. She grabbed a printout of the spreadsheet she'd been working on and pushed it at Griffin. "These are only down and dirty numbers, but I think you'll see very conservatively it would help the town without displacing it."

He picked up the spreadsheet and studied it with intent. He was an accountant by trade, and numbers were his business. He nodded. "Sophie, this is brilliant. The question is, how? I mean, it's a great idea, I love it, but obviously this would require investors, and the project seems too small to be attractive to anyone in the hotel game."

She beamed. "I've already thought of that."

"Of course you have." He chuckled. "What was I thinking?"

This was what she loved about her job. What she was good at. Finding opportunities other people overlooked. It was how her blog had become so successful. Everyone knew the flashy places, the big scores, but she'd sought out the hidden gems. The ultra-cool places with a unique vibe. She always recognized it when she saw it, and her instincts had never failed. She didn't think they would fail her now.

"I know a lot of people. More specifically, a lot of rich people. I'm thinking we could do some sort of investment consortium. I'm not sure if it would work—or if they'd be interested, but we could invite them all for the weekend and try and sell the opportunity. For most of them it would be a pet project, nothing that would make or break them, but I think I could sell it as a fun opportunity. We'd have a lot of things to do before that happens, but I'm going to Chicago in a couple of weeks, and if you're okay with it, I'd like to talk to Shane Donovan, who has ties already in the community and uncanny business acumen. He's also a no-bullshit guy. If he doesn't think it would fly, he'll say so. But if he does, and he's interested, we can come up with a plan. What do you say?"

Griffin blinked at her and shook his head. "Darcy's right, I am a little bit in love with you."

She laughed. "So you're in?"

"I'm in. What do you need to put together for Shane?"

Excitement bubbled inside her, and Sophie realized she cared about this job. She cared about Revival and wanted the town to be a smashing success. Even if she wouldn't be here to see it, she'd leave this place better than she found it. "I'll put together a list. We have a few weeks and Ryder is going with me, so we can talk to Shane together."

"The two of you are very convincing." Griffin met her eyes. "You make an awesome team."

"I think so too." Because she did. Together they fit and she loved being with him, loved working with him, and loved everything about the way he thought. "Should I set up a meeting for the three of us to sit down and brainstorm?"

"Please." He stood and turned to go, only to stop in the doorway. "Soph, I'm glad you're here."

Pleased, she smiled. She'd always loved doing a good job. "So you don't regret taking a chance on me?"

"You were never a risk. I knew I was getting a bargain."

"It's been fun, and I'm glad to help."

A sly expression crossed his features. "Any chance I could convince you to stay permanently?"

Her heart skipped a beat. She laughed and waved him away. "Get out of here."

His head tilted and he shrugged. "We'll see."

He walked away and her throat tightened. She didn't like the reminder she was leaving. Not because she didn't want to go home, but because it reminded her of how deeply invested she was in Ryder. How much she needed him and wanted him. How *he* was starting to feel like home. An unusual and unheard of feeling. Home was something that happened to other people, not her.

She looked down at her phone. He'd texted her. *I'll be there in fifteen minutes with Starbucks.*

She texted back. *You're a god among men.*

I get that all the time, darlin'.

She had no doubt that he did. He was a keeper.

An ominous shadow dimmed her happiness.

A keeper she wouldn't get to keep.

"Whoa!" Maddie looked up from the stove where she cooked dinner and gave Sophie a long wolf whistle. "Holy shit, Sophie."

She grinned and tugged down the minuscule skirt of her dress. "Good?"

From the table where Mitch had been entertaining Lily with funny faces that made the baby howl with laughter, he gave her a long once-over. "That's quite a dress."

It was. It was black and slinky, barely covering the curve of her ass and dipping dangerously low. Her cleavage spilled out of stretchy fabric that looked painted on and hugged every single one of her curves. She completed the outfit in sky-high four-and-a-half-inch stilettos.

Mitch's expression turned serious as he looked at his daughter. "Now, Lily, don't let Aunt Sophie give you any ideas. While she may cause a heart attack in the male population, you are only allowed to dress in a nun's habit."

The little girl with her shock of red hair gave her daddy a big, wet raspberry.

Sophie smoothed her hand over her hair and leaned down to mock whisper, "He's wrong, Lils, you wear whatever you want."

Mitch grinned, shaking his head. "Remind me to never let you take her shopping when she's a teenager."

"No promises," Sophie said, chuckling.

Maddie waved a hand over Sophie. "I'm assuming you're meeting Ryder?"

"Of course." She'd completed her transformation into high-priced slut by curling her hair into wild, messy waves and darkening her makeup to smoky, completing his fantasy with dark red Chanel lipstick.

She looked seriously hot. She knew that. She smirked. "I have plans."

"May God help him," Mitch said, his tone dry.

"Indeed." Sophie picked up her bag. "Thanks for letting me get ready here. I didn't want to risk running into him at home. I cleaned everything up, but now it's time for me to run."

Mitch winked. "Have fun, Soph. Don't break him."

"I make zero promises." Sophie turned on her high heels and blew a kiss to Maddie. "I'll talk to you tomorrow."

Maddie put down the spatula and glanced at her husband. "Can you watch the stove while I walk Sophie out?"

"Sure thing, Princess," Mitch said.

Sophie pushed open the swinging door of their kitchen

and started walking down the hall, Maddie at her heels. When they got to the door, Maddie grinned. "Now, remember to use protection."

They always did, although she was on the pill and thinking tonight might be time to throw caution to the wind. Ryder had gone to the doctor a few weeks ago for his annual physical for the department, and Sophie knew she was clean. She wanted him inside her, with no barrier. Wanted to feel him hard and hot, sliding deep. But it wasn't a discussion she wanted to have with Maddie. She didn't want to be late.

Sophie laughed. "All right, Mom."

Maddie tucked a lock of hair behind her ear. "You're having fun, right?"

"I'm having the most fun." Sophie's heart beat fast every time she thought of how much.

"Good. This is exactly what I wanted, for you to have fun while you lived here." Maddie wrinkled her nose and cleared her throat. "I have a confession to make."

Sophie raised her brows. "What's that?"

"There was another house for rent and I picked this one because of Ryder." She shrugged her shoulder. "I thought you guys might hit it off."

Sophie shook her head. "You are such a brat."

"When you first met him I thought it backfired, but I knew when I forced you into blind dates it was on. The look you gave each other was priceless."

Sophie couldn't be mad. How could she? When the results were so freakin' awesome. But she still huffed and put her hands on her hips. "Oh my God, Maddie. What about poor Bill and Cheryl?"

Maddie waved a hand in dismissal. "Please, those two are meant for each other. They're just so nice and accommodating they couldn't see what was right in front of them."

"Okay. You need to stop playing matchmaker."

"Why? Can't you see how good I am at it?"

"I see you're impossible."

Maddie winked. "Rumor has it those two were in a heated make out session in front of her house two nights ago."

Sophie laughed. "Good for them."

Maddie's expression creased with smugness. "I mean, it's tame compared to what you and Ryder are doing, but not just anyone can handle that kind of wild."

Sophie put her hand on her chest. "Oh my God, Maddie. I don't even mean the sex . . . I mean, everything."

Maddie tucked her bottom lip between her teeth. "I've never seen you like this over a guy."

"I know." Sophie didn't want to go down that road, so she glanced at the door. "I have to go blow his mind now."

Maddie hugged her. "You have fun."

"I will." With Ryder there was no other option.

Chapter Twenty

His back to the door, Ryder sat at the bar nursing a beer and didn't see Sophie walk in. But when the bartender looked past him, his eyes widening, Ryder knew she'd arrived. Picking up the bottle, he took a sip, turned to watch her approach, and started to choke.

Jesus fucking Christ.

"Damn," the bartender said, which was pretty much the understatement of the century.

Sophie sauntered toward him wearing a scrap of black fabric Ryder supposed could pass as a dress and mile-high heels. Her hips swayed to the beat of the music playing in the background, and all the blood rushed from his head and straight to his cock.

He growled to the bartender, "She's mine."

The bartender laughed. "Lucky guy."

"You have no idea."

She was practically making men drop like flies in her wake as she walked to the empty stool next to him. She smiled, her full red lips holding the same sins as the apple Eve held out to Adam. When she spoke her voice was a husky purr. "Is this seat taken?"

Ryder immediately caught her game. His whispered

fantasy to her a few weeks ago. And suddenly her wanting to meet him instead of driving together made sense. His mind started to spin with all the directions he could take this.

His gaze flickered over her wild hair, crimson lips, and tiny body. She looked incredible. He gestured to the seat. "It's all yours, darlin'."

"Thank you." She slid onto the chair and smiled at the bartender, who looked at her like he wanted to eat her for dinner despite Ryder's warning. He would have taken offense but couldn't really blame the guy.

Her tongue darted out to wet her red lips. "Can I get a dirty martini?"

The bartender shook his head as though clearing it from a daze. "Sure thing."

She crossed her legs and shifted her attention toward Ryder. "I'm passing through and my car broke down."

He met her gaze. "So you're stranded?"

"Yes." One bare shoulder shrugged. "I need help, but my cell phone's dead, and with the bar right here it seemed like a sign I should come in." She gave him the most obscene look and licked her lips again. "You wouldn't happen to know anyone trustworthy, would you?"

He put his drink down on the bar and slid his hand on the counter, facing her more fully. "Today's your lucky day."

"Why's that?" She batted dark, thick lashes.

"I'm a cop."

She pursed her lips and sighed, "Ooohhh, that is lucky."

The bartender returned and set her drink on the bar.

Ryder didn't look away from Sophie. "It's on me."

"Sure thing, buddy."

"Thank you." She put her hand on his knee and leaned forward, and Ryder practically fell into her cleavage. "That's very sweet of you."

"I'm a stand-up guy." Palm searing his skin through

his jeans, she squeezed before moving away to pick up her martini.

She took a sip, glanced pointedly at his erection, and smiled. "I can see that."

He didn't even miss a beat. His gaze dipped to her breasts spilling out over the fabric. "Where are you going dressed like that?"

She puffed out her bottom lip. "I had a date, but he stood me up."

Wouldn't happen in a million years, but he clucked sympathetically. "Poor thing."

"I know, right?"

"His loss."

Her eyes roamed hot and hungry over him. "Maybe this night isn't a disaster after all."

He leaned close to her. "I can guarantee you it won't be."

She sucked in a breath and lowered her lashes. "Oh?"

"You have my word." He wanted to take her off the stool and impale her right this second, but he wasn't going to do that. She'd gone through a lot of trouble for him, and he'd play along until they both couldn't take it anymore.

Unlike a stranger in a bar, he knew her now. Knew all her kinks and secrets, exactly what turned her on the most, and he'd pull out every trick in his considerable arsenal to make her so on edge, so wet, she begged for his cock.

They were alike this way.

She took another sip of her drink before fishing out the toothpick that skewered two olives. Slowly, seductively she slipped one between her lips. His mind went numb when she swiped her tongue across the olive's flesh before she bit down and took it off the stem with her teeth.

He bit back a groan.

She chewed and swallowed before saying, "It's such a relief to run into a man who can help me. Thank you."

His tongue felt a bit thick and he cleared his throat. "That's what I'm here for, to protect and serve."

She tucked a lock of wild blond hair behind her ear. "Do you have a gun?"

"I do." He wanted to bite her.

She shifted, turning so her legs knocked against his. He opened his knees and she slid her clasped thighs between them. She leaned closer and whispered, "Handcuffs?"

He dipped his head. "Why? Do you need to be arrested?"

"Maybe." She licked her lips. "I've been told I'm very bad sometimes."

"I can handle you." He moved to her ear. "I'm not above restraining you if the situation calls for it."

She sucked in a little gasp. "My name's Sophie."

"Ryder."

They moved back to a reasonable distance apart, neither ready to end the game.

They were just getting started.

Sophie was a crazy person. Absolutely out of her mind.

They'd been playing at seduction for over an hour, each growing increasingly bold. She was so hot she might go insane.

He slid his hand onto her thigh and met her gaze. "Are you wet?"

"Yes."

His silver eyes, burning like molten steel, hooded. "Spread your legs so I can find out for myself."

She glanced around the bar as though she was nervous.

As though she shouldn't. Even though they both knew this couldn't be more up her alley.

The place was reasonably crowded, perfect for their game, and they still sat at the bar. There weren't so many people that anyone stood over them, but there were enough to make it interesting.

She licked her lips. "What kind of woman does that make me?"

He leaned close. "The fun kind." Even closer. "The kind that gets off by being touched in public." Still closer, so their lips were inches apart. "The exciting kind."

Her legs were still situated between his, and she spread them before saying in a throaty whisper, "I never do this."

"There's a first time for everything." His grasp on her leg tightened. "Open for me."

"This is so inappropriate." Which was exactly why she liked it. She spread her legs, just enough to give him access.

The hand closer to the bar slid between her thighs. A second later his knuckles brushed over her damp panties. They were barely there, black and thin mesh. She gasped at the contact, his touch like an electric shock through her system. The excitement was that much greater because they were surrounded by people.

"That's a good sound." He rubbed his knuckles up and down where she wanted him most. "If I kept going, would you come?"

She was so on edge it wouldn't take long, and she wasn't about to deny it. "Yes."

His expression turned feral. "Right here at the bar?"

"Yes."

He hissed out a breath. "I'd like to see that."

She'd anticipated everything, not necessarily the particulars of how things would play out, but the highlights. She tilted her head and moved to his ear. "I probably shouldn't tell you this, but my panties have ties holding them together."

He growled. "Undo them for me."

He bracketed her body, pulling her chair closer and putting his feet on it to shield her just enough. She reached to the side of her hip and pulled the string loose.

"Do you guys want another round?" the bartender asked.

With two other people this might have broken the spell, but with them, it just upped their excitement.

"No." Ryder's voice was clipped and thick with lust at the same time.

There was shuffling, and Sophie slipped the bow on the other side.

He tugged at the fabric, baring her to him. Again his knuckles rubbed against her slippery flesh. "Someone's wet."

She shifted, tilting her hips slightly into his hand. "Well, someone's been a real tease."

"I think you like to be teased."

"I think you're right."

"How long do you think you can keep this up? Being close but not going over?"

"I don't know. Why don't you find out?"

And he did.

She made it twenty minutes with him rubbing his knuckles over her clit, pulling back when she got close, before she started begging. She clutched at his shirt and suddenly, just like that, the game was over and shit got real. In a breathless moan, she said, "Ryder."

"Had enough, darlin'?" His voice was harsh, almost guttural.

She gasped. "Please."

"Please what?"

"Fuck me." She scraped her teeth over his jaw. "I swear I'm going to come the second you take me."

He moved his hand away from where he tormented her, dragging her panties from between her legs and shoving them in his pocket. He stood, took her hand, and called out to the bartender, "We'll be right back."

The guy gave them a smirk, nodding.

Ryder pulled her through the tables, past the dance floor and down a corridor before he came to a tiny alcove. He tucked her into the corner and said in a voice thick with desire, "This isn't going to be pretty."

She gripped him around the neck. "I don't want pretty. I want what only you can give me."

"And what's that?" He lifted her leg, and she planted her foot on the wall while he unbuttoned his pants and slid his zipper down.

"Dirty, raw fucking." She had no shame around him, and best of all, she didn't have to pretend otherwise.

He kissed her, hard. It was demanding and ruthless. All tongue and teeth and snarling. Like they were two animals that didn't care about civility. Which maybe, together, they were.

He pulled back and gripped her hair tight in his fist. "That's right, only me, Sophie."

"Only you." She tilted her hips and glanced at the hallway. "Anyone that comes down the hall is going to see us."

"Do you care?"

"Nope." He slid a hand into his pocket where she knew he carried condoms, since as he said, they couldn't go anywhere without it being a possibility, and she grabbed his wrist. "Take me."

He paused, and when he met her gaze his eyes smoldered. "Bare?"

She reached between him, grasped his cock, and slid up and down the length. "I don't want barriers."

He made a feral sound in the back of his throat, gripped her hair tighter, and claimed her mouth, his kiss so filthy her knees went weak. He pushed away her hand and guided his cock to her entrance. But instead of entering her, he rubbed the head along her clit, pulling away to whisper on a harsh breath, "Is this what you want?"

"Yes." She rocked back, wrapping her arms around his waist and digging her nails into his back. "Yes."

On the next pass, he impaled her and she cried out. With one hand still tight in her hair he put his hand over her mouth, thrusting into her.

They went a bit wild. Held up only by the wall at her back and the brace of her leg against the wall, she let him do all the work, pounding inside her, and when he hit a particularly good spot, she bit his hand.

"Fuck, Sophie." He moved faster, harder.

Head lolling back, her eyes fluttered closed. Trapped against the wall, one of Ryder's hands in her hair, the other covering her mouth, his hot, harsh breath in her ear, she'd never felt so completely taken.

She dug her nails harder into his skin as she tightened, coiling tight on the very precipice.

He tilted her head and ordered, "Look at me."

Her lashes blinked open and their eyes met.

"Don't look away." He released his hold on her mouth, covering her lips with a kiss before pulling back to look into her eyes.

What she saw there stunned her. A need and burning desire that matched her own. The same feral wildness that lived inside her. She whispered, "Ryder."

"I know, Sophie." He thrust hard and she keened. "You're mine."

"Yes."

"No matter what happens, you and I . . ." He trailed off.

She gripped him around the neck, pulling him closer. She didn't know where the words came from, but when she spoke them, she knew they were true. "You're it for me."

"Yes. Nobody else."

"Nobody." He was her home. The only place she'd ever truly belonged.

"Come on my cock, Soph, show me." He shifted angles, hitting the perfect spot, and she went over the edge.

The orgasm stormed through her in a blinding rush. She came so hard it blurred her vision and left her without sound as it racked through her body in powerful, heart-wrenching waves.

Eyes locked, he followed her over. And in that moment, she opened, like she'd never opened to anyone in her entire life. She surrendered to it, and Ryder, giving in to what she wanted most.

To belong. To him.

Ryder rolled off Sophie, panting for breath and staring up at the ceiling. He ran his hand through his sweat-damp hair. "Holy shit."

Next to him, she laughed. "No kidding."

The interlude at the bar had only whetted their appetite, and after they'd left they'd gone straight to his bed and hadn't left. It was like something had broken between them, and whatever barriers they'd kept had been stripped away.

She felt like his now. Like she'd crawled inside and

become a part of him. He wanted her to stay. There was no getting around that fact. He wasn't ready to bring it up, but he was ready to do something else.

He turned onto his side and, propping his head on the pillow, slid his arm around her waist. A stirring of nerves danced across his skin. He knew her now. How she'd grown up. How she was disconnected from her parents. And while it didn't seem to bother her, it made her detached from a family unit, and he wasn't sure how she'd respond to his question.

Not that it would stop him. "I want to ask you something."

She was all lazy and satiated, content like a cat, and she smiled. "What's that?"

He cleared his throat. "Sunday I'm going to my parents' for dinner. It will be them and my sisters."

She tensed, fractionally. "All right, I can find something to occupy me."

He tightened his hold on her. "No, I want you to come with me."

She blinked. "You want me to come?"

"Yes."

She bit her bottom lip. "But . . ."

"Don't say no. I want them to meet you."

"Why?"

"Because it's important to me." He leaned down and brushed a kiss over her lips. "I want them all to meet you, but especially my mom."

"Why her especially?"

He grinned. "Because she's going to love you."

"Are you sure?" Sophie's expression creased with concern.

"Positive." He pulled her close, rolling over onto his

back so she was draped on top of him. "Please come home with me, Soph."

She relaxed into him. "All right. I will."

"Thank you." He tickled down her spine, like he knew she liked.

She rolled off him, staring up at the ceiling, silent for several minutes before she pulled the sheet up over her breasts, tucking it tight around her before her hands settled. "Ryder?"

"Yes, Sophie?"

Her fingers tightened on the sheet. "I . . ." She trailed off.

He rested his open palm on her stomach. "Do you want to tell me?"

She blinked at him, her dark eyes luminous and filled with secrets. "Tell you what?"

"Whatever it is in your past that makes you leery?" He brushed a kiss over her lips. "I want to know. I've been waiting for you to be ready."

She tugged the sheet higher. "You have?"

"I have."

She shook her head. "I don't know if I can say it."

"I think you can. I think you want to. You're just afraid. But don't worry, I have you."

Her brow furrowed. "I actually believe that."

"Because it's true."

She took a deep breath. "I've never had that before."

He pulled her close. "You have it now."

"It scares me." She shivered against him. "I don't want to lose myself in you."

"You won't." He kissed her temple. "You're too strong for that."

She was vulnerable right now. Maybe more vulnerable

than he'd ever seen her. The desire to protect her, to comfort her sat heavy in his chest.

She clutched at his arm. "That's where you're wrong."

Arm curled around her waist, he tightened his hold on her. "Tell me, and it will lose some of its power over you."

"How do you know that?"

"Because confession is good for the soul."

"Maybe." She bit her bottom lip and sighed. "I want to tell you."

"And I want to hear. So let it all go, darlin'. I'll catch you, I promise."

She nodded. "You know my parents left as soon as I was eighteen."

"I do."

"It wasn't like they gave me a ton of supervision, but they were still around. But suddenly there I was, still a kid, off on her own. I was as crazy as you would think I'd be. I partied, hooked up with guys, was up for anything. It was fun, or at least that's what I told myself. All manic, wild energy. I loved anything dangerous and risky. When I met Tony, he was everything I'd ever wanted in a guy." She darted her gaze up to him. "He was so dangerous, so exciting."

As her words clicked into place with what he understood about her, things started to make sense. He nodded, wanting her to continue. "Go on."

"It started just as you'd expect. We met at a party, and from the second we laid eyes on each other, it was game on. We were like glue from that moment." She cleared her throat, shrugging. "It was crazy. We were crazy. And it felt like I'd finally found my person. That thing I'd lost when Maddie had her accident suddenly found a new home, only it was better because it was with my boyfriend."

"I understand," he murmured, not wanting to interrupt her too much and ruin her flow.

"Over time, things started to change. He started making excuses not to see me, or canceling plans. Sometimes he'd show up hours late, and when I called him on it, he'd tell me I was crazy. I thought he was cheating on me, and he made me believe I was nuts. It went on and on until my life became about him, and his moods, and how he felt about me that day." She smiled, all sad and full of loss.

Ryder squeezed her tighter, wishing he could take it all away from her. "It's okay. Get it all out."

She clutched at the sheet, her knuckles whitening. "Of course he was cheating on me. He made me dependent on him and then made me feel insane for being addicted. It was awful." A tear slipped down her cheek. "And you know the worst thing?"

"What's that?" He smoothed his hand over her tense muscles.

"He left me." She shook her head. "Can you believe that? I didn't wise up, *he* left *me*. And when he did, it felt like the worst kind of abandonment. I lost it. I crawled into my bed and didn't come out until Maddie and Penelope dragged me out. It was the worst time of my life, and once I got my head on straight, I swore I'd never fall for anyone like that again."

He nodded, slowly, and said softly, "And you kept your promise."

"I did." She blinked up at him. "Until you."

He cupped her cheek and ran his thumb down the smooth skin. "I'm not him, Soph."

"I know that." She bit her lip. "But the way you consume me feels the same."

It was a huge admission for her, and all her resistance

and instinctive response to him fell into place. "I won't take advantage of it. Can you at least believe that?"

"I think I can. I want to."

"That's all I can ask for."

She sighed. "This is getting complicated."

It was, but he had faith. Someone this perfect for him couldn't be an accident. "Would you change it?"

She shook her head against his chest. "No, I wouldn't."

"Then that's all that matters." At least, that's what he wanted to believe.

Chapter Twenty-One

Okay, so she was nervous. Sophie didn't have a lot of experience meeting the parents. She kind of stayed away from meeting the parents. But here she was, dressed in a pretty red and white print sundress, ready to meet Ryder's entire family.

She stared at the door leading into the big frame house where he'd grown up. Ryder's childhood home appeared as idyllic as he'd claimed. The two-story home was white with black trim, with a big wraparound porch. It looked exactly what it was, a family home in small-town America.

Completely foreign to her. Everyone who mattered to Ryder was behind that door. She attempted to tug her hand from his, but he tightened his hold as he moved to open the door.

Right before he did, she experienced a swell of panic. "Ryder."

He turned to look at her. "What's wrong?"

She shook her head. "Nothing . . . but . . ."

He shifted, curled his hand behind her neck, and brushed his mouth over hers. "Trust me. They're going to love you."

She clutched at his arm. She couldn't believe how

nervous she was. Butterflies didn't dance in her stomach; they were slamming around in there like it was the head-bangers' ball. "Okay."

He kissed her again.

She closed her eyes, loving the feel of his mouth on hers, wanting it to soak in before she had to be proper for the next five hours.

So, of course, his mom opened the door.

He lifted his head and turned his attention to the older woman with shoulder length chestnut hair and amused blue eyes. He flashed her a grin. "Hey, Mom."

She raised a brow. "I thought I heard you."

Sophie flushed to the roots of her hair. Oh dear God.

Still holding her hand, he tilted his head at her. "This is Sophie."

"I'd hope so, all things considering." Her expression appeared amused, but Sophie really had no idea.

She cleared her throat and held out her hand. "It's nice to meet you, Mrs. Moore."

The older woman waved her hand away and held out her arms, laughing. "None of that." Then she swept Sophie up in a big hug. "I'm so glad you came."

Sophie immediately relaxed and hugged the other woman back. "Thanks for having me."

Ryder's mom released Sophie before waving a hand. "And please, call me Catherine. Even after thirty-six years of marriage, Mrs. Moore still makes me feel like my mother-in-law. Come on in."

They walked into an airy foyer with taupe walls and white trim.

Catherine pointed down the hall. "We're all out back."

The house was modern, light and happy. While Sophie had a hard time picturing the man who did such devious things to her as a boy, she had no trouble seeing raising a family in such a place.

"Your house is lovely," Sophie said, her tone polite.

"Thank you." Catherine craned to peer back at her. "We'll give you a proper tour later, after you've met everyone."

"I'd like that," Sophie said, following the older woman.

Ryder gave her fingers a little squeeze. In response, she squeezed back, realizing what a couple thing it was to do. That somehow, in the last month Ryder had become her significant other, an unexpected turn of events she still wasn't ready to think about. Later she would, but for now she'd focus on having fun and getting a glimpse into the boy he'd been and the family he came from.

They walked through a large, open kitchen—with a table big enough to hold a family of five nestled into an eating nook—before exiting out the back door and onto a spacious deck.

Three sets of eyes turned to look at her from an outdoor table covered by an umbrella.

Ryder's dad smiled at her with the same silver eyes as his son, but his hair was a light dirty blond touched with gray. Except for the coloring, it was like staring at a future version of Ryder. "Well, hello there."

Ryder tugged her forward. "Hey, Dad. This is Sophie." He turned to Sophie and made a gesture that encompassed the whole table. "This is my dad, Ron and my two sisters." He pointed to a striking woman with long dark hair and light silvery-blue eyes, maybe a few years younger than Sophie. "This is Jessica." Then he pointed at a honey-blond girl with blue eyes like her mom's. "And Hailey."

Ryder's sisters were gorgeous. Absolute stunners.

This was one beautiful family, and all of them had clearly hit the genetic jackpot.

Sophie smiled at them. "It's nice to meet you."

"Come on, let's go sit." Catherine walked over to the table and took a seat next to Ryder's dad.

They did, and as soon as Sophie got comfortable, Jessica leaned over the table. Her unusual eyes sparkled with amusement. "So you're the one."

"The one?" Sophie asked, feeling a rush of nerves again.

Jessica laughed. "The one that's got my brother calling and asking what to bring you to eat."

Sophie shrugged. "What can I say? He's a good neighbor."

Ryder rolled his eyes. "Let's get her something to drink before you grill her."

Catherine gestured to the cart next to the table. "What can we get you, Sophie?"

"I'm not at all picky. I'll take whatever's closest."

There were a few minutes of drinks being passed, filled with polite, slightly awkward chitchat. Next time Sophie looked down, a big glass of vodka splashed with lemonade was plopped in front of her.

"I figured it might help take the edge off." Hailey winked, pointing at the pale drink. "This meeting-the-family stuff is hell."

Sophie laughed. "It's not the most relaxed I've ever been."

Jessica picked up her own pale drink and leaned back in her chair. "That's why anytime a guy I'm dating gets any ideas, I instantly break up with him."

Catherine clucked her tongue. "Don't listen to her. She's terrible."

Ryder scowled. "Yeah, don't give her ideas, Jess."

Jessica grinned at Sophie, shrugging. "What can I say, I'm terminally commitment-phobic."

"For no good reason." Catherine shook her head, giving her oldest daughter an exasperated glare. "You grew up with two loving parents and a stable home."

"I like my freedom," Jessica said.

"Yeah, Mom, she don't need no man," Hailey added.

Catherine huffed. "You girls."

Hailey put her crossed arms on the table and said to Sophie, "So tell us everything about you. And we do mean *everything*."

Sophie ran her hand over her glass. "Well, okay, let's see. I'm thirty-one, I live in Chicago, I work in public relations and marketing, I'm an only child and my parents are eccentric, meditating Buddhists that travel the world." She turned to Ryder. "I think that sums it up, don't you?"

Ryder put his hand on the back of her chair. "Not even close."

Hailey turned to her brother. "And what would you add?"

Ryder gave Sophie a once-over and she had to admit she was curious about his answer. "She's smart, funny, high-spirited, and never, ever boring."

Sophie's heart did a quick pitter-pat before she about melted into his gaze. She beamed at him. "Thank you."

He brushed a lock of her hair from her shoulder. "That's just scratching the surface."

Their gazes met and held, and all of a sudden it felt unbearably intimate between them. She glanced away to find four interested people staring at her with smiles on their faces.

She took a drink of her lemonade-spiked vodka and prayed for a change of subject.

Ryder was putting dishes in the sink when his mom finally cornered him. It had been a good afternoon, filled with lots of embarrassing stories about him. They made Sophie laugh, so he didn't mind too much.

He smiled at his mom. "Are you here to grill me?"

"Not grill. I never grill." She leaned back against the counter. "I do like her, though."

"Good. So do I." He opened the dishwasher.

"Do you?"

He turned his attention toward his mom, his instincts going on high alert. "What does that mean?"

"It means I think you more than like her." Her expression turned smug. "In fact, you're in love with her."

He laughed. "It's only been a month. Don't get ahead of yourself."

"I'm not. A mother knows. And you're in love with her." She picked up a pretzel from the bowl on the counter. "You just don't recognize it because you've never felt it before."

His brow furrowed. That was going too far. Yes, he liked her. Yes, he liked her more than any other woman he'd ever been with. But love? It was too soon for love.

"Mom." His tone filled with warning.

She held up her hands. "I know. I know."

He put a cup into the dishwasher. "But I'm glad you like her."

"I do." Her expression creased with worry. "What are you going to do when she leaves?"

Panic about kicked him in the gut. "I'm not going to worry about that right now. She's here, everyone loves her, she's doing a great job, and we're having fun. That's all I'm focusing on at the moment."

"Ryder," she said, her voice taking on that motherly tone from his youth.

"Mooommm." He gave her a quick hug. "It will be okay, I promise."

She smiled. "I don't want you hurt."

It was already too late for that. There'd be no getting around being hurt unless he somehow managed to convince her to stay. Convince her they were worth it. "I'll be fine."

She nodded. "I really do like her, but more than that, I like the way you look at her."

"And how do I look at her?"

"Like she matters. There was a time I'd thought you were incapable of that. I'm happy to be wrong."

He grinned. "I wasn't that bad."

She popped another pretzel into her mouth, chewing slowly before she swallowed. "You've always been a wonderful son and brother, but you've always stayed detached from women. I don't know why you and Jessica are like that. Maybe we raised you too comfortable."

"There's not one thing wrong with how you raised us. You gave us an ideal childhood. There's no fault in that. It's the dream, right?"

"I suppose." She glanced out the window to their family sitting around the table. "But I wonder if maybe we gave you kids the impression that it was easy, so it lost its value."

"Mom, that's not true. You guys are what I value most."

She smiled. "And now you add Sophie to that list."

"I do."

"Then I'm going to give you some unwanted advice."

He sighed, wiping his hands and giving her his complete attention. "All right."

"However it looks, what your father and I have, it's not easy. You have to work for it. Fight for it. Show up every single day and refuse to let it go. That's what it takes to love someone for the long haul."

He glanced at Sophie laughing at something Hailey said. Her blond hair shimmered like gold in the late-afternoon sun. After the initial awkwardness of meeting everyone, she'd slid right in, and he could tell by the way his sisters glommed onto her that she was one of them.

They tried on her Chanel sunglasses, oohing and aahing over them, even though to him they were just sunglasses. They had an extensive discussion about shoes that had his eyes glazing over.

But the biggest tell was that Jessica and Hailey had asked Sophie to their next girls' night out. They loved her. She fit with them.

With him.

He nodded. "I'll remember that."

"Good." His mom gave him a quick hug and tilted her head toward the door. "I'll meet you outside."

She took her leave, and he once again started to load the dishwasher. It would only take him a short time and his mom would be grateful, so he was happy to do it.

Five minutes later, Sophie walked in, smiling at him. "Hi."

He dropped the dish towel and walked over to her, putting his arms around her and brushing his mouth over hers. "Are you glad you came?"

"I am." She rose to her tiptoes, and he bent down so she could whisper in his ear. "But there's one thing I want to see."

"What's that?" He rubbed a hand down her spine, already thinking illicit thoughts.

"I need to see pictures of you as a kid." She leaned back to gaze up at him. "I'm finding I have a hard time picturing it."

"Baby pictures, huh?"

She nodded.

He raised a brow. "What are you willing to do for them?"

"What do you want?" She chuckled huskily.

He had ideas, but he wanted hers instead. "Make me an offer."

She tilted her head, pretending to think about it. "What about your handcuffs?"

And look at that, they were thinking the same thing. He nipped her bottom lip. "You want me to handcuff you to the bed so I can torture you for a few hours?"

A sly cunning lit her brown eyes. "Nope. I want to handcuff *you* to the bed and torture you for a few hours."

He laughed, chucking her under the chin. "Never going to happen."

"Don't be a chicken."

"I'm not, but we both know we like it best when I'm in control."

She batted her lashes. "True, but I want to see how wild I can make you for precisely that reason."

"I can't wait to hear this logic." He grinned down at her, loving everything about her.

"Let me have my way with you until you can't take it anymore." She lowered her voice until it was all smoke and heat. "I know you. I know how you are. The crazier you get, the more domineering you become."

He raised a brow, catching her line of thought. "And?"

Her smile was pure feline. "When I finally let you go, I get to reap the rewards of all that mean, raw sex. A win-win, for both of us."

See, what other woman would want that? Would get that about him? Nobody but Sophie. She was like him that way, insatiable and dirty.

He growled and fisted her hair. "That does sound like a good time."

Her pupils dilated. "And it can be all yours for the low, low price of some pictures."

"Deal." He kissed her, hard and fierce, before pulling her

toward the living room where there was a fireplace mantel full of pictures.

When they stood in front of it, she picked up a picture of him when he was about five, seated on a bike. She smiled. "Is this you?"

"It is." He wasn't looking at the picture, but at her.

She traced her fingers over the wooden frame. "You were adorable."

He chuckled. "Don't I look like a badass?"

"You look like an angel."

He mock scowled. "No way. Look at me, I'm a rebel." In the photo, he wore a Star Wars R2D2 T-shirt, Darth Vader Underoos, and gym shoes.

She laughed. "Do you think your mom would give it to me?"

"Like I'd let her. There is no way I'm handing over blackmail material with your evil streak."

She turned her attention to him, her eyes narrowed with menace. "Mark my words, this picture will be mine."

He rolled his eyes at her.

She laughed and moved on down the mantel that contained his childhood memories. She picked up one picture after another, studying it carefully, asking a few questions and moving on.

She reached the end and picked up a family picture of the five of them from a couple of years ago. "Where was this from?"

"Christmas." He curved a hand around her hips. "We have a cabin in the woods, and every Christmas we go up there, just us."

Her head tilted as she stared at the picture. "Does your mom make hot chocolate?"

"Only if it's laced with alcohol."

She laughed, the sound shooting straight through him. "Do you have traditions?"

He squeezed her. "Yeah."

The wistfulness in her tone almost broke him. "What are they?"

"We go up a few days early and decorate the tree. Then we laze around. We talk, play games, and bake cookies, eating half the dough and making the other half. Then on Christmas Eve we have a big dinner and my mom gives us Christmas pajamas."

She jerked her head up. "You have Christmas pajamas?"

He chuckled. "Yes, more than I care to admit to."

Her whole face lit up. "Will you wear them for me?"

"That will require additional negotiation."

"What a hardship." She puffed out her bottom lip in a pout before returning her attention to the picture. "And then what?"

He walked her through the rest of their Christmas tradition. "We stay up late, drink and eat too much before going to bed and waking up to open presents the next morning."

She rubbed her hand over the frame again, and when she spoke, her voice was longing. "It's like a Hallmark card. What's it like to grow up like that?"

He thought of her parents, giving her a roof over her head but no real home to latch onto. How must that have been for her? Especially in contrast to her best friend's big, loving family.

He put his arm on the mantel, and looked down at her. "It was really awesome."

"You're lucky, I hope you know that."

"I do." There were shadows hidden in her eyes as he asked her, "What did you do for Christmas?"

She put the frame down and shrugged. "Nothing. My

parents thought Christmas was too commercial and didn't want to support the consumerism economy. Usually, if they weren't hosting some sort of hostel for strays, they made me go to a soup kitchen and help the poor." Her smile quivered in the corners. "So at least I was doing something good for humanity."

He scowled. "They didn't give you anything?"

"Only handmade gifts we were allowed to spend zero dollars on."

He shook his head. "That explains some of your shopping habits."

Some of her tension lightened and she batted his arm. "I'm a girl. That explains my shopping habits. But it wasn't too bad. Once I got older and had a job, Penelope, Maddie, and I exchanged gifts, and Mr. and Mrs. Donovan always let us come over late on Christmas. So I got to experience the holidays by proxy."

He looked down at this tiny slip of a woman who'd thrown his entire life for a loop, and he wanted to give her everything. He leaned down and kissed her. "You deserve a proper Christmas."

She shrugged. "It was fine."

It wasn't, but he could tell she wasn't comfortable talking about it any longer. So he let it go. "When we go to Chicago, are you going to show me your pictures?"

Her face lit up. "Do you want to see them?"

"I want to know everything about you, Sophie."

Her eyes grew bright, as though it surprised her. "Okay."

Deep down, two things hit him at once.

Sophie was surprised because she'd never had someone want to know all about her before. Yes, her friends loved her, but her foundation—her parents, who clearly put their own ideology before their daughter's happiness—she had no idea what that was like. The only boy she'd ever loved had manipulated her and abandoned her. She had no real concept of something he'd been given so freely and unconditionally he'd taken it for granted. He wanted to change that for her.

His mom was right.

He was in love with Sophie Kincaid.

Chapter Twenty-Two

Sophie sat at Penelope's table and took a deep breath. She was back in Chicago. As she and Ryder had driven down Lake Shore Drive, the top to her Porsche down, she'd gazed at the skyline that represented everything she'd always associated with home. Her thoughts were overwhelmingly on how glad she was that Ryder was with her.

After they'd settled into their hotel, they'd headed over to Evan and Penelope's. The four of them had lunch, and then the boys had gone off to meet Shane and play some sport to blow off steam from the car ride to Chicago, and she got to catch up on her girl time.

Everything was perfect.

Sophie grinned at her friend. "First things first. We need to go shopping right this second. I'm in withdrawal." She held up her hand and started ticking off her fingers. "I want to go to Nordstrom, Bloomingdale's, Sephora, and Agent Provocateur. If we still have time, we can cruise down Michigan Avenue."

Penelope laughed. "Let's digest a bit and catch up. Then I promise we'll hit the town and you can spend all your money."

Sophie rubbed her palms together. "I can't wait. I miss it so much."

Penelope jabbed a finger at her. "Hey! I think you miss shopping more than me."

Sophie shook her head. "Not true. In fairness, I've seen you more, and we FaceTimed last week. I also called you two days ago and we talked for forty-five minutes. All we've missed by me living in Revival is lunch dates."

Penelope raised a brow. "True. And look at the benefits you get in return."

"So true." The dreamy sigh escaped from her lips before she could stop it.

"Hmmm . . . It's like that, is it?" Penelope picked up her iced tea. "I'm not sure I've ever heard you make such a girly sound."

Sophie wrinkled her nose. "It's obnoxious, isn't it?"

"No, it's great." Penelope's voice took on a serious quality. "He really makes you happy, and that's a good thing."

Sophie bit her lip. "It's like he fits me somehow, you know? And he's up for anything and everything I want to do. I told him maybe we'd go to Great America on Sunday, and he just laughed and agreed. What kind of man would agree to go to Great America on a weekend just to make me happy?"

Penelope tucked a hand behind her ear. "Not many. Evan wouldn't."

"Ha! Evan would so totally do that for you, not that you'd ever do anything crazy like go on a roller coaster."

All prim and proper, Penelope straightened in her chair. "Thrill rides are overrated."

"Speak for yourself." Sophie winked. "I'm sleeping with my own personal thrill ride every night."

Penelope grinned. "I guess that explains the drive to Agent Provocateur."

"Duh." She always had to talk Penelope into buying anything impractical, so she patted her friend's hand. "I insist you shop too, and Evan can thank me later. We'll get you something super slutty and completely unlike you to shock him with."

"I'm not sure Evan can be shocked."

"You'll have to test the theory."

"Sounds like a plan." Penelope tilted her head to the side. "Have you thought about what you're going to do?"

"About what?"

Penelope shrugged her shoulder. "About your relationship with Ryder?"

"I don't want to think about it yet, I just want to enjoy what we have now."

Penelope slowly nodded. "So you haven't talked about it?"

By unspoken agreement they didn't discuss their relationship. It was like once they'd decided they were too invested to walk away, they only lived in the moment, not wanting to think about all the reasons they'd been throwing at each other since they met. Sophie shrugged. "We have time, there's no hurry."

"Have you considered staying in Revival?" Penelope's tone was light, curious.

Her chest did a strange little squeeze. "Why would you even think that? You know I live here."

Penelope took a sip of tea before placing it gently on the table. "Honestly?"

"Yeah, honestly." Sophie's chin shot up.

"You seem really happy. Not just with Ryder, but with everything. You are excited about the work you're doing. The friends you're making. When I talk to you, you sound happier than I've heard you sound in a long, long time."

Sophie bit her lip. Maybe she'd stopped complaining

about living in Revival, and yes, she was having a good time. Yes, she'd even made new friends. She and Darcy Strong had hit it off so well, they'd taken to weekly lunches. And maybe she'd started thinking about her blog again, and a different angle niggled at her, but that didn't mean she wanted to leave Chicago. Chicago was the only foundation she'd ever had. She couldn't lose it.

Sophie shrugged. "I'm making the best of it."

"The only thing you seem to miss is shopping." Penelope creased her napkin into a razor-sharp edge. "It's something to think about."

Sophie looked away. "I don't want to think about it right now, okay? I just want to have fun."

Penelope studied her. "You know you're in love with him, don't you?"

Sophie gaped at her friend in horror. "I am not."

Penelope's brows furrowed. "Yeah, Soph. You are. And he's in love with you. It's written all over the both of you."

Panic, bright and pure, shot through her. She could not handle this right now. She didn't want to think about it. She screeched, "Ryder is not in love with me and I'm not in love with him. We're having a good time. Don't go and ruin it."

"And being in love would ruin it?"

"Yes!"

"How?" Penelope's furrow deepened.

She didn't know quite how because she didn't even know what to do with the information. She *did not* love Ryder. That was impossible.

Yes, she spent all her time with him, and they practically lived together, and she wanted to talk to him all the time, and they texted all day when they were apart, and he knew all her innermost thoughts and understood her like no one else, and they had the best sex on the planet, but that didn't mean she *loved* him. And there was no way he could love her.

That was just crazy.

Sophie rolled her eyes. "Oh my God, Pen, don't be such a planner. Are you ready to go shopping?"

Penelope's mouth creased, and she studied Sophie for a few moments before she nodded. "All right, let's go."

Ryder and Evan had played racquetball and then ended up at his house shooting the shit and watching a Cubs game while they waited for their women to return from shopping. The last time he'd spoken to Sophie, she sounded like she'd been let loose in a candy store and rode a sugar high.

"I'm scared." Ryder tossed his phone on the table after Sophie sent him a picture of red shoes. "I'm getting texts about shoes now."

Evan laughed. "I have no experience with a woman who loves shopping, but I fear for your soul. Penelope's too practical to get caught up in the adrenaline rush other women seem to experience."

Ryder shook his head. "How exactly did they become best friends? They're so opposite."

Evan shrugged. "Penelope keeps Sophie and Maddie from going crazy, and they keep her from becoming a workaholic."

Ryder thought of Sophie's parents and figured Penelope provided the grounding presence she lacked growing up. "I'm glad she has them."

A sly smile slid over Evan's features. "Sophie's always been a bit of a wild one, I never thought anyone could tame her."

He laughed. "I haven't tamed her. Don't see the point. I like her wild."

Loved her wild. But since he had no idea what to do with that piece of knowledge, he avoided thinking about it too much.

"Good point," Evan said, scrubbing a hand over his jaw. "So what are you going to do about her?"

"Do about her?"

Evan grinned. "Figured we'd better get to the point instead of beating around the bush."

"Do you mean about her coming back to Chicago?"

"Yeah."

Ryder shrugged. "I don't know yet. I'm letting it play out for a bit longer."

Evan narrowed his eyes. "Are you hoping she'll stay?"

The hope sat in the pit of his stomach. "Yeah."

Evan shook his head. "I can't imagine her living in a small town."

"Why's that? Everyone loves her, she's great at the job she's been hired to do, and she's having fun."

"It's just hard for me to picture." Evan shot him a sideways glance. "You could move to Chicago."

"I could," he said carefully. Although it was premature, he'd entertained the idea. But he had a job that didn't exactly translate to Chicago PD, and his family was in Revival. And, well, he couldn't quite get rid of the notion that she was supposed to stay in Revival.

It was like she belonged there, if she'd let herself.

Although maybe that was wishful thinking.

He didn't want to discuss it further, so he shrugged. "We're a long way from that."

Evan chuckled.

Ryder raised a brow. "What?"

"Nothing. It's nice to be on the other side of this."

"Side of what?"

"When everyone sees how deep in you are except the two people involved. It hasn't been too long since I was there. It sucks when you're in the thick of it, but turns out it's pretty fucking funny from the other side."

Ryder sat back and didn't say anything. He knew he was in the thick of it, but he was pretty sure Sophie wanted no part of that discussion. And he was content to ignore it. Content to show her how good it was between them.

The front door opened and Sophie bounded in, followed by a more poised Penelope, who looked at her friend with a loving exasperation.

Sophie dropped about twenty bags onto the floor before rooting around in the middle of them to come up holding a pink and black bag. She ran over, held it out in front of his face, and said, "Do you understand what I hold in this bag?"

Ryder hadn't a clue. He sat back on the couch. "Can't say I do, darlin'."

She shook the bag, which had tufts of tissue paper sticking out of it. "This is going to rock your world."

He laughed. "And how's that?"

She shook it again, her entire face practically glowing with excitement. "The contents of this package come from the best lingerie store known to man. Do you understand?"

"I see." He grinned at her, loving her enthusiasm.

Evan peered at Penelope. "You don't happen to have one of those bags as well, do you, Pen?"

She gave him a very prim look and crossed her arms over her chest. "Of course."

"Excellent," Evan said.

They seemed to share a private look that told Ryder that Penelope Donovan was only proper on the outside.

"I think both you guys are going to be happy," Sophie said.

"On that note." Ryder glanced down at her. "You ready to go?"

"Yeah." She beamed up at him, and his heart skipped a beat.

He leaned down and whispered in her ear, "You know you're still going to get fucked before dinner."

"Oh, I know." She brushed her lips against his cheek. "Just not in expensive, slutty lingerie."

"How slutty?"

"You'll find out."

"Tease."

"Absolutely."

She was the absolute best.

Over the third course of their meal, Sophie smiled at Ryder. "So what do you think?"

His gaze hooded. "I think it would taste a lot better if I knew what you were wearing under your dress. Other than it not being black, I can't tell a thing."

Sophie wore a white dress that dipped onto her shoulders, hugged her curves, and fell to her knees. It was form fitting and she couldn't be happier with how it looked on her, but it was nothing compared to what was underneath.

She took a bit of goat cheese, sliding it off her fork with her tongue, moaning a little at the tangy flavor. She waved the utensil. "Do you like the restaurant? I chose it with you in mind."

"I do. Is it places like this that made your blog so successful?"

"It is." She glanced around the upscale pub. It was one of her favorite places in the city, so much so that she'd become friends with the owner and his significant other. "This was one of the last places I reviewed. I love hidden gems and this was a unique idea. Whoever would have thought of combining upscale dining with pub food?"

He sat back in his chair and took a sip off one of the beers in his flight, a dark amber ale made locally. "Do you miss it?"

"Chicago?"

Jaw tightening, he nodded. "You haven't mentioned it in a while."

Fear knotted tight in her sternum. This wasn't a conversation she wanted to have. Not now, when everything was so perfect between them. She smiled. "You've been keeping me so busy it's hard to mind."

His lashes flickered. "But do you?"

She shrugged one shoulder. "This is my home. Of course I miss it."

"What do you miss?"

Time to distract. "Wouldn't you rather find out what I'm wearing under this dress?"

He studied her, intent and coplike, and she resisted the urge to squirm in her seat. "Can't we do both?"

Ugh. First Penelope and now him. She didn't want to talk about this. She wanted to have fun, show Ryder the city, and have sex all night. She didn't want to think about anything serious. Her mind scrambled for what to say, but she was saved when she heard her name behind her. "Sophie, darling girl, you've come back to me."

A muscle in Ryder's jaw jumped as he looked over her shoulder. Sophie peered around to see the chef and owner coming their way.

She sprang from her seat and opened her arms to her friend. "John-Paul! It's so good to see you."

The man, a few years older than her, swooped her up in a bear hug. Very handsome, he was around five-ten and had sharp cheekbones, brown eyes, and sandy hair.

He kissed her on both cheeks, saying in his French-accented English, "You vixen, why didn't you call?"

She laughed. "I wanted to surprise you."

"I am. I am thrilled you're here. I've missed you, and François has been asking for you." After she'd written her review, he'd called her personally to thank her for the glowing recommendation and invited her to a private dinner. Sophie couldn't refuse such an offer, and she'd become fast friends with John-Paul and his partner, François.

John-Paul looked past her and gestured. "And who do we have here?"

Sophie turned to face Ryder, whose expression appeared too calm, contrasting the tension radiating off him. "This is Ryder, my . . ." She trailed off and realized she had no idea how to identify him. She'd never needed to. In Revival, everyone knew they were together. "My . . ." Friend was too impersonal, boyfriend too juvenile, and significant other too clinical. "My . . . person."

John-Paul beamed and held out his hand. "Well, hello, Sophie's person."

Sophie said, "John-Paul is the owner and chef of this place."

Ryder shook the offered hand, nodding. "Nice place you have here."

"Thank you." John-Paul put his arm around Sophie's shoulders and pulled her close, kissing her temple. "Your handsome man is looking as though he may murder me. Perhaps you should put him out of his misery."

Sophie laughed, tilting her head. "John-Paul is married to a French media mogul named François."

Ryder's expression instantly eased and he had the good nature to shrug. "Sorry. I'm feeling . . . protective."

John-Paul graciously lowered his head. "I understand." The door opened and he glanced over in that direction.

"Ah, how lucky, there's François now. One moment, I'll bring him over, as I know he would love to see you."

He returned a moment later with an equally gorgeous man with jet-black hair and vivid blue eyes.

François swept her up, again kissing her on both cheeks. "Sophie, I've been thinking of you and was going to give you a call, but here you are. What a happy coincidence."

"Oh? How so?" she asked, winking at Ryder.

He didn't wink back; instead he studied her as though he'd never quite seen her before. Before she could think any more on it, François's voice pulled her back to him.

"My vice president of marketing left for a job in New York, and you are the perfect person to fill the position. Of course, we'll need to go through the formalities of an interview with other members of the team." He laughed, waving a little. "But I am the boss and have the final say. As soon as he handed me his resignation, I told John-Paul you were the only person I'd accept. I'm hoping to get you in for an interview in the next couple of weeks."

Sophie's heart leapt with excitement. This was huge. François's company was one of the top companies in Chicago. A job with him would make her entire career. And he was in media, so she'd be invited everywhere. Attend all the best parties, travel the world.

She'd get to come home. She'd have her old life back, only better.

She turned to Ryder, ready to share it all with him. Ready to jump up and down in elation. Everything stilled. The excitement drained away. As reality sank in, her stomach turned to lead.

But it would cost her Ryder.

Chapter Twenty-Three

The ride back to the hotel had been virtually silent. Ryder looked out the window at the Chicago skyline, took a sip of his scotch, poured from a tiny bottle out of the mini-fridge, and mentally prepared himself to have his first fight with Sophie.

Because it was coming.

It hung in the air, thick and dark and dangerous.

She'd kicked off her shoes and sat on the edge of the bed, looking unsure and remote. Expressions he wasn't used to seeing on her face.

If he was honest, he didn't want to start, even though he knew deep in his bones they couldn't avoid the discussion any longer. Only, he didn't know where to go from here.

This hadn't been what he'd anticipated.

He'd planned on being in her by now. Not sitting here in silence, without a clue what to say.

They'd carefully avoided any and all thoughts of their future, but now it had caught up with them and refused to be denied.

Sitting there in that room, he came face-to-face with the truth. For the first time in his life, he was in love, and it was a goddamn mess.

He'd be more hopeful, more sure something would work out, if only it hadn't been for the look on her face. The resignation that crossed her features and told him she wasn't even considering a future with him as an option.

He had no experience with heartbreak. But from what he could tell, he didn't want any part of it.

She shifted on the bed and cleared her throat. "Even if something does happen, I won't leave before the festival."

His attention snapped toward her, and his expression must have been as fierce as he felt, because she shrank back a little. In a harsh voice he asked, "Do you think I'm upset about the damn festival?"

Her hands clenched, twisting in her lap, a gesture so unlike her he could only guess how uneasy she must be. "No, I was just trying to say . . ." Another tug at a ring she wore on her middle finger. "Well, that if I get that job, I won't leave right away."

He blinked at her, and the irony sank in a little deeper. He scoffed, his laughter harsh and bitter.

"What?" She made a helpless gesture. "It might not even happen. Yes, it's possible, maybe even probable, but you never know with these companies. Things change all the time at a drop of a hat. So let's worry about it then."

More than anything, he wanted to agree. He could see it all play out. He'd nod, she'd stand up, strip out of her dress. He'd see her in her fancy, slutty underwear, she'd walk over to him, and he'd pull her down on his lap, sink into her mouth, and forget all about tonight.

They'd go on their adventure tomorrow, spend time with her friends, and go back to Revival. Once they returned home, they'd spend all their time together and continue to ignore the elephant in the room.

It was what she wanted.

It was what he wanted too.

But he couldn't open his mouth and speak the words that would make it happen.

Instead he said nothing, just drank his scotch and looked out the window.

"Ryder?" Her tone was tinged with a bit of desperation. "I didn't know, but it's premature to get worried about it now."

He turned to face her and couldn't stop the truth from coming to his lips. "I saw your face when he told you about the job."

Her brow furrowed. "What do you mean?"

That this was the first thing to pop out of his mouth helped him pinpoint exactly what upset him. Helped him acknowledge that the hope he'd been harboring had just been just that.

Hope. Foolish wishful thinking, really. Nothing more, nothing less.

For Sophie, he was a pit stop on the way back to her regularly scheduled life.

For him, she was his life.

He forced the words from his throat. "I mean I saw your face. You were excited."

She bit her bottom lip and shrugged. "It's a fantastic opportunity. This is one of the best companies in Chicago. This will make my career. Bring me back to my life. Should I apologize for that?"

"No. You shouldn't." Because she shouldn't. She should be thrilled and happy, and he didn't want to ruin it for her. "I'm happy for you, Soph. You are brilliant and charismatic and a force to be reckoned with. You deserve the life and career you want, and François would be a fool not to give you that position. Congratulations."

"Don't congratulate me yet. It's nothing definite."

He blew out a breath. "That's not really the point."

Silence grew like a thorn bush directly between them, making him feel distant and removed from her.

Her brow creased. "What's the point?"

"Do you want to talk about our future?"

Fear darkened her expression. Almost violently, she shook her head. "There's nothing to talk about yet. Can't you see that? Nothing has changed."

But it had changed for him. He peered out the window. He was invested in her. He tightened his hand around his glass. "I'd like to at least discuss it. Talk about options."

"No!" The word was sharp on her lips. "Let's forget it and focus on having fun."

He was in love with her and wanted to talk about a future, or at least the possibility of one, and she wanted to have fun. He'd been fooling himself. She didn't see a future with him. That wasn't even on her radar. It wasn't even a consideration.

Now that he knew, he couldn't un-know, and as much as he wanted to pretend this changed nothing for him, that wasn't an option. So he forced the words from his tight throat. "We're at an impasse, Sophie."

Panic filled her face, and a flush broke out on her chest. She shook her head. "No, we're not. Why are you doing this? We don't even know what's going to happen. Just forget about it until I tell you it's serious. Okay?"

He leaned forward on his elbows and dug his thumbs into his eye sockets. "You don't understand."

"What don't I understand? It's the same situation as always since we started this."

"And what's that situation as you understand it?"

Her gaze skittered away. "We're having a good time. We laugh and have great sex. We like each other. We knew it was stupid to get involved and decided to do it anyway.

I don't understand why a potential job offer needs to change anything. Why stop until we're forced to?"

Shit. Had he misread the situation or what? He shrugged. "I'm sorry. Maybe it's unfair. Hell, it probably is. But I don't think I can be your fuck buddy anymore."

"I didn't say that." She bounded off the bed and pointed an accusing finger at him. "Don't twist my words. I never called you a fuck buddy."

He gave her a level look. "You want me to give you a good time and orgasms until you take off back to your real life, isn't that what you're saying?"

She screamed, a short burst of sound. "Why do you have to make it sound like that?"

"How else can it sound? Explain how I'm wrong, Sophie." His voice rose as the barely repressed anger beat at his ribs.

"What's wrong with what we're doing? Everything is great between us."

"Yes, it's great. You're great." He shook his head. "I'm sorry, but it's not enough."

It wasn't, no matter how much he wanted it to be. No matter how much this conversation was killing him.

She jerked back as though he'd slapped her. "Not enough? I'm not enough for you?"

"Don't you understand?"

She shook her head. "No, I don't understand at all. You've always known I was leaving, Ryder. I've never pretended anything else. We've never had a future. If I get the job, it will take at least a month to go through all the interviews and make sure everything is good in Revival. So what's the difference between one month and three? If anything, it's better. You're not being fair."

The difference was he loved her, but that was his problem, not hers. He'd gone and changed the rules, not her.

"You're right. You've always been up front. You're not to blame. This is on me. It's my problem. I'm sorry, but I just can't do this anymore."

"Why?" Her voice, strained and helpless sounding, tugged inside him and made him ache.

He wanted to yell at her that he'd stupidly gone and fallen in love with her and convinced himself that was enough. His mother's words that day at the sink came rushing back to him. She was right.

He'd believed it was easy. Believed love and hope and optimism were enough. But he'd been wrong.

And he refused to lay that at Sophie's feet.

He shrugged, scrubbed a hand over his jaw, and told her not the why, but still the truth. "It's too hard for me, Soph."

Tears filled her big brown eyes, and she shook her head. "I don't understand. How is being apart better than being together?"

"It just is. For me, it is. I'm sorry." He clasped his hands and looked out over this fucking city.

For her, their relationship began and ended with her time in Revival. He was a diversion. He'd seen it in her eyes. The prospect of "them" wasn't on her radar. He'd even pressed her to talk about it, to stay and figure it out, but that she wouldn't gave him no other option.

"So now what?"

He glanced at the bed, rumpled from the time they'd spent in it that afternoon. All the things he'd done to her, driving them both to the very edge, before pulling back and starting all over again. He studied her in her white dress, trying to picture never touching her body again and finding he couldn't. He couldn't stand the thought of living without her, but he couldn't ignore the truth anymore.

He loved her and she didn't love him in return.

He dragged a hand through his hair. "If you give me fifteen minutes, I can get out of here."

"But where will you go?" Her voice shook.

"Back to Revival."

"How will you get there?"

"I'll find a way." They'd taken her car, but and even if they hadn't, he wouldn't leave her stranded there. He could probably rent a bike to get him home.

She chewed on her bottom lip. "I'll go with you."

"Sophie."

She blinked bright eyes at him. "What?"

"Stay."

"But—"

He shook his head. "I can't be around you right now."

"Oh." She frowned. "Okay." She pointed to the door and picked up a key card. "I'll just go down to the bar until you . . ." She swallowed hard and he knew she fought back the urge to cry. "Leave."

Then she turned on her heels and was gone.

He picked up his cell phone and pressed Charlie's number.

He answered on the second ring. "What's up? I thought you were in Chicago."

"I am."

"Then why are you calling me instead of in bed with the lovely Sophie?"

"Long story. I need a favor."

"What's that?"

"Help get me the fuck out of here."

Silence ticked over the line. "That bad?"

"That bad."

"Give me five. I'll get you transport and hook you up with the details as soon as I have them."

"Thanks." He hung up.

So that was that. Now to figure out how to pick up the pieces and go on with his life.

Without her.

Sophie sat on the barstool shaking all over. She couldn't believe this was happening. Ryder didn't want to see her anymore because of a job that might not even happen?

It was so unfair.

She thought about calling Penelope, who'd come to her in a heartbeat, but couldn't make the call. She couldn't admit to her friend he'd abandoned her. Was this forever to be the story of her life?

It was a complete one-eighty, and no matter how she attempted to wrap her arms around it, nothing about his actions made any sense to her.

How could he leave her like this? Didn't he understand how much she needed him?

It served her right. This was why she never depended on anyone. When it came down to it, there was something missing inside her that made it easy for people to detach from her.

Maybe she was just unlovable.

Her phone beeped and her heart surged at Ryder's name on her screen. Silently praying he'd changed his mind, she scrambled for the cell. Her stomach dropped to her toes when she saw the words written across the screen. Two little words that changed everything.

I'm gone.

He'd left her. It was over.

She felt exactly how she'd expected to feel when it ended. Crushed. Defeated. Hopeless despair. The weight sitting on her chest, threatening to destroy her from the inside out, didn't surprise her. She'd prepared for it.

But what she didn't understand was why he'd chosen to have this soul-sucking heartbreak now instead of later, when they would be forced to be apart.

They could have weeks, months together—so why?

How could he not want to spend what time they had left together?

The bartender came over, an older woman in her fifties with a friendly, warm motherly smile. "What can I get you, doll face?"

Sophie took one look at the woman and burst into tears.

The woman didn't even blink an eye. She just patted her hand and tsked. "Hang on, I know just the thing."

Sophie picked up a napkin and attempted to sob discreetly until the bartender returned and put down a drink. "It's a mint julep. My mama was Southern and said it was the only drink for heartbreak."

Sophie hiccupped. "Thank you."

"Boy troubles?"

Sophie nodded, sniffing. "Men suck."

"Yep, they do. Want to tell me about it?" The hotel bar was nearly empty, and she winked at Sophie. "It will kill the time and make you feel better."

Sophie wept for a good minute before she sobbed out, "I met this guy, and he doesn't live here and I do, and I might have a job offer and he left me because of it."

The bartender frowned. "You don't want a man that doesn't support your career."

"I know, right?" Sophie wailed, bursting into fresh tears. "I'm so confused. I don't know what to do."

"Maybe you could try talking to him, telling him how important your job is."

Sophie shook her head. "He told me he can't do it anymore. That it's been fun, but that he can't be my"—she sobbed—"my . . . my . . . fuck buddy."

"Hmm . . . that doesn't sound right." The older woman tilted her head. "In my experience, there's only one reason a man would ever give up sex."

"Why's that?"

"Love, doll face. When they're in love and they don't know what to do with all their feelings."

Sophie wanted so badly to believe that, but she knew it wasn't true. She'd seen how love worked. She'd never experienced it herself, but she'd seen it with the Donovans all her life. When you loved someone, you stuck it out. You fought. Clawed your way out of the wreckage for it.

But Ryder had left and said he didn't want anything to do with her.

She might not know for herself, but she knew how it was supposed to look. Bailing wasn't it.

She shook her head. "Trust me, he doesn't love me."

Nobody did. That was just the way things were for her. She'd accepted that a long time ago when her parents got on a plane and didn't look back.

Deep in her heart she'd thought Ryder was different.

Turned out, she was wrong.

Chapter Twenty-Four

Heartbreak was far worse than she'd imagined. Far, far worse.

Sophie had stayed with the nice, motherly bartender for a couple hours, pouring out her troubles while the older woman listened, clucked, and sympathized.

Sophie had assumed she'd feel better after, because talking always had a way of making her feel better.

But instead she felt like there was something vital missing inside her.

When talking hadn't worked, she'd wandered aimlessly around the city, even though it was far too late to be out by herself, trying to piece together what exactly had gone wrong. In the end, she'd determined she should have followed her instincts and stayed away from Ryder. Her gut had tried to steer her away from him, but she'd gone and dove in headfirst and now she had to pay the price.

Only the price was far too steep.

She'd ended relationships with men she'd cared for before, and yeah, it hurt and it sucked and she'd cried, but this was different.

This morning, she'd finally broken down and called

Penelope, who would be arriving at any minute. After, she'd go back home to Revival and finish the job she'd been hired for. As much as she wanted to run away and never have to see Ryder again, she couldn't do that to Griffin, or the town. She cared too much about the job she was doing.

And she didn't tuck tail and run. That wasn't her nature.

There was a knock on the door, and when she opened it, Penelope stood there with a tray of two huge coffees and a box from one of her favorite places, the Doughnut Vault. One look at her friend and she started to cry.

Penelope's face creased. "Oh dear." She walked into the room in that efficient way she had, putting her offerings on the table before turning back to Sophie to give her a big hug.

Which only made her cry harder.

Penelope rocked her. "What happened? You guys were so happy when you left. And why didn't you call me sooner?"

Sophie sobbed and sniffed and generally made a spectacle of herself, hoping at the end it would act as a cathartic release. Cleanse her and put her back on the track of feeling human again.

It didn't work.

At the end, her misery wouldn't abate.

They moved to the couch, and she huddled in the corner with a blanket on while Penelope shuffled around the room to bring her coffee and other girl necessities. When everything was set up to her satisfaction, Penelope sat next to her and patted her knee. "Tell me what happened."

"I took him to John-Paul's pub last night, and his partner, you remember François, showed up and he said he wanted me for his VP of marketing." Tears spilled over

Sophie's cheeks. "It's my dream job, Pen. It blows my last job out of the water. And I'd be awesome at it."

"Ah, I see," Penelope said, as though it explained everything.

"Ryder wasn't happy."

"What do you mean he wasn't happy?"

"He said he saw how excited I was about the job and he couldn't be with me anymore." She took a tissue from the box Penelope had brought over and wiped her eyes. "Why is it wrong for me to be excited?"

"Oh, Sophie. Of course you should be excited. It's a huge opportunity for you." Penelope shook her head.

"Exactly."

"Is there more?"

Sophie shook her head. "He wanted to talk about our future, but I can't. Not yet. I'm not ready and don't want to face it."

"Maybe it got to be too much for him."

"*What's* too much for him? Why can't he enjoy the time we have left? Nothing has changed."

"Sometimes, your emotions and what you want changes." Penelope's forehead pulled as her brows creased.

"But my time in Revival has always been temporary. I've always been clear about that. Six months, tops."

Penelope patted her leg. "Things happen, and it throws you for a loop. It crystalizes your feelings, and once you know the truth, you can't go back."

Sophie twisted her damp tissue. "I don't understand."

Penelope sighed. "It's like when I had that pregnancy scare when I first got back together with Evan. It scared me because deep down it forced me to confront what I really wanted. A life that included Evan. A tie to him that couldn't break us. It felt . . . weak somehow for me to want that. I hated it, but what was even worse was I couldn't pretend it wasn't true. So I did everything I could to push him away because I was terrified he didn't want the same thing, despite all the evidence to the contrary."

Through her misery, Sophie tried, but it eluded her. "What are you saying?"

Penelope's expression filled with concern. "I think, maybe, hearing the job offer made Ryder realize the truth."

Sophie blinked watery eyes at her friend, this woman who'd been her rock for twenty years, hoping she had the answers. "What's the truth?"

Penelope glanced over Sophie's shoulder out at the city skyline. "He had hope, Soph."

"That I was going to stay in Revival?"

Penelope shrugged. "We can't know what he hoped. But I think he hoped you had a future, or at least the possibility of a future. Who knows what that looked like to him."

"But that's impossible. I live here. He lives there. We never had a future. We just have now."

Penelope tilted her head. "There are always options. He could move, you could move. Look at James and Gracie, they go back and forth. There are plenty of options you could talk about."

Why didn't Penelope understand that it didn't work that way with her? "You don't get it. I have to take this job, and there's no way I can ask Ryder to move with me."

"Why?"

"Because. His life is there. His friends and family and job. He belongs in Revival. I won't take that from him." She couldn't. She'd always been an obligation, and she refused to be that for Ryder.

Penelope's expression creased with concern. "And that's why he can't continue to be with you."

Sophie started to cry again, feeling hopeless and lost. "I don't understand!"

Penelope gripped her hand. "Sophie, the man is in love with you. You can't seem to see it, but it's obvious to everyone else. He loves you and you're leaving. In simplest terms, he just can't take it. Being with you, knowing you're already gone is worse for him. You're going to have to accept it and let him go."

Sophie shook her head. "It can't be."

"Why?"

Sophie scoffed. "Because guys don't fall irrevocably in love with me. That's how it is with you and Maddie. That's not how it works for me."

Penelope raised her eyes to the ceiling. "You're so stubborn."

"He left, Pen. Left." Anger erased some of her grief. "Look me in the eye and tell me when you acted like a complete butthead by pushing Evan away, that he ever left your side."

Penelope's gaze lowered. "We had different issues."

"But the actions are what matter. Ryder chose to leave. Evan wouldn't have ever left you and you know it. That man is like glue on you, same way Mitch is with Maddie, and Shane with Cecilia, and James with Gracie. Ryder—" She waved a hand in the air. "You get the picture. Ryder bailed over a job I don't even have yet. How is that love?"

Penelope took a deep breath and slowly exhaled. "I don't know how to make you understand."

Indignant, and ready to latch onto it instead of the grief, Sophie plopped back against the couch. "That's because you know I'm right."

Her friend tilted her head, her mink-like hair swaying over one shoulder. "Do you love Ryder?"

The question made her heart do a strange pitter-patter. "I don't know. I care about him a lot. I miss him. I want him. I feel horrid. But I don't even know what love is. Why do I have to define it?"

"You're scared."

She was. Terrified. Only she didn't know what she was so afraid of. It was like staring into a dark abyss she didn't understand or couldn't make sense of. She didn't want to think about it. It was too hard. She saw the glimmer of something she'd never had before with Ryder, but she didn't know what to do about it.

Not that it mattered, because they were over.

She shrugged.

"He gets you, Sophie. *Really* gets you. And that's rare."

She wanted to reject it, because it was true but it was over. It was too hard to think about what she'd just lost. She frowned. "We have chemistry and awesome sex."

Penelope sighed, full of exasperation, before she spoke. "Evan told me something Ryder said to him yesterday that I think you should hear."

"What's that?"

"Evan said he'd never thought he'd meet a man that could tame you. And do you know what Ryder said?"

Tears fell on her cheeks and she shook her head. "What?"

"He said he hadn't, that he didn't see the point, because he liked you wild."

Sophie's chest squeezed tight, so tight she could barely breathe.

"That's what love is, not wanting to change the wild. How many men do you think come along like that in a lifetime?"

Sophie started to cry again. Not many.

* * *

When Ryder moved to Revival, he'd done it because he'd needed a change. To do something new and break out of the routine of his life. The last thing he'd expected was to gain a group of friends, which wasn't what he thought he'd needed but sure seemed nice now.

Ryder, Charlie, and Griffin sat at Sam Roberts's bar, drinking beer and watching a game on TV as Ryder nursed his broken heart and tried not to think about Sophie too much. They didn't ask him a lot of questions, didn't bring her up, but he knew they were all there for him, making sure he didn't drown too much in his misery.

After the long drive back from Chicago, where there'd been nothing but the roar of the motorcycle he'd driven, the endless stretches of cornfields, and silence, he'd had far too much time to think about her. He wanted to take it back because he wanted her that much, but he couldn't.

"Another?" Sam said, pointing at his almost empty beer.

He nodded. Charlie and Griff had collected him at about three, and this was where they'd been for the last five hours.

Sam slid a bottle in front of him. Ryder drained the last of his current beer and handed it over. He was well on the way to stupid drunk, and that suited him just fine. Numbness was preferable at this point.

Charlie sat on one side of him, Griff on the other, bookending him in silent support. He took a drink, put the bottle down, and frowned. "Why did I think giving up casual sex was a good idea again?"

Surprised he'd spoken out loud, he blinked.

Griff laughed. "Because you're in your thirties and it gets old as fuck."

His brow furrowed. "I was wrong. It's much better." He turned to Charlie. "Maybe you have it right. How the hell do you sleep with a woman for months and not get attached to her?"

Charlie shrugged. "Easy."

"How was it easy?" Sophie had him from the first time he'd kissed her in the Rileys' kitchen.

Charlie grinned. "You want me to tell you where you went wrong?"

"Yeah, I do." Because he'd sure as hell gone wrong. He'd known from the second he'd laid eyes on her she was insanity. He'd gone into it fully comprehending that he wanted her and she was leaving. They were supposed to have an affair. He wasn't supposed to fall in love with her. Where had he detoured so absolutely?

And why the hell couldn't he make what she was willing to offer him enough? It should be enough. Because being without her was awful. Half of something was better than nothing, wasn't it?

Only, something inside him couldn't take it. He couldn't articulate why, but it was true.

Charlie pointed to Sam. "In deference to Sam, I'll leave Gracie out of it."

"I appreciate that," Sam said dryly. "And if James was here, I'm sure he'd appreciate it as well."

Gracie Donovan was married to James now, but once upon a time she'd had a friends-with-benefits type of relationship with Charlie that everyone seemed pretty cool about. Her husband included.

"But here's where you went wrong," Charlie said, scrubbing his jaw as though thinking through what he wanted to say. "You picked Sophie."

Ryder blinked at him. "That is no help."

Griffin laughed. "I get it."

"So do I," Sam added.

"Well, I'm lost as shit." Ryder's brain hurt.

Charlie sighed. "You don't pick women like Sophie for casual. Women like Sophie don't reach inside you because they're pretty and have a nice rack. They reach inside you because they are the total package." He grinned.

Charlie clapped Ryder on the back. "I have a simple strategy for picking the women I bed. I have to be able to look into her eyes and know she's not bullshitting me about a relationship." He pointed at Sam. "Gracie was like that when I met her. That woman wanted nothing to do with commitment. Not sure I'd ever met a woman less interested in a relationship. That's why she was so perfect. Hot as hell, up for anything in bed, and had no desire to talk about feelings."

Sam rolled his eyes. "I'll tell James you said so."

"I'm sure he knows what your sister is like in bed."

Sam scrubbed a hand over his face. "Why do I have to be friends with all my sister's hookups? A brother isn't supposed to know these things."

"Back to the point." Charlie held up a finger. "You have to have attraction, of course, but the insane chemistry you have with Sophie that rolls off the two of you and drives everyone crazy, I'd stay the hell away from that."

"I tried." He had. He slammed down the rest of his beer. "I really, really tried."

Charlie gave him that eagle-eyed look. "You didn't try."

"I did." She'd just been too addictive to ignore.

Charlie scoffed. "How long had you known her before you had your hands all over her? Less than twenty-four hours, I'd bet."

Ryder scowled. "Obviously you've never experienced it or you'd understand."

"I haven't," Charlie said, laughing. "If I ever ran into that kind of compulsion, I wouldn't touch her with a ten-foot pole. I'm not an idiot."

"How was that being an idiot?"

"Because it's common sense. Everyone knows once you know what she tastes like, you can't stop."

Ryder was starting to feel a bit wobbly on his stool. "What do you have against relationships, anyway?"

"We're not talking about me." Charlie took a swig off the bottle. "I've got nothing against them. They're just not for me. I'm not good husband material. I play to my strengths. It's that simple."

Ryder called bullshit, but knew Charlie well enough to know that was as much as he was going to say on that subject.

He turned to Griffin. "You have anything to add?"

He shrugged. "Maybe next time, if you don't want to fall, pick someone a little less awesome. Did you know that last week, Sophie got Mary Beth to change her mind? And she did it so smoothly I don't think Mary Beth even realized she'd ended up doing what Sophie wanted in the first place. Somehow she made Mary Beth think it was her idea."

Ryder nodded. "Okay, so no commitment types, attraction but not chemistry, and dumb. Is that all?"

Sam tilted his head. "Maybe one that isn't so daring and adventurous."

"Pretty, low maintenance, dumb, and boring. Got it." God, no wonder Sophie had knocked his feet out from under him. That had been his type for as long as he could remember, and the thought of eventually going back to it made him want to stab himself.

He shook his head. "This sucks."

Griffin nodded. "It does. I remember."

"At least it worked out for you in the end." Ryder's voice sounded angry and hostile, but nobody took offense.

"It can still work out," Sam said.

All three of them turned to look at him. Sam was an enigma, kind of quiet and watchful. Charlie and Ryder never questioned him about it, but he had a sixth sense about things.

Sometimes when they were stuck on a case and the trail seemed dead, they'd come to Sam's bar and casually bring it up. Seventy-five percent of the time, Sam would drop a single line that would set them on the right path. The rest of the time, he just shrugged and stayed mute.

Ryder knew to listen carefully to what he had to say now, and all his senses went on high alert.

"How?" Ryder asked.

Sam's eyes narrowed, and a distant look entered his expression. "She just doesn't see it clearly."

That made zero sense to him, so he cautiously probed. "Doesn't see what clearly?"

"Don't know," Sam said, unhelpfully. "She's . . . cloudy. She doesn't understand."

"What doesn't she understand?" His tone was impatient now; he wanted answers to the niggle bothering him.

Sam met his gaze. "I'm sorry, I don't know how to explain it exactly."

"Well, can you try?"

"She has blinders on, and until she takes them off, she's only able to see things one way."

"Is there anything I can do?" The beat of hope pounded in his chest, mixing with the alcohol and making him dizzy.

Sam frowned. "You're not going to like it."

"What?" He'd do anything.

Sam sighed. "You have to leave her alone for a little bit. She needs space to sort it out."

Well, fuck, that sucked.

Chapter Twenty-Five

At work Monday morning, Sophie stared at herself in the bathroom mirror and counted to ten in an attempt to calm herself. When that didn't work, she counted to twenty.

After that, she gave up and walked back to her office.

In fifteen minutes she had a meeting with the project team and would see Ryder for the first time since Saturday night. After spending the day with Penelope in the full throes of their breakup rituals established back when they were in high school, she'd gotten home late on Sunday night. Ryder's house had been dark, and she tried not to think about him inside, his long body stretched over his bed where she'd spent countless hours.

Since this was a small town, people already seemed to know things had gone to hell between them. She saw it in Griff's face when he'd offered a soft "good morning." In the pitying look his stern-eyed secretary had given her. And countless other ways.

She'd talked to Maddie on the way home, driving down the highway in the middle of nowhere, crying her eyes out as Maddie attempted to console her. She'd cried more tears in one day than she had in the last five years combined.

All she could hope was to get through this meeting without a breakdown. At the moment, it seemed too much to ask.

A knock on the door had her starting in her seat, and even though she didn't want to talk to anyone, she called the visitor in. Anything to distract her in these last minutes before she was forced to see him was welcome.

The distraction didn't work.

Ryder stood in the doorway, dressed in his uniform, looking like shit.

Throat tight, she blinked.

They stared at each other. The silence suffocated her.

He cleared his throat. "I wanted to talk to you."

Unable to speak, she nodded.

He walked forward and handed her a file. "I thought it best if I skipped today's meeting. You have it covered anyway."

That wasn't what she wanted to hear. She wanted to hear he was as desperate for her as she was for him. That he couldn't stand not being with her. That he needed her and would take any time they had together. All the things rioting around in her heart, she wanted to hear from him. But instead he confirmed what he'd said the other night.

That he could no longer be around her.

She clenched her teeth, grinding them together so hard her jaw ached.

He shoved his now-empty hands into his pockets. "I talked with Griffin, and he's fine with me backing off the project. You've done most of the heavy lifting since you came to work here anyway."

Her bottom lip quivered. She wouldn't even have an excuse to see him. Even though they lived next door to each other, she knew he would avoid all contact with her. He was systematically severing all ties with her.

She managed to squeak out, "Okay."

"I can't imagine you'll need anything, but if you do, you know where to find me. I'll help if I can, but for now I think this is better."

Better for whom? she wanted to scream but kept quiet. It was better. At least this way he wouldn't be sitting there staring at her with those silver eyes.

"Do you need anything before I go?"

She shook her head.

Their gazes locked, held together, and a thousand silent things passed between them. A muscle in his jaw twitched. "Take care of yourself."

"You too."

Then he turned and left, closing the door behind him.

Tears welled in her eyes and she brushed them away. She had a job to do.

He gave her no choice but to put this mess behind her. All she needed to do was get through the day. Then the next one. And the one after that. Every day it would get better. Easier.

Time healed all wounds. Or so they said.

Two weeks had gone by.

She wasn't any better.

In fact, she was worse. Ryder avoided all contact with her. If she was outside, he was in. If their paths happened to cross, it was awkward, brief, and filled with tension.

Only a week away, the Fourth Festival thankfully kept her so busy her days were filled. One thing she'd learned about her time in Revival was small-town citizens were far more involved than Chicago ones ever seemed to be, and they barraged her with constant questions and suggestions.

It filled the endless hours, and that was all she cared about.

This afternoon, she sat in Earl's Diner across from Maddie, pretending to eat. She'd lost weight and was starting to look model thin, so at least she had that going for her.

"Soph?" Maddie asked.

Sophie blinked her into focus. She'd drifted off again. Her brain was always so fuzzy, so clouded and hazy. "What?"

"I asked if you were okay." Her friend's face was creased with concern.

"I'm fine," she lied, before clearing her throat and delivering the news. "François called this morning. I'm going in for the first round of interviews the Tuesday after the festival."

Maddie's pretty face pulled tight. "Is that what you want?"

"Of course." It was the only bright spot in her life at the moment. "It's a great opportunity."

Maddie's brows furrowed. She opened her mouth and closed it again, shaking her head.

"What?"

There was silence before she finally sighed. "I know it's a great opportunity, but I guess I'm asking you to think about it. Think about what really makes you happy."

Defensiveness sat heavy in her stomach, and short on sleep, she snapped, "Why is everyone putting this on me? What? Because I'm the girl, I need to give up my entire life for a guy?"

"What? No!" Maddie ran a hand through her red hair. "It's not that."

"Then what is it?"

"You're just so unhappy."

"I'll get over it." She was sure she wouldn't, but she had to believe this would pass.

"All I'm saying is Ryder wanted to talk about a future. Would it be so horrible if you at least heard what he had to say?"

"For what purpose?"

"Did you ever consider maybe he'd want to go with you? If Chicago is really what you want?"

Sophie's mouth fell open and she sputtered. "Of course not."

"Why? When it's so clear you guys are miserable apart."

"Ryder isn't going to give up his life to move to Chicago with me."

"How do you know that?"

Sophie took a deep breath. "Why on earth would he?"

Maddie's head tilted and she touched Sophie's hand across the table.

She snatched it away. She couldn't stand sympathy right now. It would break her.

Maddie sighed, and when she spoke, her voice was soft. "Because he loves you, Soph."

Even if it were true, why would it matter? It wouldn't, but she was tired of explaining that to everyone, so she didn't bother. She shrugged. "It's over. In case you haven't noticed, he wants nothing to do with me."

Maddie shook her head. "I haven't noticed that at all."

Sophie turned and looked out the window onto Revival's Main Street. It really was pretty here. Getting prettier by the day as the town took on new life. A life she'd helped build. It gave her an unexpected satisfaction.

In Chicago her work sometimes felt indirect, hard to quantify outside the numbers the accountant types loved so much. That's why she'd started her After Dark blog in the first place. She saw the direct fruits of her labor when a previously unknown gem suddenly exploded with business.

Her work in Revival was like that too. Maybe that was

why she hadn't really missed her job too much. The citizens of the town informed her of the impact of her work . . . incessantly, whether she wanted it or not.

The bell over the door rang and she glanced toward the sound. Everything inside her stilled at the sight of Ryder and Charlie. All her muscles stiffened. She bit her lip.

The morning when she'd first come to town and sat in this diner with him rushed over her. They hadn't sat together that day. Had barely spoken. But even then she'd known it was on. She remembered the way he'd flirted with her, giving her that smile of his and those slow, heated once-overs.

It seemed like a lifetime ago.

Charlie waved to them, and Maddie waved back, but Sophie stayed frozen. Ryder wore a baseball hat today, low enough to shadow his eyes. He tipped the brim at her and moved off to a booth as far away from her as possible.

"You okay?" Maddie asked, her brows creased, her mouth pinched.

She nodded and offered a bitter smile. "Small towns, right? Bound to happen."

"Maybe you should go talk to him."

"And say what?"

"That you miss him," Maddie suggested, as though it was the easiest thing in the world.

Sophie shook her head. "Then what?"

"I don't know, maybe he misses you too, and hearing it will help break the tension between you."

They were pulled so tight it felt like they could snap at any second. Out of the corner of her eye, she glanced at him, and her heartbeat sped up. As gorgeous as he was, that wasn't what she missed. And it wasn't the crazy, insane sex either.

It was *him*.

The way he laughed at her antics when they watched *I Survived*.

The way she put her feet on his lap and he cupped her ankle, stroking absently over the bone.

The way he drove out of his way to get her Starbucks when she was having a hectic day.

And acted like he'd constructed a ten-course meal when he made her nachos.

How he wanted to hear everything about her. Or told her funny stories about trying to maintain order over his deputies.

But mostly, how she felt complete whenever he was around.

There were a thousand things she missed about him.

Her entire world stilled. The room quieted, and she could feel her breath too fast in her chest as her heart galloped like she was running a race.

And just like that she understood.

Understood why she wasn't getting better. Why this wasn't getting any easier. Her eyes filled with tears, and she looked at Maddie sitting across from her, twisting her hands with obvious worry.

She blinked and whispered, "I'm in love with Ryder."

Maddie nodded. "I know."

Panic sliced through her, blocking out that one second of understanding and blaring in loud brightness all around her.

She shook her head. "I need to get out of here."

"Okay," Maddie said, already raising her hand to signal the waitress. "Go ahead. I'll take care of the check."

Sophie picked up her purse and, without looking in Ryder's direction, rushed out into the warm air, sucking in breath like she was asthmatic. She raced down the street in the direction of Maddie's car, and when she cleared the diner's window she sagged against the building, putting her hand on her forehead and tucking her head down to quell the light-headedness.

She loved Ryder.

For the first time in her life she was in love.

And it changed absolutely nothing.

Her life was still in Chicago. His life was here. There was nothing to hope for, no joy in the knowing, just utter panic and blinding despair.

"You okay?" Charlie asked as Ryder stared at Maddie at the cash register, frowning.

"Yeah." He nodded, not looking away from the redhead.

Sophie had clearly been upset. She'd practically run from the restaurant, and she wasn't a runner.

But the worst was, he'd seen her face. Her pale complexion, the shadows under her eyes, the strain across her now-prominent cheekbones.

He clenched his hand around a water glass, suppressing the urge to follow Sophie out just to assure himself that she was okay. He narrowed his eyes at Maddie.

He could stay away from Sophie but still find out how she was doing. Maddie was right there, waiting to pay.

The women were fiercely loyal to each other, so he didn't expect any betrayals of confidence, but he could at least make sure. It was something to help deal with this need for Sophie, who was like a drug in his system.

"Give me a second." He got up before Charlie could say anything and walked over to Maddie.

She glanced up at him, with a frown. "Hey."

Ryder didn't intend to beat around the bush. "Is she okay?"

The frown deepened, and she shrugged. "What do you want me to say?"

"The truth." Ryder lifted his baseball cap and ran his hand through his hair before pulling the cap back low over his eyes. "She looks terrible."

"You don't look too great yourself."

"I'm not important."

Maddie glanced around the restaurant, tucking a lock behind her ear. "She's my best friend, you know I can't say anything about her to you."

Desperation was an ache in his chest. "I'm not asking for that. I just want to make sure she's okay. The way she left, she's worrying me."

Maddie nibbled on her bottom lip, much the way Sophie did when she was thinking. It didn't surprise him they shared similar traits, considering they'd spent more than half their lives as friends, but it didn't cause the same reaction in him.

Maddie cleared her throat. "Honestly, Ryder, I don't think she's okay."

It was like a punch in the gut. He felt helpless and impotent. "What can I do?"

Maddie pointed to an empty table, getting them out of the way of other people trying to pay for their meals. They sat and she shook her head. "I don't think there's anything you can do. She needs to get through it on her own."

Ryder ran a hand over his jaw. "I hate that I'm hurting her."

"I know." She looked over her shoulder before blowing out a breath. "When Evan and Penelope got together, I was so mad at him."

Ryder didn't have a fucking clue what this had to do with him and Sophie, but he kept his mouth shut instead of snapping in frustration the way he wanted.

"When I talked to him, I chastised him and said he should have picked Sophie." Maddie met his gaze, her green eyes intent and level on him. "I said Sophie could take it. That she'd be able to get over him because she was Sophie."

He nodded, not trusting the words that might come out of his mouth.

She sighed. "I see now I was wrong. She's only like that because she's never really cared before. I think, after this, I see now how she views things."

The fine hairs on his neck lifted and he leaned forward. This seemed relevant to the cryptic shit Sam had spouted that night in his bar. "And how do you think she views things?"

She was silent for a bit, staring at the table like she was attempting to puzzle something out. "You know, right? How she grew up?"

He nodded.

She blew out a breath. "It's hard to explain, I'm not sure I entirely get it, and I know she doesn't. But in her mind, because her parents always chose each other and their endeavors over her, she just doesn't really expect anyone to love her. To choose her. Not because she has low self-esteem, like it would be for most people, but it's more like it never occurs to her. Like she has some sort of a mental block about it."

What Sam had said fell into crystal-clear focus, and everything made sense. "I don't think I can fix that for her."

Maddie narrowed her gaze. "Did you tell her you love her?"

He shook his head.

"Why?"

He didn't want to shift the conversation to him, but Maddie had been so forthcoming he couldn't deny her the answer. "She doesn't see a future with me. I'm not saying she doesn't want it but that she doesn't see it. I didn't want to lay that on her when I know where she wants to go."

"I think that's the wrong choice."

"She wants to go back home, Maddie."

"Maybe you are her home and she doesn't realize it."

"I don't know. I hope so."

Maddie glanced toward the door. "I need to go. She's waiting for me."

She got up to leave but turned back to him. "You know, one of you is going to have to break down and take the risk. I think it's going to have to be you."

He had nothing to say to that, so he nodded and watched her go before getting up and returning to the table where Charlie sat.

Charlie raised a brow at him. "Feel better?"

"Nope." He slid into the booth, mulling over what Maddie said, what Sam had said, and what he understood about Sophie. The things nobody else knew about her but him.

The truth was he didn't know the answer, didn't know what direction to turn, but there was one thing he could do, and he'd take care of that tonight.

Until then he'd need to bide his time until the answers became clear.

Chapter Twenty-Six

Sophie stared up at her ceiling when her doorbell rang. God, she hoped it wasn't Maddie. She couldn't take one more second of gentle inspiration. All she wanted was to be left alone.

It rang again.

She contemplated ignoring her, but since her friend knew she was home she had no choice but to answer. Maddie wasn't the type to be dissuaded. With a sigh she rolled off the couch and walked like a zombie to the door, flinging it open.

She froze, mouth falling open. It wasn't Maddie.

It was Ryder.

She blinked, wondering if he was a mirage she'd conjured because of all her obsessive thinking about him. But when she opened her eyes, he was still there. Dressed in the same clothes from this afternoon, hat still pulled low, he held a fast food bag in one hand, a large drink in the other.

She shook her head. "Ryder."

His gaze flickered over her. "Let me in."

It wasn't a request and she blinked again. "What?"

He pushed past her and she stood there as he walked toward the kitchen. When he returned he was empty-handed.

He came over, took her hand, and pulled her with him back to where he'd come from.

Startled, she frowned, but his fingers clasped tight on hers, so familiar and strong, she didn't protest.

When he got to the table, he pointed to a chair. "Sit."

She did, managing to squeak out, "What are you doing here?"

He didn't answer, just moved around her kitchen, gathering a plate, napkins, and ketchup from the fridge before he returned. He opened the bag, pulling out a hamburger and french fries and placing them in front of her. He grabbed the drink and set it next to the pile of food.

She looked through the plastic top to see it was a strawberry shake. Her favorite.

He sat down on the chair opposite her and crossed his arms over his chest. "I'm not leaving until you've eaten every last bite."

It was so like him, so incredibly him. It was everything she missed about him. Loved about him. Needed about him.

Her throat went tight and her eyes welled.

He frowned, pulling his hat lower. "You need to eat, Soph. Do this one thing for me."

She shook her head, her throat so constricted there was no way she could swallow. "I can't."

"You can and you will."

She didn't know what to do.

Having him there in her kitchen, despite her misery, made her feel the best she had in weeks. Everything about him sitting across from her felt right. All her emotions bubbled inside her. She forced them back down, trying to contain them, but ended up taking a gasping sob.

"Fuck." The word was half moan, half growl. He grabbed her and lifted her straight off the chair and into his lap before wrapping his arms around her. He tucked her close, kissed her temple, and whispered, "Let it all out, darlin'."

And she did. She curled her arms around his neck, tucked her face into the curve of his shoulder and cried. Big, hot tears that streamed down her face and fell onto his skin as he held her tight.

This, right here, was why she loved him.

She had no idea how long they stayed like that, her weeping in his lap, but they didn't speak. He didn't try and talk her out of her breakdown or show any impatience with her. He just sat there and held her until she finally calmed and fell silent.

At long last, he stroked her hair. "Better?"

She nodded against him, clutching him tighter, not wanting to let him go.

He smoothed down her back, rubbing slow circles along her spine.

She pressed closer. She hated how weak she was. That nothing felt as good as his arms. That his palm, heavy on her back, made her feel safe. She barely moved for fear he'd stop. Eyes closed, she took a deep breath to soak in his scent, that spicy, clean smell. She needed to be close to him. She burrowed deeper.

His fingers brushed the bare skin where the hem of her shirt didn't quite meet her shorts.

She gasped, her lips touching the skin on his throat.

He tensed.

The air between them thickened.

Heat cut through her sadness, making her ache all over.

He skimmed his fingers under the cotton of her top, and she felt him grow hard against her hip.

Their breathing quickened.

She shifted, fractionally, wanting to get closer. Wanting to sink into him.

His hand gripped her hip.

She arched, sliding her legs down his thighs so they parted.

He pressed his palm flat against her stomach.

Every movement between them was jerky and brief. As though that way they could pretend not to notice.

Her pulse hammered in her throat.

His fingers snaked under her top and brushed her belly.

She moved her thigh flush against his hard cock. He traced her ribs, his thumb brushing the underside of her breast.

She hissed, all the air leaving her lungs.

Don't stop. She squeezed her eyes tight. *Please don't stop.*

His thumb kept rubbing the curve of her breast, not moving close to where she needed him most. She bowed, thrusting into his hand.

"Sophie." Her name was a moan on his perfect lips.

She tilted her head.

He lowered his.

Their mouths met, not hard like she'd expected, but a soft glance. His tongue touched hers. Danced against her. His thumb swiped over her nipple and she groaned against the sensation.

All of a sudden he stiffened and pulled back, his hands retreating to safer territory and his head lifting, taking his sinful mouth away.

He shook his head. "This isn't why I'm here."

She'd never felt so rejected in her life. She'd have done anything to keep him touching her. There wasn't anything on this earth that would have made her stop, but he'd pulled away.

She straightened and mumbled, "I'm sorry."

She got up from his lap, but he gripped her wrist, and

pulled her back before taking her jaw and forcing her to look at him. When she met his eyes, she saw how shadowed they were, the blueish tint under his lower lashes. The strain in his face.

He suffered. Because of her.

"Sophie, you have to know I want you."

She did. She wanted to say something light, something that didn't reveal how emotionally on edge she was, but instead said, "I couldn't have stopped."

His expression searched hers. "It's not because you want me more."

"Then why?" She hated asking the question but couldn't help herself.

"I want you to eat." He let her go and she pulled away.

That explained nothing.

She sat down in her chair and stared at the food in front of her. She wanted to protest, but that was childish. Eating seemed like a concession. So she just sat there, damned if she did, damned if she didn't.

Which pretty much summed up her entire relationship with Ryder.

"Eat. I can't stand watching you waste away." His voice was strained, worried and concerned.

She didn't look at him but knew he watched her. Instead she stared at the food. This, right here, was something she could do for him. So she picked up a french fry and popped it into her mouth, chewing mechanically. Her stomach felt hollowed out when the food hit it. He was right. She was wasting away. And it was hurting him.

She picked up the hamburger and ate every bite, even though she felt like throwing up.

When she finished, she finally looked at him. She couldn't deny she felt clearer. Not good, but not so much like she walked around in a fog, removed from the world. "Are you happy?"

His jaw hardened. "No, I'm not, but at least I don't have to worry about you passing out for a couple more days."

She crumpled up the hamburger wrapper, swallowing hard. "Thank you."

"You're welcome."

Uncomfortable silence, now thickly laced with sexual tension, filled the air. Their gazes caught and held. He glanced at her mouth, at her chest, and then back up again. "I need to go."

"Okay."

He stood and she went to stand too, but he shook his head. "Don't walk me to the door, Sophie. Just stay here until I'm gone."

She did. Not because he asked, but because she didn't trust herself not to throw herself at him and beg for him to take her. So she could feel him at least one more time.

To be connected to him for just a little longer.

How could he not want that too?

Ryder went home, changed, and went running to deal with his sexual frustration.

It didn't work.

He took a shower, tried to read, but gave up, throwing the book against the wall in his agitation.

Now he lay here in bed, in the dark room, wanting Sophie like he'd never wanted anything in his entire life.

He knew she thought he'd rejected her. That he had some willpower over their attraction she lacked, but it wasn't the truth.

He'd fought a mental battle of epic proportions in his head.

It was just too hard to be around her. And he'd been too worried it would set them right back to square one, so he'd managed to resist. But it hadn't been easy.

He dragged his hand through his hair, remembering the last time she'd been in his bed. She'd been on top of him, her head thrown back, circling her hips as she rode him, driving him crazy. She'd kept stopping when they got close, slowing to a crawl to stave off—Fuck!

He punched his pillow. He needed to stop.

His phone chimed and he looked down to see Sophie's name. *Are you awake?*

He went from hard to granite. He typed back. *Yes, you too?*
I can't sleep.

He couldn't help it. He fisted his cock. *Why's that?*

It took thirty seconds for her to reply. *I miss you.*

He groaned. *I miss you too.*

I've been drinking.

Are you drunk texting me?

Her response was immediate. *Yes.*

He stroked his shaft, wondering if she was over there touching herself. It was foolish, he knew that, but he couldn't stop himself. *Are you touching yourself?*

Yes.

Christ. Fuck it. *Where?*

Everywhere. Is your hand on your cock?

Grip tight, he slowed his movements. He was so on edge the urge to come almost overwhelmed him. *Yes. Play with your nipples and tell me how it feels.*

A minute went by and he waited, his breath too fast. He'd slowed his pace to a crawl. Even though it was stupid, he didn't want it to end.

His phone beeped. *It's not as good as when you touch me.*

He'd never sexted before, and he wanted to hear her voice, but if he heard those breathy little moans of hers, there was no way he wouldn't go over there, so he resisted the impulse to call her. Knowing she was right next door, her hands on her body, thinking of him was enough for now.

Tell me why.

Because you touch me without fear.

He took his hand off his cock to type out his reply. *I knew from the second I saw you how you needed to be treated.*

How do I need to be treated?

Hard, and rough, and dirty.

I'm thinking about it now.

Which time?

In the bar, I can mimic how you rubbed my clit with my hand. It helps me feel like it's you.

He groaned. Remembering how he'd pushed her, and how hot it made her, the way she soaked his fingers. He wanted her to feel that same ache.

Another text. *Ryder . . .*

Yes, Sophie?

This is the first time I'm going to come since the last time.

He gritted his teeth, fighting the urge of his body. *But you're still coming with me, aren't you?*

Yes. I don't want to, not yet . . . but I'm so close.

Here in the dark, he could tell her *I want you so bad.*

I want you too.

This was crazy, he knew that, but he couldn't stop. *Tell me what you're doing.*

I'm touching myself the way you do, wishing it was you instead of me.

He stroked his cock. He wouldn't last much longer. So he typed. *Come.*

Then he dropped the phone, and his fist tight on his shaft, he closed his eyes and got lost in the pleasure. Picturing Sophie in a million different ways, in a million different scenarios, going over the edge at an image of her, smiling at him, her hair bright in the sun, her brown eyes flashing.

When it was over, he lay panting for breath until he heard the beep of his phone.

Ummm . . . hi.

He laughed. It was so her. *Be a good girl and get some sleep.*

You are so evil.

Right bdck at ya, darlin'.

Good night, Ryder.

Good night, Sophie.

This woman, she'd be the death of him. No question about it.

Chapter Twenty-Seven

Since that night, four days had passed, and Sophie had no idea what she and Ryder were doing. They still weren't seeing each other. Still weren't talking. By all accounts they were still avoiding all contact.

Except at eleven o'clock each night when they texted each other from bed, saying all sorts of filthy, dirty things until they came and went to sleep. By some unspoken agreement neither called, or suggested calling, but the things he said to her while she lay there drove her crazy.

It was . . . odd. But she wasn't complaining. It was better than nothing. At least she'd started sleeping again, started eating, and stopped walking around in a fog. She didn't feel so horrible, but she suspected that was because their nightly texting connected them.

The interview in Chicago loomed in her mind like a dark cloud hovering over her. The festival was this weekend, and it would be crazy and busy, so she wouldn't have time to think about the interview, but she drove back Monday night. She hadn't said anything to Ryder, not wanting to ruin this brief respite of time with him, but she'd have to tell him soon.

But tonight, she was going to do her best to have fun.

She took a deep breath and climbed out of her car, grabbing the bottle of whiskey she'd brought for Mitch and Maddie on her way. Her friend was in the mood for a party, so after making sure that Ryder wouldn't be there, she'd agreed to go to the small get-together.

Maddie claimed Ryder was working. Sophie didn't have to be confronted by him, but she had no idea what to expect tonight at eleven. She supposed she could slip into a spare room. The farmhouse had enough of them.

She rang the bell and flung open the door, calling out into the house, "Maddie?"

"In the kitchen," Maddie called back.

Sophie walked through the swinging door, her gaze immediately falling on the spot on the kitchen counter where Ryder had kissed her the first time before skirting away. She smiled at Maddie, who wore a jean skirt and white T-shirt that definitely showed she'd gotten her pre-baby body back.

Sophie whistled. "Someone's looking hot."

Maddie smoothed her hand over her stomach and beamed. "It finally fit. All that running and doing sit-ups finally paid off."

"You look great," she said.

"She does," Gracie agreed, winking at Maddie. "Better you be subjected to James's training schedule than me."

Maddie rolled her eyes. "You're the worst."

Gracie turned to Sophie. "Ready for the big festival tomorrow?"

"As ready as I'll ever be. How about you?" Sophie asked. Now that Gracie's bakery in Chicago was up and running, she'd decided to open a Revival storefront and put Harmony Jones in charge of the operation. It opened next month, but Gracie and Harmony had a booth that would feature all the delicious pastries they had to offer.

Gracie shrugged. "Ask me six weeks from now. James is forcing me to take a two-week vacation in France after the opening and before he has to head back to school."

Sophie clucked her tongue and gave her an exaggerated look of sympathy. "Ahhh . . . you poor thing. However do you manage?"

She sighed. "It's a rough life, but someone has to do it."

Sophie laughed and Maddie's head tilted. "You're looking better."

She shrugged. "Thanks."

Cheryl walked in, and Sophie's chest squeezed as she remembered the first time with Ryder when they'd been so crazy. She smiled. "Hey, Cheryl."

"Hi." Cheryl glanced at Maddie. "I just wanted to make sure you didn't need anything."

"We're good." Maddie winked at her. "How's things going with Bill?"

A pretty flush filled Cheryl's cheeks and she cleared her throat. "Great, actually. Thanks for inviting us over."

"It's our pleasure."

Cheryl looked at Sophie, her brow wrinkling. "I guess I owe you a thank you."

At least someone had gotten a happy ending. Sophie shook her head. "I didn't do one thing, but I'm glad it's working out so great with Bill."

"It is." Cheryl fiddled with her hair and pointed toward the backyard. "I should get back."

"We'll be out soon," Maddie said.

When she left, Sophie said, "I'm glad they are happy."

Maddie turned and leaned back against the counter. "And what are we going to do about you?"

"There's nothing to do." Sophie straightened her top.

"Have you talked to Ryder?" Maddie's voice was full of speculation.

"No." The response was immediate, but to her horror she felt her cheeks heat.

Gracie pointed at her. "You have."

She shook her head. "I swear, I haven't."

"She's a big, fat liar," Gracie said to Maddie.

"I'm not, I have not talked to him."

Maddie's eyes narrowed. "It's something."

Again she shrugged, as though it was no big deal. "We might have exchanged a few texts, but we haven't spoken and nothing has changed."

Gracie grinned. "By the look on your face, I'm guessing they weren't ordinary texts."

"It was just checking in."

Gracie waved a hand. "You are a horrible liar."

Maddie bit her bottom lip and her gaze slid to the back door. "That makes me feel a little better."

Sophie's heart banged against her ribs. "What did you do?"

"I didn't do anything." She sighed. "I swear when I told you he wasn't going to be here it was the truth. But I guess his plans changed and he decided to come."

Sophie's throat went dry. "Ryder's here?"

"Yes. I'm sorry."

Sophie's stomach took a leap off a cliff. "Does he know I'm coming?"

Maddie's gaze slid away. "I, um, kind of said you weren't going to be here."

Sophie closed her eyes and prayed for strength. "How could you do this to me?"

"You texted him, that's half the battle," Gracie added helpfully. "Think of it this way, you get it over with and you guys can figure out how to be neighbors."

They didn't understand, and she wasn't about to explain. So she shook her head, "Let's get this over with."

* * *

When she walked outside, wearing tight capri jeans and a pinkish scoop-neck top, her hair loose, Ryder wasn't surprised to see her, even though Maddie had said she wasn't coming. The truth was, all his instincts promised she'd be there, and he'd needed to see her.

Needed to look at her.

Hear her voice.

He wasn't going to do anything about it, but he needed to see her face and remind himself she was flesh and blood, and not words on a screen. Of course their late-night texts were stupid. It kept them connected instead of building up the wall he needed to resurrect between them.

Every night he'd promise himself he wouldn't do it, but as soon as he slid into bed, his dick would get hard and he'd start thinking of all the things they'd done, and the next thing he knew they were in the thick of it.

He'd told himself he'd stay away from the Rileys' tonight, but here he was, unable to keep away from her.

He was weak.

Their eyes met. A hushed silence fell over the party-goers, lasting two beats before the din of conversation continued.

They'd moved on. But Sophie and Ryder hadn't.

Their gazes clung.

She sucked in a breath before wetting her bottom lip, and gave him a little wave of her fingers.

He nodded, and they managed to rip their attention away and back to the party. She sat down next to Gracie, Maddie, and Harmony at the outdoor table, and the four of them bent their heads and huddled together for some deep conversation.

He sat there with narrowed eyes and watched her.

"You're going to burn a hole into her." Mitch handed him a beer and sat down.

He took it and took a long drink, draining half the bottle. "Thanks."

Out of all of them, Mitch Riley was the one he knew the least. Between Maddie, his career, and their new baby, he didn't get out as much as the rest of them did, but Ryder liked the guy.

Mitch chuckled and shook his head. "I feel like I should apologize for my wife."

Ryder raised a brow. "Did she plan this?"

Mitch shrugged. "I'm sure in her mind she didn't. I'll ask her tonight and she'll have some perfectly plausible explanation that will sound really good. But it won't change the fact that while she might not have been outright manipulative, she still put the dominos in place and hoped they'd fall in her favor."

Ryder's gaze slid to Sophie, who hadn't looked in his direction once since she walked in. He shrugged. "It's not a big deal. This town is small, our friends are connected, it's bound to happen sometimes."

"Maddie means well, you know. Her friends are like sisters to her, and she can't stand to see them upset."

Ryder couldn't stand to see Sophie upset either, which was how he'd gotten himself into this weird limbo mess to begin with. "I'm glad she had such good friends taking care of her."

Mitch pointed to his beer. "You want something stronger."

Ryder looked down at the bottle, remembering how he'd licked salt from Sophie's neck that first night he'd kissed her. "Yeah."

Mitch got up and Ryder turned his attention back to Sophie. James had joined the women and his hand rested on Gracie's neck, his fingers stroking over her skin. He gazed down at her, and Ryder's body tightened, recognizing the look he gave his wife for what it was. He'd given that look to Sophie many times, letting her know with a single glance her respite was over and he was going to take her the first chance he got. That he expected to have his way with her. That it was his right to do so. That no wasn't a word he expected to hear from her.

Not that she ever said no to anything.

He both was and wasn't surprised to see the professor wearing it. Ryder had obviously never thought too much about the guy's sex life, but he couldn't miss what he witnessed in front of him. The guy had a quiet assurance about him that was hard to miss, so Ryder guessed it made sense. James tightened his grip on Gracie's neck, leaned down, and whispered something in her ear.

Her spine straightened. She turned and said to her friends, "I'll be back."

Then she slid her hand into James's and they disappeared in the direction of her house.

The remaining women rolled their eyes at each other and kept right on talking, letting Ryder know this was not an uncommon occurrence.

Mitch returned and handed him a glass filled with brown liquid. "It's whiskey. Sophie brought it."

"Thanks." He downed half of it in one gulp, looking back at the woman in question.

He missed it. Missed what he had with her. Missed being with her. But he had to put it out of his mind. At this rate, he wouldn't make it another ten minutes, let alone the rest of the night.

Maddie looked toward them, beaming at her husband and crooking her finger. "Wanna play Cards Against Humanity? I bought an expansion deck."

Mitch chuckled and shook his head. "God, she's devious."

Having fondly been on the receiving end of his own devious woman, he asked, "Well yeah, but would you have it any other way?"

"Nope." He stood.

Ryder followed, sliding onto a chair across from Sophie. Their gazes met.

The cords of her neck worked as she swallowed.

Maddie opened the black box and said, "Let the games begin."

Sophie's attention dipped to his mouth, and her tongue snuck out, licking over her bottom lip.

He stifled a groan. This was going to be a long night.

Three hours later, Sophie's head spun. As the night wore on and drinking ensued, the awkwardness between Sophie and Ryder faded, but the sexual tension between them was enough to choke her.

They still hadn't really spoken, other than to pass each other chips or drinks or talk about the game. They didn't flirt.

But their chemistry was like an electric current.

His attention dipped to her mouth.

She bit her lip.

His silver eyes darkened.

She traced a path over her collarbone and he tracked the movement with predatory eyes. They'd abandoned Cards Against Humanity after it got old and moved on to poker.

He was the dealer.

He met her gaze. "How many, darlin'?"

She sucked in a little breath. God, how she'd missed the sound of that. She took two cards out of her hand and pushed them across the table to him. "Two, please."

Their fingers brushed, sending a rush of tingles up her arm.

He smirked at her.

She narrowed her eyes.

He gave her two cards, his thumb brushing over her palm. She picked up her cards and saw the chance she'd taken by ditching her low pair had pulled her a flush.

Mitch bet, then everyone called. When it came to her she went to raise, but then she met silver eyes. Suddenly she couldn't stand it one more second.

He was making her crazy.

She was sitting there, her skin oversensitive, her breasts achy, insatiable heat between her thighs distracting her. She needed five minutes away from his penetrating stare to collect herself, because right now she felt like she did when he brought her close to the edge, only to pull back, wait until she cooled, and start all over again. Except there was no cooling off part.

She was just on fire.

She put her cards on the table. "I fold."

She got up and left the table. Instead of stopping in the kitchen, where she'd be further reminded of things she'd done with Ryder, she walked down the hallway and into the office. She sank onto the chair and attempted to collect herself.

He was the devil. Pure evil. He had to know what he was doing to her.

She put her head between her legs and took deep breaths, jerking up when she heard a noise. She looked up.

It was Ryder.

He said nothing, just stared at her long and hard, with an intensity that made her want to shift in her seat.

Heart hammering in her chest, she stood. "I should get back."

"You should."

Neither moved.

They just stood there.

Her breathing kicked up.

He reached behind him and shut the door.

And then they were on each other.

Their mouths hot and hungry and mean. They always kissed like they were starving but now they were crazed, all clashing lips, dueling tongues and teeth.

Their hands moved everywhere, clutching and pulling. Raking over their skin.

She warred between the desire to touch him and wanting to sink into the feel of his big, strong hands on her body.

He growled, low and deep in his throat, before swinging her around and slamming her against the door. She let out an oomph. He captured the sound with his mouth before bending at the knees and picking her up. Her legs wrapped around his waist and she clutched at his shoulders, her head falling back against the door, and he ground his hard cock against her needy center.

He fisted her hair and yanked her head back. "I'm not going to stop."

"Good," she whispered. "Don't. I need you so bad."

He made a fierce, feral noise. Whipping her around, he pushed her to the floor. His fingers snaked up her under her top, covering her breast and rubbing over her nipple. He murmured in her ear, "You need my cock, darlin'."

She raked her teeth over his jaw, loving the sharp intake of breath he made, and told him the truth. "I need *you*."

He moaned, covered her mouth with his. He stroked against her tongue, licking her lips, feasting on her. She raised her legs and arched, circling her hips, silently begging for him.

He unhooked her bra and pulled at the hard peak, twisting

and pinching in that way she loved. Movements frantic and jerky, he levered up, yanked her top above her breasts, and covered her nipple with his lips.

With hands, tongue, and teeth he tortured her until her hips were moving and she moaned incoherently. "Ryder, please."

He lifted his head. "I can't get enough of you."

"Me either."

"I want to drive you crazy, punish you for all the time I haven't touched you." He met her gaze. "But I want you too much to wait."

She squeezed her hips with his thigh. "Take me."

Their gazes locked, and a silence thick with emotion made her breath stall in her chest.

Everything slowed.

She reached up and touched his face, her fingertips brushing over his high cheekbones. His teeth scraped her palm, holding the flesh captive and laving her with his tongue.

Unable to hold it in any longer, she whispered the words she'd never told anyone before, meaning them with all her heart. "I love you."

His whole body stilled and she saw the surprise flash across his features before they softened. "I love you too, Sophie."

Her eyes welled with tears. "I've never been in love before."

"Me either."

She half laughed and sobbed. "It totally sucks."

He laughed too, before smiling. "It totally does."

She tilted her head, and he kissed her.

It was soft and sweet for about thirty seconds before it turned raw and demanding, hinting at desperation. He pulled away, leveraging up and peeling her jeans off before pushing his jeans down his hips.

She'd think about everything else later. Right now all she cared about was him inside her, taking her, claiming her. Making her his.

In this moment, all she wanted was to pretend it was easy.

So she did, and when he slid inside her she felt at home.

They pulled into their separate driveways and got out of their cars, and just stood there, staring at each other.

Ryder shoved his keys into his pocket and gazed at her. Her mouth was swollen from when he'd kissed her, her hair disheveled. When they'd returned to the table, they'd received a lot of sly glances because it didn't take a genius to figure out what they'd been doing, but no one made any comments.

As mind-blowing as the sex had been, that wasn't what floored him. He'd been shocked she'd told him she loved him. It was the last thing he'd ever expected. He'd known, of course, because only love could make someone as miserable as they'd been, but he'd never thought she'd admit it. Or even recognize it.

Love wasn't easy for Sophie. And as much as the primal part of him was satisfied with hearing her say those three little words, the rational man knew they still had a lot to talk about.

She took a deep breath and seemed at a loss for what to do.

So he crooked his finger and said, "You coming with me, darlin'?"

She glanced at his house, an expression of longing

washing over her features that took the air right out of his lungs. She clutched at the strap of her purse and bit her lip.

He tightened, prepared for her rejection.

She swallowed and stepped toward him. "I have to tell you something."

Dread settled tight in his stomach. "What's that?"

She squared her shoulders. "I have an interview for the job on Tuesday."

It was like a kick in the stomach.

Not even for tonight could he pretend she wouldn't be leaving. That there was nothing he'd be able to do about it. Regardless of what he did, if he stayed away from her or not, it was going to gut him. Denying himself wouldn't save him. Nothing could save him. So he nodded. "Are you coming with me?"

She blinked. "You still want me?"

He walked over to her and slid one arm around her waist and the other around her neck. He dipped down and brushed his lips over hers. "I will always want you, Sophie. You're a part of me now, and there's nothing I can do about it."

Tears spilled over her cheeks and she rose to tiptoes to press herself against him. "I'm sorry."

She buried her face in his neck and he held her tight. He kissed her temple. "We sure made a mess of things, didn't we?"

She nodded. "I love you."

"I love you too, Soph." Sometimes it wasn't enough, and maybe this was one of those times. She still didn't seem inclined to talk about a future, but he could make this offer, to show his support. "Do you want me to come with you to Chicago Monday?"

She pulled back and searched his face. "You'd do that for me?"

He rubbed his thumb over her lower lip. "There's nothing I wouldn't do for you."

Something eased in her expression before her face clouded over once again. She shook her head. "This is something I need to do alone."

He didn't question her, just accepted this was what needed to be done. "Just as long as you know you don't have to do it alone."

"I know. The offer means everything. Thank you."

"Sophie." He took a deep breath and told her the truth. "I want a future with you. I don't want to be without you. If you want, I'll move to Chicago with you. You going back home doesn't have to be the end."

Instead of her expression easing, she frowned. "Can we talk about it when I get back?"

His chest tightened. "Do you promise we will?"

"I promise."

He'd let himself have this weekend. Let her do what she needed to do in Chicago, but then when she got back they'd have it out and see where they stood. He'd move. He loved her enough to move. He loved her more than Revival. He could make it work. "Tonight will you sleep in my bed?"

She kissed him, long and deep and soul-searching before pulling back to whisper against his lips, "There's nowhere else I'd rather be."

He took her hand. "Then come with me."

And she did.

Chapter Twenty-Eight

Sophie had smiled so much her cheeks ached as she shook another hand of a Revival citizen. The day was perfect. The sun was shining, it was warm but not stifling, and the new town square was so pretty it could be in a movie. They'd set up the festival so the booths and community sponsors lined the area, so as to not mar the beauty of the new center. Fresh green grass was the perfect contrast to the giant white gazebo where the city orchestra played.

Sophie made sure huge, lush flowers hung in pots, dripping foliage in bright colors. She'd also lined the gazebo with twinkle lights and strung them across the old trees. It was gorgeous, and she experienced a sense of immense satisfaction at the outcome.

She couldn't wait to see it all lit up.

Mary Beth Crowley hugged her. "This is beyond my wildest imagination."

Sophie laughed. "It was a group effort, as you well know."

"But still, I'm good, but I know when I've met my match." The petite blond spitfire shook her head. "Seriously, without you it would have been nice, but you took it to a whole other level."

"Thank you, I'm glad you're happy." Sophie couldn't deny the event gave her a different type of satisfaction than she'd ever experienced before. What she loved was that the rewards were so immediate. Yes, there'd been the normal chaos, and craziness, and last-minute disasters that accompanied these types of things, but it was all worth it when people came up to her to thank her so enthusiastically. It's what she'd always loved, to take something rough and unpolished and make it shine.

Mary Beth smiled. "Griffin told me about your idea for the forest area at the end of the river."

"And?"

"I love it. It's genius." She winked. "Best of both worlds, you know?"

"I do." Over the small blonde's shoulder, Sophie's attention caught on Ryder talking to a couple people she didn't recognize. As though he sensed her gaze, he glanced at her and smiled that smile he had just for her.

Somehow, admitting she loved him had lifted a weight off her chest. And last night she'd poured every drop of energy into showing him how much he mattered to her. They were low on sleep, but it was so worth it. She'd think about everything else on Monday, on the road back to Chicago. But she was determined to enjoy this time with him.

After all, it could be her last. She didn't delude herself. When she got back to Revival she'd have to tell him he couldn't move with her. She wanted to pretend, but she knew the truth. He didn't belong in Chicago. They'd end, and there'd be no coming back. This, right now, was a temporary respite.

So she'd enjoy it while she could.

"I know that look." Mary Beth's voice shook her from her trance.

Sophie jerked back to the present. "I'm sorry?"

She laughed. "You do know you're crushing the dreams of all the single women in Revival."

Sophie shrugged. She wasn't going to explain those dreams might still be alive. Instead she said, "He's quite a man."

"That he is." Mary Beth turned to peer over her shoulder. "It took a lot to get him here, but it was worth the effort. Some people just fit, you know?"

"I do know." And she understood what Mary Beth meant. Ryder did belong there. He seemed like part of the fabric and flow of the town. It was why she knew she couldn't take it away from him.

It would be unfair.

Mary Beth touched her arm. "You could be one of those people."

Shocked, Sophie blinked at her. "What?"

"This town, it needs people like you. I'm just saying you wear Revival well."

"Oh." Sophie didn't know what to say, or even what to think, but it felt a little like her worldview had just tilted. She laughed, awkwardly. "That's just because you've never seen me on Michigan Avenue."

Mary Beth nodded. "Maybe."

Sophie knew where she belonged, and it wasn't Revival.

Later that night, as a local band played covers of eighties classic rock, Sophie lay with Ryder on a big blanket and looked at the stars. It was late, and this was the final show before everyone went home for the night. Sophie experienced an unexpected burst of longing that this, right here, would last forever. That she would never have to move from this time and space and she could exist here, holding hands with Ryder.

"This reminds me of being a kid." His tone was happy and a bit wistful.

She looked at him, his perfect profile, strong jaw, and corded neck. How was it possible this man loved her? She had no idea. "How so?"

"In my town, during the summer, every Friday night there would be a concert in the park. My mom would pack a picnic and we'd go up there and listen to music and eat cold fried chicken. It's one of my favorite memories. Once a summer we all get together and go for old times' sake."

She rolled on her side and propped her head on her open palm. "I can't imagine what it would be like to grow up like that."

He looked at her. "I'm lucky. I know that."

"Why'd you leave your hometown and come here when you're so close to your family?"

He put his hand under his head. "I love my hometown, but I started to feel like everyone saw me one way and I wanted something different. My grade school teachers always wanted to get out of speeding with a warning. And when I went out with a woman, she'd already heard everything there was to know about me an hour after I asked her out. I guess I got to the point where I wanted to build a future based on who I wanted to be versus who I was growing up."

One of the things she and Ryder shared was wild beginnings, and she knew all about his past exploits. She teased.

"You know, no matter how respectable you are, you're always going to bring out a woman's wild side."

He pushed a lock of hair from her cheek. "I don't care about other women, all I care about is you."

She bit her bottom lip. "I'm not sure what I did to deserve you."

"I could say the same."

She shook her head. "I feel like I'm ruining your life."

He met her gaze. "Sophie, no matter what happens, you are one thing I'll never regret."

"Why's that?" She wanted to know, wanted to feel it down in her bones that he felt the same way about her that she did about him.

He pushed her back so she lay flat on the ground before putting his hand on her stomach. "Because with you, I don't have to hold anything back. Most people, even if they fall in love, don't get that. I don't take the privilege for granted."

Yes, that was exactly how she felt. Even in this mess they'd created, he understood her. And she understood him.

She draped an arm over his neck. "I want to say, to promise we're going to work this all out."

"I know, so do I."

"I keep thinking if I could just go back and stay away from you, we'd be saved." She kissed the line of his jaw. "But I understand now that was never going to happen. The pull is too strong. I was gone the second I laid eyes on you."

He squeezed her tight. "Is that why you were so sassy?"

She smiled. "I didn't understand I'd just met my match. All I understood was when I looked at you I needed to be careful."

"Are you sorry?"

She shook her head. "It's selfish, but I can't be."

"Me either." Then he kissed her under the stars while the band played on.

The rest of the weekend past in a blur of activity and increasingly depraved sex, each time becoming more desperate as the hour for her to leave drew near.

And now there they were, in what felt like a blink of an eye. Sophie stood in front of him, bag at her feet, ready to leave. Ryder had just dragged her up from the floor where he'd stripped her naked and impaled her. Claiming her in the most visceral way possible. Communicating all that he wanted from her in the only way he knew how.

He encircled her waist. "Call me when you get there?"

"Of course."

He bent and kissed her lips. "I'm assuming eleven o'clock orgasms are on the table."

"I wouldn't miss it. Can we graduate to phone sex? All that sexting is hard to coordinate." She lifted to whisper in his ear, "And I like how you sound when you come."

"Sophie." He fisted her hair in his hand and kissed her, long and deep and fierce. Kissed her like he was dying, because in a way he was.

The knowledge that this could be the last time lay unspoken and heavy between them.

When he pulled away, tears wet her cheeks, and he brushed them away, hating to see her sad. "Don't cry."

"I'm trying. I just—"

He kissed her again, cutting off the words. Not wanting to hear them. They both knew when she returned, that would probably be it.

She wasn't going to ask him to come with her. But he

understood now, in a way he hadn't that night back in Chicago, that it wasn't because she didn't love him but because she did. She couldn't ask him to make the sacrifice.

And he wouldn't be able to lie. It would be a sacrifice.

He couldn't imagine a life in Chicago, and the only reason he'd go was because of her. He'd do it, but she knew him too well.

On Wednesday, he'd look at her and tell her he'd go with her, and she'd say no.

He'd insist. She'd refuse.

Nobody had ever made the sacrifice for her before, and she wasn't going to start with him. Because ironically, she loved him too much to ask him to make it.

He'd insist, but he had no idea how she'd respond. He'd have to see what happened when she returned.

"I know." Their lips met again. Mouths fused and melded as tongues twined. And when he could stand it no more, he released her. "I love you."

"I love you too." She clutched at him, wringing the very life out of him. "Please know how much."

He rubbed her back. "I do."

He wanted to tell her to come back to him but didn't. Instead, he kissed her one last time and let her go. He stood on his porch and watched her get into her girly Porsche. Top down she backed out of the driveway. Once in the street, she stopped and looked at him.

Her hair was back in a ponytail, her oversized Chanel sunglasses that screamed "city" in place. She looked exactly how she'd looked the first time he'd seen her. Full of sass and sunshine and hot summer breezes.

She waved.

He waved back.

And then she was gone.

Chapter Twenty-Nine

As soon as Penelope opened the door and handed Sophie a wineglass, Sophie burst into tears.

Penelope frowned and ushered her inside, closing the door behind her.

Evan was in their living room, and through her tears, Sophie saw his expression widen in surprise. Penelope made some gestures and Evan stood. The old Evan that had been a wild, manwhoring jerk-off would have gotten the hell out of dodge, but this new Evan scowled and came over to her.

He grasped her arm as Penelope said, "Evan, no."

He ignored her and turned Sophie to him. He pulled her close and patted her back. "Did he hurt you, Soph? Do we have to take him out, Donovan style?"

Sophie laughed through her tears and shook her head. "No. He's perfect."

"Ahhh . . . I see." He pulled back and rubbed a brisk path up and down her arms. "Chin up. These things have a way of working out."

She doubted that, but her throat was too tight to speak.

Penelope smiled at her husband and tilted her head toward the staircase. "I'll take it from here."

He nodded and walked upstairs.

Sophie sputtered, "I-I'm s-sorry."

"Shhhh . . . None of that." Penelope walked her over to the couch. "Sit down, I'll go grab the bottle."

She hurried off and Sophie texted Ryder. *I'm here.*

Thirty seconds later: *Good. In the middle of a work thing, I'll call you at eleven.*

Okay. She could barely wait.

Penelope returned with the wine, joined her on the couch, and got right to the point. "I thought things were better."

She looked into her glass, the dark red color that clung to the sides as it swirled. "I'm in love with him."

"Of course you are. I've known you were going to fall for him since the kitchen that night at Maddie's."

"Why didn't you stop me?" she wailed.

Penelope scoffed. "You have never listened to a word I've said. Besides, it was time."

Sophie scowled. "Time?"

"Yeah, time. You've been sitting smug on the sidelines long enough."

Sophie couldn't help the wry chuckle. "You're the meanest friend ever."

"I know." Penelope clucked her tongue. "And he loves you too."

"He does." Sophie bit her lip. "I don't know what to do."

"Well, not to get all logical and pragmatic on you, but there are only two options. Break it off and go your separate ways, or stay together and one of you move. Have you talked about it?"

She shook her head. "Wednesday we said we would." Her eyes filled with tears. "Can I ask you something?"

"Always."

"What happens if Evan gets a coaching job in another city?"

Penelope's blue eyes darkened and she took a slow sip. "We hope that doesn't happen, but if it's for his dream job, I'll be moving to another city."

Sophie blinked. "Just like that."

Penelope nodded. "Just like that."

Her friend was a huge workaholic. She loved her job, thrived on the pressure, the thrill of helping Shane run such a big company. She had a huge job with a matching salary and even bigger bonus. She loved her job.

Sophie shook her head. "You'd give it all up? For Evan?"

Penelope shrugged. "It wouldn't be giving it all up. It would just have to change. Understand, nobody wants that. Evan has made it clear to the organization he wants a future with them. But Shane and I have already discussed and come up with three or four different options in case that happens. My scope would change, but that's life."

"But you love your job."

"I do. I love Evan more."

"It sounds like you're the one making all the changes."

Penelope smiled, all blissful and happy. "Nope. We agreed the only job we'd move for is a head coaching job for an NFL team. That's it. His sacrifice is he'll pass up any other opportunity to stay here, even if it means getting him to his end goal faster. It's a compromise we can both live with. Besides, having those conversations with Shane was good because it forced me to think about life beyond work."

"How so?"

"You know Evan and I want a family. We want to be married for at least a year first before we try, but the reality is I can't work twelve-hour days with a baby and be the kind of mother I want to be. It's not bad. It's just that life changes, and no matter who you are or how much money you have, everyone has to make choices. It's not like I want to be a stay-at-home mom, but I don't want to be absent either. Having those talks about options with Shane helps me put work into perspective. It's good for me to think about because it opens up opportunities for my life regardless of whether I'm here or some other place."

Sophie sipped her wine and thought about Ryder. She looked at the fireplace, dark and abandoned. "He offered to move to Chicago for me."

Penelope's expression brightened. "So let him."

She shook her head. "I can't."

"Why's that?"

"Because it's all wrong for him." She pressed her fist to her stomach. "I feel it deep down. I'd be the only reason, and I can't ask him that."

"Maybe he wants to do it."

"Just because he wants to, and he would, doesn't make it right. It's something he'd never choose."

"He's getting you in return."

Sophie's eyes welled and she looked at her best friend, who'd been here for her since before she could remember. She swallowed hard. "I'm not my parents."

Penelope's expression clouded with confusion. "What do you mean?"

"I mean I'm not willing to force him into my life. Growing up, I hated knowing my parents were only living the life they were because of me. Hated listening to them talk about when they could leave and do what they wanted to do when they were no longer stuck with me as a dependent. Sure, they settled down to give me a childhood, but they never let me forget it. I don't want that for Ryder." Tears spilled down her cheeks. "But more than that, I don't want that for me. I don't want to sit with him at dinner in some high-rise apartment he hates instead of the farmhouse he's planning on building and know he's only suffering through this because of me. I can't live like that again. I don't want to. Is that selfish?"

Expression turning troubled, Penelope lowered her gaze. "I hadn't looked at it like that."

"I'm not just being stubborn. I'm not refusing to see the possibility. I don't see how either of us win with him moving to Chicago."

Penelope was silent for a few minutes before she said, "Can you see a win if you stay in Revival?"

Sophie drained the rest of her glass. "I don't know. I can't pretend I haven't enjoyed what I'm doing. Or that the idea of starting up the tourism trade isn't exciting to me. I've also been talking to Darcy about other ideas for a blog. But it feels like Chicago is all I've ever wanted, and I don't know if I want to give up the job of my dreams to move to the middle of nowhere."

"Can I be honest with you?" Penelope's brow creased.

"Of course." Sophie needed honest now more than ever. Her future was at stake.

"You didn't really seem happy to me. You seemed active and busy, but not fulfilled." She tucked a lock of hair behind her ears. "Maddie and I talked about it, but we couldn't figure it out."

Was that true? She thought of all the events and constant outings she'd planned, like she was trying to fill up every second of her time. And then it hit her like a ton of bricks. She'd been . . . lonely. Penelope was married, Maddie was married. The world had been moving on without her, and it brought up all those old feelings of abandonment. She'd been manically creating nonstop excitement in her life to avoid the loss.

Like all revelations, it seemed totally obvious, followed by a big ol' "now what?" But she couldn't lay that on Penelope, who would take it to heart when she'd done absolutely nothing wrong. She'd lived her life. That's what she was supposed to do.

Now it was time for Sophie to do the same. She shifted her attention to her friend, her sister not by blood but by heart. "I don't know the answer. But I'm hoping the next couple of days will help me figure it out."

"I hope so." Penelope reached out and touched her hand. "But while you do, remember one thing, okay?"

"What's that?"

"As someone who spent a lot of years in love with someone I couldn't be with, I guess I want you to think about the fact that some people aren't replaceable."

"So you think that Evan was your one and only love?"

She tucked her hair behind her ear and sighed. "I think it's more that I wouldn't have let myself love that way again, if that makes any sense at all. If we'd never found our way together again, would I have eventually fallen in love with someone else and gotten married? I don't know. Probably. But it wouldn't have been him, and I wouldn't have loved in the same wild, soul-crushing way." She chuckled a little. "Which, as you know, isn't always an advantage, but tends to be very worth it."

"I know what you mean."

"Desperate, needy love is a pain in the ass, but I wouldn't have it any other way."

"Is it still like that? Even married?"

She sighed. "Yeah, it is. It doesn't have the angst. Doesn't have that sinking pit in my stomach, warning we're about to implode at any second. But it's still a storm, you know? A good storm, like the kind we used to go run outside in, screaming like banshees as it poured and the skies rolled while the sun blazed. That's how it feels to be with Evan."

Sophie nodded, her throat unbearably tight. "I'll remember."

Sophie sat in the reception area of François's office, her legs crossed, waiting for him to come get her. She'd been in interviews all day with key staff, and he was the last on the list. It had been a long day, but as soon as she'd walked into the building she'd slipped right into PR mode, despite the horrible night's sleep she had.

As luck would have it, Ryder had a work emergency and hadn't been able to call her last night. Not talking to him made her restless and agitated, unable to settle in enough to rest.

But when she'd woke, she'd dressed to the nines, put on a bright face, and knocked every single interview she'd had out of the park. And with each interview she passed with flying colors, the more she confronted the truth. A secret part of her had hoped the job was hype, that it wouldn't be what she wanted, or she'd hate the people.

But none of that was the case.

Simply put, the job was a dream. It was everything she'd ever envisioned for herself. It was multimedia, high profile, connected, fun, and challenging and called on all her skills and abilities. Everyone she'd met had been warm, welcoming, and excited about her coming on board.

And with every conversation she had, the pit in the bottom of her stomach grew. This was her job. She felt it in her bones.

She'd be able to buy a condo, shop every day, go out to

fancy restaurants and be invited to all the best places, and travel to Europe.

All she saw was Ryder, and something else that surprised her.

She saw them watching TV on her couch, his arm around her, his lips brushing her neck.

Her small office overlooking Main Street filled with plans for the tiny houses resort.

His body covering hers, his bare chest against her breasts, his weight heavy and delicious.

Walking into a storefront and shaking the owner's hand, talking about new opportunities.

Sunday mornings on the deck, reading the news, her eyelids still heavy as she melted into the sun.

And a blog. A blog about a big-city girl and small-town life.

That was what she'd thought about, been distracted by.

"Sophie, darling." François's voice ripped her from her thoughts.

She smiled at the handsome older man and stood, holding out her arms while he kissed her on both cheeks. "So good to see you."

He pointed as they walked down the corridor.

"How's everyone been treating you?" he asked as they made their way into a sleek office with spectacular views and floor-to-ceiling windows.

"Fantastic," she said, stepping to look at the skyline before shaking her head. "This is pretty spectacular."

He came to stand beside her. "Isn't it, though? I figured if I have to work all day, I might as well feel like I'm outside."

"It's breathtaking." Because it was, it just . . . she didn't know . . . that feeling of being home was distant and far away. She turned her attention to the man poised to become her next boss. "How's John-Paul?"

"Good, working hard as always." François pointed to a round table in the corner next to a wall lined with bookshelves. "Come, let's sit down."

They situated themselves and she gave him her brightest smile. "Thank you so much for inviting me in. Everyone has been a pure pleasure."

He laughed. "I told them to be on their best behavior so as to not scare you away."

"Mission accomplished."

"So tell me about your morning. I'd like to hear your thoughts."

Sophie had always been quick on her feet, and she quickly summarized each interview, commenting on things they'd discussed as needs and coming up with various solutions or possibilities on the fly. But her responses were automatic. Not filled with excitement. Instead, she found herself drifting to Revival.

She finished her speech and François nodded. "Good, good. You know the job is yours, I already told you I wanted you on board. We both know you'll be an excellent addition, and I can tell by what you've talked about already how many ideas you have. You'll probably have more ideas than we can possibly implement. But tell me, what's your greatest reservation?"

To her horror, the second he asked the question, her eyes welled with tears. She shook her head. "Oh my God, I'm so sorry."

His brow furrowed and he plucked a tissue from the shelf behind him. "Oh dear, what's the matter?"

"Nothing, I'm totally fine." She wiped under her eyes, took a deep breath to control herself, and squared her shoulders. This was a business meeting. "I apologize. So, anyway, about your current strategic plan—"

He held up his hand, cutting her off. "Is this about that gorgeous man you were with?"

She fought to keep herself together, using every trick she could think of to collect her emotions and tuck them away until a much more appropriate time. But then she looked into François's concerned gaze, and all the fight and vigor seeped out of her. She nodded.

He gave her a gentle smile. "What's the problem?"

She lowered her gaze. "He doesn't live here."

"Oh, yes, well, that is a problem." He sighed. "Do you love him?"

"Yes, more than anything."

"And does he love you?"

She nodded.

"You'll have to work it out, then, there's no other choice." He sat forward and put his elbows on the table. "Would you like some advice?"

She waved her hand and gave a harsh bitter laugh. "Sure, why not, everyone else seems to have their input."

He grinned. "Well, bear with me."

"I'm listening." God, she had such a headache, and she was so, so tired. All she wanted was to go home.

"Do what makes you happy."

She blinked at him. "That's it?"

He laughed. "You don't understand, Sophie girl. Not what you *think* makes you happy, but what you *know* will make you happy."

She pressed a finger into her temple and rubbed. What did all of that mean? "I'm not sure I understand the difference."

"Did John-Paul ever tell you I was engaged to be

married?" With a wicked grin, he lowered his voice. "To a woman?"

Surprise lit through her. "No. How scandalous."

He laughed. "I grew up in a nice, conservative household and my entire future was mapped out for me. Of course, I had nigglings. The inappropriate crush on a friend, a couple of random make-out sessions I chalked up to being a horny teenager. But I had my plan of what I wanted, and it sure as hell didn't include hooking up with men. To be honest, I wanted no part of it."

It was hard to imagine, he was so comfortable in his own skin.

He waved a hand. "I won't bore you with all the details, but basically one day something snapped and I decided there was a difference between what I thought made me happy and what really made me happy." He winked at her. "Never wore a polo shirt again."

"Thank God." She laughed.

"All I'm suggesting is that sometimes we need to get out of our own way. That it's the decision that is filled with angst and chaos, but once you choose, accept your path and truth, life gets a whole lot clearer. I don't know what the answer is for you and your man. Maybe it's here, or maybe it's there. That isn't really the question on the table."

Throat tight, she asked, "What's the question on the table?"

"Do you choose him? Does he choose you? Make that choice, and decide the rest together."

"Thanks." She glanced out the window, thinking about Ryder and home. She sighed.

"Why don't we do this." François's voice shook her back to the room. "You have the job. It's yours if you want it. But go, take a week and figure out what makes Sophie happy under all the noise in your head."

"I will. Thanks." She stood and they hugged. "I'll call by the end of the week."

He kissed her head. "Be happy, Sophie darling. You deserve it."

She said her good-byes and intended on walking back to Penelope's but instead found herself jumping in a cab. After fifteen minutes she stood by the lake, staring into the vastness of the water, shoes dangling from her fingertips, as the icy water licked at her toes. She used to come to the lake when she was a kid, wandering by herself when she'd been way too young.

It had always soothed her.

Back then she'd walk until she finally made her way onto one of the piers, gazing into the water, making plans and dreams about her life and what she wanted to become. She'd grown up watching shows like *Friends* and *Sex and the City*, plotting her own glamorous city life filled with shoes and shopping and brunch with her girlfriends. So different from the relentless toes-in-the-earth spiritual dogma she was surrounded with at home.

In her mind, that was what she thought made her happy.

The wind whipped through her hair, and as she gazed out, she gave it all up. She stopped trying to figure it out. Stopped trying to come up with a solution. She took François's advice and quieted the noise in her head.

Despite her fancy suit, she sat down on the sand, closed her eyes, let the breeze blow over her, and listened to the sound of the water lapping on the shore. She sat like that for a long, long time.

Not focused on the past, or her problems, but on herself. To what called to her. Home. That was what she'd been thinking about all morning. What she'd kept longing for as she fought traffic and sat in endless meetings. She'd kept longing for home.

And somehow home had started to look a lot like Ryder's. As the knowledge settled over her, peace stole through her.

She opened her eyes. And knew. All the turmoil settled, the spinning in her head eased, and she finally understood what she wanted. She wanted nights on the couch with Ryder. Walking down Main Street with people calling her name. Going over to Maddie's and sitting in her backyard or down by the river. Hanging out in the hot tub with Darcy and Griffin. She wanted to improve Revival and get hugged by strangers because they were grateful.

And Ryder, always Ryder.

Ryder and Revival were home. The only home she'd ever truly had. The only home she'd ever truly wanted.

At long last, she finally knew where she belonged.

Chapter Thirty

Sophie had texted she was on her way home and he paced the floor, unsure if her coming back from Chicago early was a good thing or a bad thing. He glanced at the clock. She should be there any minute, and the later it got, the more agitated he became.

His entire future was at stake.

His happiness, the life he wanted, it was all right here in front of him, waiting to happen. No matter how much she refused, he'd go with her to Chicago. She'd fight him, he knew that, but it didn't matter. He needed to be with her. He'd convince her he'd be happy. And how could he not be? He'd be with her. So he was going.

End of story.

A car pulled into the driveway, and he didn't even think about playing it cool, he just raced through the house and slammed out the back door.

She climbed out of the car and waved.

He took a deep breath and prepared to meet his future.

She walked over, and when she stood in front of him, she wrapped her arms around his waist and hugged him close, resting her cheek against his chest and closing her eyes.

He had no idea what it meant, but he pulled her tight and kissed the top of her head. "How'd the interview go?"

"I got the job," she said, her arms squeezing tighter.

Of course she did. He'd never had any doubt about that. He decided not even to give her an option. "When do we move?"

She put her chin on his chest. "We're not."

He clenched his teeth and entangled himself from her. "Now, Sophie, I don't care what you think, I'm not going to lose you. If I have to move to Chicago, I will. I'm not taking no for an answer."

"No." Her voice was light, far too light for the subject matter. "We're not moving to Chicago."

"I'm not living without you, and that's final."

"Final, huh?" She raised a brow, that sassy expression on her face.

"Yes, final." Something that felt a lot like hope stirred in his chest because she'd lost that tired, strained, stressed expression she'd been walking around with.

"Is that your final word, Ryder?" She flashed him a sly smile.

He narrowed his gaze. "Are there other options on the table?"

"Yes, I thought of one."

Please, please let it be what he thought. "Should we go inside and discuss it?"

"Yes, let's."

They walked into the kitchen and she kicked off her shoes, went into the living room, and plopped down on the couch. He followed, taking the seat next to her, twisting to face her. "So let's hear it."

"Well, I was thinking." She smoothed her hand over her hair. "That I could stay here, in Revival."

All the air seeped out of his lungs. God, it was what

he wanted so badly; all he wanted was to agree, but he couldn't.

And finally, he understood things from her point of view. Why she'd been so resistant. He shook his head. "Soph, I can't let you do that for me."

She tilted her head as though contemplating the meaning of life before she nodded. "Good."

He didn't know what to say to that, but his stomach sank and his hope died away.

"Because I wouldn't be doing it for you. I'd be doing it for me."

He blinked. "What?"

"All day when I was in that interview, talking to everyone and making plans, all I keep thinking was, I want to go home. Over and over again. From the second I stepped foot in Chicago, I wanted to go home." She crawled over and straddled him.

He broke out into a sweat as he put his hands on her hips. She leaned down, brushed her lips softly over his mouth, and he wanted to sink into it, but he wanted to hear what she had to say too much to get distracted.

She grinned and shrugged one shoulder. "I don't understand when it happened. But somewhere along the way, home started to look like you and Revival. Yes, no place delivers, and there's no Starbucks or Nordstrom, but I like it here. It feels like home. Yes, you make me happy. But this place makes me happy. I want to work on the tourism project and help Revival prosper. I want to start a new blog. I want to be annoyed by citizens who want impossible things."

"You do?" It was what he'd wanted to hear for so long, but he couldn't quite believe it. She'd been so insistent. "Are you sure?"

"I'm sure. Once I made the decision it all became clear.

This whole time I've been searching for a win-win, and every time I thought of you coming to Chicago, it felt wrong. I thought it was because I didn't want you to make the sacrifice, and that's true, I didn't, but it finally dawned on me that was only part of it. It felt wrong for *me*. I just . . ." She shook her head. "I couldn't see it. It was like Chicago and my life there was so much a part of who I thought I was, what made me *me*, I didn't even realize it stopped feeling like home. So I guess, in some weird, strange turn of events, I'm ready to become a small-town girl."

Thank Jesus. He would have done it, really he would have, but he couldn't deny this was what felt right. He gave her one more out, though, just to be safe. "Are you sure?"

"I've never been more sure of anything in my life." She kissed him, long and deep. "I already called François and told him I wasn't taking the job."

"But . . . it's your dream job. You said so yourself."

She beamed at him. "See, this is where I forget how brilliant I am. I have a solution. I offered to do consulting projects for him on a case-by-case basis. He thought it was a great idea."

He squeezed her tight, pulling her close and tangling his fingers in her hair. "I love you so much, Soph."

"I love you too, Ryder."

He bit her lower lip. "How fast can we get married?"

She jerked back, her eyes wide. "Married?"

He looked at her blankly. "Of course, married."

She swatted him. "Is that how you ask a girl to marry you?"

He laughed. "Okay, you have a point there. I'll figure something out and do it properly."

"You'd better."

"I will." He gripped her neck. "Not that I plan on taking no for an answer."

She winked and settled her elbows on his chest. "Ryder, I'm totally a sure thing."

"You're sure?" He needed her to be sure.

She nodded. "I'm positive. However, I do have some conditions."

"Name them and they are yours."

"One, if François sends me anywhere in Europe you have to come with me."

"That's fair." He'd never stepped foot out of the Great Lakes area. He'd get to expand his horizons and drive his sisters mad with jealousy.

"Two, we go to Chicago every six to eight weeks. Maybe we could get a little condo or studio as an investment."

"I like that idea. I don't want to see you when you've gone too long without shopping."

She smiled, laughing a little. "And three, I get to drive the Mustang whenever I want."

"Over my dead body," he growled.

"Now, Ryder, this is non-negotiable." Her eyes grew wide, filled with mischief, and she put her palm on her chest and said, "I'm changing my entire life for you, the least you can do is let me drive your car."

He laughed, and all his tension and unease drained away because she meant it. This was what she wanted. She'd never tease about it unless it was. He gripped her hips. "Oh, all right."

She leaned in close. "See, we can do this. It's all about give and take."

"We're doing it. And I'm never going to let you go."

* * *

The perfect time came two weeks later over takeout. They'd eaten dinner, cleared away the plates, and right before they settled into the couch he sank down to one knee. He took her hand, and she grinned down at him.

God, she loved him. Loved him so much she could barely stand it.

He rubbed a thumb over her left ring finger. "Sophie Kincaid, I wanted to take you to your favorite place in the world, but who knows how long it will take before we get to a Nordstrom shoe department."

She laughed and shook her head. This was better than any shoe department because it was her home and her favorite place in the world, but she kept quiet and let him continue.

"The truth is, I've been in love with you since the first second I saw you. And I can't wait one more second." He pulled a small box out of his pocket. "Will you please drive me crazy for the rest of my life?"

He flipped open the top, and she gasped at the perfection of the ring inside. Her heart hammered in her chest. "Oh my God, Ryder."

"Do you like it?"

"Like it? I love it." It was the best ring she'd ever seen. It was a square-cut, one-and-a-half caret stone with a thin diamond infinity band. Tears filled her eyes. "Yes."

He gripped her chin and pulled her down to meet his lips, sealing their future in a searing kiss that stole her very breath. When he released her he said, "I love you so much, Soph."

"I love you too, Ryder." She traced his strong jaw with her finger. "I can't wait until you're my husband."

"Good, because I can't wait until you're my wife." He took the ring out of the box and slid it down her finger.

She held it up to the light. "It's perfect."

He rose and sat next to her on the couch, taking her hand so they could look at it together. "Are you sure you like it?"

"I love it. It's perfect. Exactly what I would have picked." Because it was. She'd be staring at this ring for hours.

He squeezed her hand. "Thank God. Do you know how many women I had to go through to get this ring?"

She laughed and shook her head. "No, how many?"

"My mom, my sisters, Darcy, Gracie, Maddie, and Penelope all sent me five hundred texts with what I should get. It was the most confusing process of my entire life. But then I snuck away from them all one afternoon and went to the jeweler by myself. I saw this and knew it was you." He stood, picked her up, and started carrying her to the bedroom.

She licked his jaw and whispered in his ear, "You know me best."

He swung her onto the bed and she landed in a heap, laughing.

He climbed on top of her, straddling her hips. "So it's official."

"It's official."

"Can we get married next week?"

She gave him a galled look. "Hell no. Do you know how many times I've been a bridesmaid? I'm getting a wedding."

He whipped off her top. "That's what I figured. But soon, Soph, I need it to be soon."

"We'll come up with something." She flashed him a smile.

He covered her mouth with his own. The kiss was long and possessive, telling her everything she needed to know about what she was in store for later that night.

Before she got lost in him, she pulled back and said,

"Oh, by the way, since it's official, there's something we need to talk about."

"What's that?" He nipped her neck and she jolted under him.

"Have I mentioned I have a huge storage unit full of stuff?"

He raised his head and cocked a brow. "No."

She pulled him down and whispered against his lips, "So I'm going to need to take a look at those house plans."

He laughed, snaking his hand under the clasp of her bra. "Oh really?"

She blinked up at him all wide-eyed and innocent. "It's not too late to make changes, is it?"

He shook his head. "Anything for you, darlin'."

She grinned. "I promise you'll get a tiny sliver of the closet."

He laughed. "You are such a brat."

"But you love me, right?"

"More than life itself."

"Me too." She reached up, touched his jaw, and said with everything in her heart, "I fell head over heels for you, and you're the best thing that ever happened to me."

"Right back at you." He kissed her and she sank into him, letting herself drown in the feel of him. Letting it sink in, wrap around her, and make her heart beat fast.

She was home.

Love Something New?

Be sure to check out the whole series
TAKE A CHANCE ON ME
THE WINNER TAKES IT ALL
THE NAME OF THE GAME
AS GOOD AS NEW
and novella
SHE'S MY KIND OF GIRL

Available from Zebra Books,
everywhere books and eBooks are sold!

Connect with Us

Visit us online at
KensingtonBooks.com
to read more from your favorite authors, see books
by series, view reading group guides, and more.

for sneak peeks, chances to win books and prize packs,
and to share your thoughts with other readers.

facebook.com/kensingtonpublishing
twitter.com/kensingtonbooks

Tell us what you think!

To share your thoughts, submit a review,
or sign up for our eNewsletters, please visit:
KensingtonBooks.com/TellUs.